DARK
STORM

KAREN HARPER

DARK STORM

mira

mira

ISBN-13: 978-0-7783-6992-9

Dark Storm

BookClubbish.com

Printed in U.S.A.

To all the great southwest Floridians who helped others during the hurricanes, including those who helped us when our lanai caved in.
Neighbors helping neighbors; churches opening their doors.
Despite the storms, that's why Florida is the sunshine state.

DARK
STORM

CHAPTER ONE

Naples, Florida

"I can't believe you can get two seven-year-olds to work in your garden in this August heat," Claire's friend Kris Kane told her as they watched Claire's daughter, Lexi, and her cousin Jilly pull weeds from around the flowers in the Markwood backyard.

"It's the butterflies they're interested in. The brightly colored flowers and those hanging nectar pans attract them. Lexi's obsessed, says she's going to major in butterflies in college. She adores her first grade teacher, who retired last year and has a butterfly farm out past the citrus orchard just before the Glades begin."

"Oh, the place your sister works part-time?"

"Right. And speaking of butterflies, would you and Mitch be interested in a butterfly release at your wedding rather than having everyone throw rice? It's one of the ser-

vices the Flutterby Farm provides, and Nick and I would
be happy to arrange it as a gift to you."

Kris's fiancé, Mitch Blakeman, and Claire's ex-husband,
Lexi's father, Jace, were best friends and pilots who flew
together, literally into the storm, checking data on hurricanes along the east coast, clear down to Florida. They had
all joked it was best for the men to be commuting to that
job from as far away as possible. Kris and Mitch were en-
gaged to be married as soon as the hurricane season ended
later this autumn.

"I've heard of butterfly releases for funerals, but weddings?" Kris said. "I'd have to run it by Mitch but anything
having to do with flight, he'd probably be all for. Claire, I
don't know how you ever kept sane when you were married to a pilot. Sorry to bring that up, but I do worry about
Mitch, not only because of the flying, but the work itself
now that he's a storm spy, as he calls himself."

Claire sighed and stood to move closer to the huge window to watch Lexi and Jilly work. At least they were pulling weeds, not newly planted lantana this time. "I suppose
you should talk to Brittany about that, since she's married
to Jace now," she told Kris. "I think it's great you and Brit
have become good friends—the archaeologist and the zoologist, no less."

"I'm sorry, Claire. I didn't mean to bring up any—"

"It's okay. Nick and I are friends with Jace and Brit, and
Lexi's close to her father. She calls him Daddy and calls
Nick Dad. But I understand your concern for Mitch's new
career. Lexi would be devastated if anything happened to
Jace. All I worry about these days is that some disgruntled client Nick defends in court will turn on him. He's in
court right now, defending an elderly lady who has been

wrongfully accused of fraud. He never knows what's coming next."

She turned back from watching the girls. "We've been through enough dangerous situations that I've become a worrywart, and Nick's even worse. He's so protective of me. But I've been happy just running my website and doing some forensic psych consulting lately, mostly on corporate fraud. Our detective friend at the Collier County Sheriff's Department still wants me to work there part-time, but for now, I've turned him down. It's been a great—and quiet— year, staying home, taking care of little Trey and keeping an eye on my mad butterfly gardeners when Darcy's working. She takes them to work with her some days. But try not to worry too much about Mitch chasing storms. Hurricanes or not, he and Jace know what they're doing in the air."

"Both of them are danger junkies to the core," Kris admitted. "I've noticed Trey's walking great for a sixteen-month-old," she said with a glance at him standing up in his playpen.

Observing people as closely as she did, Claire thought it was a pretty smooth attempt to change the subject. "Sometimes he's walking *too* great," she told Kris, going over to the playpen to give him the football-shaped beanbag he'd thrown onto the floor. "Good pass, future Florida Gators quarterback!" she teased, and bent to kiss the top of his head.

"He's into everything," she added with a smile, and waved at her darling son, Nick's pride and joy. "I don't like to have him in that playpen too long, but he's out and about enough to do me in."

The little guy waved back and said something only he

understood. But quarterbacks in their huddles used secret language, anyway, Nick had said.

Smiling at that thought, Claire picked up her cell on the coffee table when it sounded. "Oh, it's Darcy," she said, looking at the screen. "You know, she might be my younger sister, but she's always been one to reach out, make sure I'm okay."

"I remember from our college days, she was always calling to check in."

Claire turned away, her back toward the window. "Hi, Darcy. Are you done at the Flutterby already? The girls are fine."

"This is Darcy's sister, right? Lexi's mother, Claire Markwood?" a woman's voice asked.

Claire's heartbeat kicked up. "Yes? Ms. Gerald? Why are you calling from Darcy's phone? Is she all right?"

"I took some butterfly release packages to the post office. When I came back—well, I can't find her anywhere. And her car is gone."

"If she's not there, how are you calling me on her cell?"

"It was here on the floor in the first butterfly house. I shouted all around for her, even in the residence, but with her car gone...and some things disturbed..."

Claire's stomach went into free fall.

"I don't know whether to call the police," the woman went on. "I mean, I don't want to alarm you, but Darcy would never leave the door of this big butterfly house open. It's the one that houses all the exotics. But it was wide-open, and some of the butterflies are gone—gone, too."

"I'll be right there, and we'll call the police together. No—I have a contact there I'll call on my way. I'll be there as fast as I can."

She punched off and turned to a concerned Kris. "I can't explain right now, but can you do me a huge favor? I know you said you had errands but there's an emergency at the butterfly farm, and I need to go there now. Could you stay and watch Trey and the girls until I can get our nanny to come over? You've met Nita. She's eight months pregnant but she gets around fine."

"Sure. Of course. Anything else?"

Still holding her cell, Claire ran for her purse in the master bedroom, calling back over her shoulder, "Like I said, Nick's in court, so I can't call him right now. I may leave him a message. If you hear from him, please have him call me." She snatched her purse and sunglasses, tore back out. "Tell the girls I just had to run an errand. There are cookies on the counter and juice in the fridge."

"Claire, is everything okay?"

"I'll know more when I get here. Thanks for doing this," she called back over her shoulder as she rushed toward the garage.

Yes, something was wrong. Very wrong.

"I think I need to quit joking that our getting to fly again is like being in seventh heaven," Jace told Mitch, his good friend and copilot for this hurricane hunter flight, the first one for which they'd been in the cockpit. The roar of the wind was so loud they spoke only through their mics and muted the noise with their earphones. "Heading into the eye of these storms is damn dangerous."

"You just figure that out? Good safety record or not, the season's been bad. This storm's gonna rip up the east coast if it doesn't head out over the Atlantic, and evidently that's not the damn thing's direction of choice."

Both men were seasoned military pilots, and Jace had flown commercial passenger jets, but this new career was a challenge. Hurricane hunter planes were twin turboprops, not fan jets. Turboprops were more tolerant of hail and extremely rugged. Rugged like us, Mitch had joked.

The US Air Force and the National Oceanic and Atmospheric Administration, known as NOAA, operated these large turboprop planes that flew into hell to reach the calm eye of the storm and send back information about wind currents and direction. With the exception of when they were in the eye itself, it was one mother of a bumpy ride. The flights would last for brutal hours, but the weather info gained was essential for the safety of their fellow earthlings, as they liked to call them.

Newlywed Jace had kidded the soon-to-be-wed Mitch that it was a lot like being married: smooth at first, then the thunderstorm turbulence of a first fight, then the calm eye of making up, then rough again.

"Let's order another dropsonde," Mitch said, referring to the cylinders they released to measure storm data. "Man, this rockin' ride's something. And to think we volunteered for this."

"You know you love the challenge and danger as much as I do," Jace told him, readjusting his earphones. But he couldn't help but think of when he'd seen Lexi last week and had kissed her goodbye. His daughter kept pointing out butterflies in Claire and Nick's backyard, one beautiful gold one flitting around her like a halo.

The first big blast before the eye wall slammed them, bouncing the plane like a toy. Jace gripped the control wheel even harder. This would be an almost twelve-hour flight and the crew of thirteen weather technicians on board depended on them. At least this storm was nowhere near Florida—yet.

"Hang on. Gonna get worse," he told his friend.

Claire tried not to speed, but she was panicked to get there. She never used the phone when she was driving, but she had today, calling Nita Munez, their nanny. She had intended to call Ken Jensen, a friend and detective she and Nick had worked with before, but she decided to hold off on that. Surely Tara Gerald was overreacting. Darcy might have dropped her phone without knowing it, then run an errand and would be right back. But then there was that door carelessly left ajar at the exotic butterfly house. That didn't sound like Darcy at all.

Ms. Gerald had been Lexi's first-grade teacher last year and an excellent one, though she'd recently retired to work her beloved butterfly farm full-time. Lexi had been devastated she'd no longer see her around school, but Claire and Darcy had visited the farm with their daughters and one thing led to another. Darcy accepted a part-time job there, occasionally taking the girls with her.

Claire gripped the steering wheel with both hands as she turned off Collier Boulevard onto narrow Sabal Palm, which led to the farm. About three more miles. The road was only paved partway out.

She sped now, past a garden center, then an orchid farm. Her hands shook, and her heart pounded. Darcy had been her mainstay after their salesman father had deserted them and their mother had retreated into her books, adult fiction she'd sometimes read aloud to them. A free literature degree, Darcy had often kidded.

No one else had visited their girlhood home except sometimes their mother's librarian friend, Will Warren, who dropped off books. He'd later left South Florida and somehow made a fortune for himself. He was back at his old job now, and the kids loved it when Darcy took the girls there for story time while Claire and Nick caught up on work.

The paved road ended with a bump, and the dry dust the car kicked up obliterated everything in Claire's rearview. The skeletal melaleuca trees on both sides of the road were etched with dust, which would wash away in the season's terrible storms.

Had Darcy driven this road in the other direction? Fleeing from someone? God forbid, taken by someone? The butterfly farm was the last property on this long road before wilderness began. If only Jace was still flying small crop-dusting planes so he could look for Darcy's car out in the glades. But no, she couldn't allow herself to panic. This would turn out all right.

She passed the wooden sign with two beautiful butterflies and the visiting hours for the farm hand-painted on it. The hours included today, right now. Had someone come in to see the place without a reservation and found Darcy alone?

"Seen too much crime," Claire scolded herself. "This will be okay. Everything will be okay."

Nick heaved a sigh of relief when the judge called for a short recess. He comforted his client, gave his legal team a couple of instructions, then hustled out into the hall with a simple, "No comment at this time," to the hovering media mavens.

He walked way down the hall and turned a corner, seeking privacy. He was really looking forward to the end of this trial. He and Claire were going to take the kids north—way north—to Mackinac Island off northern Michigan, which they had always wanted to see during warm weather, since the place had been frozen during their time spent there under the Witness Protection Program. They had reservations for the last week in August, right before Lexi went back to school, if they could only pry her away from her butterfly obsession and her pony, Scout, which she rode twice a week.

He thumbed over Claire's photo to call her, his beautiful redhead with a penchant for getting into trouble. But then he should talk. They'd been through thick and thin together from the moment they'd met, but at least things were calm with nothing dangerous on the horizon now.

She didn't answer at first, must have left her phone elsewhere in the house. He was just about to leave a message when she answered. "Oh, Nick, thank heavens. Listen, Kris is with the kids, Nita's on her way there and I'm heading to check on Darcy at the butterfly farm. Tara Gerald called me."

"Check on Darcy why? Is she sick? What happened?"

"She might have disappeared—took her car. Don't call Steve yet."

"Yeah, he's working upstate. You be careful. Don't walk into anything strange. I'll call Ken Jensen to come out, if you think it's not just some...some mistake. He owes me a favor, but, Claire, wait for him if anything looks off. Do nothing on your own."

"I'm pulling in. Got to go."

"Call me back, leave a message. As soon as I can get out of here, I'll be there. Keep calm. Don't panic."

But Nick knew she was. And knowing Claire was a magnet for danger, he panicked, too.

CHAPTER TWO

Claire drove her car up the bumpy gravel drive, past the old, one-floor sprawling house with its wide, wraparound porch that had been Tara's parents' home. Behind it stood three metal-framed, white-mesh humpbacked butterfly houses that looked like greenhouses. They were filled with the vibrant-hued plants the butterflies loved. The mesh let the sun through but protected the delicate inhabitants that flitted about, feeding off the flowers and sugar-water feeders. Tara kept some of the caterpillars and cocoons in a room in the house also.

As Claire jumped out of her car, Tara came running from the nearest butterfly house. "I'm so sorry!" Tara shouted. Even from here, Claire could tell that she'd been crying, and she was wringing her hands. "I can't imagine what happened. If only I had a surveillance camera out here or in the houses. Should I call the police?"

"My husband is doing that. But just show me first," she said as she ran toward Tara. "You did look in the other two butterfly houses?" Claire was already out of breath and in panic mode. She tried to regain control.

"Yes, before I called you. Here, be careful to keep that door closed behind you. It was left open—that was the give-away, because Darcy was never careless. I didn't have time for a good count but a lot of falcate orangetips are gone."

The air inside was warm and moist, but it felt better than the humidity and strong sun outside. Claire was sweating more from her frenzy than the heat. The profusion of vibrant plants here suddenly seemed overwhelming, pressing in. Her mind flashed back to their mother's funeral—all those fragrant flowers on the casket, and she and Darcy holding hands.

"You checked through all the foliage?" she asked Tara.

"In all three houses."

"Where was—is—her phone you used?" She understood why Tara used it to call her, but what if there were fingerprints on it—ones that weren't Darcy's? Claire almost dry heaved in fear. What could have happened here in this peaceful, private, lovely place?

Tara showed her the phone, lying on a table with plants. She pointed out the grassy floor under a three-foot-tall spray of scarlet cosmos and purple zinnias where the phone had been dropped. Claire pulled a tissue from her purse and lifted the phone, wrapped it and put it on the counter. A painted lady butterfly landed on her hand as if to comfort her, but the eyelike pattern on its wings seemed to stare.

Had someone been lurking, watching Darcy? Saw Tara leave? Saw a woman alone here?

"I'm going to call my contact at the police station," Claire told her, perching on one of the metal folding chairs in the aisle. "My husband, Nick, probably already did, but I will, too, to make sure someone comes." She took out her phone. "This officer has worked missing persons before."

Tara sank into the other chair. She was a spry, wiry woman who kept her auburn hair in easy-to-tend corkscrews now frosted with silver. Claire was tall at five-ten, so Tara, at least eight inches shorter, always seemed so petite. Although she had loved her elementary school students, she'd retired at age fifty-five to grow this business she loved so much. As far as Claire knew, she had never married. Her butterflies and students had been her life.

She looked up Ken Jensen's number in her contact list and connected the call. Oh, thank God, he answered right away.

"Detective Jensen here. Claire? Nick called me, and I'm on my way out. He's going to try to talk the judge into a temporary emergency adjournment."

"Oh, thank you! There's no sign of my sister here."

"Sit tight and don't touch anything. You know the drill. And don't start interviews until I get there. So it's way down at the end of Sabal Palm?"

"Past the citrus grove, as far as you can go."

Those words echoed in her mind when she ended the call. Where did Darcy go? Her husband, Steve, was miles away in Daytona overseeing the installment of a solar community. She dreaded calling him. Darcy's son, Drew, was with Steve's parents in upstate New York for the month before school began again. And Jilly—*dear God, please don't let me have to tell her that her mother's missing.*

Ken Jensen pulled in fifteen minutes later in an unmarked car, kicking up another cloud of dust. Too bad it hadn't rained for two days, Claire thought, so car tracks in

Tara's driveway and on the road would show, maybe could be traced or molds made of strange treads so that—

No. She had to stop playing cop. She had to stay calm, objective, not fall apart as Tara had, at least not yet.

Ken Jensen always looked Scandinavian to her with his blond hair and blue eyes. He was in civilian clothes, no sport coat or tie and a short-sleeved light blue shirt. She introduced him to Tara, whose eyes were red from crying. At least she wasn't shaking like Claire was, and Jensen evidently knew it when he held her hand a bit too long.

"So, Ms. Gerald," he said, whipping out a notebook, "please show me where you last saw Darcy—her last name?"

Both women told him "Stanley" at the same time. They led him into the so-called exotic butterfly house, though Claire had noted there were Florida breeds familiar from her backyard inside, too.

"Like another world in here," Ken said. "Garden of Eden. Wow," he added as a turquoise long-tailed skipper—Lexi and Jilly had raised a couple of those at home—landed on his arm. "Go ahead, please," he said, not shaking it off.

He sat them in the two chairs while he stood, taking notes as Tara told him everything she'd explained to Claire. She pointed out Darcy's phone and where it was found.

"Glad you wrapped it and didn't touch it. If there are other prints on it—"

"There will be," Tara told him. "Mine. I panicked and called Claire on it because I didn't have her phone number."

"So what other property of Darcy's is here?" he asked. "A purse?"

"Missing, as far as I can tell," Tara said.

"Ken, the point is she's missing, too!" Claire cried, though she was trying to keep calm. "I can tell you her license plate and the make of car. Can you put out an APB for her? There's a lot of land out there," she rushed on, gesturing toward the wilderness of the Glades, where there was some dry, drivable land as well as lot of ponds and streams.

He put his hand briefly on Claire's shoulder when she tried to get up, so she stayed put. "That's what I'm going to do right now, Claire, but we have to figure this out. Why don't you try Nick again and see if he got away from the courthouse? Then I want you and Ms. Gerald to tell me anything about anyone you think Darcy might have been in contact with. When an adult disappears, there can be many reasons, sometimes generated by the person themselves."

"No," Claire said, looking up at him. "She would not skip out! Ken, she would never have left that butterfly door open if she left on her own, so I'll give you her license plate number right now."

As many years ago as it was, a sharp, stunning memory flashed at her. It was the day when she and Darcy were little and their father went missing. Her mother had insisted to the police he would never leave his family, but it turned out he had deserted them without a word or warning. That was another reason Darcy would never leave on her own. No way Darcy would do that to her own family.

"Might there have been a random visitor, Ms. Gerald?" Ken went on. "Maybe a visitor or buyer who could have dropped by? You do sell butterflies and not just, well, show them?"

"Yes. Sometimes I give tours and sell specimens, most through the mail, but I wasn't expecting anyone today."

In the humid warmth, even sitting down, Claire thought she would either faint or throw up from stomach cramps. But, of course, this was the way to go about things, calmly, rationally. Still, she wanted to scream, just scream. She wanted Nick here. They had to call Steve to tell him his wife was missing and to come back now. No way Darcy had missed him so much she would drive up to see him, surprise him, though she'd done that once before. But not without telling Claire to take care of the kids, not without her phone, unless she'd accidentally dropped it, then realized too late she didn't have it. No, she'd come back for it. She would not just leave an open door for the butterflies to escape.

Claire recited Darcy's license plate, then began to shake harder as Ken stepped away to make his call outside the butterfly house door. She kept picturing the door of their childhood home that she had stared at, waiting for Daddy to come back when she was five and Darcy was a newborn. He was on the road a lot, so maybe he was just delayed somewhere. Maybe he had finally made a big sale and stayed awhile and forgot to call them. She'd been so devastated by his desertion, still was, always would be, but Darcy didn't even remember him, that is, only through what Claire recalled and shared. And Mother was so broken—so broken by his loss that she had never talked about it to them, not even when they were old enough to understand.

Even at her age now, even a mother twice herself, Claire admitted that Darcy and Nick were still her security and sanity.

Nick tore off his suit coat and tie and tossed them in the car he'd parked behind the one he assumed was Ken Jensen's. Ken had helped them before, but then they'd helped him, too. Though Nick knew he was out in the boondocks, he locked his car and sprinted toward the three white butterfly houses baking in the afternoon sun. He was not only worried about Darcy, but about Claire—and Lexi and Jilly, too, of course, if Darcy really was missing. Surely there was an explanation, and his sister-in-law would turn up soon.

"We're over here!" Ken yelled out the door of Tara's residence before he could enter the first butterfly house. Good, Nick thought, because, unlike Lexi and Claire, he didn't like those things landing all over him, though he never let on, given how thrilled they were with the little critters. After all, butterflies were bugs, just ones blessed with gorgeous wings. He'd known people like that with fancy facades that hid motives and crimes. And that made him silently pray again that this disappearance was not foul play.

He went in through the door Ken held open for him, and they shook hands. It was dim and cool inside; an old air conditioner purred away. "Thanks for coming," Nick told him. Without another word, he followed Ken through a kitchen and a room—once a dining room, he bet—where cocoons, all labeled, hung on pegs on otherwise spotless white walls. Something called Orange F predominated, but those pegs were mostly empty alongside a lot of others. What a strange creature to go through such different life stages.

He found Claire in the living room, comforting the first-grade teacher Lexi had liked so much, the one who had gotten his family caught up in this butterfly craze.

"Since you said you were on your way," Ken told him, "I waited to get formal statements from both of them, though no one needs a lawyer."

"I need this lawyer," Claire said, and rose to hug him. She was trembling and had tears in her eyes, and Ms. Gerald had obviously been crying. Out of one trial with weeping witnesses and into another, Nick thought, but then, this was family.

"All right, I'm going to start with Ms. Gerald since this is her property and she saw Darcy Stanley most recently," Ken explained. "Of course, this is open land, a commercial endeavor where outsiders could walk in, but can you think of anyone who has any sort of issue with you or this farm, Ms. Gerald?"

"I've been racking my brain, of course," the older woman said. "I mean, who has anything against a peaceful and educational butterfly farm? We did a major release last month in Fort Myers for the dedication of a children's cancer clinic, and it was so symbolic and beautiful."

"And all went well?" Ken asked. "No customers have seemed disgruntled or upset?"

"No, and wouldn't they come after me if they were?"

"Would they know the woman tending butterflies wasn't you?" Ken countered.

"Well, perhaps not, but Darcy and I don't look anything alike, if someone meant to take—to hurt me. I do have several pictures of myself on the Flutterby Farm website."

Claire held Tara's hand as she sniffed back tears and wiped under her eyes with her other hand again. "Well, now that I think of it, there is a group who are upset about our mailing practices for distant events," she said, her voice wavering. She looked away from Ken to Nick. "They threatened—I mean, mentioned—a lawsuit, because they say butterflies should not be put in special little envelopes and mailed on ice. Well, they have to be kept cold and they quickly reanimate and fly free."

Nick had been careful not to jump in on Ken's questions, but Tara had given him the opening with that look and the mention of the lawsuit. "Anything further on them?" Nick asked. "Is this group local?"

"Local and loco, if you ask me," Tara said, showing some spunk instead of looking so wilted. "They are bleeding hearts just looking for a cause and publicity. They insist it harms nature to release the lepidoptera in an area they don't know, like taking them away from their family or something like that."

Nick saw Claire sniff back a snob. She was thinking that someone had done that to Darcy? Their strong and intimate marriage let him read her mind sometimes. If Darcy didn't turn up fast, he knew she'd be questioned thoroughly about Darcy's domestic life and problems. Steve would, too. Damn, they had to call Steve with this terrible news. They'd grown closer over the last year, as different as they were, and if Claire called him with the news, she'd probably fall apart, because she looked like she was getting close to that right now.

Ken said, "So what is the name of this eco-friendly, protect-the-butterflies group, Ms. Gerald?"

"'Fly Safe,' if you can believe that," she said. "They're into protection of all sort of insects, birds and even bats, not just the beautiful, inspiring, adorable butterflies I raise. And I understand they've also branched out into the protection of marine animals like dolphins."

Nick's gaze snagged Claire's at her mention of the name Fly Safe. Jace and his buddy Mitch planned to start a flight school on nearby Marco Island in the off-season for hurricane hunting, and Fly Safe was the company title they'd chosen. Maybe, using the excuse he was checking out the domain rights of that name, he could visit the eco-group and see just how hostile they really were.

Doing their own investigations had gotten him and
Claire in hot water with Jensen before, which made him
wonder if he should he bring it up or fly under the police
radar? Claire would probably say to forge ahead. Meanwhile, he had to get Steve home and sit with Claire while
clever Ken questioned her about Darcy. He knew damn
well that adults sometimes snapped and took off, even leaving behind ways they could be tracked—like cell phones.
So had Darcy snapped? Whether she had or not, he could
sense Claire was about to.

CHAPTER THREE

Nick had made a lot of tough phone calls in his years as the lead lawyer for Markwood, Benton and Chase, but calling his brother-in-law, Steve, about Darcy's disappearance was the hardest. While Claire stayed inside with Tara, he paced along the grass next to the butterfly houses, waiting for his call to connect. At least cell phones worked out here in the boondocks.

"Yo, Nick." Steve's voice boomed over the phone amid the buzz of background construction noise. "Everything okay? What's up?"

"We've got a problem here, Steve. Darcy was working at the butterfly farm and seems to have just vanished. Claire says she surprised you with a visit once before. Jilly's with us but—"

"You kidding me? It's our anniversary soon, but that's next week. And yeah, she told Claire last time. So she didn't say anything to Claire or Jilly? I think she told Jilly before, too. Damn, hope that's it. Should I wait here, or come home? Is there something you're not telling me?"

"Her cell phone was on the floor, and the butterfly door was left open. Some of the species that are here on a special order escaped."

Steve muttered some tough language, and Nick heard him sniff hard. Silence for a minute. More swearing. Nick stopped pacing, picturing the strong, burly guy with buzz-cut hair, a square jaw and big shoulders. But he was a gentle man, touchingly so with his wife and daughter, though he loved to roughhouse with his son, Drew.

"You call the cops?" he asked, his voice shaky now. "Or do they have a waiting period?"

"Our police contact has been to the scene already, has begun interrogations and will move on this soon. That twenty-four-or forty-eight-hour waiting period is TV and movie stuff, not the way law enforcement really works, at least with adults. Detective Jensen has talked to Darcy's employer and is going to get more information from Claire. Of course, he'll want to talk to you, too, but don't panic."

"I'll bet Claire is."

"It's a detective we know well on the case, so—"

"The case? It's a case?"

"Best to err on the side of caution. Steve, you do need to come home. They'll have questions only you can answer."

"Yeah, you told me once they always look at the husband first."

"Don't talk like that. There may be an easy explanation, surely a good ending to this."

"I'll wait around here for a few more hours—the time she'd take to get here, if it's like before. She could have just dropped her phone," he said, his usually strong voice choking up.

Nick reached under his sunglasses to squeeze the bridge of his nose. His eyes stung. He started pacing again as Steve's voice, shaky now, went on.

"I can't believe she didn't tell her employer. Maybe she thought she'd call her from the car, then couldn't find her phone. But that open door—she was careful there. Damn, Nick, something's really wrong. You guys keep Jilly, okay? Explain as best you can to her."

"For sure. And if you don't like staying at your house, come to be with her. We have room for you and Drew, too, when he gets back."

"But what if Darcy doesn't come home?" Nick heard him muffle a sob. "I can't lose her."

"We'll find her. We got Lexi back when she was taken— not that that's what's happened here."

"I'm not gonna tell Drew yet, but at least he's far out of this for a few more days with my parents. I'll call my dad, tell him not to tell Drew—just to pray."

Claire told Nick she was stable enough to drive, so he followed her in his car and she did fine. Ken had already gone ahead to the Collier County sheriff's station down-town to arrange for a formal missing-persons report after radioing Darcy's license plate to the highway patrol. He'd wanted to get away from the butterfly farm and have more time to question Claire about Darcy's life and personality. Nick had assured Ken that Darcy's husband would be back soon, that he wanted to wait for a while at his job site, then at his apartment in Daytona, to be sure Darcy didn't sur-prise him with a visit as she had once before.

"Can I get you something to drink before we begin?" Ken asked Claire as she and Nick settled at a table in a small, bare room near Ken's office.

"I'm fine," she said, feeling robotic, or maybe more like a drone, like she was seeing all this from afar. This nightmare could not be happening. Not to her. Not to Darcy, too.

She remembered she hadn't taken her narcolepsy pill, so she dug a packet of them out of her purse. Life had been going so well lately that she hadn't relied on these hard-hitters, only her herbal remedies. "On second thought, Ken, I could use some water."

He got it for her, then pulled up a chair on her other side in a friendly, relaxed posture. She knew that tactic, had used it numerous times herself on a person she needed information from and didn't want to alienate or frighten. Well, she was frightened, not of Ken, but for Darcy. Women's intuition? Her forensic psychologist training? No, just a sisterly bond that had withstood so much over the years.

She took the pill. Ken produced his ubiquitous notepad, maybe another ploy not to use a laptop or tablet in this spy-on-you technology world.

"Claire, I know this is terribly hard right now, but just in case this is some sort of crime, I need to know as much as possible about Darcy. Of course, as soon as her husband gets back in town—hopefully with her—I'll talk to him, too, if necessary. So let's start with that—their marriage. All of them have rough spots, but the fact he's out of town overseeing, like you said, Nick, a large construction crew—"

"Which means," Claire cut in, "it's probably not domestic violence. They've been married ten years next week, two kids, very happy. Churchgoing."

"Steve's job takes him away quite a bit?"

"Sometimes," Claire said, "but don't go there about another woman for him or someone else for her. Especially lately, I've been with her a lot. Her extra time when her kids are in school has been spent at the Flutterby Farm, and she's even taken her kids and Lexi there for long visits. Well, not so much Drew lately, as he's spent this month with his grandparents in upstate New York."

"Don't even go there?" Ken threw her initial protest back at her. "You know we have to look at all possibilities, and many people do have dark secrets in their lives. Okay, so probably no other men in her life. It does happen, Claire. It happens, even in the best of circumstances, though I trust you to psych something like that out."

In the sudden silence, Claire said, "She does have one notable male friend, whom I know—Steve and all our kids, too—but he's old enough to be her father."

Ken had not written one thing down yet but he poised his pen over his notepad. "Tell me. Just in case we need more information from or about her other acquaintances."

"Will Warren is a librarian at the main branch here. He's in his early sixties, usually dresses up, stands out. Silver hair, brown eyes, almost six feet tall. He's also an author—on butterflies, no less, and has written a book on them. He excels at story time at the library, does voices for all the different characters. The kids love him."

That last remark hung in the air a moment.

"He writes children's books?" Ken asked.

"The one he gave Darcy was targeted at an older audience—*Butterfly Love and Lore*, I think it is called—but he does the children's story time at the library on Orange Blossom. I think he'd been doing it for years, at the library in Olde Naples before that one was built, though he was away for a while."

"He gave her his book but not you? And he works in the children's division at the library?" he said, jotting things down fast.

"Yes, that's right. We've had our kids to his story time the last several years he's been back in Naples. Everyone knows and likes him. But I think the fact that he's a butterfly expert of some kind bonded him with Darcy lately. Really, Ken, he's got to be thirty years plus older than her, and it's…it's not like that—what you're looking for. I would have picked up on it."

"I'm just taking background notes in case I go to see him. He married?"

"I don't think he has ever been, but I'm not sure. If you go to talk to him, I could go with you."

"Claire," Nick's voice cut in, "this is all preliminary, and you do not need to go with Ken—"

"No, actually," Ken said, sitting back a bit in his chair, "it might be better, especially if we don't locate Darcy right away, for Claire to gently question him without an officer or detective hanging on. If you do talk to him, do it in a safe, public place. Darcy's ties to him seem so tenuous and unsuspicious that my presence might tip him off—or set him off."

Claire turned to look at Nick but didn't pursue that right now. He gave her a mixed message of a shrug and a frown.

"So," Ken went on, "anything or anyone else? How about Tara Gerald, who, of course, seems like a far-out possibility. But I can tell she was distraught at the butterfly door being left open and those orangetips she keeps mentioning getting out."

Claire heaved a huge sigh. "My daughter and I have known this woman for over a year. She is warm, caring and supportive. During the year Lexi was in Tara's first grade class, Tara helped her regain her outgoing nature after all we've been through with Lexi's problems and setbacks. I'm sure, if you get the security camera footage from the post office where Tara took those butterflies to be mailed, you'll find her waiting in line during the timeline when Darcy must have disappeared. Yes, Tara was distraught and emotional, but no way would she strike out at Darcy or anyone else."

Ken turned toward Nick. "Is she always one step ahead of you?"

"Usually. Or two. No law degree or police badge, but you've got to watch those forensic psychs."

Despite their banter and attempts to help and support, Claire knew she was losing control again. Ken and Nick could not comfort her or lighten the mood or calm her down, however much she trusted both of them. They had to find Darcy! Right now!

"Are you going to ask me next how Darcy and I are getting along?" she demanded, her tone more strident than she intended. "I could tell you that we practically had to raise ourselves after our father deserted us and our mother became a shut-in. She even ordered books over the phone so she could read, read, read as an escape from her husband's desertion. That ruined my life and Darcy's for years. So if you ever wonder—and I know you were going to get to that—whether Darcy would have set this all up and just left on her own, the answer is no! She would never do that because she knows the horrible pain of being abandoned. Something terrible has happened to her!"

★ ★ ★

Early that evening, Claire decided she had to tell Jilly
some version of what happened, since—obviously—her
mother was not coming to pick her up and take her home
tonight. She rehearsed things over and over in her head,
but she knew she couldn't lie. Was a softened version of the
truth even possible? She chose to tell Jilly and Lexi together,
hoping they might be a comfort to each other during this
hopefully temporary loss. She and Darcy had been stron-
ger for suffering together, holding each other up through
tough times.

Since Claire had known both girls all their lives and Nick
was somewhat new in their world, she and Nick decided
he would wait in the kitchen where he could hear if she
called. She sat the girls down next to each other on the U-
shaped leather seating in the Florida room. She had closed
the blinds along the patio window so it didn't look like a
huge black mirror. Wanting to get close to them, facing
them, Claire sat on the edge of the glass coffee table, leaning forward. All her training, her counseling experience,
all she and Nick had been through—yet she didn't know
how to start. Was this a mistake to think Lexi could help
Jilly when she had been through so much, even being abducted and held captive?

It had been terribly traumatic, of course, and though they
got her back physically unharmed, off and on since then the
child had slogged through mental and emotional turmoil.
She'd developed an imaginary, hostile friend to cover her
own anger. At least her love of riding her horse, Scout, had
been like therapy for her, as had the support from Claire,
Nick, Jace and others. The nightmares had finally stopped,
but could this loss and shock set her back?

"Jilly, your mom is going to be a bit late, so you'll be staying with us tonight."

"But she's *really* late. It's dark outside."

"She left the butterfly farm earlier without telling anyone. We're not sure where she is, but she took her car, and now we have some people looking for her. I'm sure they will find her."

Jilly jerked upright and shouted, "I've got to call Daddy!"

Claire leaned even closer and took Jilly's hands in hers. The child's skin was warm, her own hands cold. "Uncle Nick did call him, honey, so he knows. He's coming home to be with you. He'll be here tomorrow morning."

"So she didn't go surprise him like last time?"

These kids were sharp. She wanted to hold them close. She could sense, even see, that Lexi was also instantly distressed, fidgeting, folding her arms over her chest, shaking her head. Maybe she'd made a mistake to tell them together where she couldn't tend to them both.

Lexi blurted, "I hope she didn't get in a car with someone bad like I did!"

Damn, Claire thought. All that counseling, all the assurances that what had happened to Lexi would never happen again. However much Claire was praying the girls would help each other through this, she wedged herself between them and hugged both of them hard.

"I'm sure your mom will be all right, Jilly. Did she say anything about going anywhere? Or about seeing your dad?"

"She said she'd pick me up here right after work, and she was so glad I love butterflies, too!" the child whispered, and twisted around to bury her face against Claire's shoulder.

Claire tightened her grip as her niece burst into tears.

Lexi, thank God, leaned over to pat Jilly's shoulder, then leaned in to hug her, too. Claire tugged her daughter onto her knees and the three of them just huddled, even when she heard Nick enter the room, though he didn't come closer.

"We'll find her, sweetheart," Claire said in Jilly's ear.

"Yeah," Lexi offered on her other side, her voice muffled. "I came back after that really bad man took me far away. But right now I'm remembering all the bad stuff, even though I got found and saved. Like, I was so scared. Mommy, I'm going to my room to talk to my friend about this, because she's back now. And she'll help Jilly, too. The three of us can sleep in my bed tonight."

Claire gasped as Lexi pulled away and ran down the hall toward her bedroom. Not that nightmare of the past, too! Lexi had been doing so well, normal now after suffering through what Claire considered post-traumatic stress disorder. But if Lexi was running to her room to resurrect her imaginary friend who had comforted her before—and made her rebellious and even nasty—Claire had made a mess of this. Now, she had to help her own daughter as well as her niece. And where in heaven's name was Darcy?

CHAPTER FOUR

At the Markwood house, no one was sleeping that night. Drained and exhausted, but wide-awake despite her narcolepsy, Claire lay in Lexi's room in the twin bed with Jilly where the child often slept for overnight visits. Hoping to ease herself off the narrow mattress if Jilly stopped crying and clinging, Claire lay outside the blankets in her jogging outfit because the air-conditioning was on.

In her own bed just across the bedside table, Lexi had finally gone to sleep after whispering to her old, beat-up doll. It was not a baby doll, but a little-girl doll that Claire had thought she'd outgrown. It was named Honey, probably because Jace often called Lexi that. The doll had helped her get through Jace's not living with them.

But now with the doll, Lexi had been imitating another voice, harsher, rougher, to make the doll whisper back. The doll's face was marred from use and being stuffed in the closet. Much of her blond hair was gone, and her glassy blue eyes, which never closed anymore, just stared. Claire shuddered. How sad to say her dear daughter's doll, back from the grave of the dark closet, gave her the creeps.

They were enmeshed in dreadful news all around. Darcy's disappearance, of course, was the worst, but Jilly's fragile state and Lexi's slipping back into her unhealthy reliance on an imaginary friend was painful, too.

Nick had come in twice to see how they were doing, but he hadn't been in for a while. Hopefully, he, at least, had fallen asleep after talking to both Ken Jensen and Steve again. He had to be in court in the morning or he'd fall into the bad graces of the judge for getting a short delay and then holding things up again. As loyal as Nick was to his own family, until he could fully prep and hand things over to his defense team, he had to defend his client, too. Claire had actually wondered if his elderly client didn't remind him of his deceased mother.

Jilly finally dozed off in sheer exhaustion. Claire had to go to the bathroom, so she carefully disengaged the child's now-loosened grip and got up. She'd use the guest bath, not the one off the master bedroom, though she was aching to be held and comforted, too, to just crawl in bed with Nick because—and this terrified her—Lexi's bad-seed alter ego was back in that damn doll. Previously, she had not needed a physical object but had pulled her imaginary friend out of thin air, but lately, the doll had become the focus. And the fact it looked like some evil voodoo-type doll just made things worse.

"Mommy, you 'wake?" Lexi whispered as Claire passed her bed.

"Yes, sweetheart. Just going to the bathroom. Be right back. Love you."

"I'm just glad my friend is back. You told me she went

away for good, but that wasn't true. I knew right where to find her."

As badly as her bladder was calling, Claire tiptoed to the far side of Lexi's bed and leaned over to kiss her. But the child pulled her doll closer and Claire kissed the cold, plastic face.

"Mommy, she says you don't like her. She changed her name, so you and Dad have to call her Princess now."

"Really? Remember that Dad, Jilly and I are your friends, so you don't need someone you put away in the closet because you had outgrown a doll—a doll that isn't real."

"But I got taken and now Aunt Darcy, too. You said the man who was bad to me died, but maybe he didn't."

"He did. You are safe. Aunt Darcy's going missing has nothing to do with you."

"Did Aunt Darcy run away?"

"Absolutely not. She would not leave her family. Maybe there was an accident, but we will find her soon and get her back, just like we got you back."

That made her remember that the police were checking the South Florida hospitals in case there was an accident and the victim had no ID. Anything to find her—anything at all.

"Princess will take care of me so you can take care of Jilly," Lexi whispered as Claire leaned over to hear. "Trey is too little to know how to help her, but I don't know how, either."

"Just being with Jilly, giving her a hug, will help."

"But if Aunt Darcy is hurt bad, will Jilly live with us or Uncle Steve?"

"Don't think like that. Say a prayer and think good things."

This time, Claire held the doll's arm and managed to plant a kiss on Lexi's cheek. She didn't try to kiss her back. Surely she wasn't jealous of the attention she'd given to Jilly.

"I'll be right back," Claire whispered, and made for the door. In the dark hall a man's form loomed. Despite the fact she knew it was Nick, she startled. What if someone was keeping Darcy prisoner, coming down a dark hall to hurt her? For one moment, she almost felt she had a brain meld with her sister, because something dark was hovering, something terribly wrong.

"Nick, just a moment," she whispered, and sprinted to the bathroom.

When she came out he was there, pulling her into his arms, holding her tight. Ordinarily, it would have made her feel so secure, so very safe. But tonight...

"I have to go back in with the girls," she whispered. "Jilly's finally asleep, but Lexi's awake and—and regressing. Maybe I should go check on Trey."

He spoke low in her ear. "I've checked on him several times. He's the only one around here who is sleeping like a rock. Meanwhile, Steve called a second time from his car. He's turned the Daytona project over to his under foreman. He'll be here in a couple of hours. No Darcy in Daytona."

She stifled a sniff and held him closer. "Anything new from Ken?"

"The highway patrol and local police have her license number, vehicle description. Until someone spots her or the car, that's it for now. He said to sit tight and he'll call you about going to see Will Warren. He can't decide whether or not to go with you, but he knows I want him along. And I filled him in on the ploy of checking the domain name of Fly Safe so I can visit that ecology group that may have been hostile to Tara—and someone working for her."

She pressed closer to him and nodded. "Maybe you can bring one of your partners up to speed on this court trial so someone else can take over? Nick, we have to find Darcy fast. We have all these dark hours ahead of us, and I'm so scared. We absolutely have to do something now!"

He held her even tighter. For once, despite all they'd been through, it didn't help.

Nick was up way before dawn, feeling like he had a hangover when he hadn't had anything but orange juice and coffee. While Claire quickly showered and dressed, he'd peeked in the girls' bedroom. Both were asleep, Lexi embracing that doll. He and Claire had checked on Trey off and on despite the baby monitor in the room. When Nick couldn't sleep, his favorite thing to do was check on Trey in person. And he sure as hell hadn't gotten much sleep last night, not to mention that Darcy's disappearance, like Lexi's once, had triggered all kind of repressed fears for him and Claire. Ah, to have no worries. He hoped his beloved little son would never go through the things his parents and sister had.

Guessing at when Steve would arrive, Nick went down to the front room and waited for him until he saw headlights slash across the windows. He met him at the door. They were such different personalities that they had only become close lately, not only because of Claire and Darcy's bond but in sharing dad duties at times. Steve's son, Drew, was twelve now, and Trey just a toddler, but Nick hoped to learn how to handle Trey from the solid relationship between Steve and his son. Thank God, Drew was not here now, but he'd have to be told about his mother.

As Steve came to the door Nick held open, they shared a rare hug. Steve had two-day beard stubble on his square-jawed face, and his usually erect posture was slumped.

"Any word?" he asked.

"Just assurances from Detective Jensen that they are on it. The girls are asleep upstairs. Let me fix you something to eat, and you can see Jilly when they wake up. Of course they were distraught. No way they could settle down at first, but sleep may help."

"I may never sleep again—not till we find her. Got to hit the john. Be right back."

Nick locked the door and hustled into the kitchen. He'd scramble eggs and make toast; he could handle that. Juice and coffee were ready. He felt overdressed but he had to look ready for court in—he glanced at his watch—two hours. Steve, of course, was a mess, but Nick understood. He'd been there, done that, when Claire got into something too deep.

Nick had the eggs in the skillet when Steve reappeared. He'd washed his face. In the kitchen light, his eyes looked even more bloodshot. He sank at the raised counter bar and put his head in his hands.

"Steve, we'll find her, get her back. Not only are the local police and highway patrol searching, but Claire and I are going to follow up on a couple of things with the detective's permission and advice."

"I'll rip this town apart, starting with that butterfly farm. I need to talk to Tara Gerald, find out who might've shown up there."

Nick jumped at Claire's hand on his shoulder when he

hadn't heard her come into the kitchen. She hugged Steve and told him, "The police and Nick and I are doing everything we can. We'll fill you in. But you can't go charging in like a bull in a—"

"In a butterfly house," Steve interrupted. "You know, Claire, you're the most hopeful evidence we'll get her back okay. You and Lexi. Both of you have been taken—held against your will—and here you are, in good shape, still strong. But I'm scared to death and she's probably scared to death, too."

Nick saw Claire flinch at the word *death*—both times. He could tell she almost told Steve that Lexi had gone back in her shell, but she bit her lip and nodded. "It looks like you guys have breakfast under control," she said. "I'm going to go check on the kids again. I'll bring Jilly in as soon as she wakes up. Did you tell Drew?"

"Asked my parents not to tell him right now," Steve said. "At least he's out of the news coverage area, because the local media will probably be pests. And if it goes national—told my dad keep him away from the TV and his cell, which might not be so hard at a cabin on a finger lake in upstate New York, I hope. Yeah, before the kids get up, fill me in on the lay of the land, what we can do, besides my seeing Tara Gerald and the detective. I know you two have taken things into your own hands before in a crisis, and that's what I—we—gotta do."

Steve carried Jilly into the Florida room and sat down with her in his lap. His emotional reunion with his daughter made Claire cry, but she turned away to give them some privacy and kept feeding Trey in his high chair. Claire overheard Jilly say, "I can help you find Mommy. It's real scary, but I'm glad Aunt Claire told me so I can help."

That made Claire wonder if Steve was wrong not to tell his son. When Drew found out, would it upset him even more that he hadn't been told and that his little sister—that all of them—knew. She'd have to talk to Steve about that. She wished she could ask Nick.

He had left for work to try to get a stay for the trial or at least talk to his client to get permission for one of the other partners to step in for a day or two. Ken had called to warn them that Darcy's disappearance had been picked up by the media from the police desk, but he said that was a good thing. He suggested Steve make a public plea for information and provide the newspaper and TV stations with a recent photo of Darcy. Nick had explained all that to Steve, and he said he'd comply—anything, even the promise of cash for tips, to help get her back. Nick and Claire had told him they'd put up a ten-thousand-dollar reward for information but not to mention the word *ransom* or they'd attract frauds, as they might, anyway, with phony leads.

Since Steve wasn't at home, Claire wondered how long it would be before the media would locate her as Darcy's next of kin. She'd finished feeding Trey, who had carrots and applesauce all over his face, and had started to wipe him and the high chair tray when Nita bustled in through the back door with "I came back as fast as I could. Not feeling too bad this morning, but this baby, she keeps kicking me black and blue."

She clapped her hand over her mouth when she saw Steve holding Jilly. "Oops!" she mouthed. "Didn't know he would be here or the girls up after everything. But you look outside?" she asked, taking Trey from Claire and cuddling him. "It's why I used my back door key for once. Oh, that must be your brother-in-law's car in the driveway, but there's a second one," she said, lowering her voice, though there was no one to overhear in the kitchen. "And up and down the street—maybe the people out there with the TV antenna truck done traced him, but there's someone else out there, asked me tell you he wants to come in the back way to find out about your sister. Here, he gave me his card, here somewhere," she added, fumbling in her pocket while still holding Trey.

The doorbell rang. Steve and Jilly came into the kitchen holding hands.

"Nita says there's a TV truck out front," Claire told him. "If you want to make a statement, you can use that picture of Darcy in our library—just take it out of the frame. Here, I'll get it for you. Didn't take them long to track you down. Wish Nick was still here, but Detective Jensen said your public plea for information might help."

She darted into the library for the photo: Darcy smiling the day Claire took close-ups of each of them last Christmas. A decorated tree graced the background, but so what? It was a good, authentic image and maybe the Christmas scene even in August would move someone—if someone was holding her.

When Claire pulled the picture out of the frame, a rush of tears in her eyes made Darcy's smile waver as if her lips were trembling. Claire's were, too.

"Jilly, you stay here with Aunt Claire and Lexi," Steve said as he stood at the library door to the hall. "I'm going out to face them, anything to help."

She handed him the photograph. He glanced at it, then

looked away, frowning. Jilly and Lexi, holding her doll, ran to the front windows to look out.

"I don't like all those people on our grass," Lexi said in her doll voice. "They will take pictures and ask questions. They are very mean."

Ignoring that, Steve went outside as Nita came into the library, still holding Trey. "I found his card—that man outside," she told Claire. "Sorry it took me a minute. Pretty sure he's not with that bunch out there—another TV truck, too, and two men with cameras. I know that one from Fox News, that is, me and Bronco seen him on TV."

Claire didn't want to be distracted from the action outside as Steve held up his hands for quiet on their front lawn, but she glanced down at the card and gasped.

Will Warren, Librarian
Author of *Butterfly Love and Lore*
Available Now Wherever Books Are Sold
{Cherish the Winged World!}

"You girls stay here with Nita and don't get too close to the windows," she said, trying to sound calm but her voice broke. "Nita, this man's at the back door?"

"Said he would be waiting. He's a friend of Darcy's, *sí*?"

Claire nodded, then turned away from the front yard chaos and hurried toward the back of the house.

CHAPTER FIVE

"I'm starting to feel like Dorothy in that *Wizard of Oz* tornado," Jace told Mitch as they flew out of the calm, sunny eyewall of the storm into fierce winds again. "Lexi made me watch it—twice. Can't wait to see her again, though I'm going to put the skids on seeing any of her movies more than once. Besides, that Wicked Witch in it still scares her."

"Can't quite picture having kids," Mitch told him through their headsets. They had been talking on task for hours and had completed their mission—except for getting this big plane and crew home safely. They were both exhausted but still in battle alert mode. After all the new jargon with their scientist crew, it felt good to let down a bit.

Mitch went on. "Man, I hope the predictions of a busier than usual hurricane season are wrong. What if one hits when Kris and I are supposed to get married?"

"Don't even think that, because that would mean one was threatening Naples. We don't need any kind of chaos there. Thank God things have calmed down after all Lexi's

been through. It will be great to get home for a while between storm duty to peace and quiet and…no damn bumps
in the road, not to mention in the air," he said, though the
first blast of turbulence rocked them as if a giant, invisible
fist had hit the plane. He leveled them out and flew on.

Claire didn't see Will Warren at first, so perhaps the
crowd in front of the house had scared him away. How
long had the poor man been out here waiting—if he was
still here?

She spotted him over by the corner of the yard with the
small butterfly garden. Of course that was where he'd be.
At least now she wouldn't have to go looking for him to
find out if he knew anything about visitors to the butterfly farm or where Darcy might have gone. Ken Jensen had
mentioned it might be good for her to talk to Will without
Nick or the police along. Nick hadn't seemed too pleased
about that at first and had requested that he be with her if
she spoke to Will, but he would have to understand since the
man had come to her. She could be nonthreatening, and she
had known Will Warren years ago, though not well. It was
Darcy who had taken to him, but Claire and Lexi had also
attended many of his library story hours, a second generation enthralled by his children's tales and variety of voices.

He turned to face her with a striped tropical blue wave
butterfly on his arm. At least, even with the pain and pressure, she remembered which kind that was.

"Mrs. Markwood," he said, gently blowing the butterfly
off its perch. "I regret I seem to have called at a difficult
time. I especially regret what I heard from Tara Gerald this
morning." He frowned. His eyes looked watery. Surely he
had not been crying, too. His usually melodic voice seemed

scratchy. "Is Darcy still missing, and is there anything I can do to help?"

"Please come in the house," she said. "You were wise to come to the back door with the reporters out front."

"Like hovering hawks, though I pray they can help. Then it is true? She has disappeared and not returned?"

Claire nodded as they walked toward the house. Darcy was right to describe him as an "old-fashioned dandy." He would have looked just right in a bowler hat with a pocket watch vest and a carnation in his buttonhole. He wore a long-sleeved, light blue shirt and jeans, which looked as if they'd been ironed. And a bow tie, his signature piece, she recalled from years ago when she and Darcy were the kids at library story time. And he had come to their house with books for Mother once and stayed to tell them a story in their very own living room.

"Please have a seat while I check on how things are going," she said, gesturing toward their seating area in the Florida room. "Darcy's husband is meeting with the media out in front."

He ran his finger under one eye where a tear had puddled. Perhaps something in his own past—someone missing—made him especially moved. The fact he had come to visit rather than just waiting for news seemed most unusual. Perhaps he did know something that could help.

As he headed into his office, loosening his tie before yanking it off, Nick told his secretary, Cheryl, "Now that the news is out—I just called home to learn the newsmongers have descended on our house—I did talk the judge into a two-day delay. Two days, that's it." She came right behind him with her notepad. "Mrs. Lacy says she can use the rest. But with the weekend," he went on, "that's four days to find Darcy and support Claire and Lexi—Darcy's family, too."

"See, some judges have blood and not ice in their veins."

"Yeah," he said, grabbing his briefcase and slamming it shut. He also tried to shut out the picture he had when she'd mentioned blood. He'd seen too much of it and prayed Darcy wasn't lying cut or hurt somewhere—or worse.

"Nick, I do have to tell you one thing before you go," she said, glancing at her notepad.

"Someone called about Darcy or our reward for information? I didn't think that was out yet, so—"

"No. Not that. I just need a yea or nay about whether you will commit ASAP to interviewing that guy who owns the deep-sea fishing boat, ah—Larry Ralston, highly connected in town somehow. The mayor actually called, said to let him know if there was anything he could do to help find Darcy—and he put in a plug for your helping Ralston if he goes to trial. The guy's connected to a wealthy family, I think, probably contributors to the mayor's reelection campaign."

"Can you stall him until next week? Or can someone else in the firm meet with him?"

"He—and the mayor—want you."

"Larry Ralston is going to be fined big-time or may even face prison time because he netted that protected dolphin—which he denies, right?"

"Right. The environmental people will be all over this. You always say everyone is innocent until—"

"Yeah, I know. Listen, he'll have to wait until next week if he wants me to represent him. Besides, I don't need the eco-groups down here, at least not the ones who seem like they are foaming at the mouth, to be after me or the firm right now. Maybe give our resident tech genius Heck a call. Have him look into Larry Ralston and whoever he's tied to, so we know what we're really dealing with."

He locked his case and grabbed his coat and tie. *What we're really dealing with*—the words echoed in his head. What—who—were they dealing with for Darcy's abduction, if that was what it was? Intentional? A random crime of opportunity? Darcy wasn't an obvious target for an abduction, not well-known, not rich. His stomach churned. He prayed it wasn't someone trying to get back at Claire or him for something, because they were the ones who'd made enemies in the past. Meanwhile, he had to go check out that Fly Safe pro-butterfly group who had given Tara Gerald flak.

"Sorry, Nick," his longtime, faithful secretary and friend said, making him realize he was standing there frozen, lost in thought.

"Call me if anything turns up, okay?" was all he could manage before his voice snagged. He patted her shoulder on the way out the door.

"Darcy's husband is giving a press conference out there," Claire told Mr. Warren when she returned to the Florida room where he had risen and was pacing, staring out at the fenced-in yard. "I'm tempted to go out to back him up, but I've been through too many confrontations like that. Still, if I thought it would help Darcy, I would."

He nodded so strongly she thought he just might march out there, too. She had to get herself together. She had to settle down enough to take advantage of asking this man what he knew about Darcy that she might not even know.

"I appreciate your stopping by," she said, sitting at an angle to him when he came back to the couch. He perched there, leaning forward, somehow not sinking into the soft leather cushions.

"I came to ask if there was anything I might do. To learn the facts. And to see how Darcy's daughter was—is—getting on."

"Not well, I'm afraid. Nor is my daughter, so I need to get back to them. Let me be frank, Mr. Warren—"

"Will. Please call me Will."

"Will. I suppose you didn't know her that well, but can you suggest anyone who might want to hurt Darcy?"

"Or, if she was taken, could they have misidentified her as Tara?"

"Yes, but surely not for long. Unless, of course, they immediately incapacitated her so she couldn't explain or protest. Her purse was missing, so that would have been full of ID. Her phone was found on the floor and someone—surely not Darcy—left the butterfly door to the exotic house open."

He sat even more forward on the soft seat. "And were any of the exotics missing? Has Tara taken a survey—a count?"

"I don't know. She said some orange somethings were missing, though—can't think of their name now, though I know it."

That made him sag back a bit. "The falcates. It had to be the falcate orangetips. Valuable and not indigenous to this area, though they like the sunny south and adapt well. Their native turf, if I can put it like that, is over in Louisiana."

"The falcates—valuable how?" she asked, even as she heard a racket from the front of the house. The girls' shrill voices, Steve's...

She vaulted to her feet and ran with Will puffing along behind her.

"What happened?" Claire asked Steve as Jilly clung to him around his waist in the front hall and Lexi just hugged that doll.

"The kids cheered me when I came in," he said. "I think most of the crowd is breaking up, good thing, too, 'cause I about lost it answering some of their damn questions. Oh, Will," he said, tipping his head to see the man behind her. "What are you doing here?"

"Just here to see if I can help."

Claire was surprised they knew each other, since Steve often worked out of town and wasn't the type for story time.

Lexi's doll voice said, "If you came to tell us a story, Mr. Will, make it a happy one, 'cause we are all going to cry over losing Aunt Darcy. It's just like me being taken away. Very, very bad."

When Nick came in from the garage, Claire threw herself into his arms as if he'd been the one taken and had come back at last.

"I have at least four days off," he told her. "Let's see what we can do."

"Will Warren showed up, but I hardly had time to question him. I did say I'd go with him tomorrow to help Tara do a careful count of the butterfly breed that is evidently missing, the falcate orangetips. I guess they're valuable because they're rare around here."

"He just showed up? You didn't invite him?"

"Absolutely not, so I don't expect a scolding from you or Ken Jensen. But for a double-whammy, Lexi has really regressed, not just last night but this morning. I was hoping she'd kind of sleep it off. Nick, I'm afraid to just take that old doll from her. Last time she went off the deep end. She didn't use or need it as a prop but just had that imaginary friend. This time, I think I'd better try to wean her away from it, carefully talk her out of it."

"Maybe we could replace it with another one."

"Doll shopping is down on my list right now, but that might be worth a try. It used to be a darling doll, but it's so—so worn and tattered now that it kind of haunts me. Finding Darcy has to come first, but I'll keep working on finding some good, healthy substitute for that doll. You see, when Jace and I split up, it did comfort her. So I need to spend time with her, help her through this and, if I can't again, get her some counseling. I swear, Trey's the only normal one right now, and I think even he senses something's wrong. However pregnant Nita is, I'm so grateful she can still help with the kids before her own arrives at least."

They still held tight, not moving farther into the house. "Got a call on the way home," he told her. "Heck's coming over tonight to report on some research he's doing. And though he doesn't know it yet, I want him to look into that Fly Safe group. Probably research Tara, too, even Will Warren."

"Will is advertising his new book on butterflies, *Love and Lore*. I have his card. By the way, he said he thought Darcy might've had that book with her since she was reading it, so maybe whoever took her took that, too. It would have fit in that big purse of hers. Oh, Nick, where is she? Is she—is she all right?" Claire cried at the thought of what she'd almost asked: *Is she alive?*

CHAPTER SIX

They stayed up late that night, going over possible contacts and scenarios, laying plans, talking to Ken again about further police strategy and trying to bolster Steve. Finally, feeling like the walking dead, they got a bit of sleep.

The next morning, as soon as Nita arrived to take care of the children, as they had decided late last night, Steve and Claire headed out to go look through Darcy's things for any clue as to where she might have gone—or who had taken her. Claire had decided to delay going to help Tara count butterflies and question her carefully.

"Let's get going to look through Darcy's things," Claire said. "We should have done that immediately, and I've promised the police I'll report in if we find anything that could help—give us any clue. I'm glad I'm going with you," she added over their adults-only breakfast since Nita was eating on the patio with the three children. "Despite how close the two of you are, it would be good to have my point of view, too."

"Yeah," Steve said, and heaved a sigh, staring into his half-eaten bowl of cereal. "You're the next closest to her, not counting the kids."

Nick nodded. "Meanwhile, like we planned, I'm going to take Ken Jensen at his word that it's okay for me to check out this ecology group Fly Safe. They have a big website but also an office. I'll make it all about Jace and Mitch wanting that name, too. Though, actually, this group had it first, so they have dibs, as I used to say in prelawyer days."

"Wish I could go back to prebutterfly days," Steve said, picking up his cereal spoon again, then just staring at it. "Yeah, Claire. I can use your help since I don't want to leave Jilly for long, either."

Claire looked out through the Florida room glass door at the children. Nita was letting Trey stuff Cheerios in his mouth, so at least one of them was eating. The girls looked slumped, silent for once. Yes, she needed to go with Steve, but she wouldn't stay away long, either. And this afternoon, if she could get the girls to take the naps they now thought were beneath them, she'd drive out to see Tara again. No way could she stay here, sit still and just wait for news.

"Glad I caught you, boss," Heck called to Nick as Nick opened his garage door to head out to talk to the Fly Safe group.

"Glad you're here. I was hoping you'd get here earlier."

"So I hear, but I was in Miami with Gina and came right back when I got the message. I know this is tough. Didn't mean to let you down."

"You never do, my friend, but I need your help."

Nick slammed the car door without getting in and met Heck in the opening to the garage.

Heck's face was somber. "So sorry about your sister-in-

law. How's Claire doing? How are Lexi and Darcy's Mil-
lie?"

"Jilly," Nick corrected. "The girls and Claire are really distressed, of course, and Claire's thrown herself into
looking for clues. She's with Darcy's husband, Steve, at his
house going through things now. Lexi's gone back into her
hostile imaginary friend routine. This time she's carting an
old doll around who is the imaginary friend."

Nick leaned back against the trunk of his car and sighed.
"Nita's inside with the kids, and both Kris and Brit are
coming over to help entertain the girls. Jace and Mitch
are on their first hurricane flight over the Caribbean, so
I appreciate everyone is pitching in. Claire said she'd be
back soon, but I've got to see some people who...who may
know something."

"Or may be guilty? I know that look, boss. Want me to
go along?"

"What I want you to do is what you're the absolute best
at, Heck. I need you to do a thorough search on a local
flying-animal protection group called Fly Safe, which I'm
going to check out in person now."

"Got it," Heck told him with a nod. He took no notes,
but never really had to. The guy was a computer genius
who had bailed Nick out of trouble more than once. Hector
Munoz was a friend, too, and Nick had tried to bolster him
throughout the guy's off-again, on-again relationship with
his Cuban fiancée, Gina, who was in med school in Miami.

"Also," Nick went on, "I need bio dossiers on a couple
of people. Tara Gerald, who owns the Flutterby Farm out
on Sabal Palm. She used to be an elementary teacher, had
Lexi in her class. Also a guy named Will Warren—probably William—who works at the library now but, in the

past, left town for several years. He's an author, a butterfly expert, published a book recently."

"Probably a website and Facebook page at the least," Heck said with another nod. "I'm on it. And, boss, you be careful, too. We been in things before where one thing— one crime—led to another."

"That's what I told Claire, to be careful, but she's upset that I was upset she'd spent some time with a character witness—damn, don't mean to be talking like this is a trial—here at the house. She said I interrupted what she was starting to learn from the guy—Will Warren—but I told her we'll go to see him together. You know Claire. There's no way to hold her back or protect her from this tragedy, not with Darcy gone."

Nick shoved away from his car and put a hand on his friend's shoulder. "Almost forgot," he told Heck. "Check out Larry Ralston, too. Owns a deep-sea fishing boat down on the Naples pier. I think the boat's called *Down Under*."

"Good name for a charter fishing boat, right? Does he tie into Darcy's disappearance, too?"

"No, law firm business, which I almost forgot. I think he wants me to defend him on illegal netting of a dolphin charge. Find out if and how well-connected he is in town, because the mayor called over it. You know, Heck, I feel I'm at sea right now, and I'd definitely name my boat that."

"It feels funny, going through her stuff—so glad you came along," Steve told Claire as he turned on Darcy's laptop to look through email, and Claire headed toward the master bedroom to go through the drawers in Darcy's dresser and bedside table. They figured they were barely ahead of the police possibly confiscating her laptop and searching the house if they could turn up any proof of foul play in her disappearance.

Steve had slightly pulled out the drawers that were Darcy's so she'd know which ones to search. Claire saw that the table on her sister's side of their king-size bed had books piled on the open shelf under the single drawer Steve had pulled ajar, surely not to search himself but so she'd think to look in it.

What in the world was she looking for? She knew her sister better than anyone except Steve. No way was Darcy hiding something like a lover or trouble with Steve. It couldn't be that she owed someone money. She was not despondent. They were never going to turn up something like a farewell note or—God forbid—a suicide note.

Just the usual in the bedside table drawer. Silk eye shades to sleep better in the light, lip balm, a comb, tissues, a pencil and small notepad—blank.

"I'm blank, too," Claire whispered, sniffing back tears. "I have no idea what could have happened."

She made certain nothing was stuck between the books on the lower shelf, then went to the dresser and carefully examined the clothing in the drawers, much of the shirts and shorts familiar-looking. She sifted through the lingerie drawer—some sexy stuff, a black nightgown and lacy panties. She even checked for notes or photos under the drawer liner paper, which gave off a faint floral scent.

She looked under the bed, amazingly dust free, and through Darcy's half of the closet, which Steve had opened for her. Hidden under folded garments on the top shelf above the hanging clothes, she found a present already wrapped for Steve for their anniversary. If—if Darcy didn't come back soon, should she give it to Steve?

Nothing in the two extra purses, nothing in the shoes on the floor rack. Claire sat back on her haunches and sighed. She'd go see how Steve was doing, maybe look through bathroom and kitchen drawers and storage cabinets.

But then she remembered that their mother often filed notes within the pages of books she read. Darcy used to do that, too. She'd just flip through the books in the bed-side table.

Two books on butterflies. Neither one was by Will Warren, but this one had a beautiful cover. She took it to look through. Darcy had a sticky note in it with *falcate oranget-ips* scribbled on it, and yes, that was what the entire double page was on. That breed kept coming up so maybe she should read up on it. Tara and Will had mentioned those. Tara had said some were missing from the exotic house, and Will had seemed interested. She and Nick had both noticed that same breed had cocoons missing from pegs in the butterfly room inside Tara's house.

The other books included one on child rearing and a couple of novels. Claire's brain flashed back to the diary she'd found in German that had held important clues for one of Nick's key cases—and hers. No diary here.

"But have I read this one?" she said aloud, studying the cover. No, she thought, but she recalled now why it rang a bell. This book by author John Fowles called *The Collector* was one of the many too-far-over-their-heads novels Mother had read to them. After their father left, that was evidently her way of "taking care" of them.

Claire decided to take it along with the nonfiction butterfly book. But wasn't there something in this novel about butterflies? She racked her brain for a dark memory that would not quite surface. It was something about Mother reading to them, scaring them as if they were to blame for Daddy's desertion.

"Claire? You okay? I've been calling for you."

Steve stood in the door of the bedroom, his fist raised to knock. Or had he knocked?

"You find something?" he asked.

"A couple of her books I'll take with me, if that's okay. The one ties into butterflies—maybe the other one, too."

"Yeah, fine. Let's go look through her desk where she paid bills and stuff. Maybe there's even something in the monthly paychecks from Ms. Gerald. There was nothing strange on her laptop except she's been searching articles on hibernation—of bears and even dolphins, of all things. You ever hear dolphins can sleep with half their brain and keep the other half alert?"

"No. Can't imagine how that ties to butterflies," she told him, getting up with the two books. "I suppose when they're in the cocoon, that's a kind of hibernation. I'll re-search that."

As they approached Darcy's desk, Claire noticed two five-by-seven photographs she hadn't see before perched on top of it. The familiar, somewhat beat-up desk was a rolltop that had once belonged to their father. When their mother had died, they had split up some of her things, and Darcy had wanted this. Its curved roller top was open now and Claire saw the cubbyholes were stacked with various bills, receipts and other items. She leaned closer to look at the photos under glass with gold metal frames.

One was obviously taken at a wedding reception, but not someone Claire recognized. Oh, she saw why Darcy had it on display: in the background was a large butterfly release. Reception guests looked up as a spiral of bright butterflies flew skyward. She recalled that Darcy had gone to several such events for or with Tara Gerald. No wonder Claire didn't know anyone in it.

"Darcy took the butterflies there," Steve said. "It was in Bonita Springs. And that other picture—wish she wouldn't have put it here. A release of nearly a hundred yellow and blue ones at a funeral out on Marco Island. The deceased was on the University of Michigan football team years ago, and their colors were maize and blue. Crazy, huh?"

"Who would think of that?" she said, squinting at the faces in it. "Oh, I do know someone here. See—Will Warren. So did Darcy go with him to this?"

Steve shook his head. "We were busy that day, so I said let him do it on his own, though he'd asked her. The guy attends a lot of funerals, she said. Don't want him releasing butterflies at my funeral…" His voice trailed off. He shook his head and shuddered.

"Do you know him very well?" Claire asked. "Nick and I are going to talk to him soon to try to learn more than I did at the house yesterday."

"Darcy liked the guy and—same as you—she had good sense about people, so I just let it go, her friendship with him. But a guy who likes to go to funerals—not my type."

He sank into the chair, propped his elbows on the desk and put his head in his hands. "Let's look around, but I think searching for stuff here is a dead end," he told her. "Didn't mean to say it that way. We've got to find her—trace her—somehow."

It frightened Claire that it sounded as if he'd shifted his thinking. Did he now believe that Darcy was not coming back, could only be traced, hopefully found? But with a final dead end?

CHAPTER SEVEN

When Claire returned home from Steve and Darcy's house, she called Tara to see if she and Steve could come out to the butterfly farm for a visit. But a friend of Tara's answered the phone. She said that Tara had gone to bed with a migraine headache. Though feeling bad for her, Claire was actually relieved.

She knew it would be better to go there with Steve tomorrow morning. He still seemed to be seething silently, ready to explode, not acting out his anger, but rather suppressing it. And some of that seemed focused on Tara. Suppressing his feelings was somewhat typical of a take-charge man like him. He was acting as if he were emotionally drugged. But in case he exploded, she had to accompany him to Tara's. That way, she could be a buffer, if needed, as well as psych out how each of them were handling this tragedy. Helping Lexi came first, but Claire was worried about Steve and Jilly, too. No doubt, anyone in her situation would be concerned, but she had the extra burden of all that psychology training making her overly obsessed.

But she felt it would be best if she stayed with Jilly and Lexi now while Steve went for his formal interview with Ken Jensen, who could hopefully calm him. Jace's new wife, Brittany, and Kris Kane were at the house. Claire could tell they had already cheered the girls up when she saw them all drinking juice and eating Oreos on the backyard patio where she joined them.

Both Kris and Brit had lively personalities, so that must surely help. Kris, an archaeologist, suffered from what was commonly called face blindness, a disability that kept her from remembering people's appearances, even of those close to her. She would soon marry Jace's best friend and copilot, Mitch. She looked the part of a Florida girl with her straight blond hair and blue eyes. She was even working on a tan.

Brit had sharp blue eyes and a glossy mane of sandy-hued hair she often wore pulled straight back in a ponytail or up in a messy bun. She was petite compared to Kris and Claire. A zoologist who worked with big cats at the Naples Zoo, Brit was always so animated that she almost gave off sparks.

She'd seen before that both women were able to translate facets of their fascinating careers to elementary school level. Both, Claire thought, would make great mothers someday. Before she sat down with them, everyone shared hugs and greetings. She wedged a chair in between Lexi and Jilly.

"Butterflies are way cool," Brit told the girls, evidently picking up on an interrupted conversation. "We love them at the zoo, wild ones and the ones we buy and raise, not that you can ever tame a butterfly. You know what? In the old days, the Greeks and Romans thought butterflies symbolized—I mean, kind of stood for—the human soul, like what is in people that makes them special. Claire, did you know the Greek word for butterfly is *psyche*?"

"All my psychology classes and I missed that," Claire admitted.

"And," Kris put in, "I have a friend who once worked at excavating—that means digging out, girls—a temple dedicated to butterflies outside Mexico City. It's almost like people in the old days worshipped them."

"But not anymore, right?" Lexi asked.

She still had that doll on her lap, but at least, Claire thought, she was showing an interest in something else.

"Not anymore, not worship exactly," Kris said. "Still, in some places like Korea and China—especially Japan— people are crazy about all insects, especially the kind with the beautiful wings. I mean, *obsessed*," she added, emphasizing that word and rolling her eyes at Claire.

"Obsessed how?" Claire asked. "I have a book on butterflies I'm going to read, but I never heard that."

"It's true. I read a stat somewhere that something like ten percent of Japanese men are passionate butterfly collectors. They have clubs where they trade them. Some keep beetles, crickets and butterflies as pets and will pay thousands of dollars for a certain butterfly specimen. Huge prices online for them. I looked once. I remember one went for over sixty thousand dollars—probably illegally caught and smuggled ones—but I won't mention how they display them," she added with another roll of her eyes for Claire when Lexi wasn't looking.

Claire was grateful Kris hadn't gone into how dead butterflies were exhibited or stored. The girls had mostly seen live ones, not the ones put in envelopes, chilled and sent far away for releases, not to mention stuck with pins and shown under glass among avid collectors, although they had seen Tara Gerald's prize displays. But with Lexi, Tara could get a pass for anything.

Suddenly back in her doll Princess's lower voice, Lexi said, "If those Japanese people love butterflies best, then cats and dogs might like to kill them and eat them—the butterflies, not the people. Lexi and me think it's sad they get caught with nets."

Claire saw Kris and Brit startle, so had Lexi's doll been silent lately? Or maybe Kris's emphasizing the word *obsessed* a minute ago was a tip-off that the doll had been speaking as a separate person before Claire joined them?

Lexi went on in that awful voice. "Ms. Gerald said the nets don't hurt them if you do it right. But I still think that's like mean people catching good people and trapping them, like what happened to Lexi and maybe Aunt Darcy."

Silence descended with a thud. Claire's heart fell, and she bit her lower lip to keep from yanking that horrid doll out of her daughter's arms or trying to explain to Kris and Brit. More and more, Lexi was making her doll speak for her as she had not before with her invisible friend.

Patience, Claire told herself. Patience and love to keep Lexi from slipping back more into her past with disassociation and hysteria triggered by fear. Yet Claire felt she herself had been snared by terror when what she, too, needed was a safety net.

Nick found the offices for Fly Safe on Commercial Boulevard wedged in among larger establishments and warehouses. Clearly, he thought, someone in this organization had money to own or rent a space in the midst of this busi-

ness park. The sign in the single large window read Butterflies Are Free and So Should All Wildlife Be.

He hadn't called ahead as he wanted to explain himself
on-site. He rang the buzzer and heard it sound within.

A gray-haired, middle-aged woman with huge, horn-
rimmed glasses that made her look like an owl opened the door.

"Butterflies are not free, but should be," she greeted him.
"May I help you—if you are not soliciting."

"I'm attorney Nick Markwood. I wanted to discuss your
domain name, Fly Safe, with someone in charge."

"You mean like it has to be patented or something like that?
Not interested," she clipped out, and started to close the door.

"No, nothing like that," he told her, wedging his foot
against the door. "I have friends and clients interested in
that name for their small company and wanted to discuss
sharing the title, since—I believe—your endeavors and
goals are very different from theirs. I'd like to discuss that."

"Oh. Well, maybe for a donation. I'm Nora Delancy, but
you understand, I'm sure, that we have to be careful here.
Eco-groups like us do have naysayers, even enemies to put
it nicely, just as the birds and bees do." She smiled at him as
if she'd made a joke. He felt her attitude toward him shift.
"Please come in," she said, opening the door wider, "and
I'll get our board member who's here right now. Just have
a seat there," she said, indicating a rocking chair, which
faced another. Both looked like antiques, and the rest of
the office furniture and decor had a "down-home" feel.

"I'll explain to Lincoln Yost and be right back," she
added, and disappeared into the back room. He could hear
muted voices within.

Nick quickly looked around to assess the place. Photos
of various South Florida wildlife, even a dolphin cresting

a wave. The endangered Florida panther drinking from shallow water in the Everglades. Several bats hanging upside down from a rafter. And yes, four pictures of butterflies. Also, a photo of what looked like what Darcy had described as a butterfly release. Weird, but it wasn't at a wedding like Claire was talking about for Kris and Mitch. No, he realized as he stood up and leaned closer, it was at a funeral, because the coffin had not yet been lowered into the ground, and he could see headstones. And the man releasing the butterflies sure looked like—was—Will Warren, the guy who had been at their house when the TV vans were there.

He squinted to see what had been hand printed across the bottom of the picture: *These butterflies might as well be buried, too!*

So, if these people could ID Will, would that mean Fly Safe had it in for him? And maybe knew that he was associated with Tara Gerald, and went out to the farm to free butterflies but found Darcy alone there, who protested, and one thing led to another and...?

"Sorry," the thin, very tall, African American man said when he came into the room, "but Nora didn't get your name. I'm Linc Yost."

Nick rose and shook hands. "Nick Markwood, an attorney at Markwood, Benton and Chase here in town. Did Ms. Delancy mention I'm here for information and a favor—perhaps a mutually beneficial one?"

"We've had this name for four years," he said, gesturing with his big hands. "We thought about Fly Free but chose Fly Safe instead. All our indigenous wildlife—so much of it threatened—needs to be safe, which is the same as free in most cases."

"I can tell by looking around here—and your sign out-side—that you are very dedicated to your cause. Do you promote it through publicity or active protests or what kind of—?"

"Yes, anything we can do to stop offenders and get sup-port," Yost interrupted, as if he'd read his mind. "The unfair cruelties of expansion and aggression by so-called civilization need to be met with decisive action as well as mere words. So, have one of the rockers," he said with a gesture, and they sat, but neither of them rocked.

This man spoke well and with conviction. He had a lightning bolt shaved into both sides of his hair above his ears. He was dressed in new-looking jeans and a T-shirt that read Naples High School Golden Eagles.

"You're a NHS graduate?" Nick asked with a nod at his shirt.

"A while ago," Yost said. "I teach biology there now and feel I'm educating the next generation about the cause. So exactly what can I do for you?"

"I'd appreciate talking to you about whether your proj-ect could see sharing its name with two pilots who intend to give private flying lessons out of Marco Airport starting this winter, since the goals of your endeavor would be so different from theirs. Maybe we could even work out a deal about their pulling one of those popular banners behind a plane for you above the beach once in a while. They've talked about filling in their flying time with that sort of advertising. Their main career is hurricane observational flights, but that's seasonal."

"So they're already working for a good cause. If we can be forewarned about devastating storms, that could help animals, too—if we can help them." As rigid as the man was sitting in the rocking chair, he sat up even straighter. "I'd need to talk to others on our board, but it sounds intriguing. So, I assume you have a business card?"

Nick nodded and pulled one out of his billfold.

"We can always use funding and promotion," Yost said, taking the card and glancing at it. "Besides, you never know when a fight-the-good-fight project like ours could use some legal advice, but I see you're a criminal lawyer, and it wouldn't be that. We don't so much as trespass—unless our pleas and warnings haven't been heeded. Our cause, our mission, is that important and sometimes that desperate."

Nick nodded. He thought he'd found out all he needed here—plus that Jace and Mitch, for a donation, could probably use the project's name. He'd almost come to believe that this Fly Safe group would work hard to keep animals safe, but not at the cost of human safety. Yet the vibes of suppressed anger he was picking up from this well-spoken man, especially just now with the frown and steely shift of voice, made him wonder. Was there more than frustration and maybe desperation behind that controlled voice and pleasant personality for the Fly Safe cause?

"Would you mind sharing a list of your board members?" Nick asked. "I would like to send them a letter of request, just to be certain everything clears. By the way, I see one man in that photo back there who reads books to kids at the library."

Yost squinted at the picture. "That guy is sure as hell not on our board! Actually, he's part of the enemy army. He may read cute books to innocent minds but he's one of the snakes in Eden—one hiding in a butterfly bush."

Nick didn't argue because he didn't want to let on that he'd just received verification to his silent assumption that this group could be militant. And, as he often did, he wished he had Claire with him to read this guy even better.

"We need a meeting of the minds," Ken Jensen said at their kitchen table late that afternoon.

Claire was grateful that Nita was still here with the kids—outside looking at butterflies—while she, Steve, Nick, Heck and Ken conferred in person this time, to be certain their investigation kept rolling. Steve had spent much of the morning at the police station, talking to Ken, and they seemed to have come to an agreement to work together.

"I regret to tell the rest of you what I told Steve," Ken went on, "that neither the NPD nor the highway patrol have seen any sign of Darcy or her vehicle. Claire, Steve told me that you found nothing unusual or incriminating in Darcy's personal effects."

Steve still looked as if he might explode. His hands were clenched on the table; Claire feared for him despite the fact that Ken's not searching their house himself made her think he believed Steve was not a possible suspect.

"And Nick says he got a mixed message from his visit to Fly Safe and his talk with Lincoln Yost," Ken went on. "By the way, Linc Yost is a former local high school basketball star who went to the University of Kentucky on a full athletic scholarship. He was good there, too. Can't say I know him, but I have friends who say he's an excellent teacher, gets the kids involved in projects like protect the dolphins, this and that."

"Did he play pro ball?" Nick asked.

"Had an injury before the draft," Ken said, shaking his

head. "I'm sure that really changed his life, from possible big bucks as a rich pro NBA prospect to a teacher's salary."

"He seemed on edge, but it's a stretch to think his protect-the-flying-wildlife volunteer work would include kidnapping someone," Nick insisted.

"Or kidnapping those falcate orangetip butterflies," Claire said. "I noticed in a book Darcy had that she'd been reading up on them, and they are the breed that's most obviously missing from the farm—some of their cocoons inside Tara's house, too, remember, Nick? I want to ask her about that."

He nodded. "It's a stretch, but that needs looking into. By the way, this dolphin tie-in interests me. There was a dolphin picture in the Fly Safe office, though there were other pics of animals there that don't fly. Ironic that I've been contacted at the firm to defend a man who is being charged with killing a dolphin. Heck, keep researching the dolphin angle. Are they endangered, even though we see so many around here?"

"Got it, boss. I'm still looking into Fly Safe like you asked—especially since Yost wouldn't give you the backers' names. I'm tracking down Will Warren's past, too. Looks to me like the guy actually lived in Japan for a while."

"Japan?" Claire echoed, and sat up straighter.

When she said no more, Ken frowned but madly scribbled something down in his notepad. "I'd say there's no connection between butterflies and dolphins, a stab in the dark," he said. "But in police work we always say there's no such thing as mere coincidence or circumstance, especially when we're desperate. Everybody stay safe—fly safe—but keep me informed. So far, we're clutching at straws—or in this case, at delicate butterfly wings."

CHAPTER EIGHT

Claire's body screamed with exhaustion and her mind was in a million pieces, but she fought to keep calm as she convinced Lexi to take an afternoon nap.

She sat on the edge of the child's bed. Nick had said to let him know if she needed him, and that he'd be playing with Trey before his nap. Jilly was with Steve. Unfortunately, Princess the doll was in bed with Lexi, eyes eternally open and staring, her well-worn body carefully tucked in next to Lexi under the sheet. The only good thing Claire could think of regarding the child's obsession with the doll was that it suggested she didn't judge people, even things, by their looks.

"Lexi, sweetheart," she began, raising her voice over the rain drumming against the windows, "I'm sure we will find Aunt Darcy soon. We are all working hard on that."

"Maybe the bad person took her in a car, then a plane like they did me. So she could be really far away."

At least that was in her own voice. Claire had several approaches to take here, so she'd try the one she hoped was the best.

"Wherever she is, we will pray for her safety. But you need to realize that the people who took you are either dead or in prison. It would not be the same people, so what happened to you is long over, and you are safe here with us."

"Daddy should be here, then I'd be a little safer. I know you and Dad take care of me. Nita, too. But I heard you tell Daddy when he left to go flying into storms to be very careful, so is he safe?"

"You know your daddy is a very good pilot, and he's with Mitch, who can fly planes, too. So—you've been worried about Daddy as well as Aunt Darcy?"

"Of course!"

The doll's voice. Lexi reached over and sat Princess up.

"Lexi, honey, I just don't want you to—"

"And I heard you tell Lexi's dad, who lives here, that this storm is the way out bands of the hurricane. Is there a hurricane coming, the one Daddy's flying in?"

Trying to ignore the doll, Claire leaned closer and put her arms around Lexi to lift her up into her embrace. "I said this rain and wind are the outer bands of the storm— way far out. Your daddy and Mitch will be back soon, safe and sound, and we're all safe here. Please, Lexi, just calm down and take a little rest and everything will be fine. Your daddy will come back, and we'll find Aunt Dar—"

"You keep saying that, but so far it isn't true!" Lexi made the doll say. "We just want to find Aunt Darcy. Jilly does, too, or all three of us are going to go looking for her ourselves!"

When Claire finally calmed her enough that she laid the doll down again, Lexi went to sleep almost immediately, obviously exhausted. Weren't they all, though, physically, emotionally? But now, one more fear: she had to tell Steve and Nick, Nita, too, that it was possible Lexi and Jilly had talked about finding Darcy on their own.

That night, again, no one slept well and not just because of the rain. Despite the baby monitor, Claire went in once or twice to check on Trey and then Lexi, who was so sound asleep she had hardly changed positions. Claire was tempted to rip that doll out of her arms and destroy it, but the repercussions from that could make things worse, if that was possible. At least Jilly was sound asleep, too, in the other twin bed.

Claire padded barefoot back into Trey's room to check on him—yes, thank heavens, someone was sleeping like a baby—then headed back to bed, hoping not to wake Nick, who had tossed and turned before finally dropping off to sleep. Outside, the rain and wind thrashed the palm fronds against the roof. A distant rumble of thunder made her wonder if the butterflies outside had found shelter.

"Lexi okay?" Nick whispered when Claire slid back in bed. So he was sleeping fitfully, too.

"Still out. I thought you were asleep."

He reached over and drew her to him, pulling her back against his chest with her bottom cradled in his lap. He kissed the nape of her neck, then her bare shoulder before whispering, "Sleep, sweetheart. That's the best thing you can do for yourself right now and for the rest of us. I'll go check on Lexi and Trey next, just for my own sanity. Think we could save some money being our own baby monitors? And did you take your narco meds?"

"Yes. I hate to be back on those heavy-hitters but I need

them for now. If I don't get some rest, I'll fall asleep on my feet, and I have to go see Tara as soon as possible and research some things."

"That's all for tomorrow. We'll go together. For now, just sleep."

It felt so good, so safe, in their bed, in his arms. If only this lurking, dark horror about Darcy's fate would not hold to her, too.

Claire was drifting, but at least Darcy was here, too. Mother was reading aloud to them when they'd much rather watch TV or play outside with the other kids. But Mother collected books, had ever since their father had left without a word—at least without a word to his daughters. Why did he leave? Where was he, and why didn't he come back?

Oh, Mother was reading from a book called *The Collector*. There was a butterfly and a door key on the cover. But the same book she had from Darcy's house was different—a headless woman held down with tape.

Claire shuddered. She knew she was dreaming and wanted to escape, but she had to stay. She had to know about the story. No, she could wake up and find her own book, the book Darcy had. And here, she thought Darcy had hated Mother's stories. Mr. Warren's at the library were so much better, funny, fun books, things Claire could understand.

Now she remembered. This story called *The Collector* was about a man who was obsessed with a woman. He usually collected butterflies, but he drugged her with chloroform and kidnapped her and kept her prisoner. But what was also sad was that his prisoner wrote letters to her sister she knew would never be delivered. She tried to escape but she died—she died!

With a gasp, Claire sat straight up in bed.

"Claire, what is it? Are you all right?"

Nick's voice yanked her back to reality, but could that fictional book have been real—an omen? Now she remembered why she and Darcy had hated it. That Mother had read it to them made her angry now. How dare she read a horror story with an abduction and sexual obsession and a tragic ending to her daughters, who had been traumatized years before by their father's strange desertion! How much she had tried to love Mother, how much she missed her and felt sad for her, but that was bordering on child abuse!

But did Darcy know someone who was obsessed with her, so she'd picked up a copy of that old book she remembered because—because...

"Claire, did you hear me? A bad dream?" Nick asked, gently pulling her into his embrace.

She nodded. They both jumped as a crash of lightning nearby shook the house. The dim light in the master bath went out; the bedside alarm clock began blinking its 3:17 a.m. red numbers, then dimmed to black. Their security alarm began to beep.

"A bad dream but maybe good," she whispered to herself as they both got up to check the house and their children.

"Hope the electricity comes back on soon," he muttered. "I'll turn off the alarm."

She fumbled for the small flashlight in her bedside table drawer. "Nick," she whispered, shining the thin beam ahead of her in the pitch dark, "I just realized I have to talk to Will Warren again. Soon."

The electricity came back on in the morning. Once Nita had arrived to stay with the children, Claire, Steve and Nick headed out to the Flutterby Farm. The three of them hoped to catch Will Warren at the main library later, though Claire would rather go alone. Steve was adamant about talking to him, too, and she and Nick didn't want Steve facing down anyone alone.

Tara had phoned Claire to tell her that her migraine was under control, and she would like to see them, so they drove out immediately in Nick's car. Claire was relieved he was going along, because she still felt Steve could be volatile. She prayed he wouldn't blame poor Tara.

The curtains were drawn and no lights were on inside the old house, because Tara had said on the phone that helped her "poor aching head." Although Claire was hoping they could ease into an interrogation, Steve asked right away if he could see where Darcy had been taken. Claire volunteered to show him so that Tara wouldn't have to go out into the bright sun. Nick went along, too, since he had not examined the scene.

"I see the so-called butterfly door is double-netted," Steve observed. "So how did someone leave it open, if that's how some of them escaped?"

"As I understand it," Claire said, "both netted curtains were shoved aside, which allowed some of the exotics to get out. At least, they were missing. On her own, Darcy would never have been so careless."

"So," Steve said, "it was someone else's fault, deliberate or just ignorant."

Claire said, "I'm thinking the netting must have been left that way for a while for close to twenty orangetips to escape. Actually, I looked that breed up in Darcy's butterfly book, where she had them bookmarked. They're properly named falcate orangetips, commonly called just orangetips. The males, you might know, have showy orange spots on each wing, while the female is plain white. They're not large, and they don't live long."

At that last wording, Steve's and Claire's frowning gazes clashed before Steve looked away. *They don't live long* hung in the air with their thoughts again on Darcy.

"So," Nick put in during the awkward pause, "are orangetips worth a lot of money for some reason? Rare? Special?"

"That's one of the questions I have to ask Tara," Claire said. "I do know they're not indigenous to South Florida and prefer a woodland setting—Louisiana and Kentucky, places like that. Not the Everglades and swamps."

The two men looked around at the plush tropical growth of the plants most butterflies loved. Claire pointed out where Darcy's phone was found—with Tara's prints on it in her panic. Nick looked jumpy when the butterflies landed on him and he blew them carefully off. Steve just shifted away from them. They would hardly, Claire thought, make obsessed fans like the Japanese men Kris had mentioned.

"Let's go talk to Tara," Claire suggested. "I hope the dimness in her house helps her, and I'm sure loud sounds would startle her," she added, hoping both men took that as a hint to avoid raising their voices. She could tell they were both frustrated, but so was she.

Carefully closing both butterfly doors, they headed for the house.

Jace was pleased to be back on land where his phone worked. He wanted to call Claire so he could talk to Lexi. He checked his texts, then his emails. Damn, no "Welcome back to earth, Daddy" message, so he'd just call Claire and have her get Lexi on, then call Brit. Or he could call Brit first. She'd said she'd make an effort to see Lexi while he was gone.

He went to his texts again. Yep, several from Brit. He opened the latest one.

Claire's sister, Darcy, has disappeared from her job. Police on it. Big local news. Darcy's husband here. Jilly distraught but Lexi worse, hiding behind imaginary friend and some old doll. Call me when you land.

"Everything okay?" Mitch asked when Jace stopped walking and just stared at his phone.

"My former sister-in-law, Lexi's aunt, is missing. Gotta get home. Out of the hurricane and—and back into a storm."

CHAPTER NINE

Even in the dimness of Tara's house, Claire noted the living room walls were covered with framed photos of Tara with her friends—all women, one including Darcy.

Claire looked at it closely but quickly. It must be a blowup of a selfie, because it was blurry and not a very good photo of either of them, maybe because the camera was too low. Darcy looked merely content; Tara was beaming and had her arm around Darcy. Although Darcy had not worked at the butterfly farm for long, Claire wondered if Tara, an only child and childless, regarded Darcy almost as a daughter. Claire berated herself for wishing she had an older friend and mentor like that. Despite resenting Mother's treatment of them, Claire had tried to close that gap in her life. Yet she admitted that she missed her selfish mother and traitor of a father.

But on the other wall, opposite of where she, Nick and Steve now sat on a flower-print sofa, they all seemed to admire not just the photos, but the beautifully framed rows of butterflies, meticulously arranged by size and color under glass. Claire skimmed the many specimens for the orangetips she'd seen in Darcy's book. Yes, there—both a male and female with wings perfectly outspread, pinned, motionless, dead.

Claire waited for Tara to answer Steve's questions, some things she, Ken and Nick had already been over. Tara was openly weeping now, wringing her hands and apologizing again and again for Darcy's disappearance, for going to the post office despite the fact she'd done that many times before while Darcy worked in the butterfly houses.

"No, Steve," Tara said to answer his question. "Darcy did not seem one bit upset or despondent, and she was looking forward to your coming back on the weekend for your anniversary. She had just learned from someone that the tenth wedding celebration was symbolized by tin or aluminum. She said at first that sounded cheap, but she'd found out the point was that items made from either of those metals could be bent but not broken—a milestone of love and lasting duty."

"But now, it may be all broken," Steve muttered, leaning forward and staring at his hands gripped between his knees so hard his fingers went white. Perhaps he was holding his panic and anger in because he saw that Tara was obviously grief-stricken, too.

"Tara," she said, partly to change the subject, "tell us a bit about the orangetips that seemed to be disproportionately missing. Darcy was reading up on them."

"They are exotic—meaning not from this area. They make their home from Louisiana to Kentucky, points north," she told them, wiping tears from under her eyes. "We were trying to take very good care of them in all three of their stages—you may have seen their pupae in their cocoons—in the other room. You see, they were paying guests, and we needed that."

Nick said, "That breed—the ones with so many missing were 'paying guests'? How so?"

"I accepted about thirty of them nearly four months ago to protect and breed. My client wanted to see if they could be introduced here. It was for a master's degree thesis project for a local biology teacher, that's all. Needless to say, I'm all for education, and the grad student is one I've known for years, admired and followed his up-and-down career after he was in my elementary school class a good while ago."

Claire saw Nick sit up straighter. She was sure he was thinking of Lincoln Yost. He asked Tara, "Could you share his name with us?"

"I suppose I shouldn't until I get his permission, especially since this might become a criminal investigation. And he asked for privacy. I'll ask him and let you know. Actually, his thesis is on extended hibernation in two animals as different from each other as—well, as day and night. I am as proud of this person as I am of all my pupils, including your darling Lexi. He was an excellent athlete as well as a fine student, and when he had an athletic career–ending injury, he did not mope around but channeled his interests in another direction. He's been forced to take a different career path, but he's managed to still live on a teacher's salary and live well, something not easy to do in South Florida, as I could well tell you."

Claire held her breath, wondering if Nick would insist on knowing more, but the careful, circumspect lawyer came out in him, whereas she would have mentioned Lincoln Yost's name and his connection to the Fly Safe group. No doubt Detective Jensen would have brought it up if he'd been here. Of course, the Yost connection could be wrong, but something right had to turn up soon. Jensen had said to never ignore an apparent coincidence.

"No, that's all right," Nick told Tara. "Don't bother whoever it is over this. We all have more important things to worry about now."

"I've been thinking he'd contact me since the media has mentioned some butterflies disappeared, too. I suppose that many adult orangetips could have made their way out the netted doors since there were so many inside, but a few of the pupae in their cocoons were missing from inside, too, which did not make the news. I suppose Darcy could have moved them outside as she's done before since several were ready to emerge. With her being missing, I didn't give those a second thought—and then my migraine just drained me, scrambled me," she added, looking distraught and shaky.

"We should have mentioned the loss of the pupae or cocoons earlier," Claire blurted out, trying not to sound as upset as she was both at Tara and herself. "Detective Jensen could look for fingerprints or DNA—something in that room, since there was nothing like that in the butterfly house."

"I—I'm sorry. I was upset that someone would have come into my house. When I first feared Darcy was gone, I ran in here to look for her in a panic, but didn't glance at the cocoons until later. At least the middle stage of their metamorphosis, the worms, were not taken from the exotics house. I'd best call my client and tell him all that, but I fear the repercussions—the financial fallout, too. He—it—was quite generous."

"I don't mean to accuse you of anything," Claire told

her, reaching out to take her hands. What had happened to all her interview training and experience? she scolded herself: keep calm and build up the interviewee so they talked more freely. Here she'd worried that Steve might explode or that Nick might question the woman more rigorously than he had when he'd probably held back so he could visit Lincoln Yost again without him being tipped off.

As they left the house, Claire followed Nick's lead not to tell Steve about Lincoln Yost yet or he'd be likely to accost him. Besides, the orangetip abduction was of little consequence: it was Darcy they had to find and get back!

While Nick drove, Claire checked their phone messages to see if there was any news. Nothing except a text from Jace saying Brit had contacted him about Darcy and he'd soon be back in town for a short stay. Meanwhile, Steve, checking his phone in the back seat, announced, "Lots of condolences, as if she's gone for good. She's not dead, damn it! I can feel she's out there! That she needs me!"

Nick said, "We've got to hang in and hang together on this. Claire, see if you can call the library to learn where Will is today—working or home. Actually, I'd like to see his place. Didn't you say he told you it was out a ways on the edge of Golden Gate?"

Again she thought of that dreadful story in *The Collector*. The kidnapper had a house at a remote location where he kept his victim. But no. No way! She had to stop such thoughts.

"I'll call the library first to see if he's there," she told Nick. "But I'll bet we can get his address from Ken Jensen if we need it." She asked her phone assistant for the number to call and punched it in.

"Collier County Library headquarters on Orange Blos-som Drive," the sweet voice answered.

"I'm wondering if Will Warren is in today. Our daugh-ter has loved his story times."

"Why, yes, there's a story time in this building at two this afternoon, though he's here now. He is so very popular, one of our library's treasures. If you would like to leave him a specific message, I can connect you to his voice mail."

"No, that's all I needed to know. Thank you," she said, and punched off.

"That's not all we need to know," Steve muttered. "I didn't give it much thought before that he seemed to 'spe-cially like Darcy. Who doesn't like Darcy, but I think she always had Jilly with her around him. Unless he came out to the butterfly farm," he added, his tone darkening. "I might carefully question Jilly about him, 'cause she's very perceptive."

"Lexi, too," Claire whispered.

Steve said, "Let's go there right now, Nick. I think the guy's on our side, but maybe he liked her too damn much!"

"On our way, but you need to keep calm," Nick told him as he sped faster down the endless dirt road toward town.

The headquarters of the Collier County Library always reminded Claire of a huge hacienda or Spanish mission with its white columned portico entry, brown tiles and rimmed fountain. A few people sat in the metal chairs in the shade, chatting or reading. The spacious interior was a far cry from the small library in central Naples she re-called when she and Darcy were growing up and had gone to Will Warren's story times.

Nick and Steve waited just inside the door while Claire

headed for the main desk to ask for Will, but then she noticed him walking toward her.

"I saw you come in," he said, looking concerned—and as nattily dressed as usual with his striped bow tie. "Any news? Nothing bad, I pray!"

Again, she was startled at this man's intensity. She judged it to be real and heartfelt, and she came to like him even more, hoping Steve would learn to also. Will was probably just proud of Darcy as one of his "story students" from years ago, just the way Tara was proud of Lexi.

"Nothing new—still nothing," she told him.

"I wish there was more than the media's news," he rushed on. "We have to get Darcy back!"

She saw him make an obvious effort to calm himself. He'd even spoken loudly in a library. He took her elbow. "I was going to go out for an early lunch. I know we both have more to say. We must put our heads together and do whatever we can."

"I'm with Nick and Darcy's husband, Steve," she said, pointing toward them. "Could we all talk somewhere? Things were so rushed with the media when you were at our house."

"Tell me before we join the men, how are they—you, too, and little Jilly—doing?"

"Holding up somehow. The police and highway patrol are watching for her car. But nothing, that is, so far."

They walked toward Nick and Steve as Will shook his head. "Except in children's fantasy books, people don't just vanish. We will find her and someone will pay the price."

His voice had suddenly become so ominous that she startled. One of his pretend people voices when he read children's books aloud? Or a sincere swell of anger and passion that someone had taken—maybe hurt—Darcy?

The men shook hands all around, and Will expressed his sympathy and concern to Steve. "I understand there is a reward for information," Will went on. "I'd like to add my own ten thousand dollars to that, if you will accept."

Steve's eyes widened, and Nick's eyebrows rose. "That's really...v-very generous," Steve almost stammered.

"Anything to help. You see, I have no real family of my own, so I've become especially fond of Darcy and Jilly—and as you may know, the butterfly farm is very special to me. I'm a great supporter of Tara and her work staff of one—Darcy."

He indicated they should go outside and led the three of them to a wrought-iron table and chairs in the shade away from other people. The splashing of the fountain and the lovely, calm setting seemed too pretty and gentle to Claire. So, so wrong.

"How else can I help?" he asked as they sat close together.

Steve said, "With your interest in butterflies and Tara's farm, you have probably been out there a lot. Can you think of anyone who might drop in, anyone except the so-called Fly Safe group that might have a beef with Tara and netting the butterflies or selling and taking them away for events?"

"So you've looked into the Fly Safe group. I can't imagine they'd stoop to kidnapping. Picketing, protesting, pressure, verbal threats, sure, but not that. Still, they have sent more than one letter to Tara strongly objecting to her keeping butterflies 'cooped up' and especially to her distant releases where the butterflies are cooled, put in glassine envelopes and sent through the mail. Actually, they don't like the nearby releases, either, and have shown up at a couple of funerals to harass me—though they have been smart enough not to make fools of themselves in front of the bereaved families."

"Darcy's done some wedding ones," Steve said. "Could she have been harassed, too?"

"She never told me so, and weddings aren't always announced ahead in the paper the way funerals and burials are. Tara hasn't said anything about problems at weddings, either. As for me, despite that group, I still try to do as many at funerals as I can," Will said, leaning toward them across the small table.

"So," Steve said as Claire noted Nick was evidently content to let him lead the way here, "this Fly Safe bunch could want to create havoc because of sending the butterflies into foreign territory?"

"Exactly. Certain of the 18,000 butterfly breeds in this country are indigenous to particular areas and so some are released far from home. The Fly Safe people insist that's cruel, though the butterflies simply—mostly—adapt. These ceremonial releases actually keep Tara's breeding operations afloat, though. That and an occasional paying customer who buys pretty ones for their own area or backyard."

Nick's gaze slammed into Claire's. Someone local was a paying customer, paying to have the orangetips bred here.

"We heard," Claire said, "that a lot of orangetips escaped the day Darcy disappeared. Darcy was evidently reading up on them, because she had a page about them bookmarked."

"In my book I gave her?"

"No. I'm thinking that disappeared with her. It was another one."

He heaved a huge sigh, which seemed to deflate him. He looked into the distance, across the patio, as if he were seeing someone or something there. "Tara told me quite a few of that breed went missing when Darcy did," he said, his voice almost a whisper now. "But I wonder if *they* are the missing link to finding Darcy, so to speak, because *they* were taken, too."

Claire said, "What missing link? How?"

"Their secret," Will said, frowning, "their very valuable secret. You see, orangetips have the unusual gift of being able to suspend themselves in cocoon stage for years, then, apparently when their environment is suitable to them, they emerge beautiful, alert and alive. In other words, they can exist in self-suspended animation. So far, I don't think many scientists are paying attention to that, though I've been contacted for information about them by a local guy who's working on a master's degree in biology."

Nick's gaze slammed into hers once more. Lincoln Yost again.

"But I believe," Will went on, "if mankind could find out how the orangetips suspend themselves and then re-animate, it would make a hibernating bear's short winter nap or the way dolphins can sleep with half their brains still alert mere ABCs. Frankly, I fear there are some people—entire nations—who would do anything to have the priceless, powerful secrets behind self-suspended animation in their control."

Claire didn't bring it up then, but there was a possible dolphin-butterfly link. The dolphins had some sort of control over suspending half their brains, and the orangetips could suspend their entire existence at will. But all that sounded like something from a *National Geographic* TV special or a sci-fi movie miles and millennia away from finding Darcy.

CHAPTER TEN

When they got back to their house, Heck's car was parked in front, as well as Nita's. "Good," Nick said as he pulled into the garage. "I asked Heck to do some business research for me."

He wanted to talk to Heck before he got Steve hyped about possible new information or leads—namely, that all roads led to Lincoln Yost's research about the orangetips right now. At least Steve had decided it would be good to try to do something "normal" with Jilly, so he was taking her to walk the beach. And Claire was ready to spend some time with Lexi.

"But shouldn't we tell Steve about Lincoln Yost?" Claire whispered.

"I want to finesse that, and I still think Steve's ready to strike out at someone. Not now, okay?"

"I don't want to hold things back from him, but let's go see Yost, then tell Steve," she said. "And maybe tell Ken, too. He'll also have a fit if he thinks we're going behind his back."

"We'll tell both of them when we have something beyond the fact that orangetips know how to sleep and then wake up."

"It does sound so far out, but then Darcy had that page bookmarked."

"Maybe just because there were so many of them in that butterfly house. You said she tried to read up on different breeds. But we're on it, we'll pursue it, then inform the others—or not."

They hugged quickly and went into the house. Claire sniffed hard, and he saw her blink back tears despite her decisive nod. He thought she finally might be out of tears, but he hoped to God she wasn't out of hope.

Nick could tell Nita was excited but holding something back, perhaps waiting until Steve and Jilly were out the door. Jilly waved madly to Lexi as they pulled away. His pulse kicked up. Heck, too, seemed on edge, so he must have found something they could use, but if it was really key, why had he let Steve and Jilly leave? Unless it was bad news—and they were all trying to protect Darcy's family from more agonizing pain, if that was possible.

"Okay, you two, what's up?" Nick asked before Claire could chime in. She was hugging Lexi to her despite that wretched doll pinned between them, but then Lexi pulled away and walked back to the front screen door to look out.

Heck said, "I have the intel you asked for, but Nita just told me she's got exciting news, too."

"Let's hear it," Nick said as Claire glanced at Lexi, then

left her to stare out the front screen door as if Jilly—or her aunt Darcy—would magically reappear.

"Okay," Nita whispered, so excited she was shaking. She glanced over at Lexi to be sure she couldn't hear. "You won't believe this. I didn't have time to tell you this morning, but I won a walking-talking doll from the store where I ordered some baby furniture. It's a gift from God—for Lexi. It's a real pretty one called Smart Dolly. You been so good to Bronco and me, helping us through our finding that body and giving him such a good job working security at the law firm."

She lowered her voice. "Even if Bronco and me are having a girl, I want Lexi to have the doll, 'cause she's slipping back so bad, and our baby wouldn't want it for a long time. I hid it in the library. Come and see."

Heck followed, too. "It really is a smart doll," she went on. "She can respond like a person, even programmed to answer questions, chatter about horses, so won't Lexi love that? Bronco and me thought," she said as she bent to reach behind a big armchair and brought out a blonde, pretty, little-girl doll. "Lexi might go for it and ditch Princess. Since this doll talks for itself, maybe Lexi will stop that awful voice and the things it says."

Nick saw tears in Claire's eyes. "It is lovely," she said. "What a blessing, what timing, that you won this. Thank you so much!"

"It all happened real fast. I got a phone call from a man at the baby store that I won just from being a random customer there. It was delivered by UPS, free shipping, too," Nita said, beaming.

Claire hugged her. "It's worth a try until I or someone

else can get through to Lexi with counseling—or when we get Darcy back. I'll call Lexi in."

"Maybe you women better handle this," Nick said. "But we should buy the doll. It's obviously an expensive one."

"A free one," Nita insisted. "You two been so good to Bronco and me that we're excited to give back some. When that woman was found all laid out in our freezer—couldn't have gotten through that without both of you. Let's hope little Lexi and little Smart Dolly get on real good."

Claire was trembling as she called Lexi to the doorway of the library where Nita waited with the doll behind a pillow on the couch. How to handle this? How to keep from setting Lexi off? She'd love to grab that ugly doll and trash her, but that would just make things worse.

"Lexi," Claire said, still standing in the doorway with her, "Nita and I realized that Princess is very tired and kind of—well, injured—and that she would like you to have a new doll while she just sleeps and gets better."

"Princess would be better if Aunt Darcy came back, and I wasn't lost once, too," the child insisted.

"Yes, I know. Of course. But Princess wants a new doll to talk to you, just like she did, only with her own voice, not yours."

Lexi squinted up at her. Claire could see the wheels turning in that little mind. "Where is she—the new Princess?" She loosened her hold ever so slightly on the old doll. Could Lexi's fierce protection of that battered body and face be her way of protecting herself? Claire prayed that the pretty, confident image of the new doll would help.

"Here she is," Nita said from across the room, and pulled

the doll out to stand on her knees. "Smart Dolly," Nita said to the doll, "say hello to your new friend Lexi."

"Hello, my new friend Lexi," the doll said in a sweet voice. "I am so happy we can play together, and I will be friends with your family, too."

"Ohh!" Lexi gasped, and set Princess on a chair as she rushed toward Nita.

"I'm a smart little girl, just like you," the doll said. "What will you name me?"

"Mommy, she's a real princess!" Lexi said, still staring only at the doll. "She looks like Cinderella with her yellow hair even though she has a short skirt and sneakers. I will name her that, but we won't call her Cinderella, but Cindy for short."

Claire was so grateful that she was almost tongue-tied for a moment. How had that so-called "smart doll" picked up on Lexi's name so fast?

"That's a lovely name for her," she said, and knelt to hug Lexi and the doll—Cindy. Claire thought of the dead woman in the freezer, who's name had been Cyndi. But she shoved away the idea that was a bad omen, because this was like a gift from heaven.

"I like all of you. I want to stay with you," Cindy said.

"Wait till Jilly sees my—our—new friend," Lexi said, hugging Claire back, then Nita, too. "Wait till we find Aunt Darcy, because she'll be happy, too!"

"So let me know what's what," Nick said after he poured coffee for Heck and himself and they carried their mugs out to the patio.

"I'll start with Tara Gerald first, boss. Her paternal grandparents were early Irish settlers on that same piece of land. Her parents inherited, both died in the last couple of years, then left the place to Tara. Her father worked at the South Naples Citrus Grove down the road, driving equipment, working in the orange orchard store in season. Tara had no siblings. Never married. Guess her teaching—and then butterflies—were her life. No legal problems I turned up. Probably just making ends meet with her retirement and some sales from the Flutterby Farm. Has a real close lady friend."

"Meaning?" Nick said, putting his mug down on the patio table.

"Meaning nothing," he said with a shrug. "Another retired teacher who lives in East Naples."

"But she doesn't help with the farm, evidently."

"She may be an investor. Anyway, she would, no doubt, drop by now and then. Found a picture of her. Looks like she walks with a cane so I can't see her as a kidnapping suspect. Okay, on to William Spencer Warren. I have his address if you want it. Like you said, wrote a book on butterflies. Library degree. Botany degree. Married briefly in his twenties, divorced, no children."

"Botany, not biology? No kidding."

"I don't make this stuff up. Besides, botanists are valuable to lepidopterists. You impressed with what I picked up so far? See, certain butterflies like and need certain plants to flourish, to feed and breed. Anyway, for years, Warren worked at the library here, which you knew, but then took a five-year sabbatic—what's that word?"

"Sabbatical?"

"Right. To Japan, no less. And as far as I can figure out, because I obviously couldn't read the online ads in Japanese, he sold butterflies."

Nick sat farther forward. "Ones he got or caught there in the US?"

"Don't know, but some damned pricey ones. I could at least read the prices from the yen, then convert that to dollars. Big bucks. Thousands for one sale sometimes."

"I wonder if they were exotics."

"What?"

"Never mind, butterfly expert. Anything on Larry Ralston, deep-sea fishing guide, who may be my new client?"

"You were right that the name of his boat is *Down Under.* Nick, it's a big one. A fifty-four-foot sport fishing vessel, with several ads for taking out fishing charters online. It's at the dock at Crayton Cove, you know, near that restaurant you like called The Dock? And yeah, he's under investigation for netting a dolphin and killing it. He says it died while he was trying to free it, but no one buys that with the video evidence."

"That's one thing I researched myself," Nick told him with a sigh. "It was a bottlenose dolphin he might have accidentally netted but then not released. Witnesses were in another boat. It's a twenty-thousand-dollar fine for that and up to one year in federal prison, though someone in Texas recently had a good lawyer who got that reduced to one year of probation and a ban on fishing with fifty hours of community service. But for a professional fisherman, that year ban on fishing could ruin him. I think I'll be meeting Ralston Monday morning at the office, so I'll psych him out there, as Claire would say."

"He's well-connected. His father owns funeral homes up and down the Florida west coast, two here in town, and has contributed lots of dough to political campaigns. Larry

Ralston also got a brother who lives in Collier County, not sure what he does yet, but I'll keep looking—ah, father's name is Aaron, brother's name is Clinton. Couldn't find a picture of the brother, though I looked."

Nick told him, "Besides giving everyone a defense and highlighting the need to protect our environment, the only reason I'd take Larry Ralston's case is to highlight how important, valuable—and smart—dolphins are. A far cry from little, delicate butterflies."

"Man, I'm still thinking about that year in prison and twenty-thousand-dollar fine for harming one of them."

"At least butterfly theft from a farm, display facility or protected park is only a misdemeanor, so I wonder what the Fly Safe people would say about that discrepancy. But let's go see how that smart doll is going with Lexi. We have smart phones, smart everything lately—except the smarts to find where Darcy is."

"I feel so much better about leaving Lexi again, now that she seems entranced by the new doll," Claire told Nick after lunch. Heck had stayed and the three of them still sat around the patio table in the shade. Steve and Jilly were not back yet, though Lexi was going crazy waiting to show talkative Cindy to her cousin. Nick had told her he had put Princess "to sleep" in their closet this time, not Lexi's. Claire doubted Lexi would even care now that she had the new doll in her arms as she wandered over to sit with them. And the rule, gently given by Claire more than once, was that since the new doll had her own voice, she would not talk for Lexi.

Claire put her arm around Lexi as Nick said, "Hey, Heck, before you leave, almost forgot to ask you to look up an address for Lincoln Yost, that biology teacher at Naples High School I mentioned to you."

"Oh, yeah, and board member of the Fly Safe organization," Heck said, reaching down on the floor to dig his iPad out of his backpack. "I couldn't find the names of their board members, but Yost is well-known in town. Local basketball star about fifteen years ago, lots of old newspaper articles. Okay, I'll grab his home address."

"Good. Even if school was in session, I'd try his house," Nick said. "Security at the high schools is pretty strict these days, and I could not just go walking in to see him."

They all jumped when the doll piped up. "I love to go to school. Summer vacation will end soon. I will work hard to get good grades. I wish my friend Jilly was here."

"It must pick up on keywords and have rote things to say," Heck said. "The tech term is *interactive*."

"I believe the correct term is *invaluable*," Claire put in, stroking the doll's silky hair. "So where does this guy Yost live?"

Nick glanced at the screen Heck held up toward him.

"Okay, 661 Turtle Bay Drive. Impressive," Nick said, "especially on a teacher's salary. A house on the edge of Pelican Bay, no less. He's got to have a sideline or be making way over what Tara must have earned, or maybe he has a rich wife."

"Maybe he inherited it like Tara did her house," Heck said.

"That's the least of what I want to find out from him," Nick said. "Claire, if you're going, too, let's head out. I think your presence—and observation—will really help."

"I like to help people," Cindy said as Lexi put her up on the table, and everyone watched as she took a few stiff-legged steps, as if on her own. "Tell me how I can help you, Lexi."

Claire noticed again that the doll had learned Lexi's name. So amazing, the things even a toy could do in this modern world. Why hadn't she even seen this doll advertised for sale? It must be so expensive. She would research it online later.

Lexi told the doll, "You can help me, Cindy, by helping us find Aunt Darcy, who got took from the butterfly farm."

"I think butterflies are pretty, and you are, too," said the doll.

On that obviously prerecorded thought, Claire got up, hugged Lexi again and ran to get her purse. In a way, she felt guilty they didn't wait for Steve, but the fact that he wasn't here was a good excuse not to involve him further until they found out more from the high school biology teacher.

After Heck left, he waved to Lexi and Nita, who were standing in the front door. When Nick backed them out of the driveway, Claire told him, "Wait a second. I see a bouquet of flowers in a vase off to the side on the porch."

Leaving the car door open, she got out. Evidently curious why, Nita came out as Claire bent to lift the heavy glass vase loaded with roses, lilies and foliage. A note was stuck in one of those little forked plastic holders. She handed the flowers to Nita, but opened the note and read aloud.

"Darcy's church family will be praying for her safe return at both services tomorrow morning. Please do not hesitate to call Pastor Hayes if we can do anything to help. A bouquet just like these flowers will be on the altar tomorrow morning. Love to Darcy's extended family and, of course, to Steve, Drew and Jillian.

"How lovely," Claire said. "Nita, please give these to Steve and Jilly when they get back from the beach. We need all the help we can get and strength from above..." Her voice caught, and she blinked back tears. "We will move heaven and earth to find Darcy and soon."

CHAPTER ELEVEN

Nick rang the doorbell to Lincoln Yost's home. He lived in a large house on a beautiful street in one of the most desirable sections in Naples. Just before Nick rang again, a pretty woman opened the door.

"Sorry, but it says No Soliciting," she said, pointing to a sign he hadn't noted in the window because they'd been surveying the landscaping. Claire had promised to let him do the talking, so he'd just see how long that lasted.

"We're not soliciting. I met Mr. Yost briefly at the Fly Safe office the other day and wanted to follow up with him. I'm a lawyer, Nick Markwood. Sorry to bother you at home, but—"

"Oh, okay, but he's not here right now."

Nick heard at least two kids arguing loudly inside but the woman didn't so much as blink. "I just had some follow-up questions about the butterfly breeds we were discussing."

"If it was the orangetips, they're quite special and precious," she said with a nod and a slight smile. "He's at Doctors Pass on the gulf right now with a couple of his best students who are gonna be seniors. Loves to tutor bright, promisin' kids about butterflies, dolphins, whatever, even durin' summer vacation."

A screech sounded from somewhere behind her, then a young voice. "Mom, he hit me!"

"Wish he'd see to his own kids," she said with a shake of her curly head. She had long hair and a soft Southern accent. Big gold bangle earrings swung from her earlobes, and she had a chunky bracelet that looked like real gold, too. Yeah, the Yosts were living large.

"Anyway," she went on, "he'd be easy to find there. They're set up with a telescope to record movements of dolphins and manatees when they swim in or out past the breakwater rocks. You want to leave a card or somethin'?"

"No thanks. We'll just see if we can catch him there. He sounds like a very dedicated teacher."

"Oh, he is. Always learnin', always teachin'."

Nick caught a glimpse of their front room before she closed the door. White carpet with young kids? White leather furniture and a huge abstract painting on one wall. Money talked here, so he hoped the owner of this place wouldn't mind talking more, too.

The minute he landed in Naples, Jace phoned Brit at the zoo, knowing she was working this weekend. He told her he'd see her soon but he was heading to see Lexi and find out how the search for Darcy was going. Through connections he'd left his car here in the Naples Municipal Airport pilot's parking lot. Mitch had, too, and he waved to his buddy as he peeled out to head for Kris's condo.

"So glad you're back for a while," Brit said. Her voice

sounded so good over the phone, though he heard animal cries in the background. "Claire mentioned wishing you could fly over the land out behind where Darcy was taken, even though the police chopper searched briefly from the air. Maybe you could help with that."

"Yeah, anything I can do, but task number one is comforting Lexi, maybe supporting Steve and Jilly, too, if they're still at the house."

"I think they are. Jace, Claire says Lexi's kind of off the deep end again, flashing back to her own abduction, I think."

"I was afraid of that. They need to let her do something to actually help look for her aunt Darcy. She's been through a lot, but then, haven't we all?"

"Did you know Darcy well when you were married to Claire?"

"Oh, yeah. A tight sister act for sure. Their dad deserted them and their mother was a little screwy, so they really leaned on each other. Darcy—lively, stubborn, strong, too, like Claire without the drawback of Claire's disease. But they're both tough. I hope—" his voice broke "—it helps them both get through this. But hey, love you. Talk to you later, maybe bring Lexi with me so we can both support her. I can at least stay a day or two unless another bad hurricane starts to form, and there are a couple lined up out in the Atlantic. I'm definitely on call. Mitch is here to see Kris and probably nod his head a lot over wedding plans."

"Ah, shades of our past. But, Jace, really, is there any chance you and Mitch could borrow a plane from one of your buddies at the Marco Airport to do a flyover of that area? Claire and the police need all the help they can get. You know where it is, right?"

"Yeah, just west of that citrus grove out by Sabal Palm. I'll make a quick phone call on that but gotta see Lexi before I fly. If I do, maybe I should take her along, make her feel like she's helping."

"You're good at that, picking up the pieces like you did with me. Miss you. Love you. Bye for now."

He started his car, but then decided to call the Marco Island Airport first, so he sat there with the engine idling and the AC spewing out cold air. A friend at the airport who had a small Piper Cub there owed him a favor. But he had to see and hug Lexi first.

"Nick, I feel guilty we're here without Steve, but we can always say it was best he spend time with Jilly if he gets upset. That is, gets more upset. I know I'd be ready to explode if something like this happened to you. I'm devastated over Darcy, too—terrified."

"I know, sweetheart, but we're doing all we can," Nick assured her, and took her hand as they left their car at Lowdermilk Park and began to quickly walk the beach north toward Doctors Pass.

The man-made entry to the gulf was lined with black boulders and, on a weekend like this, it was busy with everything from Jet Skis to yachts. Condos and houses lined the shore, and the foam of warm waves washed in nearly to their feet. The screeching seagulls seemed to want to warn them away, but once on the rocks, the warm sun and fishermen made the scene seem almost normal. Nick tried to ignore the scudding storm clouds on the western horizon. Never good to be caught out on big water if there was lightning, but it seemed far away right now.

"Careful along here," Nick said, and gave her a hand up

to the top of the boulders. They both skimmed the area. He'd assumed teacher and students would be on this southern side, and he hoped they didn't have to drive around. Yeah, there they were, Yost and three students, all boys, out a lot farther.

"That's him. Watch where you step," he told her. "When the tide's up or there's wind and spray, the rocks can get slippery. And don't step where there's green algae growth."

He went slowly, picking his footholds carefully as she followed him. With the water sloshing on both sides, even in the no-wake zone for boats, footing was iffy. Despite distant storm clouds, it was bright out here with the sun off the water, even with sunglasses and a visor.

"Linc!" Nick called when they were out nearly to the four of them, and raised his hand in greeting. "Nick Markwood and Claire, my wife," he added as Linc came closer. He spoke up so the wind wouldn't grab his words away. "Sorry to bother you when you're with your students, but your wife told us where you were."

Several fishermen casting off the rocks turned to glare at them as if talking loudly way out here with the crash and suck of waves would keep the fish from biting.

Linc came closer and called to them, "Hey, I read what happened to the missing woman in your family after Tara Gerald phoned me to ask if it was okay if she gave you my name. I think I surprised her when I said I'd already met you. So sorry," he added in a quieter voice, now standing close to them and turning toward Claire. "I mean, that your sister disappeared from where I board my butterflies—and some of them disappeared, too. Sorry for your loss."

"She isn't lost, only missing!" Claire blurted. She hoped she had not come on too strong, but his condolences were what someone said when someone died. "We're trying hard to track her, and if you could just answer a few questions..."

"I wouldn't know anything about that. I was at Fly Safe that day, not the Flutterby Farm."

"I didn't mean that, but—"

"Something about my butterflies, then?" he asked. "Mr. Markwood, you should have told me you were hoping to learn about more than Fly Safe that first day."

"At the time I wasn't. Listen, it would help us if you could share the names of others on the Fly Safe board of directors."

"Like Tara correctly did to ask first, I'd have to check. Some of them are investors, some advisers, et cetera, but I'd need to ask permission to disclose their names, especially to an attorney at a large, local law firm."

That annoyed Nick and set off alarm bells, but he'd seen that sort of privacy paranoia with groups that could be contentious, including a case he—Claire, too—had worked not long ago with big-name people protecting local historic buildings at any cost.

"Okay—" he tried another tack instead of arguing "—so it would also help us to know more about your orangetips that Darcy was tending for Tara Gerald."

"Sure. So," he said, turning back a moment to look at the three boys who were taking turns watching the entrance to the pass with the telescope, "we're tracking and counting dolphins and even manatees out here, but, of course, anything I can do to help with the butterflies, I will."

Figuring that Claire would call that trying to change the subject, Nick said, "That's much appreciated, because, since you know what we have at stake here, you'll understand our desperation for fast answers. We are not accusing you of anything, but we're hoping as an expert on the orangetips you may have an idea who might have wanted your butterflies—and took Claire's sister along because she could identify them or was in their way somehow."

Nick could tell Linc was frowning, even in the shade of his baseball cap. The guy also tightened his lips, so what would Claire say about that face language? He'd heard her sniff hard more than once to keep from crying—or maybe from screaming.

"I can't tell you much, really," he said, shrugging and shifting position again despite standing on the rocks. "Orangetips are rare in these parts. But they could be unrelated to her disappearance. I was assuming they escaped from the open netted door someone left open."

"But we understand that breed has an unusual talent," Claire said. "Isn't it true they can suspend themselves and then wake up—not the expected metamorphosis, but something way beyond that? No wonder you're using them for your thesis."

Nick saw Linc's eyes widen. He nodded jerkily. "It is… quite unusual and interesting," he said. "But then the same can be said for the dolphins—not SA—but an intentional turning off half their brain for a while, so they never really have to completely sleep. But all this is under wraps right now. So, did Tara give you my name and tell you my thesis topic? I only gave her permission to give you my name this morning."

"No," Nick said, "she protected your privacy until you gave her permission, but in her brief description of you, I thought I saw similarities and made a guess it was the man I had recently met." No way was he going to admit he'd had his tech guru checking up on him.

Yost suddenly seemed even more antsy, but then he probably wanted to get back to his students. He glanced again at them on the outer rocks, or maybe he was assessing the distance of the storm. But Nick could understand his concern. And he got the other message: Linc Yost did not want to talk about the strange talent of the orangetips, at least not now.

They said thanks and goodbye and waved to the boys before heading back down the slippery pile of black boulders toward the shore.

"We made him nervous and upset," Claire said from behind. "And not just because we might have guessed his thesis topic. Dolphins aside, he's obviously looking at the orangetips' secret gift and its import. Otherwise, would a biology teacher be so at ease with the topic of suspended animation that he would refer to it as SA without defining that for us amateurs? Nick, he sounds like an expert on that subject and you know Will said it was a lucrative and cut-throat field. He implied some people would do anything to have that priceless, powerful secret in their control. So maybe someone thought Darcy knew more about that than she obviously did—does."

"Man, I could use you in court or strategy sessions," he said, and stopped to hug her before they went on. She was tense, her muscles tightly coiled, and shaking.

As they hurried down the beach toward their car, still hashing things over, Nick's phone sounded, and he fished it out of his shorts. "Text from Heck," he told her, squinting at the screen in the sun. "A long one. Oh, Jace showed up and spent time with Lexi, so that should help. Gina's there with Heck."

"That's right, she's home for the weekend. I hope they

can work everything out, but that's the least of my worries. I'm glad Jace is there, too."

"Apparently Gina thinks the doll is amazing, and Jilly loves it, too."

"So if Jilly's there, that means Steve's back. We'd better get home and fill him in on things."

"No—wait. Heck says Steve left Jilly with Nita and headed out somewhere, but decided not to go with Mitch and Jace after Heck filled him in some. Our flyboys got ahold of a small plane and are going to do a flyover of the Flutterby Farm area. And Lexi begged to go with them, had a fit when he tried to leave so soon. Claire, they took Lexi with them. Nita was afraid to let him, but he is her father."

"Maybe it will help her to be helping," Claire said, pulling a tissue out of her shorts and blowing her nose. "Jace and Mitch both have great safety records and know what they're doing. I'll bet she took that new doll with her. I just hope he brings her back soon."

"I'd trust him to do that, and it really may help her. So here's the rest, probably the reason he sent this since Jace and Steve were in too much of a hurry to call us. Heck's found another board member of Fly Safe besides Yost, and guess who?"

"Not Will Warren or Tara?"

"No, but a name I'm familiar with. Lawrence Ralston."

"The guy who wants you to defend him for netting a dolphin?"

"Yeah, maybe for killing it. But an observer in a big sailboat near him says he captured it intentionally."

"Let's go find him now before heading home."

"I'm supposed to see him in my office on Monday morning. It might spook him to question him now if the Fly Safe people have anything to do with harassing the Flutterby Farm. Yost, now this Ralston guy. Something's starting to smell about Fly Safe."

"Nick, Larry Ralston might suspect less if you question him in your office, but time is precious! The so-called golden hours we might find Darcy are already tarnished, if not gone! Jace took decisive, quick action and we, too, should follow any trail for information. Can't you just say we happened by—'Hey, nice boat. So, are you the guy I'm supposed to see on Monday morning? Can we chat a bit now?'"

"Yeah, you're right. A risk, but worth a try. He needs me, evidently, as much as I need him right now. If his boat's in, it's at Crayton Cove, so we can say we were at the restaurant there. Steve's not home to bring up to speed right now, anyway. Before that storm comes closer, let's go."

CHAPTER TWELVE

It was about a fifteen-minute drive to Crayton Cove where Larry Ralston's charter fishing boat was docked. Nick parked the car not far from the maze of docks lined with everything from sailboats to yachts. Noise and laughter poured from the open-air restaurant called The Dock.

"If that rain comes up," he told Claire, "they just roll down those window flaps over the screens and let it pour."

"I've always loved being here under better circumstances," she said, taking his hand. "Darcy and Steve announced their engagement there, and it was one of the first places we went when our lives returned to normal, remember?"

"Even after we managed to save Lexi and get back here in one piece, when has life been normal?"

"True," she said with a nervous glance at the sky. "I hope Jace and Mitch keep an eye on that rainstorm since they have Lexi with them."

"Sweetheart, they are hurricane pilots. They are used to

watching the sky and dealing with storms—much bigger ones than that."

"Since they are usually in such dangerous ones, they might think this little one coming is nothing. But I know it will help Lexi to be with them, and the few times he's taken her up before, she's loved it."

"And, no doubt, she'll feel like she's helping find Darcy. Now, let's see what we can do here."

"Starting with finding the *Down Under* among all the watercraft along these docks. We'll have to ask someone. How about that guy over there?" she asked, pointing at a wiry, sun-bronzed man coiling a rope near a small sailboat. "I'd guess with his captain's cap he's an owner or at least works here."

Who belonged and who didn't, Claire thought, was easy to figure out. The tourists were obvious, the ones who just walked the docks looking at what her father used to call "boat flesh," most of which, despite the worsening weather, were not docked today since it was the weekend. But they figured Larry's boat would be here since Nick had heard he was not allowed to take fishermen out until a hearing. No wonder he needed a lawyer fast.

She saw a couple of young kids eating ice cream cones with their parents. More than once when she and Darcy were growing up, on the way back from getting library books, before Mother became completely agoraphobic, they had stopped here just to ooh and aah over the boats.

"Hiya," the thin man greeted them. "Looking to buy? A couple for sale."

"Actually," Nick said, "we're looking for a specific boat, a charter fisher called the *Down Under.*"

"You two don't look like journalists," he said, squinting up at them from his perch on a wooden bench on the dock. "Guy that owns it's in hot water for killing a dolphin. Lots of TV and newspaper types been around lately. And another guy looking for him a short time ago."

"No, I'm just a business acquaintance he wants to see."

"Down at the very end of this main dock, turn right, end of the line. Big boat, big info about taking a charter painted on a sign."

"Okay, thanks."

They followed his directions. Claire was glad to see the other visitors seemed to have no interest in boats this far out on the dock, and, thank heavens, they saw no prying journalists. All they needed was for Nick to be recognized as a local criminal lawyer if this Larry Ralston was in trouble. Dolphins and manatees—many breeds of birds, too—were protected and almost sacred around here. She wondered if the news coverage of Ralston and perhaps a future trial would be either helpful or dangerous publicity for a group evidently as aggressive as the Fly Safe people. But even if Ralston became Nick's client, none of that mattered to her compared with finding Darcy.

Nick whistled low in awe when they saw the boat. "Heck said it's a fifty-four-footer, but it looks bigger—and new," he said.

It was a handsome two-deck boat with the captain's chair observation deck on the top in a partly glassed-in cockpit. It had all kinds of radar and satellite gear poking from the top deck and a large live tank at the back of the stern for keeping catches fresh until they were cleaned and packaged. Places for fishing rods studded the stern taffrail, and swivel fighting chairs were prominent.

"He's got a place here where his charters obviously clean

their fish," Nick added, pointing to a large plank tray that had been scrubbed clean.

Evidently Ralston was washing his nets, because a big one draped over the side between the dock and the boat was riding up and down partly submerged in the waves. Maybe that was an easy way to clean a large net.

"Wonder if he usually keeps a catch of big fish that don't fit in the live tank in the net," Nick said, staring down at where the net disappeared into the blue-black water. "That would keep them fresh until he can clean them. Man, that net's big enough to hold a big fish. If I take him on as a client, I'll advise him to get rid of that before a trial, but then it looks pretty new, doesn't it? Maybe it was already confiscated and he replaced it. I mean, it's so white while the other nets we've seen have gone brownish from the salt water."

They read the painted sign the man on the dock had mentioned. Bright letters offered half-or full-day deep-sea fishing on the *Down Under* with the chance to catch sailfish, mahi-mahi, bonito and skipjack tuna. In case Ralston was not aboard, Nick scribbled down the phone number of "Captain Larry" and stuffed it in his pocket.

"Hello!" he called out when no one appeared. "Larry Ralston? Captain Larry!"

No sound but the wash of waves against the big wooden pilings holding up the dock, the buzz of muted voices from the restaurant and the screech of a seagull that swooped in to sit on the sign, evidently thinking they were about to clean some fish he could get part of.

"Larry Ralston!" Nick called again, cupping his hands around his mouth.

"I hope you don't have to wait until Monday in your

office," Claire said, annoyed her voice sounded choked up. Every little setback loomed so large. They had to get more information on Fly Safe, on how their board members felt about something like a butterfly farm, and Nick would have some leverage over this guy. Had someone visited the farm the day Darcy disappeared? Did anyone know of someone else who might have a beef against the Flutterby Farm or Tara Gerald?

"I'll bet he's just taking a nap or stepped away for a minute," Nick observed, pointing at the mooring ropes holding the boat close to the dock. "If he was not around, he wouldn't leave everything as open as it looks. And on a seat cushion in the stern, I saw a cell phone just lying there."

"I saw that. It made me think he'd be right back. He'd surely be eager to see you, and we need any kind of help we can get right now," she said the obvious again, gripping his hand. "Let's maybe go on board and knock on the galley or cabin door."

Nick looked at his watch, then glanced at the clots of gray clouds coming closer.

"Let's give it a few more minutes. If he's not here, we've got to go home, hope Steve's back and bring him up to speed. I'd hate to just try to calm Steve over the phone. Can't say I blame him, but he seems to be waiting to explode."

Despite the desperation of their mission, Jace was amused at the comedown this little Piper Cub airplane he'd borrowed presented when he and Mitch were used to much bigger aircraft. And that tiny storm on the horizon was a far cry from the behemoths they were used to seeing and flying through. This bright yellow plane he'd borrowed from a friend had its pluses, though: Lexi and her new doll liked the bright color, and the thing had floats as well as wheels in case they spotted anything interesting and needed to put down on water or grass in this fringe-of-the-Glades area.

"I hope we see her car," Lexi called up to them for the fourth time. At least it was better than the voice of that doll she wouldn't let go of.

"Yeah, Lex," Jace said over his shoulder. "But you can see there aren't many good places to drive a car out here."

"So maybe she didn't go far, then left her car and walked. Or waded. She likes to wade in water, like at the beach, but I'm scared there might be gators or those big snakes down there to hurt her."

Jace and Mitch exchanged frowns. Yeah, there wasn't much good news here and no sign of a car or even a person except a couple people on an airboat that was leaving a large trail below. And then he heard a crack of thunder.

"Gonna loop past that little storm and head back," Nick told Mitch. "If we didn't have Lexi, I might go farther east but I can't see it."

Lexi piped up again. "I can see the storm, and it's not too scary. I want to find her, Daddy!"

"Me, too, honey. But we'd better go back home and we'll keep looking more later."

"But I'm not afraid! Unless we lost her!"

Jace frowned as he banked the plane back toward the west. Mistake to bring Lexi, evidently. But he had really wanted to spend time with her and help in the short time he might have before another flying assignment.

Although he prided himself with nerves of steel in the air, he jolted when that robot doll's voice came from the back seat.

"I'm not afraid, either," it said in that sickly sweet mono-tone voice. "Lexi and I want to know what will happen next. Where are Mommy and Nick now? But I am sure we will find Aunt Darcy, and she will be just fine."

Jace whispered a swear word only Mitch could hear.

"Remember the basics we had pounded into us," Mitch told him, his voice nearly muffled by the noise of the en-gine. "Any problems—aviate, navigate, communicate."

"Not with that damn doll," he whispered back. "I swear it likes to eavesdrop." He added in a louder voice, "Head-ing home for now, Lex."

Claire realized the rainstorm was larger than it had looked. The drops were heavy, and gusts of wind drove them sideways. She was instantly soaked but at least it was a warm rain.

"He should be here by now!" Nick shouted, taking her elbow. "Let's take shelter under the boat deck on board. He won't mind when he hears who I am."

He steadied her across from the dock to the boat. Teth-ered by ropes, the big craft was barely rocking in the waves. They huddled on the lee side under the slight overhang above the stern, clinging together. It felt so good to put her arms tight around Nick's waist as he held her to him. But a blast of wind somehow yanked open the galley door, which nearly bumped into them. It banged against the wall.

They both turned to look. Claire figured Captain Larry had heard them and was coming out. Suddenly, she had a terrible thought: What if he was armed, what if whoever took Darcy had been armed, had used a gun?

But no one stood in the doorway.

Nick shouted again, this time through the door. "Larry! Larry Ralston! It's attorney Nick Markwood!"

No sounds but the whine of wind and drumming of rain. And another rumble of thunder. That scared Claire, not for them but for Lexi with Jace and Mitch in a plane. Surely he'd head back and land.

To her surprise, Nick tugged her hand and went through the open door into the cabin of the boat. A light was on over the small sink, so Ralston must be here.

"Larry! Larry Ralston! Nick Markwood and my wife, Claire, to see you!"

Claire was grateful for the shelter, though being here like this—actually trespassing—made her nervous. She told Nick, "He must have just run out for something, then the storm hit, so he stayed put for a while."

"Yeah. As soon as this quits, we'll head out, and I'll call him to explain. All we need is someone in another boat nearby calling the cops, then Jensen comes to arrest us for breaking and entering—or trespassing at best." He shook his head and gave a little grunt of a laugh.

They both looked around the cabin. Not exactly what they called "shipshape," so didn't Captain Larry keep things organized here or hire a first mate who did? The lamp, which was lighted, was still attached to the wall, but hung askew. Claire saw that broken glass—a bottle of liquor?— from the small bar was smashed into gritty shards she felt underfoot. A back cushion from the seat along the wall under two portholes was on the floor.

She saw Nick was taking that all in, too, frowning, puzzled.

"And," she said, "I'm glad we didn't touch his—or someone's—cell phone that was out on deck, even though this storm may ruin it. There's been a struggle here, right?"

"Looks that way. Maybe he was hurt and went for help, didn't close or lock up, but I don't see any blood around."

He loosed his hold on her and took several steps toward the cabin, then evidently changed his mind. "We better not touch anything," he told her. "Let's get out of here, and I'll try to phone him to see if he's okay."

They hurried outside and back onto the dock. The rain had let up a bit, but not enough to keep them dry. Nick bent over his phone, and Claire tried to block the sprinkles. She saw his hand shook as he pulled the paper out of his pocket and punched in Ralston's number.

The phone lying in a puddle on the back deck rang. Again. Again.

"Nick, that's his phone."

"I hear it. Something's wrong. Really wrong."

"Disappeared just like Darcy? Related somehow?"

"Don't jump to conclusions, but I'm calling Ken Jensen. Hope he's working today, but I guess he's always on call."

They huddled. Claire could tell that Nick's call to Ken went to voice mail, so he described the time, place and what they'd found, even mentioned that Ralston was on the Fly Safe board they had discussed.

Claire quickly called home to see where Jace and Lexi were.

"They're not back yet but they landed," Nita told her. "They didn't find nothing. They gonna be back here soon. Jace is going to see Brit at the zoo even in the rain."

As soon as she said goodbye to Nita and explained Lexi was fine, Nick said, "I hope Ken calls back soon—and that he won't be mad as hell at us for checking on people with possible information. Maybe we should go wait in the restaurant, get some coffee at least. Don't know how to make sense of what we found."

Claire nodded, but she kept watching the rise and fall of the large net over the side of the boat. Since the water was more turbulent than earlier, something white kept showing beneath the waves, then sinking. It must be the belly of a fish, surely not of a trapped dolphin that was the cause of Captain Larry's troubles.

"Nick, look," she said, pointing.

Like her, he leaned over in the lessening rain to stare down between the boat hull and the dock. In the next surge of water, it surfaced again, a white arm, which led to a bare white shoulder.

Claire sucked in a sob. She screamed and fell to her knees, reaching far down into the net. No! No, it couldn't be! Not Darcy!

CHAPTER THIRTEEN

Claire sucked in a sob. She reached down so far into the net that Nick yanked her back.

"No!" she screamed again. "No, it can't be!"

But the minute she pulled free from Nick and lay on her stomach to reach for the submerged arm again, she saw it wasn't Darcy. The arm, as Nick helped her pull it up, was muscular, large and looked fish-belly white under the surface despite its dark hair.

"Oh, thank God, thank God," she cried, but then someone was dead. And the more likely conclusion was that Larry Ralston had leaned over the live tank, slipped somehow and fallen in. But was that actually likely with a professional fisherman who had to know this boat and dock so well?

"Here, let me," Nick said, hooking the man's elbow through a woven space in the net, but not pulling him up farther. "I'm calling Jensen again."

Claire knelt on the dock, staring down, both grieved yet

grateful. Again, she agonized, how could a charter captain used to waves and water have slipped in that small space without being able to grab the dock or the boat—the net at least. If this even was Captain Larry Ralston.

"Not sure if you got my message—we're at the boat dock at Crayton Cove," Nick said into the phone, his voice trembling. "Came to see a potential client of mine, a charter fishing boat captain. We found him here—at least we think it's him, but he's dead, caught in his own net, maybe drowned… Yeah, yeah, I know, but no way we could just sit home waiting… Okay, send the ME. If you don't want a crowd, better not use your sirens… What?"

Nick frowned. Claire could hear Ken's voice raised, but with sounds of the wind and waves, couldn't tell what he was saying. Still, she could guess.

"No, we're not taking over your case, Detective. Of course we're being careful," he said with a shake of his head at Claire as she leaned closer to hear. "It's just we are even more desperate than you to find Darcy and we couldn't just sit there… Right… Yes. Okay, we'll just sit here now until you arrive."

Nick saw Ken was more than upset; he was furious. The three of them and two uniformed officers waited on the dock for the ME and the forensic team to arrive. So far they hadn't even tried to retrieve the body Nick had hooked into the net.

"You went inside, too?" Ken demanded, gesturing at the *Down Under* when Nick explained what had happened and how they had known to try to talk to Ralston. "And you're one of the top criminal defense lawyers in South Florida? And Claire a forensic psych? You two are going to end up persons of interest with this if you don't stay home, damn it."

Claire decided to speak up, though he was glaring mostly at Nick. "Captain Ralston was going to be Nick's client," she said. "And we are absolutely desperate to find any lead from anyone who might know something about Darcy, since nothing official seems to be forthcoming!"

"I got that, Claire. But Nick's the one who should have known better. I don't care if it was raining. You actually went inside and found signs of a struggle? And here I'm waiting for a warrant to check this boat out."

Nick said, "At least we found a body before it drifts away or something down there eats it. And there's probably going to be hell to pay, not for us, but for you, because evidently Captain Larry here is well connected in this town, so good luck with that!"

"And not hell to pay for you two?" Ken flared back. "Are you kidding? You not only found a body but probably have your DNA all over the crime scene. As for good luck, you got that right," he muttered. His anger seemed to deflate a bit. "Look, the ME has arrived and their gurney's drawing a parade of onlookers. Got to have my officers get the crime scene tape up. You two, wait down the dock a ways and do *nothing* until I'm ready for complete statements, understand?"

Claire said, "I'd like to get home to my daughter and son."

"Not yet. You know that," Ken said, his voice quiet now as he moved away to meet the ME's people.

The two of them went down to the end of the arm of the dock. Claire's legs were shaking so badly she sat down on the edge, dangling her feet. Nick sat beside her and put his arm around her.

"Good thing we didn't touch that phone in the stern," he said. "Truth is, I don't think we touched one damn thing inside the boat, either, since the door was opened by the wind and is still that way. We've been totally honest with Ken. Just remember, never lie to the police and never lie to your attorney."

"Is that a joke to obey my husband or are we going to need one?"

"If Larry Ralston didn't kill himself—accident or intentional—someone did."

They looked down the dock. The ME's people were holding up a tarp so the gathering crowd, which two officers were holding back, could not see the body brought up, but she and Nick could see. A man wearing jeans. Barefoot. Buzz haircut like Jace and Mitch still wore.

Ken came toward them. "Can you two ID him before next of kin arrives?" he asked. "If not, I'll ask people on the dock. He has no ID on him."

"Never met him before," Nick said. "But there are some pictures online, advertising charter fishing, if you don't want to start asking around in the crowd."

Ken grabbed his phone from his pants pocket. "Hate to do it this way, but I don't want to call next of kin—his father and brother—if it's not Larry. Yeah, I know about the family. I'm still mad as hell at both of you, but we're now unofficially working together on two cases—only one murder case, Claire," he added hastily. "The other strictly a missing person."

Claire nodded. Exhaustion and grief swept through her. Her body felt wooden, yet her mind surged like the sea.

They watched as Ken kept sliding his finger across the screen, obviously looking at several pictures.

"It's him," he told them. "Now I've got to make that phone call. His father's a wealthy funeral director and friend of the mayor's and who knows who else?"

As he walked away, Nick muttered, "And just in case Ralston knew anything at all about Fly Safe and Darcy, there goes our lead!"

A good hour later, with a finally delivered search warrant in hand—actually on his cell phone—Detective Jensen was preparing to go on board the *Down Under* with a forensic team. Nick and Claire both shook his hand after their separate statements to him on a nearby yacht, which the police had been given for a temporary office. He had spent about half an hour with each of them. His demeanor and questions had been professional and calm, not angry like earlier.

They were about to get off the yacht and head home when three men came nearly running down the deck toward where an officer had pointed out Detective Jensen. The two men in front greatly resembled each other. The other man was tall and thin with silver blond hair.

"The first two resemble the deceased," Ken said the obvious. "Next of kin. Here we go. Stay here until I have them make an ID, then you can head out, and I'll talk to them here on the yacht. So, Nick, you think they brought a lawyer?"

When Claire got a closer view of the men, she was content not to pass them on the dock right now. It was understandable, of course, that family and perhaps a friend would be distraught.

All three looked furious, the first two men panicked while the blond man emanated rigid control. Perhaps because the day was still cloudy from the rain, none of them wore sunglasses. And yes, two of them must be family of the deceased, especially the younger one, perhaps a brother. Those two were very tanned with dark hair and similar stocky builds. All three were dressed well in slacks and golf shirts. The older man evidently had on golf shoes because she could see the cleats, so they were probably tearing up the wooden dock. From the looks of them, they planned to tear up Ken, as if this were his fault. So would they blame her and Nick, too?

"Aaron and Clinton Ralston," the older man introduced them as they stopped in front of Ken. Both nodded; neither shook his hand.

With a quick look at the blond man behind them, the younger Ralston added, "And my associate Jedi Brown."

"You're sure it's Larry?" the older man interrupted. "I'm his father. I need to see him, claim the body."

Ken said, "We are very sorry for your loss and would appreciate an identification. But this is a police matter, possibly foul play, so the body will need to be autop—"

"Look here, we understand you have a job to do," the older man went on. "But you said he was submerged, so it's possible he fell in—no foul play. He's been under duress for something he didn't do, something not his fault, this harmful dolphin charade."

"Sir, I'm certain you realize you cannot just claim a body involved in a police investigation even if you are next of kin."

"He has—had no wife. Divorced. No children. Just me and his brother here," he added with a nod, "and I'm sure you can make an exception for family. If not, I will have to go over your head."

"If there was a murder here—" Ken's rising voice floated to them, even though he was facing away, "—you certainly want it investigated and someone brought to justice. We are about to examine the interior of his boat, and we have taken possession of his cell phone, which was found on the back deck, so all that may throw light on whether this is an accident, murder or suicide—"

"Look." The young man—Clinton—spoke. "If you cannot release him to his family at this time, I have a legal document here, a living will so to speak, in which my brother claims that whenever and wherever his death occurs, his body be immediately given into my possession. Time is of the essence. It may help that he was in the water, but—"

The father interrupted. "Not released to you, Clinton, I don't care what that document says you two kept secret from me. He's going to be properly buried!"

"Now they are going to turn on each other," Claire told Nick. "So much family volatility. Ken will have to look into that. I should tell him their body language shows—"

"You need to stay way out of this," Nick interrupted, gripping her wrist. "You are not working for the police, so you should tell him nothing."

"What is this?" Ken demanded as he bent his head to read what Clinton had thrust at him.

"Just what I said," he insisted. "A legal document ordering his body be immediately transferred into my possession."

"No way!" his father burst out. "That is not what I have planned. You two went behind my back?"

Claire did not have to strain to hear. Even if water carried sound, both men were almost shouting and at each other.

"You know," Nick said only to her, "I just remembered my father was buried by Ralston's Funeral Home, but I've never seen the son. Sorry to put it this way, but the senior Ralston is very hands-on."

"And wants to control both his sons. They must know they can't have the body right now, if there was a possible murder."

"Even suicide—I hope not," Nick said, and she put her arm around his waist as they stayed back on the end of the dock.

"I'll need to call a judge on this," Ken said.

"It's not to be made public," the dead man's brother insisted. "Absolutely private information. Call it classified. I'll sue you if your holding him makes a difference in terms of proper timing. Read that third paragraph."

"Since you two cannot even agree on where the body is going and what is going to happen to it," Ken told them, finally putting the paper he was skimming down to his side, "I'm telling you, we need an autopsy."

"Then let me have his head first!" the brother insisted, pointing at the paper again.

The older Clinton looked aghast, but the Jedi guy only nodded.

"Did I just hear that?" Nick whispered. "What in the world...?"

Claire pulled her phone out of her purse and checked information on Clinton Ralston of Naples, Florida. Amazingly, nothing came up. Did he just live off his wealthy father? Work at one of the Ralston funeral homes? He was as good as a ghost. There was plenty about Aaron Ralston, though, and really, that blond guy hovering seemed like more of a bodyguard than an associate, whatever that meant. And was his name really Jedi?

That reminded her of *The Last Jedi* movie she and Darcy had finally agreed to watch with Lexi and Jilly last year. She even remembered the lines from the trailer she and Darcy had watched several times while agonizing over whether the kids would get nightmares from the film. But it was Carrie Fisher's last movie, so she and Darcy had wanted to see it, too—and then Carrie had died and where was Darcy?

Strange but she recalled the scary voice narrating the teaser with the young female character who wanted to learn the ways of the wise Jedi, something about *I need help... You have untamed power...*

"Anything about him online?" Nick interrupted her memory.

"No, but maybe if we get out of here, Ken can talk more to them and then talk to us about what he learned."

"Their family mess—I can't see how it links to Darcy, and tracing her has to be our first priority."

"I just wish Larry Ralston had actually become your client, so you could have some say in this—a right to know what they're arguing about at least. Let's go now before these men link us to finding the body, even though I suppose they'll find out eventually. We've been gone too long from Lexi and even from Steve."

"Yeah, okay."

Ken was still arguing, but at least the men were walking away to where the body was covered by a tarp. That gave her and Nick a chance to leave without being part of a confrontation. And, she thought as they turned away, the emotions she had seen displayed by the dead man's relatives puzzled her. Not grief or even shock, really. Anger, yes, but at Ken and at each other—so strange for family members just learning their brother and son was dead, maybe even murdered.

A little ways down the main dock, Claire turned back for one last glimpse. Clinton Ralston turned his head to look at them and her eyes locked with his steady stare for a moment. He did resemble his dead brother quite a bit. Were they twins? But the dead one's picture was easy to find on the internet and this man's was not. And what had he planned to do with his brother's body—or, for heaven's sake, his head?

When she glanced back once more, the blond man named Jedi Brown had turned to watch them.

The *Star Wars* movie darted through her mind again: *I need help… You have untamed power.*

CHAPTER FOURTEEN

When Claire and Nick finally got home, there were hugs all around. Jace even gave her a quick shoulder hug after he shook hands with Nick. Nita was beaming to see her back—and, probably, to finally get away from Lexi's and Jilly's questions—and go home to Bronco. But where was Steve?

It was getting dark. Fireflies lit the lawn and twinkled through the patio window to make the reflections of everyone gathered around seem to sparkle. In her continued fear and grief, Claire hoped, wherever Darcy was now, that she might be comforted by memories of happier times like when they used to catch what they then called lighting bugs. As girls, they used to put them in a jar and they would light up their room at night...

"Mommy, did you hear what Cindy just said?" Lexi's high voice broke her reverie.

"No, I'm surprised I didn't. What did she say?"

As Jilly hovered close, Lexi said to the doll in her arms, "Can you say that again, Cindy?"

"I am glad you are home, Mommy. Tell us where you have been," the doll said—no, actually commanded. So did this little robot give Lexi stern orders sometimes, too?

That's all she needed, Claire fumed, to be ordered around by that doll. And since Jilly was here, she wanted to ask her where her daddy was. Perhaps exhausted, lying down at last.

"Mommy," Lexi repeated as if she were the interactive doll, "where have you been?"

Darned if she or Nick were telling these kids they'd found a body, so Claire said to her daughter, not to the doll, "Dad and I have been to the beach and talked to some people we saw there."

But the doll answered. "Oh, that's nice. But Lexi is sad, even though we took a plane trip. Where is her aunt Marcy?"

Lexi said, "It's not Marcy, Cindy, but Darcy, with a *D*."

"Oh, sorry," the doll said. "Tell me more about Aunt Darcy."

"Well, that thing made one mistake at least!" Steve's voice came from across the room. "I swear, it's smarter than me."

Everyone looked his way. Claire gasped, and Nick asked, "What in the world happened to you?"

"Gotta admit I had a couple of brews at the sports bar and fell going out to the car. Hit my head, got scratched up."

A moment of silence followed as everyone stared at him, and Jilly went over to take his hand to comfort him. He had a bump on his forehead slowly turning brownish blue. Claire noted the beginning of a black half-moon under his left eye and a swollen lower lip as well as a few cuts on the backs of his hands and arms. So he fell on the *backs* of his knuckles, not put his palms out to catch himself?

"I don't want to talk about it," Steve said in the awkward silence. "My mistake. Yeah, okay, I got into it with a guy there who asked if the little lady ran off with someone else—you know," he added with an I-don't-want-to-say-more look at the girls. "He was no one I know. After our disagreement, he left. I bribed the manager not to call the cops. So, if everyone would please stop staring, let's figure out our next move."

Claire put the girls to bed—including the walking-talking marvel doll—then hurried back to the Florida room. Nita had left a hefty tray of snacks and a pitcher of iced tea; Claire and Nick were famished. Nick had Heck on speaker phone so he could explain his latest research. Steve, looking sheepish for once, didn't take any food and kept fingering a tooth that looked to Claire like it might have come loose.

"We could try another public plea," Nick was saying, "but that means letting the media mavens poke around again. It could help, but they could get in our way if we do more investigating on our own."

"And then," Claire said, "Detective Jensen might lock us up just to shut us up. He's already ticked off at us for overstepping. Here's the full story of what Nick and I did today."

They explained their attempts to question two members of the possibly militant Fly Safe pro-butterfly protection group, Linc Yost and Larry Ralston. Everyone was aghast at their retelling of finding the body in the net and the arrival of the dead man's next of kin. Nick concluded things with, "So the one guy clams up and changes the topic from butterflies to dolphins, and the other ends up dead before we can talk to him. Just the sort of puzzle my private business, South Shores, looks into. Was Captain Larry Ralston's death natural, accidental, suicide or murder?"

Nick's investigation and support outreach was known to those present, so he didn't say more. Those closest to him knew the reason he tried to help families whose loved ones had committed suicide—or was it suicide? His own father had been murdered but the scene was staged to make it look as if he had killed himself. Nick had finally tracked down the murderer. Then, through investigation and legal support, his South Shores project became his way of helping others who had gone through the hell that he had faced.

"And," Claire added, "does this death link to Darcy's disappearance or not?"

"More important, where the hell is Darcy?" Steve muttered, tears in his eyes. "Can she—she be gone, too? Or is she dead, too?"

"We can't jump to conclusions," Claire put in. "Detective Jensen assured me her disappearance is officially still a missing-persons case."

"But what happened to her?" Steve said, and his voice broke. The big guy's hands were shaking. "How can she just be missing? I'm scared to death for her."

Claire reached out to cover his hand with hers, and he flinched from the bruises there. Thank heavens he hadn't been arrested for a barroom brawl. They really needed to keep him home, but then she thought that was exactly what Ken Jensen wanted from them all, and they could hardly stay home and wait around for someone else's news. Things were taking too long.

"Like I told you," Heck said on the speaker phone, "even though the focus is obviously on butterflies, the fact that Larry Ralston and Lincoln Yost were both involved with dolphins might mean something. I'll look into that as well, along with trying to learn more about this mystery man Clinton Ralston, since there doesn't appear to be much about him online."

"Sounds good, my man," Nick told him. "Heck, I'm going to have to go into work Monday because that trial delay I asked for is over, so be aware I may not have access to a phone right away, depending on how it goes. At least that still gives me tomorrow to help here."

"I'll leave you a message and let Claire know, too," he said. "Bye for now."

Claire had a feeling Nick didn't want Heck feeding her information while he was in court, but she didn't mention that. Not with everyone here and again not later when they went to bed and tried to get some sleep, as exhausted as they were. While she said her jumbled, panicked prayers, she asked that Steve not lose control again and for Darcy to be somehow, somewhere safe. After all, she'd read news items where captive women, like that terrible case in Cleveland, finally made it free, and the abductors and rapists were arrested. She shuddered, just admitting that possibility to herself.

Tired as she was, she carefully edged out of bed so she wouldn't disturb Nick. Heck was going to research dolphins. Yet she had another obsession right now. She needed to skim that book she'd taken from Darcy's house, *The Collector*, about the butterfly freak who kept an innocent woman prisoner in his isolated house. Maybe there was a clue in that story. Besides, something about Will Warren, butterfly expert and very helpful friend, kept haunting her—his soft heart toward Darcy and obsessive concern over her disappearance, his drifting through their past...

Could he have become overly fond of Darcy years ago or even now? Like the demented kidnapper in *The Collector*, Will evidently lived alone in a fairly isolated house.

And she could not get seeing that bloated body of the boat captain out of her mind. She and Darcy had once gone swimming with the dolphins down in the Caribbean when they were on break from college. How ironic that Captain Larry had hurt a dolphin and then had ended up swimming with them, paying with his life as if he were now cursed? Surely it was not God's justice—payback—for him going to Tara's place to protest her butterfly "prison" and finding Darcy there and one thing led to another. But if he was murdered for that, who was behind it?

She turned on a light in the den and opened the lid of her laptop. In the search box, she typed in *Dolphins + Suspended Animation*.

Claire's brain took in the information and her amazement kept her somehow awake in the heavy silence of the house. She read and printed several articles she would have to show Nick. One was about how susceptible these marine mammals were to sonar. Navy ships emitting pulses of sound had been blamed for a mass beaching. The animals talked to each other with sounds. But she also found proof of what she'd heard before: dolphins could put themselves into a partial sleep while swimming, resting half their brain at a time, before switching to the other half. They controlled their breathing, and one eye at a time kept watch. But they were still quite functional.

So that, she thought, was like the butterflies in the regard that these animals had control over suspending some or all of their lives and then coming back to full or half consciousness at will. Granted, if mankind could master that, as Will Warren had said, that would be information leading to great riches and power. Not only would that mean overcoming the long distances and time in space travel, but it could lead to a sort of extended life, a step toward immortality.

Yes, as kind and concerned as Will seemed, she had to find out more about him. But how could this arcane information lead to finding Darcy?

She nearly jumped out of her chair when Nick spoke behind her. "Sweetheart, don't just go off like that. Not with your sister missing. When you weren't in Lexi's room, I nearly freaked out."

"Sorry," she said, swiveling toward him in her desk chair as he sank into the club chair nearby. "I wanted to look up the dolphin info and take a look at a book I took from Darcy's bedroom."

"Listen, Heck said he'd do the dolphin research, and we can try to further nail down Yost. Seems he wants to talk about that at least," he said, trying to stifle a huge yawn. He looked exhausted, hair mussed, his cheek with a wrinkle from his pillow; his eyes, even in this fairly dim light, were bloodshot.

"We need to get you back to bed," she said. "You have tomorrow, but then court the next morning."

"I hope we know more by then. When I couldn't find you—"

"Nick, I'm trying to function, to think straight. And Steve getting in a fight like that..."

"I just don't want you to go off on something iffy or dangerous while I'm a captive audience at the courthouse this week."

A captive audience—the words snagged in her exhausted mind. Was Darcy being held captive as they spoke? A random kidnapping? Or was it someone she knew, someone who had motives other than ransom? She'd be careful, all right, but she'd take a look at that book in the morning, would have done it right now if Nick hadn't woken up. They had plans for more interviews with the media tomorrow, but Monday she'd spend time after breakfast with Lexi—and that darned doll. But then she was going to make sure Will was at work and take a little trip out to that isolated house of his.

And unless she found something suspicious, Nick would never even know about it because he'd blow sky-high. But she had to take risks. She'd leave him a note about it in case anything went wrong, and take all the precautions she could. But truth be told, she'd risk her own life to save Darcy's.

CHAPTER FIFTEEN

Claire agreed with Nick that, for Lexi and Jilly's sake, they should try for some semblance of a family Sunday—at least in the morning—so they went to church. Steve didn't want questions and concerns, and Jace was home with Brit, so it was just Claire, Nick and the girls. For once, Claire was relieved that Nick had convinced Lexi to leave the doll at home by playing up the fact Cindy needed more rest. Claire just rolled her eyes but she was so grateful not to have Lexi's "crutch" with them for a while. As much as she'd tried to comfort and counsel her daughter using every psych trick she knew, until now, Lexi had not let go of that doll.

At church, everyone was supportive but also curious. Claire cried through the prayer from the pulpit for Darcy's safe and soon return.

After lunch at home, the parade of television and newspaper interviews began, all carefully scheduled by Heck, who hovered over the lineup while Gina, home from med school for a few days, played badminton with Lexi and

Jilly in the backyard. This time, instead of Steve, who still looked banged up, Claire did the sessions one at a time with the reporters and their entourage of cameramen: three TV reporters from Fort Myers and the Fox News reporter from Naples. She also gave the *Naples Daily News* and the Fort Myers *News-Press* interviews, asking for tips from anyone who might have seen or overheard anything about Darcy's disappearance. She held the Christmas picture of her sister in front of her for the video and photos.

The only ground rules were that she would not answer questions about her and Nick's "stumbling" across Captain Larry Ralston's body, but would stick to Darcy's disappearance. A few reporters tried out-the-door questions about Ralston, but she firmly declined to answer, and Nick stepped in to warn them there would be no follow-ups if they got off topic with their coverage.

When they watched the six and eleven o'clock coverages that evening, Claire noted that not only did her voice shake but also her hands. That made the photo she held look like Darcy was trembling, too.

The next morning, the voir dire went far more smoothly and faster than Nick had expected, so the jury was all seated for the trial, which would start the following day. He was even pleased with those he'd helped to select—and to have psyched them out to be sure they would not be prejudiced against his client. That reading of personalities was Claire's forte, which was why he'd probably try to get her to work with him part-time when the kids were older. That was, unless another baby came along, which he wouldn't mind at all.

But despite the demands of this coming trial, he had to help Claire and Lexi stay strong in this search for Darcy.

He'd never say it aloud, but he had terrible vibes. Too much time had passed with no rational answer. This was the fifth day she'd been missing. She and her car might as well have been spirited away by aliens.

He'd talked to Claire the minute he got back in his office. She'd been "counseling" Lexi, as she called it, despite the doll chiming in. That tech doll was a blessing and a curse, he thought as he went back to wolfing down his sandwich at his desk. His secretary, Cheryl, buzzed him, and despite having a mouthful of pastrami and rye, he punched the talk button on his console.

"Nick, Bronco says there are two men downstairs at the security desk who insist you will want to see them—a Mr. Ralston and a Mr. Brown. Bronco says if they come up, he'll come, too, and stay with them. It's about that dead man you and Claire found."

"They should go to the police."

"They said they already have earlier today. Did you know it's in the morning paper that you and Claire found that charter boat captain's body?"

"No, in too much of a hurry to read it. Jensen probably had to put it in the official report and the newspaper desk picked it up."

"I can call Detective Jensen or summon more security and have Bronco stall or remove them."

"No. Send them up. And yes, with Bronco. Also, call Detective Jensen to tell them they're here."

"Will do. Right on it."

After talking to Nick, Claire phoned the library to be sure Will Warren was there today. "Yes," the receptionist told her, "he's here now and will be all afternoon. Story time at two-thirty, so please also invite your friends and their children. We always have a lovely gathering. Will Warren is such a wonderful entertainer."

"Oh, yes. Thank you."

But she wasn't telling her friends and especially not her husband. She did, however, leave Nick a note on his desk. She wrote that Will Warren was accounted for elsewhere and she was only going to look around his place to see if there was a shed or outbuilding, or if any of the windows looked nailed shut. In this part of Florida, at least, there would be no basement.

She had read and reread the pages where the villain of *The Collector* had taken and kept his victim imprisoned. That man was such an egomaniac and psychopath that he actually thought his victim would fall in love with him. And then it had ended so badly. The captive had tried to escape, been recaptured—had died. *Villain and victim, villain and victim*, the words kept revolving in her mind as she went to tell Nita she was going out for a little while. As she left without saying goodbye to Lexi for once, she felt almost grateful for the doll the girls were focused on in the Florida room. At least that horrible machine in its cute body didn't bother Nita at all.

As Claire hit the remote to lift the garage door, she whispered the haunting refrain again, "Villain and victim. Whatever it takes, I have to find both."

Cheryl escorted the two very different-looking men into Nick's office with Bronco trailing. Nick nodded that Cheryl could go, and he shook hands with them, then indicated the chairs in front of his desk. Bronco hovered in the back of the room on a chair near the shelves of law books.

Jedi Brown was neatly but casually dressed whereas Ralston looked once again as if he'd stepped out of *GQ Magazine* or at least *Golf Digest*.

"May I call you Clinton and Jedi?" Nick asked.

"If we might call you Nicholas," Ralston said.

"Nick is fine."

"I don't use my full name," the dark-haired man said as he settled himself in the leather chair, then leaned forward as if he might leap out of it. "That is, I don't go by Clinton, but Clint. Only my parents call me Clinton."

"Clint, it is. And Jedi?"

"If we're talking parents before business," the tall blond said, "my name's really Jedidiah, the so-called blessing name for King Solomon. My parents are big Bible believers. Anyway, I was a *Star Wars* fanatic for years, so I go by Jedi. But lightsabers are not my weapon of choice."

Nick realized he must have been asked about his name ad nauseam. But the way he'd said that about lightsabers... Then what was his weapon of choice?

"Plus," Clint said, evidently impatient with the small talk that kept him shifting around in his chair, "the *Star Wars* Jedi are wise as Solomon, and this Jedi is my information gatherer, which is where you come in. You and your wife, we saw in the paper today, were the ones who discovered my brother's body."

"True. We were in the area and since Larry had requested a Monday appointment with me to talk about his defense on the dolphin case—and I knew I'd be busy then—I thought we'd take a look at his fishing boat, and if he was there, I'd introduce myself."

"Yeah, that makes sense," Ralston said, sitting back a

bit as if relaxing his stance to intimidate. "That's kind of what we figured."

Once again, Nick thought, Claire's continual reading of body language was useful but nerve-racking. As a matter of fact, as calm as he usually kept under pressure, the stares of these men were getting to him. Now that he'd admitted he and Claire had found Larry's body, what else did they want? To thank him or blame him?

Actually, Nick would like to grill this man about his occupation. Why wasn't there any info on him anywhere online? But this was not the time for confrontation. Ralston had lost someone close to him under mysterious, tragic circumstances, and he sympathized with that.

He also wasn't going to admit that he had mostly wanted to talk to Captain Larry about Fly Safe and any link dolphin suspended animation might have to the same in butterflies—and if Fly Safe had been at all hostile toward Tara Gerald. The idea sounded impossible, even as he thought of it now. And he certainly wasn't going to bring up that Larry as well as Linc Yost were possible—though it was a long shot—suspects, at least in his mind.

Nick explained, "My wife and I were trying to talk things out over her sister's disappearance, and strolling the docks seemed like a good diversion. We didn't even know which boat was your brother's and had to ask, then that quick storm came up. We saw his cell phone in the stern, saw the net bobbing, but didn't find him at first. It was quite a shock, especially because our focus had been on our own family tragedy."

"Understandable," Ralston said with a firm nod. "Sorry to hear about your wife's sister and hope you get her back soon. Families—joy and pain. So, I see you don't have any photos of your family here in the office," he said, craning his neck to look around. "Kinda unusual, but maybe, you being a criminal lawyer and all, it's one way of keeping them safe in case people are here who want something from you—or are upset at the way things went."

A sharp chill racked Nick. Were this man and his associate—or protector and enforcer—actually here to intimidate or even threaten him? Or was he just feeling paranoid to protect his own since Darcy had disappeared?

His eyes met Clint Ralston's. He stared him down in the sudden silence. Time to turn the tables, go on the offensive.

"So what do you do here in Naples, Mr. Ralston?"

"Well, don't confuse me with my father, who is a behind-the-scenes mover and shaker around here, funeral director extraordinaire up and down the Southwest Florida coast."

"I take it you are not in business with him but have your own? It seemed to me that the two of you were at odds with the police and each other yesterday."

"Our careers are in direct competition with each other, and he's always taken it personally, that's all," he said with a shrug.

And that evidently was all. Was this guy a master of deception, in on something illegal or did he just value his privacy? And was his so-called associate indeed a bodyguard?

"That paper you delivered to Detective Jensen—some sort of living will to claim your brother's body?"

"More or less. Privileged information, so the detective better not divulge it, either. Just asking for a quick handover of the body in case of an accident," he added, looking suddenly more than nervous.

With a nod and a frown, Clint Ralston rose and his companion popped up, too. Maybe this guy was Mafia or something that he didn't share his career. Most men liked to advertise what they did, even talk shop.

And when it came to this apparently well-heeled man's mysterious profession, exactly what was a career which was in "direct competition" with a funeral home? What were the death choice options besides embalming and burial or cremation and ashes in an urn?

He almost demanded to know more, but the two of them, with Bronco right behind, were letting themselves out the door.

Good riddance, he thought, and decided to call Ken Jensen with a full report. Besides, Nick needed to know what had been on that paper Clint had thrust at Jensen on the dock, privileged or protected information or not. As soon as he got home—early today after a meet with his legal team for the trial—he'd tell Claire to be extra careful since Ralston had made that carefully worded comment about his family's safety. But why?

Claire drove north on Collier Boulevard. Darcy had mentioned once that Will lived out at the end of Golden Gate Parkway, north of a dead end street called Safe Harbor Drive. She'd easily found his address online, but kept racking her brain about whether Darcy had told her why she'd been out to Will's—taken Jilly along, too, if she remembered right. Claire did recall that Darcy had said they were in a hurry and only dropped something off.

Claire was fairly unfamiliar with the area so she used her Google search. When she drove so far out that she was approaching wilderness, the area reminded her somewhat of Tara's. Actually, the wilderness was encroaching here, or else the vintage 1980 houses had encroached on the wilderness. Tall, spindly pines surrounded many of the one-floor stucco homes, most in bland beige. There it was, with his last name, Warren, on the mailbox.

The house was set back from the street with the next home a ways down the road. Widely spaced near-Naples property, however old and out in the boondocks, must be worth a lot these days. But unlike Linc Yost, Will seemed to have the resources for owning his valuable property. Heck had said Will had made a lot of money in Japan selling rare butterflies.

She got out of the car, locked it and walked toward the property as if she were just taking a stroll. No one was in sight. Of course, it was almost two-thirty, so Will would be well into his popular library story time by now, so no worry there. If, by chance, someone did suddenly appear, she could just say she wanted to see what butterfly-attracting plants were in his yard so she could enhance her own.

As she approached Will's house, Claire hoped he was as concerned and kind—and genuine—as he seemed. Steve had taken him up on his offer to add ten thousand dollars to the reward for information. As far as Claire could tell, Will's heart was in the right place, but the story of *The Collector* kept haunting her. And what she considered a terrible omen was finding Captain Larry's drowned body. At least, except for people who had a swimming pool out here, there were not even lakes. As unnerving as it was, that drowning had to be unrelated to Darcy's disappearance, didn't it?

The house had a double car garage. Claire pressed her ear to the closed door. No sounds within. She knocked quietly, then a bit louder.

"Hello! Anyone here?"

No sound. Nothing.

She walked around the back of the house. Brilliantly colored bushes galore, but no house for butterflies. A few of the bushes she could name—fire bush, flame bush, both with flitting butterflies. She glimpsed a wooden shed beyond that, not big, partly hidden by a huge purple bougainvillea. She strolled to it, took off her sunglasses, cupped her hands around her face and looked through the window. The bill of her visor struck the dusty, rain-streaked pane. Inside she saw a riding lawn mower, a tiller and a bench with neatly arranged garden tools. Well, did she really expect to find Darcy tied up here? Still, she intended to look in every window of the house.

If Nick hit the roof over her admitting she was here, she'd tell him it was in broad daylight. But then, she'd have to agree that was when Darcy was taken. For once, she almost wished they'd had a gun at home she could have brought, not that she knew how to shoot one.

She hurried toward the back of the house, taking off her visor so she could get close to the glass to peer in. If there were drapes or blinds, at least they were open.

The first window was in the kitchen. Nothing looked out of place that she could see. She moved to the next one, which was larger. Her own reflection stared at her until she moved closer and cupped her hands again.

She saw rows of hanging frames, a collection of butterflies under glass that glinted back at her, all hung on the wall next to a realistic painting of a woman in a flowing old-fashioned gown who was holding a butterfly net in one hand. Her straw bonnet dangled behind her by its blue ribbons, and her gown was a gauzy, lacy white. So lovely, so old-fashioned. And the woman—except for the long, flowing hair—dear heavens, it was Darcy!

CHAPTER SIXTEEN

Nick had just finished his last prep meeting with his defense team for the trial, which would begin tomorrow. He decided to go home early, comfort Claire, see Lexi, hopefully bolster Steve and decide what to do next about finding Darcy. Other than trying to talk to Linc Yost again, he was out of ideas. His console buzzed; it was Bronco at the first-floor security desk.

"Hey, boss, I just let Detective Jensen through to see you. Couldn't have stopped him, anyway. He said he has an autopsy report for you."

"Thanks, Bronco, and thanks for the earlier support with my guests."

"Something off about them. Good luck with the detective. He doesn't usually bring good news."

That was all he needed to hear, Nick thought as he put his briefcase under his desk so it didn't look like he was on his way out. He went to his office door and opened it himself.

"I'm expecting him, Cheryl," Nick said as Jensen emerged from the elevator and made a beeline for his office.

"I guess you have this place memorized," Nick said as he closed the door behind them. "Just tell me there's not bad news about Darcy."

"No news is maybe good news on her. Nick, I want to assure you and Claire we are not resting on this. The TV coverage Claire did was good. We've already received about thirty new tips we're looking into."

"If you can share the most promising tips, we can—"

"You two have already been too damned involved in solving this, but I understand. Come on now, you've seen how your getting in the way can cause problems—like finding dead bodies and the media coming after you for that rather than the search for your family member."

"We've declined to answer questions about Ralston's death. Besides, truth is we don't know anything about it—but do you now?"

"Yeah, a couple of things. But your finding him puts you in the puzzle, so to speak."

Nick sank into the chair next to where Jensen sat, rather than across his desk. Nick told him, "I had a logical, legitimate reason for reaching out to a potential client in Larry Ralston. But what has the ME ruled about his death?"

"Death by drowning, probably after a fall from his boat. *Down Under*, what a prophetic name," he said, shaking his head. "Time of death still being calculated by body temp tests may have been thrown off by the water. He had water in his lungs, et cetera. He did have chin, head and hand contusions, but that could have been from hitting his head on the boat or dock or trying to grab on, then being knocked around in that net by the waves."

"If he was conscious, I keep thinking he could have used the net to haul himself up to the surface. I keep thinking it's ironic that he was in that Fly Safe organization, then ended up accused of killing a dolphin. The group focuses on lots of other animals, but dolphins and butterflies are two of them—and so different from each other." But, Nick thought, they did have suspended animation in common.

"Yeah," Jensen said, "but they're also militant for manatees, lots of bird life around here. I'm looking into Fly Safe, too. Got the idea from my initial interview with Tara Gerald."

"Glad to hear that," Nick said, his faith in this guy increasing again. "Because what if Ralston or even Linc Yost went to Tara's place to protest or deface something—take butterflies or free them? Darcy's there alone, she protests or resists, says she'll call the police, and someone gets nervous or aggressive."

"Yeah, exactly. I guess cops and lawyers—criminal lawyers—think alike. Back to my visit here, a follow-up on our quick interview yesterday. So were you two actually there near the boats to check that out with Captain Larry, interview him about Fly Safe? And should I warn you to stay away from Linc Yost because you're going to question him next now that Captain Larry is gone?"

Nick swallowed hard. Once again, they were keeping information from Jensen since he'd already talked to Yost—twice. But he didn't need another lecture on overstepping right now, because Jensen would tell him to absolutely steer clear of Yost, and he had to talk to him again about the dolphin-butterfly connection.

The detective's voice hardened; he pointed a finger, suddenly morphing into an interviewer, maybe even an accuser. "And you've just given me an idea that you might have been hostile toward Ralston, thinking he'd gone to the Flutterby Farm, so on his boat you had an argument and—"

"Damn it, you know better! Claire was with me on the boat. I did not argue with, fight with or kill Lawrence Ralston! We couldn't even find him there—until we found him dead!"

"Yeah, I believe you," Jensen said, sinking back in his chair. "Partly because Claire's such a straight arrow. But either Ralston himself or someone else messed up his boat cabin. Our tech department's looking for DNA and still examining his cell phone. But—hate to put it this way considering Captain Larry's career—as a homicide detective, I do have to rock the boat. You were smart to call me right away when you found the body. And to have your secretary call the office to let me know Ralston the younger and that so-called associate of his were here in your office today. They want details of his brother's death? Were they grateful or hostile?"

"One thing I can tell you is that I asked them what was on that paper they gave you on the dock—the one they thought would make you hand his body over right away."

"Sorry, Counselor, but I think you understand about some legal documents being protected and privileged, and that one was. But I will tell you that, though it was legal, my jurisdiction over a dead body trumped it. And I'll say it was not anything that pointed to Darcy's disappearance. So tell me what else those two said."

Nick summarized their visit, including the weird vibes he got from them and the subtle threat about his family. "I'm going to have Bronco and Nita move back in with us for a few days for extra protection," Nick explained. "Someone else can fill in for him here."

"Nick, one more important thing. Since at this time, there's no evidence of a crime and the temporary ruling is accidental death by drowning, the ME did release the body to the victim's brother, and that's all I'm at liberty to say." He rose and extended his hand, which Nick shook.

"Let me just ask this, then. Never mind that mysterious legal, protected document. Why were the Ralstons at odds with each other on the dock? Was it something to do with either the body going to a Ralston funeral home or some other method of burial? The funeral home also does cremation. What's the alternative to those two options? Were Larry or Clint Ralston in some religious-freedom-protected cult, where the body is buried at sea? Or Clint didn't want his father to have Larry's body over some family feud? Was Larry ill and going to donate his body for research? Ken, I've been racking my brain. Can you at least tell me what business Clint is in?"

"That last question I can't answer because I don't know. People do have a right to their privacy if they're not indicted or under arrest. As a lawyer, you understand that. When and if I can, I'll let you know the answers to those questions. Let me say, though, as far as I can tell, that information has no link to finding Darcy."

Nick was furious but what choice did he have? He liked Ken, trusted him, but he could have grabbed him, slammed him against the wall and demanded more information. He had to be stonewalling him. Oh, yeah, he understood poor Steve losing his control over all this.

When the door closed, Nick leaned stiff-armed against

it and tried to fight off the overwhelming fear that this whole search for Darcy was in deep water.

As shaken as she was by seeing the old-fashioned painting Darcy must have posed for—or was at least the romanticized subject of—Claire calmed herself to drive home and spend the midafternoon with Lexi and Jilly. After all, looking in other windows, some of which had lowered blinds or closed curtains, she'd seen nothing else strange.

When she arrived home, Jace and Mitch had just left. Tomorrow they were being recalled to their base because it had been predicted that the next weather disturbance, which had paraded across the Atlantic from Africa, was sure to become a named storm headed for the Caribbean. And that meant, although it was several days out, it might turn toward South Florida.

Great, just great, Claire thought as her stomach cramped in foreboding again. A hurricane was all they needed to blast apart whatever time, clues and sanity they had left to find Darcy. At least, she thought as she played with Lexi and Jilly, the girls hadn't heard all that on the TV.

"Where is Darcy?" Lexi's doll asked again as if it had read Claire's mind. "We have to find Darcy."

Claire could have thrown that little interactive machine across the room. It kept asking prying questions, but then it was surely just repeating what Lexi had said. And the child's attention to the doll kept her busy, not brooding, because she had someone to take care of.

Claire heard the garage door go up so Nick must be home early. As angry as he'd be, she'd decided to tell him the truth about what she'd seen at Will Warren's house. Her plan was for her and Nick to go there when Will was back home, hopefully this evening, supposedly to thank him for his moral and financial support, get invited in, see the portrait, then question him about it. Surely there was more than he was admitting about his relationship with Darcy.

She left Lexi and Jilly talking to the doll and hurried to greet Nick as he came into the house through the laundry room. She hugged him hard, and he held her to him.

"I had visits from Clint Ralston and his associate, Jedi Brown, then later from Ken," he told her. "Ken wouldn't or can't say what was on that legal document Clint Ralston thrust at him. No new info except that the ME has ruled Larry Ralston accidentally drowned, though he did have some bruises that could be from bumping around in that net. Approximate time of death not decided yet because of the water temperature. And they're still examining his cell phone."

She nodded and hugged him harder as they both leaned against the washing machine.

"One more thing," he said. "There was no direct threat, but I didn't like the way Ralston made a subtle remark about my not having family photos in the office, asked whether that was so no one would think to threaten them. As a precaution, I've asked Bronco and Nita to move into our guest room for a while. Nita has to be here daily, anyway, and I'll have Bronco's position at the firm covered by someone else."

"But why would Clinton Ralston want to scare you or threaten us? We're no threat to him, unless he knows something he's not telling about Darcy. But what could his connection to her be? Maybe Fly Safe is to blame for her disappearance, but I would assume it was Larry involved, not Clinton."

"He goes by Clint."

"Maybe that name differential is why we can't find him online, but I think he'd show up under his shortened name."

"And he still wouldn't say what he does. If he has something to hide, why doesn't he just make something up or use a fake business front? Anyway, let's go see the girls and Steve, spend some time with them until Bronco and Nita get here."

"Steve finally took a nap. But wait—you had news but I do, too. I made sure Will was at the library for his story time and then checked out his house."

"Claire! Alone? You didn't go in?"

"Of course not, though breaking and entering is not out of the question if it would help find Darcy. Shhh, or that darned doll will be asking me about it, too. And yes, I went alone, just walked around the outside, but I did look in a couple of windows."

"Damn!" he muttered, setting her back at arm's length to frown at her. Her elbow hit his briefcase off the dryer and it clattered to the floor into an empty laundry basket, but he didn't make a move to retrieve it.

"I left a note on your desk," she said.

"Oh, very helpful if I needed to start looking for you as well as your sister. I thought we had an agreement not to go out alone. I swear I'm going to chain you to—to this washer and dryer, or something."

"Nick, time is precious. Protest and scold me later. When I looked in Will's back room window, I saw a lot of butterflies mounted under glass but also a large framed painting of a woman with a butterfly net. And her face—it was Darcy!"

His lower lip dropped. His brow furled. For once he said nothing, so she did.

"I always had a strange feeling he cared deeply for her, and obviously she liked him. What set me off on that was I was reading that novel I took from her bedroom. It's about a man who was obsessed with a woman, kidnapped her and took her to his isolated house. I mean, there are lots of houses in Golden Gate, but his is on a big lot kind of back in. I knew you were tied up with work—I just had to go."

"If I tell Ken, he'll go in like gangbusters and maybe scare Will. This has to be finessed," he said, his voice shaky.

"Exactly. As soon as Bronco and Nita get here, let's fill them in on being careful of visitors—then become visitors ourselves at Will's this evening. He'll have to ask us in. If he doesn't, I'll pretend to faint, you carry me inside. We have to either ask or confront him about how and why he has a painting of Darcy with butterflies. It's beautiful, fanciful, old-fashioned. I swear if she'd known of it, she would have been proud, would have told me, shown me."

"Maybe she didn't want Steve to know, that he'd not approve—to say the least."

"My mind's going crazy over the worst scenarios. I only looked in more windows, then ran. But her car could be hidden in his two-car garage, and maybe she's in the house somewhere behind closed curtains or blinds. If this doesn't work out, I'll find a way to follow him everywhere he goes. And I was so sure he was on our side."

Though she'd meant to be strong and steady, she burst into tears. Nick pulled her to him and held her hard.

"All right," he said, whispering in her ear. "Wash your face in the kitchen before the girls see you like this, and I'll go change clothes. It's still a long shot, but that's all we have right now. Jensen will probably kill me, but we have to try. The minute Bronco and Nita get here, we'll fill them in and, armed with questions, head for Will's house and that painting."

As they quickly left the laundry room, they nearly stumbled over Lexi and the doll standing in the doorway. Nick's briefcase knocked into the doll and shoved Lexi back.

"Hey, honey," he said, "I didn't know you were there. Sorry. You okay?"

"I guess. And Cindy is, too."

"Yes, I'm fine. We missed you, Dad," the doll said.

"I already told her I missed you," Lexi explained. "We want to know if you are home to stay or going somewhere else."

Tears blurred Claire's vision as Nick knelt to hug Lexi. "We didn't mean to shut you out," he told her. "Guess what? Nita and Bronco are going to move in for a while like they did once before. Just for a while."

As Claire knelt to hug her, too, Lexi wiped tears from under her eyes. "Yes, I like them," she said. "But last time they came it was 'cause that lady died. It's not 'cause... I mean, because Aunt Darcy is... I mean, you were whispering, and we couldn't hear everything you said so you should talk louder."

"No, sweetheart!" Claire said and hugged her harder. "We are still looking for Aunt Darcy, and Bronco and Nita are going to help. Everyone here is working hard on that, and we're a team—you and Jilly, too."

Lexi sniffed and nodded. "Just tell me if you find out who took her. Just don't whisper and keep secrets, okay?"

Claire's gaze locked with Nick's over the head of the doll, which Lexi was holding between them.

"We'll all do our best," Claire said. "We'll all stick tight and do our best."

It wasn't a real answer, but as scared as she was, too, it was all she could think to say right now. And they were not telling this child where they were going nor about that strange painting at Will's and what it could mean.

CHAPTER SEVENTEEN

"I hate that we're saying goodbye again, but I'm proud of your work," Brit told Jace. They had an hour before Mitch picked him up for a flight back to the NOAA base at Biloxi, and they'd decided to spend it in bed. "Risky, but worth it," she added, reaching for his hand. "Still, I'm hoping this tropical storm does not turn into another hurricane you have to fly through."

He pulled her close. She was a great wife, understanding, supportive. And how unusual, he supposed, that she and Claire had grown to be friends. But he hated heading back to work for more reasons than just leaving Brit. Enough time had passed that he knew they were unlikely to find Darcy alive. Yeah, it could happen but odds were against it, and pilots often flew with the odds in mind—and nerve and guts.

"Hey, flyboy, a penny—no, a hundred dollars for your thoughts," Brit said, reeling him back to the here and now. "I know you're worried about Lexi. I'll try to help with her while you're gone," she said with tears gilding her eyes. "You just keep yourself and Mitch and your crew safe. Remember your high-flying creed—one of them, anyway— 'aviate, navigate, communicate.' That means with your wife, too, not just your copilot and the ground control. Earth to Jace—don't drift off—navigate and communicate with me."

He had to chuckle. "Ma'am, yes, ma'am! Speaking of flying, time's a'wasting for you and me," he said as he reached for the hem of her nightgown and tugged it up—and up. "Let's fly."

Her arms wrapped around his neck, and she snuggled naked against him. This would make it harder for him to leave her, but he needed to do his job. It might be one way to help his daughter, his friends and family here, to measure another storm, because this one might hit close to home.

Trying to be deliberate not desperate, he kissed her hard. What if he didn't come back? What if Darcy didn't come back? What if Claire never recovered, and Lexi regressed and all was lost?

But for a little while, he lost himself in loving Brit.

"Look," Claire said as she and Nick drove past Will's house, both craning their necks. "He's parked his car in the driveway when he has a two-car garage. Now, why would he do that?"

"Maybe he's going out later and just didn't drive in. A lot of people have so much stuff in their garages they can't use them."

"True. I'm probably just paranoid."

"I'm going to turn around and go back. At least it looks like we caught him at home."

They had eaten an early dinner with Steve and the girls. He had promised to stay in tonight and watch a movie with them. Bronco and Nita had arrived, and Nita, God bless her, however pregnant she was, took right over. They had told only Bronco where they were going. Heck had texted to say he was still having trouble tracing Clinton Ralston even under his shortened first name.

They parked in front of Will's property and went up to the front door. The windows were all closed, not unusual where people had the air-conditioning on in this humid late-summer weather. They rang the bell.

It took a moment for a response. Claire saw Will glance out his front picture window to see who they were—not unusual, either. He opened the door.

"Good news, I hope," he said. He extended his hand to Nick. Will was dressed in denim shorts and a T-shirt, which had one large word on it: *Read.*

Yes, she thought. They had to read this just right.

Nick shook his hand, then Will offered it to Claire, who said, "No news is perhaps good news now. We hope you don't mind our just dropping by."

"Absolutely not and do come in," he said, gesturing. "And how is Jilly holding up?"

"She has her father and Lexi with her," Claire explained. "She and Steve are staying with us now, so she's not alone, although I know she's suffering—afraid for her mother, of course, even when we try to keep her spirits up. I've explained to her more than once that none of this was her fault—that Darcy would never have just left her."

The moment they were in with the door closed behind them, Claire panicked. She had to look at that painting close up. She and Nick had even rehearsed what they would say when they saw it. But in this front room, nicely furnished, she saw a huge painting of two butterflies alighted on an orange blossom branch next to a huge photographic blowup of his book cover, *Butterfly Love and Lore*.

"You have a lovely home here," she said, trying not to sound too nervous or too eager. "Out from the city a ways, but not far. What an interesting painting! Of course you would have butterflies in your decor. Those are painted ladies, aren't they?" she asked, moving a bit closer to the oil painting and the door to the Florida room. Will walked with her and Nick stepped closer, too.

She saw the painting was done in the same hazy, almost impressionistic style as the one of the woman in the next room. One butterfly had its dotted orange, black and white wings spread, the other had its wings closed. Her own words, *painted lady*, snagged in her brain. She had to get Nick into that back room to see the other painted lady.

"Good for you for recognizing that," Will said. "It's one of my favorite butterflies because they are so prolific, like a universal representative of the butterfly world. It's the type I asked for on the front of my book, as you can see," he added, gesturing at the blown-up photo of it. "Painted ladies, genus *Vanessa cardui*, are hardy, resilient global fliers. They've been known to migrate clear across the Saharan desert, populate Europe and Asia, even Australia, yet we have them here in our backyards. When I was young, growing up near here, I actually buried a few out back, and put little crosses over them, but they were no longer beautiful when I dug them up to see how they were doing."

That mental picture shook Claire. The idea of burying something beautiful out back... But she had to say more, to go on, before Nick stepped in as he said he might if she needed help here.

"Those black spots outside the closed wings look like two staring eyes," she observed, edging slightly more toward the door that must lead to the back room.

"They do indeed. Those are hindwing eyespots that scare predators like birds away—make them think it's a much larger insect than it is. They even resemble the eyes of an all-seeing owl."

"If you have any actual butterfly displays," she went on, "I'd love to see them."

"Some people find them boring, overly ornate, even fussy—mostly men," he said with a nod at Nick. Will didn't budge toward the back room, even though Claire had taken yet another step that way.

"No, I'd love to see them," Nick said. "And the signature on this painting—did you do this? I see it's signed WW."

"Good eyes, Nick," Claire said, leaning lower. "Will, are you an artist? Anything else around here you've done?" she asked, trying to keep her voice steady. Had he actually painted that picture of Darcy in the back room? If so, maybe he was obsessed with her and that could mean—

"About men being bored," Nick said when Will didn't answer, "I think butterflies are fascinating. And I've read somewhere that Japanese men dote on them—spend fortunes on them."

Will seemed to snap to attention. "I believe I can deduce from this visit that you two have looked into my past beyond my book's bio. Yes, I made a small fortune selling rare butterflies in Japan—not illegal, unless one gets caught."

"We're not here to pursue that," Nick said. "Frankly, we are taking a close look at anyone and everyone who had a tie

to Darcy because we are so damned desperate. We're looking for clues she might have given you about disappearing,
about someone new in her life. Will, I hope you understand."

"Oh, I do. I do."

Claire stifled a groan that Nick was going off script, but
he did have good instincts for working with devious minds,
criminals hiding the truth. For one moment, the three of
them stared at each other. Claire held her breath and bit
her lower lip hard to keep from begging this man to just
tell them the truth.

"I understand and sympathize with your desperation,"
Will told them. "Here I am, merely her friend, and I would
die or kill to get her back. So I don't know what you've
discovered about how I made my meager fortune, which
allowed me to do the things I really love," he said, looking
intently first at Nick, then at her, "but let me explain some
things. First of all, know and believe that I am on your side
in finding Darcy. I have been racking my brain and some
of my financial resources to get answers."

"We know that," Claire put in. "We are so grateful for
the boost you've given our pleas for any information that
leads to her whereabouts."

Will nodded as he bent to open the top drawer of a cab-
inet. Nick stiffened and stepped in front of Claire. Was he
expecting Will to draw a gun? But he pulled out a well-
worn, leather-bound scrapbook that looked like a photo
album.

"Come with me," he said, "for I have someone for you
to meet."

At the Southwest Florida International Airport, just before Jace and Mitch were ready to board their Delta plane

to get them back to their hurricane hunting base in Biloxi, Mississippi, Jace's phone sounded with a text message.

"Probably Brit again," Jace said. "Hated to leave her."

"With a woman you love, parting is such sweet sorrow, or something like that," Mitch muttered as they hefted their carry-on backpacks and got in line. "I hated to leave Kris, too."

Jace stared at the small screen. "Oh, not from her but Hector, Nick's tech guru. Maybe they found Darcy."

But what he read was that Heck had to drive to Miami to meet with a possible investor—Nick was his only partner so far—for the facial recognition technology supplies company Heck was setting up. And he wanted Jace to finesse something with Nick, to do Heck a favor.

"A favor like what?" Mitch asked when Jace explained.

"Still reading," Jace said. When he'd read through it, he told Jace as they edged forward in the line, "Heck clearly doesn't know I'm leaving, thinks I'm still going to see Nick and Lexi before I leave—don't I wish."

"And what does Heck want you to explain to Nick?"

"Well, I guess Heck is blaming himself for telling Steve a couple days ago that Nick was going to question Larry Ralston, a possible client who was in that eco-group that has the Fly Safe name we want for our company. Heck told Steve to just stay out of it, then realized he should not have told him the Ralston connection."

"Like why?" Mitch asked. "You mean that Steve could have traced Ralston, flipped out while questioning him, then harmed—killed—him?"

"Remember Steve came back looking like he'd been in a fight. So Heck's asking me to let Nick know he might have blown it by telling Steve. Heck thinks it would be better if someone told Nick in person in case he loses his cool."

"Boarding rows twenty-two to thirty-eight," the woman at the gate announced, and Jace changed Heck's message on the screen to his boarding pass.

Man, he thought, what if Steve did locate, argue with and fight Larry Ralston? He had to think this through, then tell Nick, as if he needed more of a mess than he and Claire already had on their hands.

Claire held her breath as Will led them into his Florida room. For one moment she considered that he could have seen them drive by or come up his walk and so he'd moved the painting. But no, there it was, nearly life-size, Darcy in an old-fashioned dress. And yes, this painting, too, had the signature WW in the lower right-hand corner.

"It was what first drew me to Darcy when I returned from Japan and met her at the library with little Jilly, though I had sort of known her—you, too, Claire—as a child," he said as Claire and Nick both stared, speechless. "It's not what you think, so let me explain."

CHAPTER EIGHTEEN

"Despite the old-fashioned clothes, it has to be a painting of Darcy," Claire insisted. "When did you do it?"

Nick took her hand as if to steady her, or maybe to warn her to be careful of what she said.

His voice quiet but not calm, Will told them, "You have heard that all of us have strangers who are doubles somewhere in the world, haven't you? It's just that we seldom see them." He hugged the album to his chest, resting his chin on it. "That is not Darcy, but my dear grandmother, Vanessa White Warren. I have her to thank for my obsession with butterflies."

There it was, Claire thought. But she didn't believe him. He must have had an obsession with Darcy, and if it was because she looked like his beloved grandmother, that didn't change her suspicions of him.

"But you never showed her this, or she would have told me," Claire accused, trying to control her voice and expression.

"No, I—I just kept it all to myself. I actually think it might have unsettled her, made her think I didn't like her for herself. But I must admit it made me want to keep her as a friend."

To keep her... Those words echoed in Claire's head. The crazy collector in that novel had wanted to keep his prisoner trapped, like a caught butterfly. So, Claire agonized, Darcy had never been here, or at least didn't see this portrait. But could she believe this man?

"Let me explain," Will said as she tore her gaze away from the painting. It seemed—how she wished—that the real Darcy could just step from the canvas, to be here, alive and well.

"Sit, both of you, please," Will said, indicating a rose-hued velvet settee under the window Claire had peered through. All the furniture in this room off the kitchen was tastefully old-fashioned, like a little shrine to the era of the painting.

They complied. Nick kept ahold of her hand, and Will cleared magazines away to perch on the coffee table in front of them, though the picture still loomed large behind him.

"Let me explain," he said yet again, and Claire forced herself to look at him. She told herself she had to use her forensic skills to see if he was telling the truth, to read his expression, words and tone of voice, his body language. He seemed uptight, emotional, but then, so was she.

He opened the old photograph album and turned it toward them on his knees. Mostly small black-and-white photographs, some evidently glued on the black paper pages, some set in little corner gummed holders so they could be removed. He flipped several pages, and she noticed his hands shook. Eagerness? Nerves? Guilt?

"Here's the photograph I painted from, though there are many others you might want to look at," he said, pointing. "Ironic that her name was Vanessa, and that's the genus for the painted lady butterfly. Ironies and coincidences do happen in life," he added as Claire recalled that Detective Jensen had always insisted there was no such thing as a coincidence in a criminal investigation.

Looking closely at the picture, Nick cleared his throat, and Claire gasped. They both leaned closer. Yes, an old photo of that woman in the painting, holding a butterfly net, though the dress was not quite the same as the one Will had painted. Claire looked up at the painting, then squinted back at the photo again.

"Paternal or maternal grandmother?" she asked.

"Paternal. She was born in 1902, died in her early eighties. I figure that photo was taken when she was about eighteen, 1920 or so, though I admit the picture looks almost Victorian. But then American styles in the wilderness of south Georgia where she lived probably did not keep up with shorter skirts and bobbed hair."

Claire skimmed the other photos on these two pages, then flipped the page to look at others of the same woman. Yes, a distinct, powerful resemblance to Darcy. So that was why he'd been drawn to her?

"So much like Darcy," she whispered, then spoke louder. "Will, under the circumstances, under all this pressure, I was certain you had painted Darcy."

"No. If I had asked her, you and Steve would have known."

"Yes. That was Darcy. She shared most important things, so if she'd intended to leave Naples in any way, she would have told me."

"I was just blown away when I returned from several years living in Japan and saw her—I think you and Lexi might have been with her and Jilly that first day—at the library for story time. Darcy's resemblance to Grandmother Vanessa is uncanny. You know, I have that very butterfly net Grandmother is holding in that photo and several others in the album. And I did plan to share all this with Darcy—someday."

He rose and went to a framed shadow box on the wall nearer the kitchen, lifted it off hooks and carried it to them. He removed the back of the box and the net. He shook it out and swirled it in the air.

"She taught me, among other things, when she was widowed and came to live with us in Florida, that there is an art to making and using a net. First, the material must be soft as a spiderweb and at least that strong."

He looked up at them. His eyes seemed glazed. With emotion? He sounded almost poetic. She would have to admit he was telling the truth with all this proof, with his intensity—wasn't he? Although he was looking at them, he seemed to be seeing someone somewhere else. And from the first day Darcy disappeared, he had always seemed genuinely distressed, even desperate, and she knew how that felt. Surely she'd been wrong to suspect this man of anything. That haunting novel about the butterfly collector had set her off, wasting time on Will when someone else must be at fault.

When she and Nick said nothing, Will went on. "You need to make a swift sweep with the net to capture the butterfly. Get the net under your prey, then with a strong move, swing it up so as not to injure the plant it may be on or just leaving. To release it, just reverse," he said with a flick of his wrist, "and none the worse, butterflies are free. Yet, there is a real art to it, you see."

Nick finally spoke. "Are those butterflies mounted on the wall ones you netted?"

"Every last one here or there," he told them with a nod. "I'm sure, given a choice, they would have preferred to live, but it is not only for my good but the good of all mankind that we catch, examine, preserve and write about them. And display them in all their captured beauty."

Handing the album back, Claire told him, "You know, just as if there were a swoop of someone's huge net, Darcy is gone—but I hope not harmed. I hope she is only being held but then released."

"We'll be sure she's found," Nick promised, and Will nodded.

But how Nick had worded that terrified her more than anything that had happened so far. Before, Nick had always said, "We'll find her."

After Will served them iced tea, Nick and Claire finally got around to asking him their other questions. The tension in the air had lifted slightly now, Nick thought. Still on the settee with the long-gone Vanessa staring at them, he said, "We know Larry Ralston's father is a prominent funeral director here and up and down this coast, but Detective Jensen mentioned his brother, Clint, claimed his body. There must be some kind of a family feud."

"Very strange," Will said, "but then the family is a bit estranged. You know, Aaron Ralston does the let-us-comfort-you TV commercials for his funeral homes. He's also quite well-known around town since he's been here so long and his father was what they used to call an undertaker before him. His funeral home buried both my parents."

"My mother, too," Nick said.

"And mine," Claire added.

Will said to her, "I believe your mother—her name was Miranda, correct?—used to patronize the library extensively, brought you two little girls to story time."

"Yes, she was the reader to end all readers, sharing books aloud with us that we were sometimes too young to understand. Darcy always kidded about our childhood honorary English and American literature degrees from having an agoraphobic, bibliophile mother. Yes, she would go out to the library or, later, just send us with her list. And didn't you drop books at the house once?"

"I believe I did," he said with a wistful little smile, yet his eyes were sad. "Yes, I remember."

Nick cleared his throat. "So anyway, you don't really know Clinton Ralston?"

Will shook his head and rattled his ice cubes in his empty, sweating glass. "I don't really know the man per se, but I've observed him closely at two funerals where I've had butterfly releases. He must have known the deceased, because he certainly wasn't there to help his father with the arrangements. I've seen and overheard some conversations he's had at community events, conversations with strangers that seemed secretive and anxious who then more or less nodded and quickly disappeared. Call me too suspicious and interested in mystery and suspense novels, but from time to time I've thought he must be into something secretive or illegal. I've tried to look more into him, but haven't gone so far as to follow him yet," he said with a short laugh. "But he seems at times to be a mystery man."

"Maybe just an investor in his father's funeral empire," Claire put in, "but one who doesn't want anything to do with morticians and death. Then why was he so intent on getting his brother's body? Maybe, since Larry was a fisherman, he wanted to be buried at sea—anathema to their father and very bad public relations for the Ralston funeral empire—so Clint agreed to take care of that and even prepared a legal document in case their father balked."

"You did see the obit in the morning paper, didn't you?" Will asked, getting up to go back into the kitchen. "I mean, there was all that further coverage of Darcy's disappearance, so maybe you missed it," he called back over his shoulder.

He opened and folded the newspaper as he hurried back, extending it to them. "Only a memorial service announcement, not visiting hours per se or burial mentioned for Lawrence Ralston." He summarized what they were reading with their heads bent together. "Even the place and time are not given here, but you have to get on his Captain Larry website for details. Sad. Quite a young man, I believe, though his age isn't given, either. Someone on the library staff thought he was divorced with no children. At least there is no mention of the court trial he's escaped regarding that dolphin, right, Counselor?"

"Correct. So, two mysteries," Nick said, putting his empty glass on a coffee table coaster. "I won't get to defend him on whether he caught or killed a dolphin. Now, the question may be who killed him."

"But the earlier newspaper article implied that his death could be accidental."

"A text came in while you were making the tea and Claire was looking through the photo album," Nick said. "The police techs that are combing his boat checked Larry's phone that was lying on a seat in the stern. It contained an email of a brief suicide note sent only to his brother."

"Really?" Will said, wide-eyed. "I hope the police checked that phone to see if there were fingerprints or DNA on it that weren't Larry's."

"If that's true, then he didn't fall in but jumped," Claire said, reaching out to grip Nick's arm. "I know a suicide is especially terrible for you, sweetheart, but you may not be able to disprove this one."

Will said nothing but pulled his chair closer. It was almost as if the three of them, in mutual trust now, observed a moment of silence for the tragedy—and Claire again feared for Darcy's life.

"I don't tell many people this, Will," Nick said, his voice quiet, "but I think we've learned we can trust you. My father's death was ruled a suicide when I was young—he had a gun in his hand, bullet to the brain. I've since founded a small group that helps people whose lives are impacted like that. Maybe the insurance company reneges on their insurance, or someone is blamed who shouldn't be, or it was a staged suicide that was actually a murder. It took me years, a law degree and Claire's help, but I proved my dad was killed and ultimately brought the murderer to justice— that is, he paid with his life."

"You don't mean you killed him?" Will asked.

"No. His own evil and the god of justice did that—actually, he drowned, so this Larry Ralston thing hits close to home even though all our efforts must go to finding Darcy. I know I for one won't rest until we find her!"

Nick was about to finally drop off to sleep that night when Claire spoke from beside him. She'd already woken him up once earlier, saying, "It was really nice of Will to send those books he bought for Jilly home with us."

"Mmm. Very nice. He's a strange guy."

"I mean, Lexi has that doll, but he's the first person who has given us something for Jilly."

"Yeah. Glad you changed your mind about him."

"He had proof that woman was his grandmother. Just chance she looked like Darcy."

"Yeah. For sure," he said, stifling a huge yawn.

Now he was ready to drop off again, swimming in exhaustion.

"Nick, we need to go to that Larry Ralston memorial. I read the invitation over twice. Out on the rocks at Doctors Pass, no less. Could that be a link to Lincoln Yost or is it just a coincidence—well, there I go again with that. And at sunset, when it will soon be dark and everyone will be way out on those rocks? They are dangerous enough in the daytime. If we stand far enough back, maybe no one will ID us. Or we could go in some sort of disguise."

Nick rolled onto his back and stared at the dark ceiling. "Claire, I don't think Clint Ralston will want the people who found his brother's body there."

"I don't care! And that's a reason to go a bit disguised. If not that, then we need to follow Clint when he leaves, at least find out where he goes, where he lives. Who is he really that he's so mysterious?"

"Sweetheart, you read Will wrong, so don't go jumping to conclusions about Ralston just because he keeps his occupation private. Maybe he's a big investor, maybe he's undercover FBI, maybe he's Mafia. I just mean, okay, I'll think about that, but it seems too cloak and dagger—in other words, damned dangerous."

"But for Darcy, damned dangerous is nothing—or everything, I don't know."

He heard her sniffle and start to cry. As tired as he was, he pulled her to him, turning her back toward him so that they were lying sideways and she was curled protectively against him. He kissed her shoulder and held her close until she quieted.

"We'll do it, but be careful," he promised. "I think— I hope—Bronco's got things locked down here if any of Clint's subtle threats were real. But we cannot—*cannot*— rile him, give him or that Jedi watchdog an excuse to come after our family."

CHAPTER NINETEEN

Nick spent the next morning in court, trying to keep his mind on this client rather than on Darcy. More than most, this client, a nervous, elderly woman, was in dire need of representation and support. At each recess he called Claire. He still was not convinced it was smart to attend Larry Ralston's memorial service at sunset tonight on the rocks at Doctors Pass.

"Nick, if we don't go, we might miss out on the chance to find Darcy," she insisted, her voice level rising. "I know we have to update Ken Jensen about Will's friendship with her—the portrait and all that—so how about I call him? Maybe he'll have something new to share or at least not be so uptight about our investigating on our own."

"All right, but do not tell him we're going to that memorial, especially disguised. Let him track down Clint Ralston's source of income, background, all that. Besides, if Heck can't turn up something online, then—"

"We could follow Ralston when he leaves the service, at least learn where he lives."

"I don't know about that. It's really a long shot to be trying to chase down Clint Ralston or the rest of the Fly Safe board members."

"Right now, long shots are all we have," she insisted, and the phone went dead.

Jace and Mitch sat together in the briefing with the rest of the 53rd Weather Reconnaissance Squadron at Keesler Air Force Base in Biloxi to get intel on the new threatening storm.

Jace kept frowning at the moving, dark orange blob on the radar map that the Air Force lieutenant colonel who was in charge kept pointing at.

"It's a possibility we will send out more than one plane because this storm looks potentially quite dangerous," the lieutenant colonel said. "One or two of you and your crews may be temporarily transferred to MacDill Air Force Base in Tampa to get closer to the action.

"And," he added, frowning, "I know several of you live in areas which might be affected, but do not start panicking about trajectory, storm level, any of that. I know it's tempting with family and friends possibly in harm's way— property, too—but I must warn you not to make personal phone calls that might start early rumors or panic. The weather service will announce the name and coordinates of this disturbance to us and the public in due time."

"Disturbance," Mitch muttered as they filed out. "That's putting it mildly. Meanwhile, you know your nearest and dearest are not concentrating on some dark storm, but on finding their missing loved one."

"Yeah," Jace said. Claire had been his loved one, and he'd had trouble getting past that, of letting go, especially when she and Nick first got together. And Lexi—he'd let down both of his girls, away from home so much as an international pilot. He'd been a real jerk when he first learned of Claire's narcolepsy, but then she'd tried to hide it from him.

"I said, you want me to go check the plane with you?" Mitch's voice broke into his agonizing.

"Roger that."

"We're both gonna have to keep our minds on this flight if we go up—more than most," Mitch said. "It's personal this time, and we don't want anyone at home to go MIA in the storm. I had a friend in Afghanistan who was declared MIA, never found his body, no parachute, no clues, just gone after he bailed out. Damn hurricanes can be like that. It leaves the family with so many questions."

Jace frowned and nodded as they headed for the hangar. Questions indeed. Darcy was MIA, too.

Claire had finally convinced Nick they should go to the beach memorial service for Captain Larry Ralston. They needed to keep their eyes open as to who was there, especially possible board members of Fly Safe, since it was the only decent lead they had as to who might have taken or hurt Darcy. If it had been some random, freak, spur-of-the-moment kidnapping or an act of passion or violence, Claire feared they'd never find her.

She had talked about fifteen minutes to Detective Jensen, who had assured her again that they were still following leads. She'd explained what they had learned about Will Warren's ties to Darcy—a cross-generational friendship—and had described the painting. She had, however, omitted telling him she'd first seen that by trespassing. At least they weren't doing that tonight, though she had talked Nick into tailing Clint Ralston when he left the memorial service.

But she had more secrecy planned: Nick had finally agreed, if they were going to the seaside service, to go, more or less, in disguise. She had pinned her giveaway crimson hair back and up under a baseball cap and she wore loose, neutral-looking clothes. Nick had totally dressed down and looked like a cross between a vagrant who'd been sleeping on the beach and a gardener from one of the nearby ritzy estates.

"I just hope the way we look doesn't draw attention *to* us instead of letting us blend in," Claire admitted as they parked a block away and walked toward the shore. "I still think we should have tried to look like some of the eccentric romantics who hit the beach every sunset to drink toasts at the end of another day."

She instantly wished she hadn't said it like that at this end of the seventh day—one entire, endless week—that Darcy had been gone. It would be a bright, new day when they found her. *If* they found her. She could almost think that but not say it or believe it.

Besides the ever-present fishermen and tourists or locals on the boulder-strewn breakwater, they saw a cluster of people farther out, near where Linc Yost and his students had been watching for dolphins and manatees. She pointed at a dolphin heading outward, its sleek gray body arching from the pink foam of waves lit by the setting sun, which shone in their eyes before being swallowed by clumps of dark clouds. It didn't look like a peaceful sunset.

"Can't make out individuals at the gathering," Nick said.

"We'll have to go closer, but not too close. Let's try blending in with the fishermen instead of the mourners."

"But we have to be close enough to hear what Clint is saying. What are the odds their 'funeral father' will be here?"

"Lousy," Nick told her, and took her hand as they began to walk the boulders on the inlet side of the pass, opposite of the way they'd walked out before. The rocks on this side were not as wet or slippery as on the other side toward open water. An occasional boat or yacht motored toward the inland waterways, seeking their docking spots in the nearby backyards of mansions or pricey condos.

Clint Ralston was easy to spot, standing a bit apart from the gathering of maybe twenty people. He had emerged from the small crowd, probably after greeting them. And of course Jedi Brown was easy to spot with his almost-white blond hair.

"There's Lincoln Yost and his wife," Nick whispered.

"I see them, but can't pick out anybody else, at least not with the sun in our eyes. Look, they have some sort of lanterns. Maybe they're going to do a release."

"They sure wouldn't do a butterfly one. Whenever this ends, we need to hightail it before people get near us, then try to follow Clint's car if we can spot which one he gets into, hopefully when it's dark."

"Nick, thanks for agreeing to this. It seems to be our only lead, since Will didn't pan out."

"But look—look who's here!" Nick said. They gripped each other's arms as they recognized Steve. "Should we let him know we're here? He must have read the obit and decided to come, too, when we thought he just needed time alone. I'm starting to get the feeling that we're trying to stay ahead of the police—but Steve is, too."

To Claire's dismay, Steve turned and saw them, even though they were standing on the other side of the rocks. He dipped his head, obviously studying them, and came over.

"I can't believe you guys are here, too," he said.

"So much for the disguises, right?" Claire asked.

"I don't think most would notice. I know you're suspicious of the Ralstons, so thought I'd hang back and just listen. Let's not stand near each other, and we can confer later on what we learn."

He turned away and started back toward the cluster of mourners, but they saw him immediately stopped by another man. Trouble? Had Ralston brought more security than his usual "associate"? But Claire thought the man speaking to Steve looked vaguely familiar.

She whispered to Nick, "That's the man we asked for directions at the cove dock to find Larry's boat."

He nodded as they overheard words on the breeze. "Seen you looking for Captain Larry the day he died," the old man said as if he had read their minds.

"He must be confused," Claire said. "He means us."

"No. Remember, he said someone else had just asked for Larry? Besides that, I didn't think anything of it since Steve has been so upset in general, but the day Jace got to Biloxi, he emailed me that Heck had told Steve who we went to find and Steve was ticked and rushed out. Maybe we've made a mistake to keep some of our investigation from Steve, so he's done things his own way."

"But surely Steve wasn't at Larry's ahead of us, because

he would have found— Well, he probably just didn't find Larry and left, so..."

She couldn't finish the thought. What if he had found Larry before they had? She felt sick to her stomach, even worse than the gnawing pain she'd had since Darcy disappeared. Steve had come back that day with those bruises and cuts...someone had evidently had a fight in the cabin of the *Down Under*.

"I greatly appreciate your attendance here this evening." Clint Ralston's voice rang out as they watched Steve walk away from the old man. Since they could hear and see from here despite the wash of waves and occasional screech of seagulls, Claire and Nick went no closer.

"I recognize the woman from the Fly Safe office," Nick whispered.

"My brother, Lawrence Andrew Ralston, loved the sea," Clint went on, his words clearly discernible. "Let me begin this sunset of his life memorial service with these words from the poem *Requiem* by Robert Louis Stevenson. 'Home is the sailor, home from the sea, and the hunter home from the hill.'

"I know many of you have had questions as to the cause of Larry's death. I have been asked why he isn't being buried by a Ralston funeral home. Simply to that I say, because his home was the sea, as vast as the unknown future. So please just accept that he left a sort of living will that requested no burial in the ground. But we are not here to ponder that tonight. We are here to celebrate his life, not his death, either accidental or intentional, his going onward, and I assure you that he will.

"You know," he continued, "most people don't realize that about seventy-five percent of what deep-sea fishermen and their charters do is catch and release. Yes, really. Reeling in delicious fish in legal season is a great thing, but most fishermen, including Larry, treasure the fight, the hand-to-hand primitive combat with a huge denizen of the deep. We all have our battles in life, don't we, but we want to go on, to live on.

"He also reveled in sometimes tagging fish for scientific study, and then releasing them to fight another day. The battle with nature but also the support of nature by letting great fish go.

"Larry had his favorite offshore or backwater spots. I'll always picture him there on a sunny day in the future, alive again. Immortality—it can take many forms, future forms. Soon, mankind will find a way."

She had no idea what he was alluding to, but the sun was sinking bloodred into blackness. She needed to listen to the weather report again, but she didn't need something else to panic her.

Other than a newspaper reporter she recognized hovering at the back of the crowd, she knew no one else, and Nick had only mentioned one beside the Yosts. Several other people spoke with memories about Larry. When it seemed the event was ending, Claire and Nick moved farther back.

"It sure got dark fast, so maybe there is a storm coming in," Claire whispered. "They're lighting those paper lanterns to send them up. I can't quite hear what they are saying anymore, but it looks like Jedi Brown's in charge of that."

"Memorial lanterns," Nick whispered. "They put candles in those things to make them lift since hot air rises. Actually, they are fire hazards if they tip too much or land sideways."

"With all this water around, maybe it will be okay."

Perhaps attracted by the lighted lanterns sailing on the breeze into the quickly darkening sky, a motorboat heading in hovered, then turned around to head back out.

"Maybe the boaters just like the sight," Claire whispered. "But what is that they are doing?"

Although the mourners were busy watching their lanterns drift aloft, she and Nick saw something else released in a dark blur that fluttered sideways, then skyward.

"What in the world?" Nick asked.

The wind was just right—or wrong—to take the mass toward the mourners. With the graying sky the winged creatures were hard to see at first. The boat sped away with a plume of white foam behind it, going over the posted speed limit.

Clint and the crowd swatted at the dark cloud at first until Jedi's voice cried out, "Black butterflies! Where from? Over the water?"

Everyone looked that way as the hum of the inboard motor faded and the boat's running lights were swallowed by the darkness. Claire felt Nick shudder, perhaps because he didn't like butterflies landing on him, and a few came this way. Carefully, she captured one by its wings, holding it as gently as she could.

"Walk slowly, don't run," Nick told her as they went farther toward the shore. "Don't draw attention, and we'll wait on the sand. Ralston could not have parked closer than we did, so we can get in our car to follow him."

"Could Tara be behind that butterfly release, or if not, she might know who ordered that many and has a boat. And black ones—to symbolize death?"

"The least of our worries right now," Nick whispered.

"I'm thinking that murderers sometimes have a compulsion to attend their victim's funeral."

"Don't even think that about Steve!"

"Let's sit down on the sand now that it's really getting dark. Keep an eye out for Clint."

"Compared to all I'm grieving for, I don't think I'll ever get upset over little things again. I just want to find Darcy, and everything's working against us!"

Before they sat down in a small shaft of light from the nearest house, Claire lifted the captive butterfly close to her face on her palm and let it open its wings. It was all black but for a crimson rim on the bottom edges of the sculpted wings. She blew gently on it to encourage it to fly, and it did. Then she lifted her hands to hide her tears.

They both jumped at a familiar voice close behind them. "I've either got to swear you two in as adjunct officers or lock you up just to keep you safe," Ken Jensen said.

CHAPTER TWENTY

Claire gasped, but Nick seemed to handle the shock of Detective Jensen standing right behind them.

"Let's just say great minds run in the same saltwater boat channels," Nick told him, steadying Claire with his hand on her upper arm. "You're not the only one who needs to know more about Larry and Clint Ralston."

"But you two don't learn, don't listen—and I'm on your side," Ken insisted, drawing them farther back into the darkness. "You have heard, haven't you, that some criminals return to the scenes of their crimes?"

"Meaning what?" Nick asked. "That everyone here is under suspicion for Larry Ralston's death—his accident or suicide?"

"I don't want to face off with you two, whom I consider friends, but I haven't discounted murder—and neither have you, right? You were on the scene of his death about the time he died."

"So the ME has established the time of death?" Nick demanded.

"No, and may not be able to pin it down. But then, there's another possible suspect here in this crowd, one who didn't make an attempt to disguise himself as you two did."

Despite the cooling breeze, Claire felt her face flush. This was her idea to try to hide who they were. But if this man thought he was going to intimidate them by suggesting blame when they were only desperate to track down Darcy, she would tell him off. But before she could react, Nick tightened his grip as if he sensed her outrage.

"Is someone else here from Fly Safe?" he asked. "If we could get some of the other names they seem to hide—"

"There may not be other names, since the group is fairly new, though it seems to be well-funded. But don't tell me you two haven't thought of the other person of interest here, or are you too close to him to get it? Darcy's husband is here tonight. He even spoke to me about the progress of the official search when he came in. Yeah, I know he wasn't anywhere in the area when Darcy disappeared, but stranger things have happened. I've seen cases where someone hired someone else to do their dirty work."

"We told you from the first, they were not having marital problems," Claire insisted.

"As close as you are to her, some people don't share things like that."

"Detective Jensen," she said, putting her hands on her hips, "look at it this way since you're watching what everyone wears tonight. Steve had nothing to hide or fear from you, no reason to be here but to get information—like us, like you—or he would have hidden or even disguised himself. And not come here at all."

"And yet another person here tonight is first mate Bernie Thompson," Ken went on, "who's always around the cove docks to help fishermen clean up—he's the janitor of the place, so to speak, the guy you asked for directions the night you were looking for Ralston's boat, so he's ID'd you, too. He's the same guy Steve had also asked for directions to find Ralston's boat before you got there. Even if Steve would never hurt Darcy, he could have lost his temper talking to Ralston. I asked him about that black eye tonight, and he said he got in a bar fight."

"It's true. He did," Claire said, but her stomach went into free fall. For one frozen moment, she just stared at Ken. It suddenly seemed so dark, so late, standing here on the shore waiting for the mourners to scatter. She almost blurted out that she and Nick had just become aware of Steve visiting Larry, but neither of them shared that now. And did Steve need a lawyer?

She felt faint. If Nick had not had such a strong grip on her arm, she might have fallen. All she wanted was Darcy back, Darcy safe. Was Ken going to accuse or arrest Steve for Larry Ralston's death? Question or accuse her and Nick since they'd been there, too?

Nick spoke, though it seemed he had been silent for hours.

"Detective, are you asking for a statement? For some sort of confession to something we know nothing about except the statements we have already given about finding Ralston's body? Do we or Steve Stanley need legal representation?"

"Not at this time, Counselor," Ken said, matching Nick's formal tone. "Still, for a while, an active investigation. But let me advise you that you should go home immediately and not question, confront or follow anyone here, namely Clint Ralston. You don't need to tangle with him or his associate, Jedi Brown. I will take care of that and keep you informed if there is any information pertaining to Darcy Stanley's disappearance."

So formal, even fierce. Claire's legs almost gave way. Nick exhaled hard. "It isn't working out for us to stay friends through this, is it, Detective?"

"That doesn't change but needs to be set aside for now. Otherwise, as you know, Counselor, it could well compromise the investigation. Claire," he said, turning to her, "I assure you again we are doing everything we can to find your sister. We are following every viable lead. We have checked each day to be certain her credit cards were not used anywhere, even outside the state, and they were not this past week. This is not just a Collier County search, or a state of Florida search, but a national search. Now, I'd walk you two to your car, but I'll trust you to do that, and I will be in touch."

He turned away and went a few yards down the beach where he could watch those leaving the memorial service. Nick still held her arm, and they plodded through the thick sand and seagrass toward the street to walk to their car.

"Caught," she said. "My fault. Nick, what about Steve since it wasn't us who hurt Larry or even saw him alive?"

"We'll have to talk to him—prepare him. Ken said he wasn't here to arrest him. If Steve needs representation, it would look bad if I do it, even if someone in the firm did."

"And here Steve came back beat up and had a story about a fight in a bar the night Larry died. I feel like the world is falling in, falling on me—on us! But I can't just do nothing. It's like waiting for this horrible hurricane to hit they keep watching for."

★ ★ ★

When Claire and Nick got home, they tucked the girls in bed, trying to assure them that everyone, especially the police, were still looking for Darcy.

"Where have you been tonight looking for Mommy?" Jilly had asked the question the doll had repeated more than once.

"We took a walk on the beach and talked to a detective about how they are looking hard for her," Claire said. "Now let's turn out the light so all of you—all three—can get to sleep."

Nick kissed both girls and went out, hoping to wait for Steve to come in. Claire sat on Lexi's bed until both girls fell asleep. But the doll's eyes stayed wide-open as if she were watching—judging. Claire had a good nerve to dig out the raggedly doll and bury this one in the depths of the closet, but of course, Lexi, Jilly, too, needed this pretty programmed machine right now.

When she heard a car door slam outside, she went to join Nick. He and Steve were just going into the library.

"The three of us weren't the only ones watching that memorial service tonight," Nick was saying.

"You mean Ralston's lackey? That tall, blond shadow of his?" Steve asked.

"I mean Detective Ken Jensen of the Collier County sheriff's office."

"Yeah, I talked to him briefly. At least he's on the case. Good move on his part to keep an eye on Ralston. He'd better hustle now in case that storm turns to a hurricane, since that will pull all the police away from trying to find Darcy. I can't stand to think of her out there—out there somewhere in a storm."

"My point is, Jensen spotted us—and you," Nick told him as they all sat down facing each other, she and Nick on the couch and Steve in the club chair. She could see that his body language had gone from tense to hostile.

"You talked to him, too?" Steve asked, narrowing his gaze.

"We did. He also talked to the guy—name of Bernie Thompson—you asked about Larry's boat the day he was killed."

"So? What is this, one of your courtroom grillings?"

"What it is, is our attempt to get you ready to be seriously questioned or worse by Jensen. You need to get your story straight—and true. Do I need to find someone to represent you if Jensen tries to question you so that—"

"I didn't kill that Ralston bastard! I only wanted to question him about his ties to that Fly Safe bunch, but I couldn't find him. I yelled for him. I got so damn frustrated at everything I went to a bar and got into a fight, okay?"

"With someone you said you didn't know who then left," Nick said. "At least the bartender or regulars there can vouch for that and that will clear—"

"You two actually thought I'd beat someone up to get information? Then kill him? I was just frantic for a useful fact, for a trail, for a clue—anything!"

"We totally sympathize," Nick insisted. "Keep your voice down, or we'll have the girls awake, or Bronco coming in here to find out what's—"

"I hear my name?" Bronco asked from the door. "Boss, sorry to interrupt but when I turned on the outside lights for a safety check before Nita and me turned in, I saw a little problem in the backyard. Someone—it wasn't the girls, Nita says—yanked up every one of them butterfly bushes and plants out there. I went out. They're not wilted or dead yet, so it might've just happened. Things were okay a little bit ago when I looked out, walked around. The girls gonna be real upset."

"Hell, *I'm* real upset!" Nick said.

The four of them raced to the back windows where Nita stood, looking out. She'd turned the inside lights off to be able to see without someone seeing her. The safety lights flooded the area.

How different things looked, Claire thought as even more adrenaline poured through her to fight her narcoleptic exhaustion. The yard looked naked and ugly along the back fence. And the message? Forget about butterflies? Your home isn't safe? These are dying or dead and Darcy is, too—or will be if you don't back off?

"We should go out and put them in water," Nita said. "Maybe replant now or in the morning. You are right, the girls will be upset."

Claire said, "No, we shouldn't rush out right now. Maybe that's what someone wants us to do."

"And," Nick said, "even throwing water on the roots or stomping around in that mess might destroy any evidence to show who did this. I'm not calling Jensen over this, either, not tonight. In the morning, we'll go out and look for anything dropped—anything else. And, Steve, what about getting you a lawyer, one not from the firm but one that would be impartial?"

"You defended one of your own lawyers over that double murder you call the Silent Scream Case. He was innocent, and I am, too!"

"I'll advise and consult, but I don't want any screwups with enemies like the powerfully connected Ralstons—the father, Aaron, at least—and I think Clint's got to be some kind of high roller around here, too. Captain Larry seemed like the exception, the rebel in the family."

"Then you believe me?" Steve demanded, getting right in Nick's face. "I didn't find and didn't hurt Larry Ralston."

"The thing is, Jensen and a prosecutor—hopefully it won't get as far as a jury—are the ones who need to believe you."

Steve nodded. "Man, I feel as torn up as those plants."

Nick suggested Bronco and Steve go to bed, but he and Claire sat in the Florida room in the dark, staring out.

"Nick, that black butterfly release tonight, then this. We have to talk to Tara Gerald again. I wish you didn't have to be in court tomorrow. Surely I can go talk to her—or have her meet me somewhere public, maybe for lunch—if you'd be worried about my going out there alone. Or I could see if Will can go along if he's not at the library until early afternoon. I think we've learned we can trust what he says, that he's on our side. Maybe there's a clue in what sort of butterfly those black ones with the red stripe were in that release tonight. I got a good look at the one I caught."

"Yeah, a public place with Tara and Will could work."

"It will only take me a minute to check that butterfly on my phone so I can tell Tara and Will what it was. Just a sec. You know," she threw over her shoulder as she got up, "I could probably ask that all-knowing genius doll what kind it was and get an answer. As soon as we locate Darcy—settle all this—I've got to find a way to wean Lexi away from that thing."

She went into their bedroom, grabbed her purse and fished out her cell phone. She sat on the couch with Nick, and her description brought up several butterfly breeds, but she was sure it was the one called red rim. She read aloud, "It is usually found in Central America and Mexico, but has been imported and bred in the United States. Because of its dark color—oh, get this—it is sometimes used for releases at funerals. Nick, we know Will used to do those."

"So he'll either know about them—or he did it, rented a boat. I think we can trust him to help us find Darcy, especially since we're running out of options, regardless of what Ken Jensen pledges about the official search."

She showed Nick the picture of the red rim but noticed the photograph of it on the small screen looked as if it were fluttering its wings. She felt faint again, so exhausted she was falling apart, but she wanted to go on, to stay up, to make more plans, even to go outside to check for clues, to call Tara right now, to assure herself she could trust Will at least to have lunch with—

"Sweetheart, you're falling asleep sitting up," Nick said, rising, then bending to scoop her up in his arms. "Your head just jerked, and you nodded off. I'm putting you to bed, and don't argue."

She held her phone, held to him, so grateful. Since Nick had turned off the outdoor lights, she caught a glimpse of herself in his arms in the black mirror of the window. At least he'd agreed she could meet with Tara and Will in public tomorrow, make some progress to find Darcy, find her sanity. And then that other storm, the real one that could become a hurricane—for the girls' sakes, she had to watch the weather predictions, get ready if fierce winds came their way.

Nick sat her down on the side of their bed, took her phone and kissed her, then walked away and brought back her nightly narcolepsy med and a glass of water. So much water if a hurricane came, she told herself as he took off her shoes and laid her down, covering her with the sheet—driving rain and storm surge, drowning everything, just everything, like that man caught in the net, but hopefully not Darcy, out there somewhere, somewhere...

CHAPTER TWENTY-ONE

Claire woke, still in her clothes. Daylight flooded their bedroom. Nick was not in bed; she heard him in the shower. Everything came crashing back, the memorial service at the shore, Ken Jensen's frustration, then the ruined butterfly bushes and flowers. Were the girls up yet?

Feeling dirty and wishing she were in the shower, she checked the clock. Six-fifteen. She went barefoot to the girls' room and peeked in. Both were asleep, so that might give them time to put some of those plants back in. She tiptoed out again. Down the hall, neither Steve's bedroom door nor Nita and Bronco's were open. She went into the guest bathroom those rooms shared, used the toilet and washed her face and hands.

She hurried into the Florida room and looked out the window again. Not only did she see dead plants but dead butterflies—black ones. She jumped when Nick spoke behind her.

"I saw you were out of bed."

She spun to look at him. He had his good slacks on but no shirt, and dampness clung to his chest hair. She saw he still held a towel.

"I used the guest bathroom," she said. "No one else is up."

"Bronco is. He's out front looking around the cars, checking under Steve's. He's upset I'll think he's not doing his job, but he can't be everywhere at once. Still, I wish he would have seen or caught whoever made that mess and left us some sort of message."

"Checking under Steve's car for what? A bomb? Have we come to that? But what we have come to are dead butterflies that might be red rims like the ones released last night at the memorial service."

He came over and put his hands on her shoulders. "Last night when we looked out there, they must have blended in with the roots and scattered soil. Let's go out and take a look."

He unlocked the back door, and they went out and over to the bizarre blur of stems, roots, strewn soil—and torn, fragile butterfly bodies. Awful—but then, maybe the red rims were dead from their flight last night and someone had gathered them up. Then that would mean whoever did this was there among the mourners—and then came quickly here.

Watching where they stepped, they moved around, leaning down to study the plants and the places from which they had been pulled up.

"But what's the point—the message?" Claire asked.

"Nothing else to make it clear," Nick said, heaving a huge sigh.

"The message is what we're looking at. Murder, but on a plant and insect scale. I think it's time we have those security cameras you talked about installed."

"I just hated to admit we'd be vulnerable again. A dead gator in the pool—we solved that. I can't stand the idea of living in an armed camp, so to speak. I thought having Bronco here for a while was enough."

"I know," she said, and put her arm around his waist. "I guess it comes with the criminal lawyer territory."

"I swear, nothing threatening is going on right now with my work. But how could something like this tie to finding Darcy? You don't think Steve's so frustrated that he was drinking again and—"

"No. No, I don't."

"Once we get through this storm, if it's coming here, we'll get cameras, front and back," he promised. "After all, Bronco will have to return to his real life soon, too."

Shaking their heads—and deeply shaken—they went back inside. Could they ever return to what was "real life" if they didn't get Darcy back?

Claire started to fix coffee and turned on the television at the end of the counter. "The tropical disturbance has become a named storm, with hurricane force winds," the weatherman said, standing in front of a moving weather radar map, flaring with bright colors. "We are still hoping that Hurricane Jenny, now a Cat 3, will stay in the gulf when it leaves the Caribbean and not approach the shores of southwest Florida. However, Governor Scott is ready to declare an emergency for the entire state if Jenny becomes a Cat 4. The governor said in a press release, 'This storm could be very bad.' Tips for how to prepare if you stay at home and advice on needed supplies at eight, so stayed tuned for—"

Claire muted the sound and turned around to embrace Nick and hold hard to him. "That's all we need," she murmured with her lips against his bare shoulder.

"I won't say when it rains it pours. Here, I'll finish fixing the coffee so you can get ready—for anything and everything."

"I'll grab a fast shower and help Nita with breakfast, then pick up some storm supplies before they disappear from all the store shelves. At least this new home is up to hurricane code," she said as she moved away, but she kept talking, energized again. "Nita, Bronco and I can water those uprooted plants and try to get them back in the ground. But I'm also going to call Tara and then Will. Nick, if he was the one on that boat with the butterfly release, do you think he'll admit it? And should I tell him about the dead ones here, or could he be behind that, like—like maybe warning us to be careful in a different way to really get our attention?"

"Maybe," he admitted as she stopped and turned toward him again. "But where would he get that many? We saw he has no butterfly house in his backyard. From Tara? Just be careful with both of them—public place for sure. Sweetheart, with that storm coming, there's a chance the local judicial system will be delayed or closed, so that would be one helpful thing that could come from a possible weather disaster."

"We've already had a human disaster," she said, turning away again. "I'm still praying we'll get a lead about Darcy. Let's face it. There's nowhere to go from here but up."

By the time she'd filled the trunk of her car with bottled water and groceries—mostly things that didn't need refrigeration in case the power went—Claire was exhausted again. Everyone had the same idea, and the checkout lines were long.

When she got home, she didn't let Nita help her unload

because she was so far along; her belly looked, well, bulbous. Bronco had gone for a little while to somewhat "hurricane proof" their own house and would be back soon. They'd asked to stay here during the storm since the newer Markwood home met hurricane standards and their house was far from that. Even before Nick left, Claire had picked up the dead butterflies, but had them in a plastic bag in the freezer in the garage to show Ken—if they were still speaking to him then, Claire thought.

The girls helped carry in water bottles. They were chattering about bad wind at night, which they thought had uprooted the plants, so the adults had let it go for now. Neither Lexi nor Jilly were old enough to recall a big, damaging storm. And as the TV weatherman had said, "This could be a bad one."

She had made Lexi and Jilly—the doll, too—promise to help Nita until Bronco returned. Steve had gone to check on his house, as well, bring some keepsakes here in case there was serious damage, and he needed more clothes for him and Jilly. He also planned to pick up batteries and get all the flashlights working—one per person and three extras.

Despite the terrible timing for a lunch out, both Tara and Will had promised to meet Claire at the Carrabbas Italian restaurant on the East Trail. A ways for Will, but close for Tara, who, with her best friend and two volunteers, were moving every butterfly they could net into the living room of her house. The structure had been damaged by Hurricane Andrew in 1992, but then that was a Cat 5. Surely Hurricane Jenny would not be worse than that or than Wilma in 2005, which had been terribly destructive. Weren't they due for some kind of a break? But Claire understood Tara's concerns and promised to make their meeting brief. Even if this storm was as bad as predicted, the butterfly houses could become flying objects themselves.

"I can't thank both of you enough for meeting me here in the current chaos," Claire told them when they were seated. Tara sat by Will across the booth from Claire, Will on the outside.

"We've been in chaos since Darcy—since she disappeared," Tara said, reaching over to squeeze Claire's hand, although they had hugged earlier. "I see they are even closing this place at one today, but who would want to be out when the weather goes downhill?"

As Tara drew her hand back, Will said, "So how have you been, Tara? Sorry I haven't been out for a while, but I've been at work—and trying to help Claire and Nick."

Yes, surely she could trust both of these people. They, too, had been terribly impacted by Darcy's vanishing. She was blessed to have people beyond the family who cared deeply, but then, that just showed how lovable Darcy always had been—was still, of course. And unless these two were in cahoots, that answered one of Claire's questions: evidently, Will had not been out to Tara's to purchase large numbers of red rims, though she didn't plan to entirely let that line of questioning go.

They ordered iced tea and ignored their menus, huddling in the greatly deserted restaurant. "Last night," Claire told them, watching both their faces as best she could, "after dark, someone yanked up all our butterfly flowers and bushes. Worse, there were at least forty dead red rim butterflies in the ruin of soil, roots and wilting leaves smeared on the patio concrete."

"Oh, my—all red rims?" Tara said, looking genuinely distressed.

"Were any of you home then?" Will asked. "Jilly—and Lexi. Are they all right? Did the girls get upset?"

"The girls were there with a couple who is living with us at the moment. They love that butterfly area. Thankfully, they only saw it after we had removed the butterflies. They haven't reasoned it out well yet, thinking the coming storm had bad winds that yanked up plants."

Still frowning, Will said, "I must tell you, red rims are one of the favorite funeral release types. The idea, I guess, of the darkness of death, but with that red stripe as the sunset—or maybe new dawn—on the horizon. A striking variety. I've seen hundreds of those over at Butterfly World in Coconut Creek near Fort Lauderdale. Since Tara doesn't breed that variety, I've ordered from several places for funeral releases so—Claire, are you working up to asking me if I left those in your yard?"

"I'm bringing them up because I want to tell you both that Nick and I—Steve, too—attended Captain Larry Ralston's memorial service at Doctors Pass last night, although we all stood a ways back. And someone, obviously not Larry's brother, Clint, who was conducting the gathering, released a huge number of red rims."

"No one saw who it was?" Tara asked, looking shocked.

"It wasn't someone at the service. It was getting dark. A motorboat pulled up in the pass and let the hoard of them go. It was obvious from the reactions, even though Nick and I had moved even farther away by then, that everyone was shocked, and we didn't hear Clint Ralston take credit—or blame—for that. By the way, Detective Jensen, who is heading up the search for Darcy, was there to observe, too."

Will looked more furious than flustered. Tara looked clueless. Another dead end, Claire thought.

"As I said," Will told them, "I've used those for funeral releases, but it wasn't me in that boat or in your backyard. Were you and Nick thinking it was? But what would someone's motive be, and who is that someone?"

Tara said, "Will, do you think someone is trying to point the finger at you? And for what? Larry Ralston's death? I mean, he was the most vocal Fly Safe member and anti-butterfly-farm speaker, he and Lincoln Yost. Well, actually, Lincoln saw the good in a safe, nearby breeding place for butterflies, including some of his own, but he was adamantly against shipping them or releasing them at events—abuse, he called it. He lectured me on that more than once. I told him he had to take the 'bad' so the good could flourish, but I never won him over, nor did he convince me."

Will just clenched his hands until his fingers turned stark white.

Yet Claire trusted these two, and wished she could think the best of Lincoln Yost, too. This was a terrible time for tracking down and questioning Yost again, but Claire knew they had to do it. And Tara had just given away more than she'd told them earlier: she had named Larry and Linc as hostile to her efforts, so if either of them had found Darcy there alone...

"Will," Claire said, "I'm sorry, but I have to ask, you are telling me you definitely were not so disgusted with the Ralstons or Fly Safe that you decided to release those butterflies?"

"Nor dump some in your backyard!" he said, and glared at the waiter who came to take their order but then backed off. "You and Nick need to trust me."

"We do, or you wouldn't be sitting here, helping as you are—you both are," she added hastily. "But who does that leave?"

"Who knows?" Will insisted. "Darcy's disappearance has been all over the newspapers, including the fact that Tara's place was the site of her abduction."

He was obviously growing angrier by the moment, but, thank God, not at her. A vein had appeared at the side of his forehead, beating madly. He'd gripped his water glass so hard she wondered if it could shatter.

"But those red rims are a clue," he went on. "A clue, but also, I swear, an attempt to smear me, implicate me, and I'm not going to take that. Ladies, if you'll excuse me."

"Will, wait," Claire cried as he started to slide out of the booth. "Can't we work together? Can you think of someone who would want to implicate you and why?"

"Why? For one thing, to intimidate me—us—from finding Darcy. The more a kidnapper, and maybe a murderer—of Captain Larry, not of Darcy, I hope to God..." His voice snagged, but he went on, "The more that person can get in our way, can obscure the truth, like smearing dead red rims and butterfly plants all over... Claire, I will be in touch," he said, and walked out.

"Well!" Tara said. "He's always been passionate about butterflies, but—I thought—not so much about people. I must have read him wrong."

"I just hope I haven't," Claire said. "He's tried to help us find Darcy, bring her back home."

Her eyes welled up with tears to make two Taras sitting across from her. But what she was really seeing in her mind's eye were those poor, delicate bodies of butterflies, dead and smeared across the soil, ready for burial. If that was a sign or symbol or threat about Darcy's fate or future, she couldn't bear it.

CHAPTER TWENTY-TWO

Despite the encroaching storm, Nick felt he was on a roll. The prosecuting attorney had asked for a delay of the trial to admit additional evidence, even though the storm was likely to delay proceedings anyway. Nick again assured his elderly client they had a strong case that would find her not guilty. Then, before heading home, he decided to stop at Linc Yost's house to try to dig a little deeper. It still puzzled him that Yost seemed to live on a CEO salary, when most teachers, sadly, in the state of Florida were lucky to live in Bronco and Nita's neighborhood. Ken Jensen had said an injury had kept Yost from playing pro ball, so no money there.

After he pulled up to Yost's house, he ditched his tie and suit coat and left them in the car. He wondered how Claire was doing with Will and Tara. He could have gone to join them, but this had to be done. He had to force Linc Yost to answer some of the questions he'd been skirting.

As he walked toward the house, he heard pounding from

around back, so maybe the Yosts were boarding up. He didn't go to the front door but walked up the driveway. A full-size basketball net with an iron base stood there, its net swaying wildly in the quickening breeze. That dwarfed a smaller, child's size, plastic net-on-wheels version. That was right, Yost had at least two sons. He had to hurry, to get home to his own son, to Lexi and Claire.

He saw no one at first, but the pounding drew him to the back of their yard where Linc was hammering nails into two-by-fours around a small, strange-looking building. A kid's playhouse? Yost, hammer raised, looked up and saw him.

"Storm coming, Mr. Lawyer," Linc said. "You better get inside somewhere safe."

"My family's been in a storm since my sister-in-law disappeared. I was hoping you could help."

"Like how? Why do you keep coming back? I've seen the media coverage, but don't know anything to help. Can you push that board closer?" he said, raising his hammer even higher.

For one moment, Nick thought he might strike him so he stood away, didn't put his head down, only reached out one hand to hold the board steady.

"This is my boys' army station, supposedly in Iraq," he told Nick as he pounded away, knocking long nails into the board and the building. "My brother's stationed there. They play soldier. They like anything in a uniform, even the police. Well, I don't want them to hate the police, anyway."

"Good. How about you? The police are working hard on Darcy's disappearance, but can you throw light on anything? I'll make this quick and honest, because I see how good you are with your students and your kids, and I admire and trust someone like that."

Linc stopped, then dropped the hammer in the grass and tightened his Naples High School baseball cap on his forehead, giving it a hard twist.

"Okay, so I boarded, so to speak, my falcate orangetips at Tara Gerald's. But I did not—repeat, did not—go out to the Flutterby Farm the day your sister-in-law went missing."

"Do you know anyone who did, or even who might have?"

"No."

"So let me get this straight. Fly Safe, which you support and work with, is against someone having a butterfly farm—"

"Hardly. I admit I've boarded some of mine there. But I hate it if any place imprisons butterflies in those little envelopes or sends them away to amuse people when they should—obviously—fly safe and free."

"Look, I admit we've covered some of this before, but you understand my wife and I are desperate for answers, for any lead. I'm concerned someone has imprisoned a young woman, a wife and mother. I take it the falcate orangetip breed of butterfly can be valuable for study because of their suspended animation technique, which could be developed for mankind, and be lucrative. Does that have anything to do with your study of them, your doctoral thesis or whatever?"

Linc's eyes widened, and his lower lip twitched. It hit Nick that he'd just struck a nerve. Maybe this high school teacher was living large because he was in on a much bigger study. And that linked to the talent the dolphins had for putting half of their brain to sleep at will, another of this man's passions. But who would be heading that up—probably secretly? And wouldn't that mean imprisoning and even killing the butterflies he seemed such a champion of? Nick decided to come at it from a different angle.

"I see you're interested in dolphins, too. Do you think Larry Ralston actually took one of those—like maybe for study?"

"And put it where? In our fish tank at Fly Safe? In my guest room bathtub here at the house? I see you've been doing your homework, Mr. Markwood, but you're not hitting the nail on the head, far as I know, and I got to do that now." He stooped to pick up his hammer again. "Unless you want to play carpenter's helper, I suggest you go take care of your own backyard because I have nothing else to say."

He started to pound again with a vengeance.

"Actually," Nick told him, raising his voice, "my backyard does need some help. Someone sneaked in after dark last night and yanked up all our butterfly bushes and left about forty dead butterflies, the same breed that were released by someone at Larry Ralston's memorial service."

Yost registered such sudden surprise that Nick, at least, chalked him off the list for that. He stopped hammering and turned to Nick again. "Listen, man, sorry to hear that, sorry about everything, really. I hope you get your sister-in-law back safe and sound. Beyond the science angle of suspended animation—yeah, I'm interested in that—I don't have anything else to add."

"Even about who I could see next?"

"I can't help."

Can't or won't, Nick wanted to demand, but he was done here for now. Maybe he could get Jensen to try shaking something out of this guy, who was in over his head and seemed really shaken about being questioned.

As Nick walked away, the hammering started again, fast and furious. The pounding almost matched his sudden headache.

When Claire described the mess in their backyard to Ken on the phone, he told her, "I'm sorry, Claire. I'm going to be busy preparing for this storm, but I will also keep following leads about Darcy."

"Nick figured you'd be on special assignment during the storm. Do you think there's any way it will miss us?"

"Right now, the forecast is landfall somewhere between Marco Island and Fort Myers, so that includes us, but it could veer off westward. Will you shelter in place or go to a shelter?"

"Our house is hurricane proof and far enough away from a storm surge, so we'll be here. We'll have another family with us, two friends, plus Steve and Jilly, in case you hear anything. I hope we can continue to work together. I just can't—can't believe she's gone…isn't showing up, I mean."

"Stranger things have happened, but everything I've heard about her makes her look very stable."

"You mean, you actually thought she might have gone off on her own? Run away or hurt herself?"

"Claire, we've been over this. We have to look at all angles. If you and Nick think of another possibility, just leave a message on my cell, if the cell towers don't go down. Sorry, but I have to go. I will not let this become a cold case, I promise you. I will keep in touch as best I can."

He was gone. A cold case? She shivered. Darcy's loss, that is, her disappearance, a cold case after one week? Never. Never in her lifetime was she stopping her search for her sister.

★ ★ ★

"Déjà vu all over again?" Mitch tried to tease Jace after they safely taxied and took off from Keesler Air Force Base in Biloxi heading for MacDill Air Force Base in Tampa. They were immediately out over the Gulf of Mexico heading south, talking only to each other now, not their NOAA crew or ground control.

"Roger that, but this storm's a real killer—and it may be on Naples's doorstep. Just glad we got assigned to scope it out. We can't be there to help on the ground at home, so we can help in the wild blue yonder—or the black storm yonder."

"Affirmative," Mitch said. "We won't be on the ground long there before we head up to take it on. Maybe enough time to call home, though we're not supposed to upset everyone, as if they aren't already. I'd like to tell Kris we're doing all we can."

"With the prep and worry they're going through, they don't need to know we're going up into the storm, anyway. Just say we don't have final orders if she asks. They'd be getting ready for the hit and still panicked over Darcy—I don't know if I'll call, as much as I'd like to hear Brit's and Lexi's voices again."

"Bet we won't even need radar or ground control to describe Hurricane Jenny—just take a look at her appearance. Jenny—nice, sweet name. Sounds like someone who should be playing with Jilly, Lexi...and that smart doll."

"I can't believe how big the outer bands of the storm in the Caribbean look on the TV radar," Claire told Nita as they fixed dinner together late that afternoon. Claire was trying to help her all she could since Nita was so very "with child." "I just wonder if Jace and Mitch will be observing it up close and personal."

"If I was their boss, I'd send someone else. I mean, wouldn't they be extra nervous and maybe not do their job if it's gonna hit their homes?"

"Nervous, maybe. But not so much that they wouldn't do their jobs, no way. Even under fire in war, men like them are trained and dedicated to do what is necessary."

Her own voice, strong and proud, surprised her. She did admire Jace, still cared for him in a way and always would, and not just as her first love or as Lexi's father. But on a personal, forever level, their relationship just wasn't to be. She was so grateful to have found Nick and to have the beautiful baby they had made together. And if that storm came here, she would die to protect her family, but then, how she wished she could have protected Darcy. She blinked back tears and tried to concentrate on what Nita was saying.

"Our new house—I mean, it is an old one—I been praying it stands so we have a room for our baby. I heard some women, they go into labor early with depressions or pressures, something like that."

"Old wives' tales," Claire told her, patting her back. But Nita's "depressions or pressures"—she was feeling that herself and had been since Darcy disappeared.

"But one thing I been wanting to tell you," Nita said, turning to Claire. "You been such a good friend to me. If the doctor's ultrasound of the baby is right—and it's a she—I'm going to name her Clarita, named for you."

"Oh, Nita!" Claire said, and hugged her hard with the big baby bump between them. "You couldn't do anything that means more to me. It helps some—since I'm missing Darcy so."

She heard Nick's voice, so he'd come in before she'd heard his car or the garage door going up. She thanked Nita again. They both wiped tears away, then Claire went to greet Nick in their bedroom, took his suit coat jacket and tie from him. She told him her good "baby" news and hugged him, too.

"Great! We really need another 'Claire' around here," he teased. "Listen, the trial's delayed, so I dropped by Yost's house on my way home. He didn't exactly say so, but I'm thinking someone might be paying him big bucks for his research on the falcates—maybe on the dolphins, too. I had the feeling he wanted to tell me more, but was scared to. His fear might have something to do with Larry's being accused of killing a dolphin, and then being murdered, like maybe Yost's afraid of talking more, talking to me."

"This is all getting too...too spiderwebby," she told him.

"But hey, I'm getting good at reading facial expressions and body language, my love," he went on in an obvious attempt to lighten the conversation again. "I'm going to take a quick shower, then we'll gather everyone to make a plan for when and if the storm hits here. I hope we have two days before that monster churns up the gulf and decides where it's going to make landfall."

"Okay. I'm helping Nita in the kitchen, trying to do some normal things. But I'm already churned up."

On her way, she checked on the girls again. Lexi's doll was telling them the storm could be bad, using the exact words that had been on the TV. The doll was a recording device, of course, but what did it record? And did it then just speak what it had "learned," or was it controlled by some outside source that had preprogrammed it before it was sold? She'd been so busy, so obsessed—and grateful the doll comforted and distracted both girls—that she hadn't really studied it.

She noticed the wind was picking up as she hurried to her laptop and put in "Smart Dolly." That led her to interactive talking dolls. She read that they were similar to remotely controlled baby monitors operated by computer software. The system both transmitted and recorded voice prints, whatever that was.

But another link led her to a site she just stared at wide-eyed. An exact picture of the doll came up—German made. But in that country, there was a huge fine for not destroying those dolls. And that brand of Smart Dolly violated US privacy laws!

She fought to calm herself. Of course there were risks with interactive devices. Lexi loved and needed that doll, but what if—

She jolted when the doorbell rang. She rose from the laptop and peered out the library window, but could only see part of someone standing on the front porch under a black umbrella. She could see wet, dirty running shoes and damp jeans, but it looked like a woman. It must be Kris or Brit.

She went to the front door, opened it, jerked back and gasped.

Darcy stood there, thinner, half-drenched.

"Sorry I'm late, Claire," she said, shaking water off the umbrella and stepping in to drop it in the large porcelain umbrella stand. "Is Jilly ready to go home? I think there's a bad rainstorm coming. What—what's the matter with you? Is everything okay?"

CHAPTER TWENTY-THREE

Claire just stared. She must be having a narcoleptic nightmare.

"Claire, I said are you okay?" Darcy asked, looking closer into her face and squeezing her arm.

This was true, really happening. She wanted to burst into tears, scream and dance. Wanted to hug Darcy—but it was Darcy who was not okay.

Her eyes were dilated. She wore not a bit of her usual makeup and looked pale. Alive, but something was so terribly wrong—with her—with all this.

Claire hugged her hard. Had to feel her, know this was real. So thankful. Answer to prayer, fear over. Or was it?

"Is it something with Jilly?" Darcy asked, pulling back. "I should have called but I lost my phone."

Lost eight days, Claire almost blurted, but she led her into the library. Either she or Darcy had lost her mind.

"No, Jilly's fine, and Steve's here. I'll call them."

"Steve! Oh, he came to surprise me for our anniversary,

after all!" she cried as tears filled her eyes. "And he came here to get Jilly, but you probably said she had to wait for me, or I'd think something was wrong."

"Yes. Yes, that's it."

Darcy was articulate, thinking straight for the world she knew. The world of eight days ago when she disappeared. Someone or something had wiped out those days.

Call Jensen first? Get Steve and Jilly? Then Darcy would think they'd all lost their minds when—evidently—she had.

"Okay," Claire said, trying to sound normal and upbeat, but her voice kept breaking. "How about you stay here a sec, and I'll bring Steve in so you guys can have a little reunion before I get Jilly?"

"Oh, boy, I don't want to ruin his surprise. I know I'm a little late. I'll bet you were worried and Steve, too. All right, I'll stay here while you get him—don't tell him it's me!"

This was insane. Or was Darcy insane—or the entire world? Claire hugged her again—yes, solid flesh—and went to find Nick before telling Steve. But Jilly would give it all away, let Darcy know she was crazy. Who or what had done this to her?

Nick was outside helping Bronco sweep up the mess on the patio. They'd thrown some plants in the trash can and put back some in the ground and watered them heavily. The area was still a dirty, muddy mess.

"Nick!" Claire called, gesturing with her hand. "I need to see you for a minute."

He left his broom and came in, clapping dirt off his hands.

"What's the matter?" he demanded when he got close and saw her face. "Are you ill?"

"Stunned. You aren't going to believe this, but Darcy's here, in one piece and—"

He gasped. "Ken brought her here?"

"She brought herself—drove up. She has no clue she's been gone. She says she came to pick up Jilly. When I told her Steve's here—"

"She's really here?" he interrupted. "But is she all right?"

"She thinks everything's normal, but she's not. Really weird. She believes it's eight days ago."

"We need to get her to a doctor, tell Ken Jensen."

"Go ahead with Jensen, but we've got to warn Steve so he doesn't say she's crazy and set her off. Something horrible must have happened to her, so bad she has amnesia or was drugged or—"

"Thank God she's back, but—but... Whew!"

He pinched his nose with his thumb and index finger, leaving what looked like dirty tear marks. She could see him try to steady himself. Yes, she had to find Steve, warn Steve.

She saw him with the girls watching TV in the den with that damned doll.

"Steve, I need to see you for a second," she said, gesturing to him.

"They say the storm is worse?" he asked as he followed her into the kitchen.

"Brace yourself for some good but strange news. Darcy just showed up, and she thinks it's the day she was taken. She's lost over a week, and I'm afraid if we tell her anything of the big search for her, it might make it worse. I told her you're here, and she thinks it's a surprise for your anniversary. I don't think she recalls anything of being gone. Steve?"

His eyes had widened, then narrowed. His jaw hung open. He just stared at Claire.

"Where—where is she? I have to see her, hold her."

"The library, but be careful what you say so—"

He rushed away. Claire wilted against the wall. Maybe she'd let Steve break it to Jilly. She was starting to shake, felt cold, but how would Darcy feel?

She exploded in tears, shoulders shaking, sobbing into the palms of her hands. Finally, she calmed herself, grabbed a tissue so the girls wouldn't see her and think the worst. She ducked into their master bedroom where Nick sat on their bed talking on the phone.

"No, only Claire has seen her and now Steve. She says Darcy's out of it, thinks it's the day she was lost. But you can't just start to interrogate her, or she might flip out."

Still shaking, Claire sank onto the bed beside him and gestured for Nick to give her the phone.

"Ken, it's Claire. Maybe she's been drugged or has a concussion. She doesn't know she's been gone. I understand you need to talk to her, but she's with Steve, and we need to prepare Jilly and Lexi."

She listened to his rush of words, then dared to interrupt him. "Yes, I realize she needs a checkup and care, but what will taking her away from us do to her right now?"

"Claire, if she was imprisoned—mistreated by someone—we have to examine her right away, find out who, hopefully why. Keep her—and Steve—calm because I'm coming over, and we'll have to have her treated, but I promise you, you can stay with her."

"Me? Why not Steve?"

"I'll explain. Try to keep her calm—Steve, too—until I get there. We won't let this hit the media cycle until we have her safely off-limits from them."

"But we can get her a doctor."

It annoyed her that Nick was not only leaning close to listen, but was shaking his head to that question and mouthing, "No."

"Listen to me," Ken said. "You've been around crimes and victims enough to know we need to take her into medical custody right now. She may well have been abducted, abused, violated. It's a police matter, the law. Ask Nick and keep an eye on Steve because he's volatile. Keep calm, and I'll see you soon."

She ended the call and handed the phone to Nick. "It's like—like she has to be committed. He said I could stay with her if I wanted to."

"Stay where?"

"I don't know. Where she's treated, taken. A hospital, I guess."

"Not Steve with her?"

"No—I don't know why. But we've got to go tell Jilly, unless Steve wants to. I'll go find out—see how they are doing. Nick, thank God she's back, but in a way, she's not really back at all."

Nick held her tight, hopefully just the way Steve was holding Darcy.

Steve had whispered to Claire that she should tell Jilly. Claire took her niece off by herself while Nita stayed with Lexi. Darcy and Steve were still in the library.

"Honey," Claire told her, "I have some really happy news, but you are going to have to help your daddy. Your mommy has come back but—"

"Yay! Where is she? Is she okay? I have to hug her right now!"

"You will, but the thing is, she doesn't remember any-

thing about being away. Maybe she hit her head or something—I mean, she is fine—but she somehow forgot she
was away for over a week. Can you try not to tell her she's
wrong until we can get a doctor to help her?"

"You mean, tell her lies?"

"No. Just agree with her, pretend everything is just like
usual and okay."

"But isn't that like telling lies?"

"We need to have her see a doctor to get straightened
out bit by bit."

"But where was she? And where is she now?"

"Right now, in the library, sweetheart, with your daddy.
How about you join them there and hug them and celebrate quietly in your own mind and heart. But just agree
with things right now until we get her some help. Then,
when she's better, you can tell her everything, and she'll
tell you where she's been, because I don't think she even
knows right now. Can you do all that to help her and your
daddy, too?"

"I can do anything to help her. It will just be pretend for
a while, not a lie, right?"

"Right," Claire assured her, and walked her to the library door, hoping to heaven Steve had not ruined Darcy's
fragile facade already.

To Claire's surprise and annoyance, not only did Ken
arrive in a squad car wearing a Collier County police uniform instead of his usual detective civilian look, but he'd
brought an ambulance and two other uniformed officers
with him.

"Do you need all this?" she asked him as the three men
entered. "She's hardly going to resist a short hospital stay,

and I'll take you up on your offer to go with her. Nita just went to pack a duffel bag for both of us with my clothes."

"How is Steve taking this?" he asked as Nick joined them in the front hall. He, too, frowned at Ken when he saw the officers.

"He insists he can handle things," Claire said. "He says he should go with Darcy instead of me. Nick advised him I should go with her, but he's protesting, says he wants another lawyer."

"He's going to need one. Claire and Nick, sorry to rain on your parade on this happiest of days. I'm ecstatic you have her back physically well, but she will need to be deposed and treated."

"We understand that," Nick said. "Claire will go with her. We appreciate that. But what do you mean Steve *needs* a lawyer? If he wants one for his own reasons, that's one thing, but *needs?*"

"Just brace yourselves—again. I'm here to arrest Steven Stanley for suspicion of the aggravated murder of Lawrence Ralston. I'll be able to protect Darcy's privacy for a few days, but not Steve's when this gets out. I wanted to warn you in case he protests. There's been corroborating DNA evidence he was in a physical struggle with Ralston on his boat just before the victim was found drowned."

Claire wavered on her feet. Too much. Too much!

"You can't—cannot arrest him in front of Darcy," she insisted. "She knows nothing of this. She's been through too much—through something."

"Then clear the way for me. Get her, and their daughter—if she's still with them—away from him. It would be best. It's why I'm telling you all this. Claire, that will mean you will temporarily be legally in charge of your sister, at least until Steve makes bail or is—"

"I'll go with him until he gets his own representation," Nick insisted.

"Fine by me. Now, I'll have these officers step aside so you can prepare Darcy to be taken to the North Naples Hospital where a psychiatrist is waiting. She'll have a thorough checkup there before being interviewed. Your psych background will help, too, I'm sure, Claire."

At first, she just stared at Ken, then at Nick. He gave a terse nod and put his arm around her waist. They were both shaking.

"I need to read Steve his rights," Ken said. "I hope you'll continue to help me—help them—as you have these last eight days, for everyone's sake."

Claire wiped tears from under her eyes and whispered, "Yes."

While Nick and Ken waited in the hall and the officers stepped into the kitchen to not be seen at first, Claire squared her shoulders and knocked on the library door.

"Come in!" Steve called.

She went in and closed the door behind her, leaning against it as if she could shut out Ken and everything awful that had happened.

"So, I think Darcy looks a little thin and tired and could use a visit to a doctor just to be sure everything's okay," she said, trying to sound upbeat but her voice quavered.

"I understand, but can't we wait until tomorrow?" Steve asked. "Thanks for all you've done, Claire. Nick, too."

"Steve, you need to step out in the hall a moment to talk to Nick first."

"He decide to represent me?"

"For what, Steve?" Darcy asked. "Do we need a lawyer? Did something happen on your job site?"

She was sitting tight against him on the leather couch with Jilly pinned to her other side. For one moment that wistful, puzzled look on her sister's face reminded Claire of Will's painting of his grandmother with her butterfly net…

"Steve, please," Claire said, and came closer to him, praying he would not see her sending him out into the hall without warning him as a betrayal. "I promise you, I will stay with Darcy."

He heaved a huge sigh and got up to go to the door. Claire bit her lower lip, feeling she'd been a traitor just now, but they didn't need uniformed officers near Darcy or Jilly, or Steve putting up another fight. Dear God, what if he was guilty of what they were accusing him of?

He looked back at his family, then went out into the hall and closed the door behind him. Claire put her arm around Darcy, and they hugged again, even as Jilly squeezed into their embrace, too.

Through the door, Claire could barely hear the muffled words, but she knew what to expect. Steve's protest and then Nick's calming tones. Finally, even more distant, Ken Jensen's voice, "You have the right to remain silent. Anything you say can and will be used against you in a court of law. You have the right to an attorney…"

"Darcy," Claire said, "you do look like you're coming down with something, so I'm going to go with you to have you checked out."

"But Steve and I are going to plan our private anniversary dinner, so that will have to wait. I'm fine, just fine."

CHAPTER TWENTY-FOUR

Rain pounded on the ambulance roof as Claire sat next to Darcy, who was strapped on the gurney. An ER nurse was with them and had checked on Darcy's vitals—normal but for dilated eyes and a high blood pressure reading, but what did they expect, whisking her away like this? At least the driver had not turned on the siren to alarm her more.

Steve had been given time to see Darcy again before Ken took him in. He'd told her he was going to check their house because of the storm and would see her soon. Nick had gone with him. How had it come to this so swiftly? The shock, the joy—then tragedy again. Steve was under arrest and poor Jilly, who was suddenly without her parents, was clinging to Lexi and that horrible doll.

But if time was a blur to Darcy, everything was that way to Claire as the ambulance drove toward the hospital. She'd taken her nightly narcolepsy meds, but she had to try to keep things straight. She empathized with Darcy, the uncertainty, the panic and fear.

"I don't think I need an ambulance, but Steve said maybe I hit my head," Darcy said as Claire leaned close and held her hand.

"Maybe. Your eyes are dilated."

"And I can't remember how I lost my phone, because I had my purse, my car keys. Can't recall leaving Tara's. I think someone came for some butterflies."

"Who was that?"

"I don't know. Maybe the men who took care of the dolphin at the zoo."

Claire was confused. There were no dolphins at the zoo. Even if there were, why would dolphin keepers want butterflies? And she realized she should not be questioning Darcy now but then she could tell Ken—if she was ever speaking to him again—what Darcy said here. But her sister wasn't making sense. Was she?

"Were you at the zoo today, Darcy?"

"I might have been."

At least the nurse didn't seem interested in what Darcy was saying, only in reading the monitors attached to her.

"I think it was raining at the zoo," Darcy whispered, as if it were a secret. "Or it might have been somewhere people were swimming in little pools, but I could only see their faces."

Oh, dear God, her sister wasn't here at all, at least not mentally. Something traumatic had happened to her, but at least they had her back and could help her. Claire kept holding her hand as the ambulance turned into the emergency entrance of the NCH North Naples Hospital. It was dry under the portico as the nurse and driver slid, then rolled out, Darcy's gurney and extended the wheeled legs.

Claire followed along, hefting the duffel bag with things for her and Darcy that Nita had hastily packed.

They went inside and down corridors, used an elevator to the area marked Psychiatric and Psychology Center. A private room was waiting; they went right in, and two nurses transferred Darcy to a bed and got her changed into a hospital gown while Claire hovered. The single room had a sofa-type bed along one wall, so she put her things there. Thank heavens, she could stay right here all night.

A tall, thin, blonde woman stepped in. Her white coat was scripted over the pocket with Dr. Lesley Spizer. Claire stood at the foot of the bed while the doctor, perhaps in her midforties, nodded to her, but stepped closer to take Darcy's hand.

"Darcy, I'm Dr. Spizer, and I'm going to help you feel better."

"I'm really all right, just tired. But maybe I hit my head because—because on the wall there," she said pointing past Claire, "it says it is August 23, and that can't be. That means I missed my wedding anniversary, but I don't think I did."

"Don't worry about that, about anything," the doctor told her. "We will do some tests to find out if you hit your head, and your sister can stay here with you. If you missed your anniversary, I'm sure you can celebrate later."

Dr. Spizer assured Darcy she would be able to go home soon, that her daughter and son could visit, so the doctor had obviously been filled in on Darcy's background. She didn't mention Steve. How much did this woman know?

The doctor said goodbye to Darcy "for now" and motioned Claire out into the hall.

Dr. Spizer assured her they would do all they could for Darcy and her family, and that, starting tomorrow when the story broke, there would be police protection here to fend off any "untoward, intrusive inquiries."

"First, of course," she told Claire, "we'll do a blood draw for tests to see if she has any drugs in her system. With those dilated eyes, it's a good bet. We will try to expedite lab results if it's anything unusual."

"We're so grateful to have her back," Claire said. "You have obviously been filled in by the authorities about her."

"Yes. Actually, I was also following the story in the media. I'm a certifiable news junkie—so I guess there's something off-kilter about all of us." She touched Claire's shoulder. "Detective Jensen said you are a forensic psych, so that will give you some knowledge about how things will go here. We'll start with her body, but we'll have to probe her mind, too."

"Anything I can do to help, to support her, please let me know."

"I have a sister I couldn't do without," the doctor said with a sharp nod. "I know it's hard, but try to make yourself—and her—at home."

It was after ten o'clock that night when a nurse came into the room to whisper to Claire that her husband was in the waiting area down the hall.

Darcy had gone to sleep after blood tests, and they had eaten a light meal, but Claire had just lain on the sofa bed wide-awake, thinking, worrying, wondering.

Though hesitant to leave Darcy in case she woke and wondered where she was, Claire hurried into the waiting room and into Nick's arms.

"How are Steve and the girls?" she asked.

"The girls are shook but both Kris and Brit stopped by

with little gifts and diversions. Steve has been booked. I got him bail bond through his company. He'll see a lawyer friend of mine tomorrow. He's been released, under Ken's temporary condition he not barge in here for twenty-four hours. I took him back to our house where he's trying to deal with Jilly and his own stupid behavior. He admitted to me he did confront Larry Ralston when he figured out from Heck that Fly Safe was hostile to Tara's butterfly farm. He admitted to me—not to the police—that he did have an argument with Ralston, shoved him around. Steve got a cut on his face there, then used a paper napkin from the bar to wipe the blood."

"And probably accidentally dropped it on his way out so the police could eventually find his DNA. Nick, I fear for Darcy's sanity already, and if she hears about Steve…"

He tugged her over to the table and pulled out chairs for both of them. At least this late, the area was deserted. "So fill me in on what's happened here so far," he said.

"I like her doctor, Lesley Spizer. They drew blood, did other kinds of tests. Results pending, at least I haven't heard. Dr. Spizer asked me for possible questions to ask Darcy, and she said I could sit in on that if I mostly listened and didn't prompt. I gave her some basic queries like 'Did you go anywhere but the Flutterby Farm? Did someone come to take the butterflies?' Darcy said someone came to take them, but she didn't know who. She said something about seeing people swimming in little pools, but she saw only their faces."

"Sounds delusional at best, but it's got to mean something. What else?"

"Questions like, 'What happened to your phone? Since you were late coming home, where were you?' Then I ran

out of questions except for going back in time to be sure
she has those memories—she knew Steve and Jilly, so...
Nick, I was terrified when she was missing, but I'm still
scared for her. Something awful happened, and she won't
be really safe until we—or Ken Jensen—find out what."

"I know, sweetheart, and—"

Dr. Spizer came into the room with her little laptop in
hand. "I heard your husband was here. Let me share some
prelim findings with both of you. I understand Darcy's
husband needs to be informed also, but Detective Jensen,
whom I called first with these results, tells me you can pass
on this early information to her husband."

Nick stood and shook the doctor's hand. She sat across
the table from them and lifted her laptop lid. The glow
from the screen lit her gray eyes.

"I asked the lab to rush the findings," she told them.
"Darcy had faint traces of a drug called propranolol in her
system. It's a beta blocker, fairly new, used to blunt post-
traumatic stress disease—and, frankly, to blunt stressful
memories."

"To make her forget what's happened," Claire said.

"Yes. It specifically targets trauma. It has even been
used for stage fright. I tend to think of it by the nickname
Prop—a prop for those who have nightmares and trauma.
Its most important uses are to help handle, even erase, such
disturbing and haunting events as war, accidents, rape and
natural disasters."

Claire gripped Nick's hand so hard he winced. He said,
"So it doesn't let the person calmly recall memories, but
actually buries them, so to speak."

"Exactly. But the sufferers may have flashbacks. Now
that she's off the drug, that could happen. But it's up to us

to pull those memories out, help her deal with them. And, of course, in this case it may be evidence for a crime.

"Claire," she went on, looking now only at her, "you mentioned her speaking of seeing people in pools, water, a dolphin. These could be fragmentary memories of where she was and what happened. However, you will be relieved to know that the physical examination we did indicates she was not forcefully violated, nor did she have any signs of a struggle. No bruises or cuts, nothing under her fingernails. She's been hydrated but not well-fed, I would surmise from findings," she said, looking down at the screen again. "It won't take long for us to reverse that, so I hope we can discover why she was given the Prop. What was it her abductors were trying to make her forget?"

"Tomorrow, we'll begin listening and counseling sessions, which I will allow you to attend if you let me take the lead and only weigh in if I ask you."

"Yes. Yes, thank you. Might I sit behind her and raise my hand if I can think of something to say or advise you?"

The doctor's gray eyes narrowed for a moment. She looked at Nick, who shrugged as if to say, *That's my Claire.*

"Yes, all right," the doctor said with a curt nod. "You handled it very well when she asked why the policeman was in the hall and you assured her it was standard procedure for this area."

"I hate to lie to her. But, Doctor, I will do anything to help and protect her. We were blessed to get her back— physically. Now we have to get her back mentally and emotionally, too."

Claire finally fell asleep on the hard sofa. The room wasn't really dark the way she liked it with the lighted

movement on the monitors and the muted glow in the attached bathroom. After much agitation, Darcy was on her
back, breathing in a regular pattern. It had to be long after
midnight. Of course, as in every hospital where Claire had
been, nurses came and went all the time, but at least they
didn't wake Darcy. But what were her dreams that made
her so restless? Maybe that was what they had to find out—
and then face.

Claire shook her head at the thought that there were two
of them here who needed help—the sister with the possible
PTSD med in her and the one with the narcolepsy meds.
What a pair, always had been. What would Mother have
thought? But then she'd had her problems, too, and could
have used tests and meds and counseling.

She thought of Tara and Will. Nick had said he would
tell them that Darcy had come back, but that she had some
kind of amnesia. He promised to thank them for all their
help and support and ask them not to talk to the media if
they came calling one way or the other.

She had also told Nick that she suspected Lexi's horrible
doll of perhaps spying on them, though they could hardly
blame Nita and Bronco for giving it to them. Someone
very clever—diabolical—must have seen Nita as a perfect,
naive way to get that doll into their lives.

"Someone must have set them up—set Darcy up—us,
too," Nick had said. "Someone who knows too much about
us. So that pretty little doll violates US privacy laws? Damn,
I'll look into that, but first things first with Steve and the
girls. You just take care of Darcy."

"What if that doll is kind of like a Trojan horse?" Claire
had asked. "You know, we take it in because it's such a gift,

and Lexi needs it, but its insides are full of deceit—a trap.
If we could just trace who set up Nita to 'win' that."

"But if I tell anyone—Ken, especially—and he takes the
doll to tear into it..."

"I know. I know," she'd said, holding to him after the
doctor had left. "Then Lexi might go off the deep end,
too."

Darcy's cry jolted Claire from that memory.

"The fish doesn't have much room to breathe!" she cried.

Claire got up and bent over her. She was thrashing, mur-
muring. It was suddenly like she used to comfort Darcy
after Daddy had left them, when Mother used to get so
strange, sobbing at night, crying out like—like this. But
Darcy was so young then...

"It's all right, Darcy. I'm here with you. Everything's
all right."

"It isn't! There's not much room, and that dolphin needs
to come up for air. I do, too—a mask, a mask on my face.
Not Halloween."

"No, it's not Halloween. You don't have a mask on your
face now. It's all right."

"People are floating. They can't breathe in there. Stop
it. I don't want to die!"

"You won't. I'm here. You're here with me now, and—"

The door to the room opened. A shaft of light from the
hall sliced across Darcy's bed.

"Her blood pressure..." the nurse who came said. "I'm
not to sedate her, but—"

"She's all right," Claire told the nurse. "Darcy, everything is all right now," Claire crooned to quiet her. Amazingly, Darcy nodded and went almost instantly to sleep. The
nurse took her pulse, reread the monitors and finally, with

a nod, went out. But Claire heard her tell someone in the hall before the door closed, "The doctor was right. PTSD from something terrible that happened."

But, Claire thought, that memory—something horrible and haunting during her abduction—was buried deep. At least, thank God, Darcy wasn't.

CHAPTER TWENTY-FIVE

"I hate to sound like I'm giving medical advice," Ken Jensen told Claire and Nick the next morning in the visitor's room on Darcy's floor at the hospital. "But I think it would be smart if you kept Darcy here where they can observe her for a while. They have excellent treatment and follow-up counseling once they have the diagnosis. They call this section the voluntary crisis stabilization unit, and I'd advise you to take advantage of that."

Claire was grateful that Nick pulled his chair tight to hers across the table from Jensen. *At least,* she told herself, *Nick is here to help.* She hadn't wanted to face Jensen alone, even though he was back in civilian clothes, not the uniform that had suddenly seemed so formal and imposing.

"Ken," Nick said, "do you have any reason to believe Darcy would not be safe if she were to stay with us or at her own home?"

"If you're asking if we've figured out what really happened to her, where she's been or with whom and why—

no. But you have to admit she has a volatile husband at least."

Nick frowned. "Wouldn't you be if your wife suddenly disappeared and didn't show up for days?"

Claire gently kneed Nick under the table. She wanted to explode at Ken, but they needed him on their side for more than one reason.

"Yeah, I would," Ken said with a sigh that seemed to deflate his rigid posture. "But I'd also trust the police. It's not like we—and I—haven't come through for you before."

Claire said, "Nick, I think Darcy could benefit from being here longer, even if I leave. I'll come back and forth, maybe still sit in for her sessions. If it wasn't for Lexi and Jilly, I'd stay another night, but the nurse came right in when she became distressed."

Ken turned to her again. "I have a detailed transcript from the doctor, but you mentioned she said some things to you?"

"From an apparent deep sleep last night, she started raving about a dolphin not having enough air to breathe. She also sounded panicked about herself wearing a mask. But it wasn't Halloween, she said. She mentioned that there were people swimming but she could only see their faces."

"Weird," Ken said. "Especially since we found Larry Ralston drowned and he had that whole dolphin business before his death."

"There's also the butterfly-dolphin link," Claire said, "that they both have the power of suspended animation. Darcy did say someone came to get the butterflies. I'll bet it was the falcate orangetips. I asked her, but she can't recall who it was. That was in the ambulance yesterday. If we could just find out who links those butterflies and the dolphins. And that—right, Nick?—has to be Lincoln Yost."

"I need to sweat him some," Ken said. "You two just steer clear of him—out of my way. So, Nick, I see you're not representing your brother-in-law. Can you tell me why?"

"Obviously, not a good idea to have any conflict of interest figure in with judge and jurors, for starters. I have another case pending as soon as this damn approaching hurricane does its worst and the court system is up and running again. Besides, Claire and I have been through so much. Our first concern is our children, especially right now our daughter, Lexi, who was abducted two years ago. How's that for a list?" Nick demanded, standing.

Claire started to speak, but, rising to his feet also, Ken cut in. "You have a good reputation for wins, Counselor. Do you think representing Steve Stanley might disrupt that?"

"You know better than to believe that—to even ask. Circumstantial evidence has turned out to mean nothing before. However distraught he has been, I'm confident Steve would never kill someone."

"Unless it was an accident. Look, Nick," Ken said, holding up both hands like a traffic cop, "we both have to be on the side of the law, however hard that is sometimes. And that means I am on your and Claire's side—Darcy and her husband, too—and I hope you realize that. Got to go, back to finding out where Darcy's been, who drugged her up, not to mention special assignment plans for this approaching storm. I hope, after everything is settled, we can still be friends."

Ken thrust out his hand, and Nick shook it. Claire extended hers, too. It was as if they had made a three-way pact.

When Nick said no more, Claire told Ken, "We'll let

you know if we hear or learn anything that could help. There have to be answers out there—and someone who took her, but why?"

Claire had decided to go home after sitting in on Darcy's first therapy session. Darcy had offered nothing new, but had repeated about the dolphin swimming in a little space, about herself fearing she couldn't breathe, although tests had shown she had no respiratory problems.

Claire needed to spend time with Trey and the girls, especially since Steve had let Jilly stay at their house while he went home alone. Jace's wife, Brit, was coming to pick Claire up at the hospital so Nick didn't have to leave Lexi and Jilly again, since Nita had gone out to run some errands. Brit would then spend time with Jilly while Claire focused on Lexi, and tried to get that doll away from her.

Brit had been busy helping the zoo staff batten down the hatches for the animals in case the hurricane hit here. It had taken a turn that could mean it would indeed make landfall nearby. But Brit couldn't come until two, and Claire was starving, so she went down to the cafeteria.

She had barely sat down to eat at a small table in front of a huge glass window when a man sat down beside her.

She gasped. "Oh, Will! What are you doing here?"

"Actually hoping I could get upstairs to see you or even Darcy, but that didn't work out. Nick told me she was being treated here. He said she's responding, but how is she doing right now?"

"He was going to call Tara, too, since you have both been so great."

He reached out to cover her left wrist with his hand. He was trembling.

"Claire, is she really all right? Nick said she was somewhat disturbed. What did he mean? Was she harmed?"

"We don't want any details made public. It's enough the media has celebrated that she's back safe and sound. At least they didn't blast it far and wide that she's in the psych ward for observation—just observation, Will," she insisted, though that wasn't quite true.

"Safe, but not sound?"

"She's had some trauma. Can't recall things."

"I was hoping she could. Any mention of who visited the butterfly house that day?"

"No. Will, like us, you have to let the police do their duty. We are blessed she's back."

"But to have her husband up for that murder... The poor girl."

"We haven't told her that yet. Steve's coming here tomorrow, so he'll explain to her. Hopefully, the police will get Larry Ralston's real killer, or she'll be shattered again."

"I know you will take care of her. Jilly, too. If Steve should go AWOL, so to speak, don't let him take Darcy's daughter. As it stands now, the child, maybe Darcy, too, are better off with you than him. But someone must pay for whatever happened to her."

Claire nodded and sat there stunned at Will's seething anger. He got up, squeezed her shoulder and walked out. It was heartwarming that Will cared that much, but was it too much?

At home that evening, Claire spent time with Trey while Brit regaled Lexi and Jilly with stories about the zoo animals. Nick and Claire put their son to bed, then Claire finally took Lexi off to her and Nick's bedroom.

Claire had insisted that the doll Cindy stay behind and listen to the zoo stories, which upset Lexi, but she had to get her alone without that eavesdropping little monster. Yet how to proceed, because the last thing she needed was for Lexi to implode. No, the last thing she needed was that thing spying on them more, if that was what had been going on. But could she gamble on telling her volatile little girl the truth?

"Sweetheart," Claire began, patting a place next to her on the recliner Nick sometimes liked to read in, "let's sit here, just you and me, like in the good old days."

Still pouting, Lexi joined her but didn't cuddle up, despite Claire putting her arm around her.

"The good old days, like when?" the child challenged, and Claire almost burst into tears at the truth of that. Calm, normal times had been few. Even her marriage to Nick had been forced at first, and there had been one danger after the other. But now that they had Darcy back—at least, once they found out who had taken her and had them arrested and Darcy returned to normal...

"The good *new* days are what I'm really interested in," Claire said, trying to keep her voice steady and light. She forced a little smile. "Days when we just rely on each other and ourselves, not on pretend things, not on outsiders."

"Outsiders like my daddy, Jace? What about Brit? 'Cause she's with Jilly."

"Of course your daddy isn't an outsider. He is very special to you, and he is a friend to Dad Nick and to me. Our friends, like Brit and Kris, are not outsiders. Not Bronco and Nita, either, because they are almost like family and are for sure our friends. Heck, too. But, in a way, your doll is an outsider. You know what I learned about her?"

"She is not! She knows all about me. We talk."

"But she isn't a real person. I learned that dolls like her are connected to people who are sometimes not our friends and family. It really isn't the doll talking but someone we don't know talks through the doll."

Crossing her arms over her chest, Lexi frowned up at Claire. "She is my friend. Nita is my friend, and she gave her to me."

"But Nita has no idea who gave the doll to her. I talked to Nita about that. She wanted you to have the doll, but she didn't know that kind of doll is made to listen to everything a family and their friends say, then maybe tell a bad person what is going on."

At least Lexi didn't react at first. She could see her thinking. *Please, God, let her have enough maturity and self-protective instincts to reason this out. Let me find the right words...*

"Is there some way to fix her?" Lexi asked. "Does she have a real brain or something?"

"As pretty as she is, she's like the voice on my cell phone. She listens, she can answer, give you information. But she's also making a recording of everything you say. But then, what if a bad person who made her—who is kind of like on the other end of a phone listening—wants to find out what we're saying? I think we could get your dad's friend Heck over here to take a look at her insides—"

"Like, cut into her?" Lexi demanded, and tears flew. "But she helps me, she likes to be part of our family and listen, she even tells me what to do!"

Claire pulled Lexi close and, finally, the child reached out for her and held to her hard.

"What kind of things does she tell you to do, sweetheart?"

"Like, go close to you and Dad when you're talking. Like where are you and Dad now? And she said don't worry, because if I do what she says, someday Aunt Darcy will come home—and now she did, see?"

Claire pulled Lexi onto her lap as if she were a baby. Indeed a monster in their midst, planted there, not by Nita but by someone diabolical, who knew entirely too much about them. Because of something in Nick's law practice? To keep a close eye on their search for Darcy? But why? Why?

CHAPTER TWENTY-SIX

Nick held Claire tight in bed that night.

"So I'll get Heck here in the morning to take a look at the doll's insides," he promised. "I know you won't like it, but he said not to tamper with the batteries or anything so we don't let on to whoever's watching that we know what's going on."

"I think we have the story on what that thing has been doing. And despite what she says, Lexi will have a fit if we dissect it. I mean, she gives it baths, dresses it. She'd see it was cut up, taken apart... I wish we could just cut off whoever programmed it and has evidently been listening."

"True, we don't need a meltdown."

"I think we can write a script that Lexi—all of us—could go along with. Like maybe Lexi could tell the doll that she wants to run away. That she's alone with the doll somewhere. Of course, Lexi wouldn't be waiting there, but we would. Maybe Ken, too."

"My love, not with this storm coming. We may not see

the worst of it, but we're going to get hit with something. Besides, Ken doesn't have time for something like that."

"But maybe it could lead us to who took Darcy?" She sighed. "If there's any chance the two things are related." All she wanted to do was find her sister, and her tired brain was making connections and grasping at straws in a desperate attempt to make sense of everything that was happening.

"Ken swore he'd charge us with interference, at the least, if we start mixing in again."

"But that's just the point. With this storm and now trying to track what happened to Darcy—Larry Ralston's death and who knows what else—as you said, Ken doesn't have the time for something like this. Nick, I repeat, maybe we can find out on our own who's behind this darn doll at least."

"Listen to me," he insisted, and gave her a little squeeze. "We have Darcy back. Yes, she needs help, but she's back and she's alive. I'm going to consult with Steve's lawyer so we can get his charges dropped. He admits he did have a row with Ralston, but left him very much alive. Then he intentionally picked a fight with a guy in a bar so that he had an excuse for his bruises. The fact the ME couldn't exactly pinpoint the time of death doesn't help, but we'll find a way to defend Steve—and to help Lexi. That has to be enough for now."

"But it isn't. Maybe we can find out where Darcy was and with whom. Because whoever had her could have killed Larry. The dolphin connection is too weird not to mean something. And those butterflies. I know Ken said he'd rattle Linc Yost's cage again, but we could, too, so—"

"No! We need to hunker down here, prepare for the storm. I can see your talking to Lexi about the doll, trying to convince her that someone bad is listening. But not something to lure the mastermind behind that doll—to bring him here."

"Bring him *or her.*"

"You're not thinking of Tara? Claire, springing traps like that can mean the trapper gets caught, too, so—I repeat— we're going to sit tight here."

"I don't think Will's sitting tight, though. He was furious Darcy came back disturbed. I suppose you're right about just hunkering down for now, but I really have a feeling Will isn't. He seems kind of like a white knight ready to charge in when it comes to Darcy, and, even with Ken on the case, I think we need that. Longtime bachelor that Will is, I still can't help but wonder if he could have been secretly in love with her."

"Pretty strange to think how close we are to our loved ones," Mitch told Jace as they flew out over the west coast of Florida toward the eye wall of approaching Hurricane Jenny, now a Cat 4 with winds at nearly one hundred fifty miles per hour. "Only we're miles up, not miles away," he added.

They were using the pilot sound system, so their crew didn't hear. The staff on board were ready to do their readings and assessments once they dropped the probes into the volatile atmosphere. They already knew that the waters of the gulf were so warm this late in August that it would kick up any precipitation into a deluge.

As he scanned his readouts, Jace told him, "Now that they've got Darcy back, I'd like to think it's a fairy-tale ending. Without an ogre under the bridge this time."

"You mean like when Lexi was kidnapped? Yeah, your little girl's been through a lot. I'm sure she's ecstatic to have her aunt back. And Markwood's house is storm-ready, so

I'm grateful they're letting Kris as well as Brit stay there if this thing takes a westward turn."

"Here we go," Jace said.

The plane fought its way into the outer bands of the eye wall, then, finally, after a teeth-jarring ride, they entered the eye of the storm into the amazing peace and a sun-lit, blue-sky day. Damn, Jace thought, but these storms were like life—rough, then calm, then brutal again.

Claire could not stand the waiting for what would come next. She phoned Tara to be sure she was hunkered down. Nothing new or unusual there, though the woman told her she and her friend would probably go to a public shelter when they opened. Claire assured her that Darcy was making progress. When she shared that someone had pulled up the botanical butterfly attractions in their backyard, Tara was quite distressed.

"Oh, what's the message there?" she asked. "You just be careful, and keep an eye on Darcy, too. There is some piece missing to this puzzle, but even if we had it, would the picture fit together? Please give Darcy my best. I suppose—well, she won't ever want to come back to work for me again and now she has her husband to worry about. But thank you for calling, and do let me know if there's anything I can do, after the storm, I mean."

After the storm... The words echoed in Claire's head. Would this puzzle be solved, the storms of life ever be over? At least her family bred strong women. Lexi had been through difficult times, as had Claire—Darcy, of course, even their poor mother. Three generations of her family's women had had it tough, but they had fought back, each in her own way. And now Lexi had promised she would listen to Claire about the doll. Claire had promised Nick she would not try to lure the person pulling the doll's strings out of hiding—yet—but she could at least mislead him or her.

She went down to the Florida room where Lexi was sitting with the doll, though she didn't have it on her lap and wasn't holding it for once. Claire crooked her finger to request Lexi come to her and, without the doll, they went into the library while the TV weather station went on about the approaching storm.

"Okay," Claire told her, keeping her voice down even here. Nick had asked Heck to sweep the entire house for listening devices a little while ago, but she wasn't taking any chances. "Are we ready to have your doll hear what we want someone who is spying on us to hear?"

"Can't we just say, 'Why are you using my doll? Why are you such a bad, nosy person?'"

"Wouldn't it be a great world if people just told the truth and didn't hide and do bad things?"

"I want to be like you, Mommy, when I grow up. You know, like, be able to help people, like help Aunt Darcy, to be able to look at a person and tell what they are really thinking—if they really like me or not, if they tell lies."

Sadly, in this world, Claire thought, it took a lot more than body language to read people, sometimes even those you thought you knew.

"All right, let's make our plan," Claire told Lexi, opening a piece of paper where she had printed their little script quite large. "We want to keep the doll away where she can't hear us make plans for the storm. So you just say, 'I am putting you to bed for a while because you are tired, Cindy. I will wake you up soon.' But then, like you promised me, you put her to bed in your room and you and Jilly don't say anything around her until after dinner—maybe longer."

"But what if she tries to talk to me?"

"You just tell her you don't feel good right now and, 'Cindy, I'll wake you up later, but you need to sleep now.'"

"But not be dead, right?"

Claire gasped. "No. We don't want— I mean, no, just sleep."

Claire soon felt like a party planner or maybe an air traffic controller as she coordinated where their "hurricane guests" would sleep away from windows, though she trusted the hurricane glass—well, mostly. But this was projected to be a big storm, and they were going to feel the effects of it, even if they didn't take a direct hit. The governor had declared a state of emergency. There had been mandatory evacuations of outlying islands and coastal buildings. Public shelters at Germaine Arena and the big First Baptist Church would be opened soon, and stores were out of necessities. Nursing homes were being evacuated, and the public was told to expect at least seven hours of hurricane-force winds wherever Jenny made landfall.

But this really was the relative calm before the storm, Claire thought. Despite the fact they would soon have a houseful of people, Bronco and Nita had gone out again to bring food from their house and finish boarding up the windows. Kris and Brit had left together to pretty much do the same to Jace and Brit's condo. Heck and Nick had gone to the law offices to, as they said, batten down the hatches there. So this last evening of relative calm, it was just, at least momentarily, Claire and the kids.

Lexi smiled at Claire. "One good thing, Mommy, is that

Heck didn't have to hurt Cindy when he checked her out today. I hope her feelings aren't hurt because she has to be alone a lot more now."

Yes, that was one break today, Claire thought as she hugged Lexi. Heck had made sure the doll didn't have a hidden camera. What a great solution this had been to trust Lexi to understand, to help. She was her mother's daughter indeed.

Both girls were exhausted, and Claire wanted them to get all the sleep they could before the howling winds and torrential rain hit, so she got them ready for bed. No problem with Trey. Amazingly, nothing bothered him when it was time to sleep.

Claire had made another of several calls to the Behavioral Health section of the hospital, and this time had been able to talk to Darcy instead of the nurse or Dr. Spizer. Darcy had talked to Steve today, too, though he still had not told her he was out on bail for murder and had promised to see her tomorrow "come hell or high water."

"Glad this hurricane didn't come calling when I was missing," Darcy told Claire on the phone.

"The hospital is a safe place to ride it out. Dr. Spizer says it's all up to code."

"But I'd rather be with all of you. Steve says you'll all be there together. Claire, I want out of here."

"But the doctor says you're remembering more, and that's good."

"None of it makes sense. None of it pinpoints a place or person. It's— I keep thinking it's like I was in a hospital while I was gone, but the police checked that out. Not in any hospital around here."

"A hospital, why? How? What do you recall that makes you say that?"

"People in breathing machines—like those old iron lungs we saw in pictures when people had polio way back when. People in lab coats, like here. Blood tests, or something like that. They even found pinpricks in my arm by a vein, but so what, since they've stuck me for blood here and say I had some drug in me to make me forget. I hope it wears off."

"I'm sure it will. And when they release you, if you want, you are welcome to stay here instead of going home right away."

"Jilly and Lexi will start school right after Labor Day, so I'll have to be home then. She can ride a school bus this year, but, like you and Jace—I mean, Nick—I'd rather drive her, drop her off and pick her up."

A mixed message there, Claire thought with a jolt. At least Darcy was clear on the details of Jilly's new school year, but she had said Jace instead of Nick's name.

"I'll call you soon, or you can call here," Claire assured her. "I'll be so happy to have my sister back."

"But I hear the phone lines may go down—cell towers, too, if it stays a Cat 4. I—I think I just heard that on TV."

"Stay safe, Darce. Love you," Claire told her, sounding to herself as if they were kids comforting each other again.

"Love you, too!"

Claire headed for the kitchen, hoping again they'd have enough canned food if—when—the power went. At least Nita, Brit and Kris were bringing an ice chest with some of their perishables, and they'd have a lot of mouths to eat things up fast if the power went off. She planned to fry and bake meat right now so they wouldn't have to worry about cooking it on the grill outside. They'd have a good old party, waiting for the hurricane to blow through.

She thought she heard the doorbell, so maybe someone

was back already. Their guests had plans to park down the street where there were no tree limbs to fall, but of course they'd bring their food here first to unload.

It crossed her mind that the last time she'd opened the door alone, it had been Darcy, back from the dead—or at least, thank heavens, from the missing.

She snapped on the light and looked out the library window.

It was Will Warren, fighting the wind, holding plastic wrap around a large item. "Oh!" she cried aloud. "That painting!"

She unlocked and opened the door, which nearly blew in on her.

"Will? What are you doing out in this?"

"My house isn't safe, so may I leave this here? And I have a note on it that if anything happens to me, I want Darcy to have it since it resembles her."

"Here, bring it in. Of course. But what could happen to you? Where are you going to stay?" she asked, thinking what problem would one more person be, but something kept her from instantly inviting him. A vibe? A hunch, or her long-honed forensic psych intuition?

"Just rest it here in the hall," she said, helping him to bring it in and lean it against the wall. Together they closed the door against the wind. The blurry, plastic-muted image of his grandmother—of Darcy—stared out at her, holding her butterfly net.

And then Claire saw what must have been making her nervous. Will was trembling—understandable enough with this dark storm coming—but it was more than that. From behind the wrapped portrait, he drew a gun and pointed it at her.

CHAPTER TWENTY-SEVEN

Claire just stared. It was a small, square black gun, but the pinpoint of its barrel seemed as big as a rain barrel.

"It's all right, Claire," Will said, locking the safety bolt on the front door. "I've seen everyone else go out, waited. I swear to you I will not hurt you or anyone here, as long as you cooperate—help me. Now where's that doll Lexi told me about on the phone?"

"You—you talked to Lexi on the phone?"

"Earlier today. What luck that she answered the phone herself, but I was calling your cell and she said you were in the shower. I told her—and she did remember who I am from story times—that I was friends with her aunt Darcy and that I had been helping you to look for her and to keep our phone call a secret."

Claire just gaped at him, trying to take in what he was saying—and what it could mean.

"I assured her," he went on, sounding both earnest and calm, "that her aunt would be fine, be home soon and that the person who had hurt her would pay for it. And I told her that was all a secret, too."

Thoughts bombarded Claire. Had Will been the one who planted the doll here through Nita? There had been newspaper articles about how Nick and Claire had helped their nanny, Nita, when a body was found in her house several months ago. Had he observed Nita, saw she was pregnant, then arranged for her to win the doll? To spy on them? So had he taken Darcy? If so, he might intend to destroy the doll now so it could not be traced to him. Strange, but despite the fact that gun was pointed at her, she didn't think he'd shoot her. And yet she couldn't take that chance. If only Nick or the others would get back soon, but then what would Will do?

"It will save us time if I have the doll," Will said.

"I can go get it, bring it out here."

"Hardly. Claire, I know you are as smart as Darcy is sweet. I can't let you call for help, and I don't plan to wake the girls. Take me to the doll, and we won't bother them at all. I assume from watching their bedroom light go out they're in bed. It's late."

"Were you watching from where you yanked up the butterfly flowers and bushes?"

He frowned. "Never would I do that, and you must not think so. But we'll settle with who did soon."

Strange, but once again she believed him. Tara would never do that. Did that leave Clint Ralston or that Jedi lackey of his?

"Will, I can't take you to the girls when you have that gun."

"I'm here to help, really to show and tell you things so

that you understand. So that you can tell Darcy when she's better, tell Jilly, too."

"Tell them what?"

"What I did for them—am going to do. Justice. You and Nick—that detective, too—all believe in justice, and you will have it. Do not be afraid and do as I say, and everything will go well. Now!"

He raised the gun. "Get me that doll," he said. "It's served its purpose, and the girls have each other. They'll get over its loss. Actually, you should have drowned that thing days ago, but I know you were looking for Darcy, too, and you probably thought the doll could distract or help the girls. But I have the answers. Now, move!"

His voice, his tone, had changed. For the first time, she was terrified of him. Her thoughts flew to Trey, asleep in his bed in the nursery across from the girls' room. Will hadn't mentioned him, seemed unconcerned or ignorant about him. But what if this was a ruse and he tried to take or hurt the girls? Could she grab a lamp from Lexi's dresser, hit him with it? Yet best not to wake the girls, alarm them—and maybe wake Trey, and then Will would have another way to make her do anything he wanted.

"Do you just want the doll, and then you'll go?" she asked, her voice quavering.

"Yes, I'll go. I need to give you answers, have you be my witness, then tell Darcy."

For some reason, as cryptic and confusing as that seemed, she believed him. Get him the doll. Listen to his story. Get him out of here. She suddenly knew with such conviction and clarity that he would not hurt the girls, hopefully not hurt her, either, if she was to be his witness, his mouthpiece. She only hoped that for some reason he did not hurt himself when all was said and done here. That portrait must mean so much to him. Was he giving away his dearest possessions? Was he going to make some terrible admission and then kill himself or someone else who had been behind Darcy's disappearance?

He followed her through the house and down the hall. Trey's door was barely ajar. Thank heavens, silence from within. The door to the girls' room stood open. The dim night-light glowed golden. They both slept peacefully, faceup, in the matching twin beds with a small table and unlit lamp between them.

Hoping he'd stay in the doorway, Claire mouthed and gestured, "Wait there." He stopped one step in.

She tiptoed between the beds and carefully lifted the doll from where it lay outside the covers by Lexi's feet. She hadn't tucked it in, hardly had it near her. Smarter girl than a smart doll, once things were explained to her.

She turned back to take the doll to Will, wanting to get him out of here, out of the room, even out of the house. But she saw he had come farther and stood at the foot of Jilly's bed, just staring raptly at her. And he was crying.

Despite the fact he held the gun, though not pointed at anyone now, she tugged at his arm to leave. Should she lash out at him now? Go for the gun? But no, not here at least.

He sniffed hard and pushed her, still holding the doll, from the room.

"I take it the others will be back soon," he whispered as they stopped in the kitchen, and she put the doll on the counter. He seized a terry-cloth towel from the rack and wrapped the doll in it one-handed, still holding the gun. He whispered, "Wrap it in more towels, maybe tin foil." She thought the wind and thudding rain probably muted their voices for the recording device in the doll, but she did as he said. And, after all, since Will was possibly behind the doll, what did he care anymore? But then perhaps he had someone monitoring it for him, since he obviously still held a normal day job—if anything was normal here anymore.

He motioned her down to the other end of the kitchen. "I've written a note to leave for your husband," he told her, his voice still a mere whisper. She had to almost read his lips.

"But you said you'd explain things to me, then leave."

"I am leaving and I will explain, but I must show you things, not just tell. You will then be the witness, the conduit, the testifier to justice and their destruction."

She pictured little Trey again, sleeping, peaceful, and the girls, so sweet. Will had said Darcy was sweet.

"I'm not leaving this house with you."

"You must. You must to understand, to keep Darcy safe in the future in case he doesn't think she's forgotten enough."

"Will, who wants her to forget?"

"You must go with me now. Your children will be all right, for surely your husband and others will be back soon."

"You— Then, you are the one who's been listening through this doll?"

He hesitated a moment. "I wish I could have gotten one for Jilly, too, but Darcy told me some backstory about Lexi's being kidnapped once—before Darcy disappeared, of course. I don't want you wounded, hurt and bleeding on our journey, so don't even think of trying to take this gun. You come now, or I'll take the girls, too. Claire, I swear, I'll have you back safe soon."

"Back soon, like Darcy? Drugged? Memory erased?"

"I will tell you one more time. I did not—would not—hurt Darcy. Now you must come with me willingly or—or another way. Yes, I arranged for the doll here and figured, from things Darcy had told me, your daughter would be the best recipient. And Darcy mentioned your nanny, Nita, was pregnant and that seemed a good conduit to get the doll here. I needed to keep track of what you were doing to trace Darcy, so I could help, lay my own plans and trap. I paid a friend to monitor the doll for me, and I don't want him to hear anything else through it now. Claire, we are leaving immediately—now!"

She thought to bluff him, to refuse. But she feared he might take Jilly then, even Lexi, and they'd both been traumatized too much.

She stared as he fished a business-size envelope out of his jacket pocket and propped it up on the counter. She saw printed on it Nick Markwood.

"That's not supposed to be from me, is it?" she asked.

"I signed it. It explains you will be back soon with enough information to free Darcy's husband from those charges and to have the mastermind of all this ungodly butterfly and dolphin research—and Darcy's drugging—arrested and put away for life, if he's alive then."

"Do you mean Lincoln Yost? Has he made money from his research from someone rich and powerful—surely not you?"

"An excellent guess, but a bit off. We must go now. If you don't, we'll go get the girls, and they don't need to see where we're going. They wouldn't understand, and it would terrify them even more than it evidently haunts Darcy."

Claire realized the portrait in the hall would testify to who had been here, even without the note. So Will had discovered who took Darcy and he wanted her to know, to see, perhaps, where he was holding that person captive?

She grabbed her purse where she'd left it in the kitchen and an umbrella—the one Darcy had come home with. At least she hadn't taken her cell phone out of her purse. After locking the door with a gun pointed at her, trusting Nick would be home soon to care for the children, she went out into the storm with Will.

"It's a monster, and it's going to hit Naples, at least damn near," Jace told Mitch as the most recent storm readings were relayed to them in the cockpit and then back to NOAA so public announcements and warnings could be prepared. "I don't care what they say, I'm tempted to call Brit when we land and tell her to hunker down. Wish we could just parachute out, not have to fly this big baby back to Tampa, then sit it out there in case we're needed again."

"Yeah, right. Pie in the sky, like they say, but we have a job to do," Mitch muttered, nodding so hard his tinted goggles bounced on his nose. "And if the phone lines and cell towers go down, it may be a while before we know things. At least—after all you and I've been through, facing the enemy, combat—it's good to know we have people we love, ones we want to go home to."

Nick drove himself and Heck into the garage. Heck had decided to leave his car parked up tight against the back brick wall of the law firm, hoping that would provide some shelter from possible flying debris, so Nick had brought him here to join the others who would be arriving soon.

"Boss, I'm really worried that Gina decided to stay in Miami for this big blow. At least it looks like it might not be as bad there. She's really dedicated to her hospital work. Something else I haven't told you and Claire—I'm gonna give her a ring for her birthday next month, ask her to marry me. If she can't or won't move here when she's ready for medical residency, I may have to move there—but I could still work for you, consult, drive here if I need to."

"I'd hate to lose you," Nick told him as they got out of the car and the garage door closed behind them to stop the rush of wind. How Nick wished South Florida had basements with protection and flooring overhead. The price—one of them—you paid to live in paradise.

"But it's more important that you and Gina be together, live together," he tried to assure Heck. "Claire and I have been through so much apart and together. We'll ride out this storm and any others on the horizon together, and I'm sure you and Gina will, too."

Nick popped his trunk and took one of the boxes of food and supplies Heck had put there. They each carried a box into the house, set them down on the island in the kitchen, then Heck went back out for more. Nick looked in the Florida room, but it was quiet there. This late, Claire probably had checked in on Trey—who would be in la-la land for the night. He was a very talented sleeper, and Nick wished he still had that in him.

He saw an envelope propped up on the counter with his name printed on the front. It wasn't Claire's writing. Whose and what?

"Just put this down here, too, boss?"

"Yeah, fine. I've got to go find Claire and check in on the kids. She probably fell asleep in the girls' room or is with Trey," he added, glancing at the kitchen clock. Only nine thirty, but yeah, the kids would have been tucked in by now.

"Make yourself at home, Heck," he said, taking the letter out of the envelope. It wasn't sealed. "Be back in a sec. Get something to drink out of the fridge."

He headed for the library and noticed the large item wrapped in heavy plastic in the hall. He turned on another light. It was that portrait of Will Warren's grandmother that looked like Darcy, so he must've stopped by.

He hit the lights in the library and opened the letter, skimming to the bottom for the signature. Yes, Will had dropped that off. This was not printed by hand but typed. It must explain about the portrait, ask them to keep it safe.

He read just a few lines and raced out into the hall. Down to the girls' room. No Claire. The kids sleeping. No doll for once.

He opened Trey's door. The little guy was lying on his back, breathing in regular rhythm. Safe. The kids were safe.

He tore toward the master bedroom. She had to be there, maybe in the shower. No one in the bathroom, not in bed. He even looked under the bed, in the closet.

"Claire," he whispered, but he knew now, he sensed, she wasn't here. Ken Jensen, not to mention everyone who would be here soon to sit out the storm, would not believe this. He didn't believe this.

He skimmed the letter again.

I know who took Darcy and he will pay. After Claire understands and can explain, I will see that she returns safely and soon with information about what happened to Darcy and information to free Steve from the murder charges.

It is the only and best thing I can do for Darcy. When I am gone, assure Darcy and Jilly that I love them, that I would—and might—die for them.

Do not try to contact me. I will not have access to my phone, and if it sounded, it could give me away.

I do not need the doll anymore to watch over Jilly and Darcy's family. I have found answers another way. Someday, some way, I will send Jilly more than the living toy I sent Lexi.

In haste to get this over, to see it all end,
William Warren

CHAPTER TWENTY-EIGHT

Claire now wished she'd fought Will for the gun. He held it on her, insisted she put handcuffs on and lie in the back seat of his car. If only Nick would get home now!

Will tied her feet together and strapped her down with all three seat belts. Raising her voice to be heard above the drumming of rain and the *whap, whap* of windshield wipers, she asked him where they were going.

"You'll see. It will all make sense then. It's an important step, one of our two stops tonight before I take you back home. I need to concentrate on driving in this rain, but it will be our friend, our ally—the element of surprise, though I must admit, I planned the timing. When we are there, I'll explain. I've arranged to get that watchdog Jedi Brown out of our way. As for your being tied, I just don't want you to change your mind about helping me."

Help you? she thought. And they must be going to Clint Ralston's house, if Will had managed to get Jedi out of their way. She knew it was a huge risk to come with Will, but he had always seemed trustworthy, and he said he had answers. At least she had kept him from bringing the girls out into this dark storm to learn and face the horror of what had happened to Darcy.

After what she judged to be about twenty minutes, he parked the car and turned off the motor. By looking up, watching overhead traffic lights at intersections and recognizing some tall buildings, Claire had guessed they were now in a residential neighborhood a few blocks off the Tamiami Trail toward the Gulf of Mexico. At Clint Ralston's home?

Will got out into the rain, opened the door at her feet and leaned in. He unhooked the seat belts and freed her feet. She didn't see the gun now, but he must've had it on him.

"The blessing of this storm," he told her, "is that no one will be expecting us at the facility once we leave here."

"What facility? And where is here?" she demanded, looking around. Through the blur of rain on the car windows, as she sat up, she could see large houses looming, some with lights, some not.

"Barely two blocks from where the bastard held that memorial service for his brother. By the way, Steve did not kill that man, just roughed him up. I didn't kill him, either, before you and Nick found him—really. I did shove him, but it was an accident that he fell between the boat and dock, when he was going to toss me in. I swear it, Claire."

Despite the fact that she was sweating, chills racked her. Will had killed him—but not? She'd learned when people protested so vehemently—and swore it was true—they were often lying. And why was he so desperate to help Darcy? Again she agonized over whether he could have loved her, wanted her, then gone on a rampage when someone hurt her. If so, he'd done a better job finding who was responsible than she and Nick had, than Ken Jensen and the police, too.

Before she could ask him another question, Will went on. "Clint, alias Stanford Clinton, lives in walking distance of Doctors Pass. It was easy for him to have someone in his own boat loose those butterflies he got from somewhere. I suppose he was trying to cast blame on Tara or me for that butterfly release, but he'll pay the price now."

"Clinton arranged it from his own boat, had someone do that while he and Jedi were in plain sight at the service? And Clint Ralston's real name is Stanford Clinton?" Despite the handcuffs, she grabbed for his wrist and held tight.

"The other way around. Stanford Clinton is the name under which he runs his quite secret business. In a local facility, but with elite, rich customers from all over the US, even a few wealthy Germans who winter here and were taken in by his—well, his sales pitch of eternal life."

"Eternal life? He's a con man? He took Darcy, then handed her over or used her for his company's work somehow? Testing drugs on her?"

"Calm down. Think it through. I knew you would believe me, speak for me later when I'm gone."

"Are you saying someone else took Darcy? But whatever Clinton's name is—we're at his house?"

"The street behind his house," he said calmly, ignoring her other questions. "Wouldn't do, even in this big storm, to park right in front or even on his street. I'll get him and bring him here through the backyards. He thinks I have information he needs on the falcate orangetips from when I was researching my book. But actually, I knew so little about their potential until I talked to Tara, then to Linc

Yost, too. But I must go. I'm afraid you'll have to wait in the trunk, since I can't take you inside his mansion with me."

"Will, even if Jedi isn't there, doesn't Clint have a family at home?"

"I believe he's sent them north out of harm's way, the fool. I'll explain later—when he shows us his palace of horrors. You know, this storm is perfect for covering my tracks, a perfect setting for all this, worthy of a detective or gothic novel, one I could tell a tale about at story time. But I'll be with you, Claire. I'll protect you even if I wasn't able to save Darcy from all she went through."

"Will, wait!" she cried as he pulled her out into the driving rain. "Don't lock me in there. What if you don't come back?"

"I will. I will, that is, until I don't."

She was trying to process all that he had said to have some sort of comeback or plea not to leave her, to let her go home. He was speaking in riddles as if they were in some alternate universe where he was an all-knowing alien and she a visitor.

"Will, just tell me one more thing, then—please. Was Darcy just your friend? What was she to you that you outsmarted Nick and me, the police, all of us, and that you are taking revenge—I mean, seeking justice—for her?"

"In time," he told her, and gave her a boost up and lifted her legs in. "I swear to you I will be back shortly, and then you'll know and see it all."

"No, don't leave me in here!" she cried as he closed the trunk lid over her to trap her in an even darker dark.

At first, Nick went berserk. Trying not to wake the kids, he tore into every room in the house and looked everywhere again, though he knew Claire wasn't here. He explained to Heck, who turned on the outside lights, then searched Claire's car in the garage. Nick spread out the letter on the kitchen table, reading it again and again, searching for clues as to where they had gone. He needed to call Ken for help, but this seemed too impossible, too terrible.

"He must have forced her to leave," he told Heck, and collapsed in a chair. "Unless she was crazy enough to go with him. Maybe he threatened the kids."

"Maybe she knew you'd be back soon."

"She's been dying to keep looking for answers at any cost—but to leave the kids?"

He shook his head and shuddered. Claire off on some crusade again, wanting to right wrongs, or caught up in something over her head? Was there a curse on their marriage, on his love for her?

He jumped up. "Will may have turned off or ditched his phone so he can't be called or traced. His note said not to try to contact him, but he didn't say not to try to contact her. Unlike when Darcy was taken, I haven't seen her phone anywhere, but her purse is gone—like Darcy's."

He punched Claire's automatic number on his cell. It rang, rang. His gut twisted. He almost broke into tears. Her recorded voice came on: "Hi, this is Claire, but I'm unavailable right now, so please leave me a message—"

He punched it off. "I'll try again in a minute," he muttered. Again and again.

"There's some missing link," he went on, raking his fingers through his hair. "A piece of evidence to lead to whomever took Darcy. And to explain why Will Warren was so attached to her. I just pray Claire isn't going to pay a big price for getting those answers."

Claire could not recall a more pitch-black place. She tried to breathe slowly, calmly, to save the air in the trunk in case Will did not come back. And if not, who could she possibly scream to for help, especially in this storm? What if one of the tall palm trees blew down and crushed this car? People were hunkered down inside their houses or heading for shelters or even driving north or east, out of this area. They would be idiots to so much as walk a dog on this street with such danger looming.

She imagined she heard the muted music of her cell phone, but that might be wishful thinking, and it was in the back seat of the car anyway. It had only been for a moment in a slight lull in the rain.

Was Will going to kill Clint Ralston? No, he'd said he would make Ralston explain things, so it couldn't be that. Or maybe Will meant that he was going to force Ralston to show her where Darcy had been those lost eight days. Or was he only going to bring him out into the storm to make him confess he had taken Darcy and why? Would Will then disappear—it sounded that way—and trust her to deliver Ralston to the police with all she had learned?

The rain thudded so loud on the trunk that she felt she was in a huge drum. The wind seemed to rock the car. Or was that her mind, her fears? Here she had thought she might have to help poor Steve raise his two children when he was away on jobs, and now Darcy might have to help Nick. She should have fought Will for the gun when they were in the kitchen, when they were not near the children, but she had instinctively trusted him, so she must be crazy. And was he?

No. No! she told herself. Will seemed protective of her, no matter that she'd more or less been kidnapped. So could he have taken Darcy, stashed her someplace, given her that amnesia drug, then let her go? Again, that horrible story *The Collector* tormented her. Was all this the price she had to pay for answers about where Darcy had been?

Worse, she could just imagine what Nick would think when he got back home. Surely he was there by now. How had it come to this, and would Nick ever forgive her—again?

But she was sure she heard a voice, a man's. Was Will back? She heard a car door unlock. The car jerked as if someone got in, then a door slammed shut. The trunk opened and wind and rain swept in on her, but she was grateful.

"We have a guest with us, my dear," Will told her, and helped her out. "I believe he knows Nick better than he knew you. From what he told me in his futile protests, he dared to try to intimidate Nick when he visited his office by subtly threatening you and the children, so he'll pay for that, too."

He helped her out of the trunk and around to the back door of the car. He half helped her get in but pushed her down and fastened the seat belts over her again, then—as if he'd read her panicked mind—picked her purse off the floor when her phone music sounded, so maybe she *had* heard it before.

To her amazement, he answered it. The light of it made his face look like a fright mask. Was he disguising his true intent to harm Ralston and her? But she clung to the gut feeling that, however desperate, he was being helpful, wanting to protect Darcy, Jilly—even her.

"Nick, it's Will, and she's all right. I'll see that she gets back, and don't try to trace this call to Sarasota or pinpoint its location, because we're moving on now. Don't call again."

She lifted her head to see him toss the phone into the outer darkness where she heard a distinct splash, perhaps as it fell into a water-swept culvert or drain. He slammed the car door.

No sound from Ralston. He must be gagged, maybe unconscious. Will started the engine, drove into a driveway, backed out and turned the car around. She was pretty sure they went out the way they had come in. As they drove closer to a more lighted area, Claire saw it was indeed Clint Ralston in the front seat, trussed up with black strapping tape, a piece of it over his mouth, so no way she could talk to him about this. Maybe he did not know where he was going, either.

Nick caught a glimpse of himself in the bedroom mirror as he paced. So Claire was with Will, evidently as his prisoner, since he controlled her phone and seemed in charge. No good to have the police check Will's house. The man was too intelligent for that. He must have been behind Darcy's disappearance, but why?

Not only was Heck here but Steve had come back, too, and Nita and Bronco had arrived with supplies. Kris and Brit were coming first thing in the morning. But Nick just couldn't face anyone, at least not their friends. He could only pace back and forth from Trey's crib to the girls' room, to his and Claire's bed, and pray that she would be all right. Why hadn't she talked to him on the phone? Was she unconscious? Tied up? Or worse?

Ken would be busy dealing with the hurricane. If Nick told him Claire had been kidnapped, what would he say? What could he do? He hadn't been able to help Darcy. Nick thought he had never felt so panicked in his life—but then he remembered all the other times she had managed to get as deep into trouble as she was in his heart.

CHAPTER TWENTY-NINE

Steve stared in awe at the portrait Nick had unwrapped in the front hall. The others had gaped at it, too, then had the good sense to melt away, leaving Nick and Steve standing there alone to commiserate.

Nick could hear the others whispering in the Florida room, except he knew Nita had gone to look in on the sleeping kids again. Both Nick and Bronco had told her to go to bed. She was almost into her ninth month of pregnancy and was carrying a huge weight. People had even kidded her she must be carrying twins, but the ultrasound had shown one baby—a girl she was determined to name Clarita, in honor of her friend Claire.

"That painting's something," Steve said, still staring. "Wait till Darcy sees it—or maybe she has. I don't care if this is Will Warren's grandmother or the Queen of Sheba, the guy's a nutcase."

"I keep telling myself that Claire has great instincts about people. And I keep clinging to how calm Will sounded on her phone. He said she's all right, and he'd see that she gets back. I think he mentioned Sarasota as a diversion, because they couldn't be there already, since I wasn't gone that long. But then he said, 'We're moving on now,' and when I tried to call him back, her phone— Well, it doesn't even ring, like it's dead."

"You gotta call Detective Jensen," Steve said. "I don't care if there's a storm coming. He has to look for Will's car, since hers is still here. Cops need to check his house, see if Will has any ties to someone in Sarasota, even if it is a ruse. And can I read his note again? I swear to you, Nick, bad as it looks, I didn't kill Larry Ralston. He was alive when I stormed out, and if Will Warren has any kind of proof of that—damn, I'm just desperate. And," he said, throwing an arm around Nick's shoulders, "I'm a guy who knows how you feel."

"Yeah, I kept hoping she'd walk in the door. I'll call Ken, even if he hits the roof. I don't know what we'll tell the girls. With Claire gone, Darcy away... And if Will is the one who set up that doll—I want to trust him, but I just can't."

Claire's only consolation was that Clint Ralston seemed more scared than she was. Or maybe that was crazy of her, because he somehow knew what was coming. He was trying to talk through his gag, kept jerking around, though Will was concentrating on his driving again as, through the rain on the back car windows, she tried to figure out from traffic lights and road signs swinging in the wind above where they were going. At least the traffic on these wet roads seemed light.

She finally glimpsed a large green-and-white sign that

marked a north turn onto I-75. They drove quite a ways at a fairly low speed, windshield wipers whipping back and forth. Will had turned on the air-conditioning, perhaps to help keep the windshield from fogging up. Ralston had quit trying to talk. He seemed to pay no attention to Claire but was now either asleep or staring out his side window with his head turned away. It was when a car passed them that she saw in the headlights his hair was coagulated in a circle of darkening blood.

Will must've hit him with the gun or something else. So was he unconscious now—or even dying? For the first time, she realized that Will was capable of things she never would have guessed from the dapper dresser and children's storyteller at the library. So if he was doing this to bring justice for Darcy's abduction, or Steve's wrongful arrest, why did he care that much? And he'd had such tears in his eyes when he had gazed at Jilly, sleeping so peacefully.

But nothing quite clicked. Answers seemed beyond her, so she had to bide her time, cooperate—and so did Clint Ralston.

When Nick finally reached Ken Jensen and told him what had happened—even told him about the doll—the detective said nothing at first.

"I thought you'd shout at me and cuss me out—or order me to be arrested," Nick said in the sudden silence after he'd spilled everything in one big rush.

"I'm thinking. I trust Claire. Yeah, she oversteps all the time, but she's savvy—and determined—and I can't fault that. It's why I've been trying to get her to consider working part-time as a forensic psych here. You do understand the Collier County police force is totally obsessed—and specifically assigned—to hurricane duty?"

"I do, but I wanted you to know in case you can at least make officers aware of Will Warren's license plate number—if anyone can even see it in this storm."

"I'll get the make and model of his car and see if there's a unit anywhere near his address to look there, but he'd be an idiot to take her where we'd look."

"He's not an idiot for sure. He's evidently learned something we didn't about who took Darcy, or at least where."

"But why does he need Claire? Just so she can tell Darcy what happened, maybe to help her get her memory back? But why does he care so much?"

"The ten-million-dollar question," Nick muttered. But, pacing back and forth, he kept passing the painting he had recently unwrapped.

"For one thing," Nick went on, trying to keep calm, "Will has a painting he did of his grandmother, who was very special to him. He left it here, and the woman in it is a dead ringer for Darcy."

"Look, Nick, gotta go. I'll do what I can. I can't believe we've run into a brick wall on this, tracking Darcy, finding out who had her and why and then letting her go. I've been assigned to Germaine Arena, which is going to open first thing in the morning as a public shelter, and it's highly likely that, if this hurricane's as bad as they say, even the cell towers will go down, not to mention power outages. So don't worry if I'm not in touch. I'll do what I can. At least you're able to sit out this storm at home. Bye for now."

Nick punched off his phone and stared at it. Ken had not really exploded at all. He'd admitted failure, tried to buck him up. And he had to give it to the guy for, like him, he had to deal with Claire, a bright, dedicated and determined woman, but one who kept getting them all into one hell of a mess.

This storm was making a mess of things, Claire thought. But more than once, Will had said it would help. He must have meant to cover his tracks, or did he mean, where they were going, the guards or staff would have been sent home because of the hurricane emergency? Everything was closed now. One reason she'd had trouble looking up through the car windows to read signs on buildings was that most of them had been turned out or gone off. She'd heard it called a killer storm. Was Will ready to be a killer, too? Or was he already, no matter that he said Larry Ralston just fell in the water? But she still couldn't grasp how Clint Ralston figured in.

"Truth time!" Will spoke at last as he pulled up next to a fairly large, two-story building. "Look familiar, CEO of Onward?" he asked Ralston as he turned off the engine.

Despite her bonds, Claire raised her head, trying to see where they were. Yes, a sign, illumined by their headlights, quite small and tasteful over the entryway of a building they had pulled up to. She read, in scripted letters, Onward. Then in smaller script: LLC, Founded 1993.

LLC meant a limited liability corporation. Claire knew that indicated that the company could be "owned" by a sole proprietorship—one man—and that it protected that owner or CEO from being sued or going into debt. And hadn't Will just intimated that Ralston was the CEO of this place? But then she saw something else on the building, something shocking that opened up so many possibilities.

"Oh!" she cried. "That logo on the building. An orange butterfly!"

"Exactly," Will said. "A falcate orangetip, the symbol of suspended life that can be brought back again. New life, taking flight."

"But what is Onward?" she demanded when he finally turned the headlights off, killed the motor and got out to open the back car door to retrieve her again.

"I—and its CEO and mastermind—will explain when we get out of this storm," Will shouted over the wind. He loosed her foot ties and finally produced a key to unlock her handcuffs. "You have to help me now," he said in her ear. "If you are on my and Darcy's side, do what I say."

He left the back car door open for her to get out. She was so soaked already so she didn't bother with Darcy's umbrella she'd brought, but did take her purse. Will had Ralston out of the car, shuffling toward the front door. The three of them stood under a covered entrance, finally out of the downpour.

Will produced his gun again, though Ralston seemed tied as well as subdued, and lifted the man's bound hands to press one of his palms to a panel on the front door. Though the entryway inside looked dimly lit, another light came on inside and the door clicked so loudly Claire could hear it over the pounding rain.

Will half dragged, half shoved Ralston inside, and she followed. More lights came on automatically. What was this place? No one was in sight. She glanced around a well-decorated reception area with a large desk. She saw a glassed-in room, probably for private conferences. Normal, so normal, until she read the sign overhead with arrows pointing down a hall; it read Your Eternity in one direction and Your Future in the other.

Was this a church? Some strange sect? Or a maverick doctor's office or beauty salon, promising women an ever-youthful future, maybe like that Fountain of Youth cosmetics scam she and Nick had exposed?

She was continually amazed as Will forced Ralston into what looked like a cleaning closet, locked him in and jammed a chair—the furniture here was modern and expensive-looking—against that door.

"Let's take a quick tour first," Will told her. "We need to be sure there is no skeleton staff or security still here, or I'll have to lock them up, too. I made a bogus call, supposedly from the local authorities, saying all businesses with large, flat roofs must be vacated, though the storm might have sent most of them home, anyway. Once this place is secure for us, Ralston will explain all—or else. We'll both have our answers before we're done with him. Come on. I haven't seen this place myself, only photos sent to my laptop as I pretended to be a potential, wealthy California client."

Client of what, for what? she wanted to demand, but she kept quiet.

She followed him through a door to where a long hall went both ways, one toward Your Eternity and one toward Your Future.

"Will," she said, unable to hold back and following fast behind him, "what is this place Ralston runs? And how does it tie in to Darcy? Did he bring her here for—for experiments, brainwashing or what? If she was given that drug so she wouldn't recall what happened to her, why?"

The air was chilly here, so the air-conditioning must be on. They both jumped when more lights went on from their just entering a spacious, open area with some sort of large, upright vats, also lit from within.

"Here's where it all comes together," Will whispered, looking as awed as she felt, but hardly as puzzled. "It's the site of animal research giving way to human suspended animation. The experimentation with drugs to erase bad memories. The secrecy, wealth—and stealth—of Onward. Claire, these capsules, called dewars, are filled with liquid nitrogen and preserved dead people who had hopes to be resurrected someday when a cure is found for their specific illness or injury."

He turned to her and took her elbow gently in his hand, not releasing the gun in his other hand. "You see," he said in almost reverential tones, "this company offers eternal life to those wealthy enough to pay for it and crazy enough to believe in it. Have you heard of cryonics?"

"No wonder it's so cold in here. That's freezing things, for preservation."

"In this case," he said as he walked closer to one of the capsules, drawing her along with him, "freezing humans shortly after death so that they may supposedly be brought back to life in the future, when—the theory goes—whatever disease or even old age killed them has been somehow eradicated. Born again, so to speak, and given a percentage of their massive amount of investment money paid to their preservers. And sometimes, for a cheaper fee and the promise of a new body later, people just have their heads frozen and preserved."

Claire gasped. "So that's why Ralston would have just taken Larry's head if the police could have had it released to him quickly. But when the ME kept his body—when

Ralston argued with his father over the corpse being buried by the funeral home..."

"I don't know why it took the police—or even you and
Nick—to track this down. It took me a while, but I managed."

She recognized that other side of Will now. Yes, a clever,
talented, creative man, but one who had such pride in his
brilliance that he could be devious and act outside of the
average person's boundaries. And he had turned vigilante
to learn and avenge what had happened to Darcy.

"Here," he was saying, "go up these steps a bit and look
in one of these dewars, which might as well be coffins.
You mentioned Darcy rambling on about lighted faces as
well as a fish that could not breathe. I'm afraid we'll find
both here at Onward."

He stepped up on the metal ladder outside the closest
gray metal dewar and, with his hand on her elbow, tugged
her up, too.

Claire looked in and gasped. Almost screamed. No hair
on its head, for it must have been shaved, but a person
floated inside, with eyes wide-open as if in surprise. But,
she thought, her eyes weren't quite wide enough open yet.
She had to know more.

CHAPTER THIRTY

"Amazing. And horrible," Claire whispered as though the bodies floating in their capsules could hear. "I've heard about this, but—to think it's here, and that Darcy was brought here. Let's go. Let's take Ralston to the police or call them."

"No, my dear. We have unfinished business with Clint Ralston for taking Darcy away and experimenting on her with that memory-tampering drug. You see, although it took me a while, when I heard that she came back remembering nothing, I knew. So many of the mothers talk to me at the library, and one was fearful her wealthy father was going to spend a fortune at this place. She said there was even a drug available here to make one forget the past sad things in a life when preserved for a new life. I comforted her but gave it no more thought because I was so busy, and it seemed so—so far out."

"But then when Darcy came back that way..."

"Even before that, because the woman had shown me

that the logo of an orange butterfly was on all her father's correspondence with Onward. True, I followed Ralston to this site, but I knew where it was before, and feared Darcy had been kept here—the butterfly connection, of course. But I had to be sure, not make a mistake where I exposed myself to Clint Ralston or to the police. Even when Darcy returned, supposedly safe and sound, I dedicated myself to finding answers—to finding all this—though I hadn't been inside before today."

"But you researched it somehow."

"I've been up day and night getting answers. I interviewed a man in California who thought I worked here at Onward, a man planning to be brought here just before he dies so that he can be quickly preserved. I found him through a so-called forward-thinking group online."

"And I thought Nick and I were pursuing answers—but nothing like that."

"You didn't follow Ralston to work, you see. And then learn that he had an alias and was hiding this Onward endeavor from everyone but his family—and his 'customers.' To preserve a deceased person, the belief is that brains must not die. The corpse—or just the head for some who want the 'economy package'—must be quickly preserved in liquid nitrogen. I take it that's what we see above these dewars in those canisters so that more can be poured in if needed. Uncap and tip those," he said, pointing upward, "and freezing liquid nitrogen pours out in the form of a frozen mist. But let's bring in the mastermind of Onward to explain things to us before—well, before we are done with him."

"And then," Claire said, wishing her voice didn't sound so shaky, "take him to the police. For kidnapping and imprisoning Darcy at the very least. They use that drug to erase bad memories in their victims—their clients. So their experiments on her were not only using the drug she was given to block her bad memories of her kidnapping and being experimented on here. The staff here must also be studying the butterflies and maybe dolphins' brains to learn how to suspend life until those preserved are ready to be brought back."

"Exactly. I regret I could not ask you to help me when I did all my research, but you would have run to the police, not to mention your lawyer husband, and we needed not only revelation but another form of justice here. Now, let's get Ralston and force him to prove all that to us, with not only a gun to his head but with the threat—yes, a threat—that all of this will be not only exposed, but ruined, if he doesn't talk."

"You mean cut off the electricity that keeps these dewars and everything going? Or by stopping the liquid nitrogen feeds? But they must have a backup generator. After all, this coming hurricane could stop the power."

"Oh, they have a huge generator out in back they could use. The man I talked to here assured me of that when he thought I would like to be part of this—in a dewar, that is, not as the one who would, and will, bring this all down."

Standing in the front hallway, Nick was talking to Ken as fast as he could, trying to convince him he should go with him out into the storm. To Nick's surprise, Ken had showed up here on his way to his hurricane assignment at Germaine Arena about twenty-five miles north of Naples on I-75. He wore a bright orange slicker, which dripped water onto the tile.

"Man!" he'd said when he first came in and saw Will's painting. "That does look like Darcy!"

"Ken," Nick was arguing now, "let me go with you. If you get a call about where Will turns up, or if he or Claire call you, I'd go with you, be there with you to help her."

"What if she calls you here?"

"We don't have a landline anymore, and Will must have her phone. If he calls again, I'll talk to him, find out where she is. If the lines or cell towers go down, I'm hoping you would know what to do to stay in touch with the authorities."

"So you're volunteering to help with hundreds of panicked people seeking shelter at Germaine Arena during the storm, and that's why I would take you with me? Simply as a concerned citizen volunteer, in case I'm asked by my boss, is that right?"

"Yes, damn it. The kids are protected here, our friends should be safe with them in this sturdy new house and the worst part of this storm is supposed to be at least a day out. Yes, if you're asked by your superiors, just say I'm a concerned citizen, say whatever, but I know as soon as we hear where Claire is out there in this mess, you could get there, and I'd go with you. It's all I can think of to keep from going crazy over her safety. It sounds like a replay of the Darcy mess, I know."

"I got that, Nick. Okay, I got you, so get stuff together fast. Maybe one or the other of us will hear from her or Will and can work together. If I get fired for dereliction of duty, will you hire me at the law firm, maybe working security?" he asked with a roll of his eyes.

"Bronco's got that gig," Nick said, exhaling in relief, that he could work with Ken, even kid with Ken. "But we could sure use a new computer genius, since Heck may be moving to Miami."

"Me doing that would be the day. Go get ready, and let's hope the winds don't put trees or branches in our way. And," he called after him as Nick sprinted away, "just keep your mouth shut in my vehicle if we get any calls. Now hurry up!"

Claire was appalled at how controlling and commanding Will could be, a man she'd seen as polite, even kindly, almost meek. He had his gun barrel pressed hard to the back of Ralston's head just above his neck, although the man's hands were still tied.

With her following, Will marched him to one of the computer consoles—a string of them, all in screen saver mode—and shoved him down into the ergonomic chair. Will ripped off Ralston's taped gag with one hand, still pressing the gun tight to him.

The screen saver read Onward to an Eternal Life with a falcate orangetip flitting across the screen.

"First of all, disable the alarms, phone system and intercom but not the internal computer system!" Will ordered the trembling man. "You're all so 'smart' here, everything is linked. I don't trust you to just give verbal commands, so do it!"

"Not—not my job description, b–but I can try," he stuttered.

His hands were shaking so badly that he messed up commands at first, then deleted those. Will hung over his shoulder, keeping an eye on each move. "Who went to pick up those butterflies that day? Your lackey Jedi?"

"Yes. Yes, it was him. Darcy said he couldn't have them

unless she checked with Tara Gerald, and she'd have to check with the client who had brought them. When he started to take them anyway, she said she was going to call the police, and he—he just lost it. He knew we needed more subjects to test with the propranolol. No one was there, even when he checked Tara's house, so he took some falcate pupae from there, too. He had chloroform along to sedate the falcates so they could be easily gathered, but he used it on Darcy when she protested and threatened him before she could phone for help."

Will said, "And when he brought her here and the news media was all over her disappearance, you just kept her to experiment on, you bastard!"

Will's voice was not his own, either. He pressed the barrel of the gun even tighter to Ralston's head. "If you don't do exactly what I say, your staff here won't even have your head in one piece to pickle in these liquid nitrogen containers for your future life."

"I said I didn't take her. I insisted she be released!"

"Yeah, after you'd scrambled her brain, kept her from her family! You made us—her daughter—suffer, too!" Will insisted. "Get her lab results and print them out. Now!"

Ralston fumbled around a few different screens, then brought up what Will wanted and sent a print command. Above the line of six keyboards with large screens, a printer jerked to life and spewed out three pages.

"Get them, Claire," Will said, and she did. Glancing at them, she saw the last page had also printed at the bottom a color photo of Darcy with some sort of a mask over her face, lying on a gurney. Yes, Darcy had recalled that, fearing the mask and that she couldn't breathe. Claire almost showed it to Will, but that could come later. He was crazed enough right now.

"So onward to a tour of this warped Disneyland," Will said, jerking Ralston to his feet but keeping the gun in place. "In my extensive research about Onward, once I figured out what you were hiding, I read people thought Walt Disney wanted to be cryopreserved, but it turned out to be rumors. You see, Ralston, I have done a lot of work on all this in a little over a week. And this week will seem like nothing when you spend the rest of your life—your lackey Jedi Brown, too—in prison. And all these poor people who believe there will be a future when they are pulled from their liquid nitrogen swimming pools someday will be lost, and so stupid to have trusted you."

"We're learning more. We'll find a way, cures for old age or what caused their disease. We'll bring them back to life! And the suspended animation knowledge from the animals will be of great benefit to all mankind—the space program, too—invaluable, lucrative!" Clint insisted, nodding toward a large drawing Claire had not noticed. In it, astronauts secured by straps, slept in their space capsule on the way, no doubt, to someplace light-years away.

Will just swore under his breath, yanked Ralston out of his chair and shoved him down the hall.

"You know," Will said, "I'm afraid you've been reading your own propaganda about the future—wealth, fame. It may all be a pipe dream, if you can't bring them back, or if the earth explodes in nuclear war, or if an asteroid hits here or—who knows? Maybe because someone shoots you."

Claire wanted to stop Will, but she had to keep him calm and bide her time now. Surely he wouldn't endanger his own future by killing this man? Besides, he must want all this to come out, to be a warning to others.

As she followed along, holding the papers that would help Darcy's testimony at this man's criminal trial, Claire wondered what else they would find in this house of horrors.

"You might know the big boys need more storm data," Mitch told Jace as they flew into the eye of the storm again after a rough ride through the increasingly powerful outer bands of Jenny.

"It may help Floridians realize how bad this could be," Jace said as he looked ahead across the eight miles of the eye of sunny sky calm, literally before the other side of the storm. He knew mandatory evacs were happening below in some areas. He fought to keep his mind on his controls and not on his loved ones on the ground.

Above the windshield the small plastic figure of Yoda from *Star Wars* finally stopped its wild swinging from the WC-130 turboprop bucking the outer band winds. One of their sister planes had Kermit the Frog for their mascot, but Jace's crew had voted for the small but wise and powerful genius Yoda. They needed that—someone really smart to figure out how to weaken, even defuse, horrible hurricanes like this. Yoda was a Jedi master, the Jedi fighters' trainer. Wasn't that the nickname of the guy that had something to do with someone Claire and Nick suspected for something? He couldn't recall exactly what they'd said, but he remembered the name.

But back—back to concentrating on every move up here.

Again, the crew measured air currents, dropping their last dropsondes with their little parachutes toward the eastern Gulf of Mexico and the coastal areas near Naples. The beautiful blue calm passed quickly. While Jace concentrated on the controls, and they headed into the northern outer bands, Mitch opened the all-call to the crew and told them, "Batten down the hatches, mates. Back into the big blow to get out of here and head back home.

"You know," he told Jace, cutting off the all-call, "for once I almost feel sick to my stomach. I skipped breakfast, and we've been up here too damned long. At least I don't have any cookies in me to toss, but maybe I'm coming down with something."

"Yeah. Prewedding jitters."

"Very damn funny. But it just makes me think we should move ahead with our idea of a Fly Safe private pilot school. Nick said he'd have no problem freeing up that name legally, despite the save-the-animals group using it, because our company would be so different."

"Later for chat. Here we go."

They bounced into the brutal outer bands again, hopefully, Jace thought, for the last time on a Hurricane Jenny mission. This baby was trouble. At least all those he loved were safe.

Claire saw the next room down the hall called Your Future was much smaller and not so intimidating. Except, that was, she saw shelves of chilled, thick plastic envelopes that seemed to be moving inside a refrigerant unit with clear doors, from which a strange, muted sound emanated.

Will said, "Glassine envelopes of butterflies, right, Ralston? No doubt falcate orangetips, doped up by the cold, yet fluttering to be free. And perhaps the black ones you released at the memorial service for your brother, thinking Tara or I would be blamed for that."

"Red rims," Claire put in. "They were, weren't they?"

"It was all Jedi's doing," Ralston muttered. "He thought the butterflies were a good idea, even when I told him to leave well enough alone. The man's unstable. He kidnapped your sister. He would've killed her outright if I hadn't insisted on using her as a test subject. I'm the good guy here! I let her go in the end, didn't I?"

Apparently, Clint's desperate pleas failed to soften Will's heart as he pressed the gun barrel against the man's head.

"Will," Claire said gently, hoping he wouldn't blow the man's brains out, "when he's arrested, we need to get Tara here and have these butterflies freed and taken care of."

"You checked out they were red rims?" Will asked her. The mention of butterflies seemed to defuse some of his anger. "So, both of us have been tracking down this maniac. I'm proud of you, Claire, proud of Darcy, too, and you must tell her that."

So reassuring, Claire thought. Will was calming down now, sounding more like himself. He was going to let her go, going to let her get back to her house and to Darcy after this nightmare, though it sounded as if he might also have plans to disappear. However awful this experience, Will kept his promises. Surely he would soon get her back home.

She sighed as they left behind the haunting sound of hundreds of butterflies fighting to be free. In the next room, a large one, she gasped as the overhead lights automatically came on. Darcy's frenzied words, her warped memory, came back to Claire as she looked around.

In a lighted tank about the size of a rental truck, swam a single dolphin, and it didn't have much room to move or rise above the surface to breathe.

CHAPTER THIRTY-ONE

The driving was so bad through increasing wind and rain that Ken pulled over into a parking lot when a call came in from headquarters. Even though the wind was howling and the rain beat on the squad car, the dispatcher's voice carried. Nervous and scared, Nick frowned out into the increasing storm as the flashing bar lights on top of the car reflected in the clinging rain.

The female dispatcher was spieling off an address near Doctors Pass. Nick turned to listen, his pulse pounding.

"See the man Jedi Brown at that address," the woman said. Her voice crackled a bit. "Mr. Brown says his employer, Clint Ralston, was taken by force by an unknown man with a gun from this address. Mr. Brown has the incident and suspect on home security camera. Can you take this on your way to the arena, Lieutenant Jensen?"

"Roger that," Ken said. "I'm not too far, will swing by on the way. Over and out."

Bingo! Nick thought. This desperate move to stick to

Ken was going to pay off. Maybe he shouldn't be so hard on Claire for taking risks.

As Ken pulled out of the parking lot and turned back the way they had come, he told Nick, "You got that? One of our favorite persons of interest, Jedi Brown, called the sheriff's desk to say that not only had his boss, Clint Ralston, disappeared from his home but that he has security camera proof of who took him by force with a gun."

"Obviously, he doesn't know who or he would have told your dispatcher."

"If he knew, I bet Brown would already be on the kidnapper's tail."

"Brown could be the guy who took Darcy—or else Ralston's kidnapper is. It can't be Lincoln Yost, because Jedi would know him. Yost had to be on the take, working for whoever is studying all those falcate orangetips boarded at Tara Gerald's, though I don't think she knows who she was really dealing with. I just hope the kidnapper's recognizable on the camera in this weather. This storm isn't really even here yet and it's one of the damn darkest ones I've ever seen."

"I agree. You know, as a detective, it's been a while since I had a partner in a squad car. But I'll leave you in it when I go up to Ralston's house, so no one knows you're on a ride along with me."

"What if I can identify the kidnapper?"

"I don't trust Jedi Brown or Ralston, not after that 'Can I have his head?' reaction to Larry Ralston's drowning."

"Yeah. I get it. Whatever you say."

"Darcy remembered this!" Claire said as the three of them went closer to the dolphin's water-filled prison.

"Pretty impressive," Will whispered. "So, Larry Ralston caught a dolphin, and gave it to his brother to conduct experiments on its brain—right, Ralston?" he demanded. The man evidently refused to talk, even though his tape gag was still dangling from his chin instead of over his mouth.

"This must be a different dolphin from the one Larry got caught with," Claire said. "It just gets worse and worse. Let's get out of here, get the authorities. We have enough on this man now, and I've seen enough for a lifetime. What an awful place for Darcy to have been kept for all that time."

"We'll go soon," Will said, his voice calm, strangely assuring. "I've sent this man's bodyguard, Jedi Brown, on a fool's errand, but he really is no fool. Eventually, he'll come looking for our villain here." He poked the gun into Ralston's neck again for emphasis.

Again, Claire was terrified the gun might go off. Will had kept his finger on the trigger. Perhaps it was his way of tormenting Ralston since he had allowed Darcy to be so terrified.

"Back into the other room with the dewars and your precious canisters of liquid nitrogen," Will ordered Ralston, and gave him a little push.

Finally, Ralston spoke. "You wouldn't dare tamper with those bodies, or it will be mass murder."

"They're already dead!" Will cried as he slapped the strapping tape over the man's mouth again.

With a glance back at the imprisoned dolphin—at least it would be returned to the sea as soon as she and Will reported all this—Claire followed the men down the hall again to the large holding room with the dewars. There, Will shoved Ralston into a chair and, grabbing the roll of black tape from his raincoat pocket, taped his wrists to the arms of a chair.

"This won't take long, Claire," Will promised, and proceeded to climb the short ladders next to each of the six dewars in the front row one at a time. She'd counted twelve of the hanging canisters of liquid nitrogen with several more farther back. Surely Will didn't intend to shut them down so the bodies warmed and the people inside, well, "died"? Or was he adjusting the canisters above each so that he could ruin the frozen liquid, make it unusable?

Or did he intend to dump them on Ralston?

Their prisoner kept trying to struggle against his bonds and protest through his gag, but Will ignored that, however much it unsettled her.

"Will, let's take him and go. The storm is only going to get worse, and it's a ways back into town to the police. What if someone shows up?"

"The palm and thumbprint for entry in front is disabled, and I want it that way," he called down to her. "You know, sadly, there's a child in one of these dewars. Some poor, sad soul wanted to keep a loved one suspended to be reborn, someone who lost a child too early."

Claire thought of Lexi and Trey, as well as Darcy's Jilly and Drew. At least they were safe. But she had to get going, even if Will lingered. Whether his plan was really to turn Ralston in or dump liquid nitrogen on him first, she really wanted out of here.

"Will, what are you doing? Let's go! We need to call the police, and I have to call Nick."

"Justice first. Get ready to run and get away from him right now."

Justice? Did he mean to punish Ralston with the cold

of the liquid nitrogen? Surely not to kill him? Ralston had
been a party to Darcy's kidnapping, so he'd definitely go
to prison. But Will seemed so overly emotionally invested
in revenge here—why?

Will was up next to the sixth dewar, the one closest to
Ralston. No matter what Will had said, she had already
started to unwrap tape from the chair that held Ralston's
arms down so they could leave.

But she heard something—a single sound from the way
they had just come. Surely the dolphin had not broken the
glass, and those poor struggling butterflies trying to flap
their wings could not make a sound like that. Had a staff
member returned, or maybe a watchman who had come
in a back door when the front one wouldn't work?

"Will!" she screamed as the shadow of a man leaped
across the floor in front of her.

She saw Jedi Brown, gun in hand—a long automatic—
pointed right at her before he swung it upward at Will.

Watching from the police car, Nick saw a man he thought
looked familiar—maybe from Larry Ralston's memorial
service—come to the door of Clint Ralston's house when
Ken rang the doorbell. It wasn't Jedi Brown. Despite the
rain and distance from the car in the driveway, the light
was bright on the entryway. Nick could even see the security camera pointed downward. So where was Jedi Brown?

Ken went into the house, and the door closed. Feeling
he might have made a mistake not to stick close to Ken,
Nick fumed a moment, then pulled his phone out of his
pocket and called Bronco's number.

"Hey, boss. Find out anything? Find Claire?"

"Detective Jensen is following a lead, but it may go no-where. So no word from Claire there?"

"Sorry, nothing. Maybe she'll just walk in like Darcy."

"I hope not—I mean, not with a lot of time gone and her mind screwed up. The house holding up okay in this wind?"

"We still got power, TV, everything. They say it's coming here, boss. Tonight, real bad. I made Nita go to bed, even though the kids are still up, so Steve and me are taking care of them. Well, Nita did put Trey in bed first. Can't believe I'm gonna be a dad in a couple weeks. So where are you?"

"Got to go. Detective Jensen is gesturing for me to go to him. Take care of everyone, especially Nita. I'll call back when I can."

It was reassuring, at least, to have everything still work-ing at home and here, though he had no doubt the entire area might lose power. That's how he felt—powerless.

He got out in the rain, slammed the door and ran for the lighted front porch.

"Nick," Jensen said, gesturing to him, "I want you to take a look at the security camera video Jedi Brown called about. While he was away, Clint Ralston was abducted. And now Jedi's not here, either."

"It's an epidemic, people disappearing," Nick muttered. "So where did he go? That was a different guy at the door."

"Jedi went out to check someplace he knew to look. This is James Parsons, the house butler, just came back from checking his own place and found his employer missing, then checked the cameras, as Jedi must have."

Nick followed Ken into a room off the front hall where a small monitor mounted on the wall played back security video. Nick wiped water from his eyes and squinted at the grainy, rain-swept video the butler reversed and started over.

Nick's head jerked as he saw Clint Ralston shuffling out the front door wrapped and taped like in some old Boris Karloff mummy movie. The man with him wore a rain-coat with a hood, but he faced the camera once.

"It's Will Warren, pretty sure," Nick said, biting back a string of curse words. "But he had to have Claire with him, and she's not there—not in the picture anywhere."

"And," Ken said, squinting at the video, too, "he doesn't take Ralston down the driveway, or out in front where you'd think he has a car—maybe her in it. He shoves Ralston around the house, toward the back. You have any back door, backyard cameras?" he asked the butler.

"Yeah, but nothing there, Officer. I looked. Too stormy, too dark."

"Damn," Ken said.

Nick feared Jedi had set them up, stalled them, misled them. But for what? And could Ralston have staged his own kidnapping to take the heat off himself? But no, he couldn't be working with Will, but then what in hell was Will doing? And where was Claire? Nick could have beat the monitor apart with his bare fists.

"So where is your best guess Jedi would go looking for Mr. Ralston to check on your boss?" Ken asked the butler.

"I don't know, Officer. Well, maybe at Onward, Mr. Ralston's private business, a ways north of town."

"Private business? Tell us where it is," Ken ordered.

When he told them, they left the house in a hurry. "Onward to Onward," Ken told Nick as they got in the squad car again. "Sit tight, because we're closing in on something bad, but damned if I know what."

★ ★ ★

Claire opened her mouth to scream, but nothing came out.

"Get down! Get back!" Will shouted to her as Jedi raised his weapon toward him.

Claire knocked it so his shot went askew, then ducked behind the nearest dewar. Bullets pinged off the metal, off something.

Will must be all right so far, because he yelled, "Get back, Claire!"

Somehow he managed to open and tip two huge canisters of liquid nitrogen above. Yes, he must have planned to do that, anyway—to freeze or even kill Ralston.

Afraid of more flying bullets, she dropped to the ground and belly crawled behind the next dewar in case Jedi shot at her. But bullets pinged off somewhere above again, so he must've still been trying to hit Will.

And then she realized what Will was doing. A spiral of cold, white, curling air slid down to the floor behind her, maybe at Jedi's position. And she knew liquid nitrogen not only made an unworldly mist but that it burned warm flesh.

Jedi was swearing and screaming at Will. He shot wildly toward his elevated position while crawling back away from the white fog. Had Jedi been hit? By Will's bullets or his own?

"My eyes! My eyes!" Ralston kept screaming. "Let me loose!"

Claire imagined his trapped butterflies shouting that, the dolphin, too. She had not had time to completely free Ralston, but they didn't need him disappearing into this thick mist.

She crawled farther toward the hallway, holding her

breath with her eyes half-closed. Enough white mist swirled across the floor at least knee-high so she risked crawling on all fours instead of her stomach. As large as this room was, Will must have moved along the top of the dewars to tip more of the canisters because she was soon scrambling into an absolute icy whiteout, a blank wall.

Behind her, she heard a man cry out in pain. Will or Jedi?

The shooting stopped after two more quick bangs. No more pings off metal, no men's voices. She feared for Will's life. She got to her feet in the hall and tore toward the reception room, but should she cry out for Will, or would that give her location away to Jedi—and why the sudden silence? No, she should run so Jedi didn't shoot her, too.

Some of the white, smoky stuff came creeping across the floor toward her. Yes, she told herself, she had to get out of here unless that front door was jammed. Since the phone system had been disabled, she'd walk the roads in this wind and driving rain until she found someone to get help.

But it was Will who staggered down the hall toward her with Jedi's weapon hanging from one hand. As far as she could tell, he wasn't bleeding.

"He got disoriented by the mist, bullet ricocheted off one of the dewars, hit him," he gasped out. "Ralston's still tied up in there, but Brown indirectly shot himself, I swear it."

She recalled how Will had claimed he had not drowned Larry Ralston, that the man had fallen in the water. Too much protest to be innocent?

Because it suddenly hit her with stunning force: if Larry's fall into the water and the net had been an accident, who had put the suicide note on his phone? Someone who wanted to keep clear of a murder charge?

By accident or intent, had Will actually killed Larry

Ralston? And did he hope to eliminate Larry's brother, Clint, now, so he would never figure that out, or because he blamed them both for harming Darcy?

Will gasped out, "Though that guard dog Jedi will go to jail for attempted murder on this night—if he survives— you can also blame him for defacing your backyard." Struggling for breath, Will stood and leaned against the wall. "You see, he very kindly just admitted that inside to me when I dragged him away from the liquid nitrogen—and questioned him a bit Life is about little details as well as big ones, Claire. Again, I apologize for using that smart doll to spy on you, but all this was necessary."

He surprised her by heaving Jedi's gun down the hall when she thought he would keep it for evidence. It skidded heavily away on the wooden floor.

"Remember to tell the police where that is," he said, his voice still raspy. "Lost my pistol in there when I jumped down in that white, cold—somewhere."

"Will, we're leaving, but your fingerprints are on Jedi's gun and your own. You didn't harm the bodies in the dewars, dumping all that liquid nitrogen, did you?" she demanded, helping him toward the front door.

"I'd planned to burn him with it, let him suffer— Ralston, not Jedi. Jedi's leg's shot up, if not more, and you didn't free Ralston enough, so they are there for the picking when the police get here. I'll let you stay to explain, but I have to be on my way—far from here. Claire," he cried, throwing an arm over her shoulders to prop himself up, "time to tell the rest."

She pulled him toward the front door in case Jedi or Ralston did manage to get out of that horrid room. The door opened from the inside, and they staggered out, but he would not budge farther. They stood under the sheltered entryway leaning against the wall as the rain thudded down around them and the winds ripped at their wet clothes and hair.

"Listen. Just listen—please," he said, sucking in a big breath of outside air. "Not much time, one way or another. So—once upon a time, I fell in love with an introverted woman who loved to read, who loved stories to escape her own dilemma because her husband was gone a lot and had another woman in another town, a common-law wife."

"You—you don't mean my mother?"

"Yes, really, no fairy tale. Miranda had only recently learned about his other wife when she turned to me for help, for comfort."

Claire was cold, shaking—but her entire body suddenly felt as frozen as those bodies inside. Suddenly, everything fit together, the jagged pieces of the puzzle.

Will was Darcy's father.

CHAPTER THIRTY-TWO

"My—our mother?" Claire cried. She could not quite believe him, but certain memories—the signs—had been there.

"Yes, yes, I loved her. She had you, your father's daughter, then. But from our union—our love—Darcy. God forgive me for not telling Darcy and you before, but I am Darcy's father. And when your father learned of our love, it was the excuse he needed and wanted to leave your mother—for good. Well, I thought it was good, that I would make my fortune abroad, then return to the US and marry her, raise both of you with her."

Claire stared at him. She had to get this straight, make herself believe and accept it all. "You are Darcy's father, but not mine? But you left her, left them?"

"I had a deal to go to Japan to make a lot of money, importing and selling rare butterflies there, some legal, some not. I promised to come back, but she told me not to, since I wanted to go—it was my big chance to make money, so we'd be well-off. She—she was so doubly wounded in her head and heart that she turned against me and turned to her books even more. I should have realized that, if I left, her depression, her…loneliness and agoraphobia would isolate her even more—from me, too. As much as I loved books, for a while, I hated them because they were her crutch, her barrier from the world and then even from me. When I came back, I could not win her back, and she turned to her fantasy world and against me."

"She buried herself in them, sometimes buried us in them, too. She never told me—never told Darcy—about you."

"I figured that out later when I came back. She died shortly after I returned. I grieved, blamed myself for chances lost with Miranda and Darcy. Later Jilly was lost to me, Drew, too, of course. I wanted to tell Darcy everything, but I was afraid to, afraid she'd blame me for desertion the way both of you had your father—that is, the man Darcy thought was her father. So I did what I could, became close to Darcy, adored my grandchildren from afar, and then closer when you and Darcy brought your girls to story time."

"I saw the way you looked at Jilly when we left the house. What about the painting?"

"It really is of my grandmother, but Darcy is her mirror image. Give her the painting, Claire. Tell her all this, that I love her and Jilly and always will—little Drew, too, of course, but he never liked story time or me, I could tell. I never had a chance to know him, to win him over, only see him, talk to him once or twice. But I can't stay here now. So tell Darcy all this and let her decide if she wants to tell her children someday."

"You did all this tracking down and ruining Ralston for her?"

He nodded wildly. "But it might not be understood by the authorities, or even by Darcy and Steve since he got snagged in all this. I did visit Larry Ralston to force some information from him, and now, with kidnapping Clint and Jedi bleeding in there, if either of them die, I may be culpable, but tell them that Steve did not kill Larry Ralston." He handed her a letter. "That's a signed confession to police. I fought with Ralston, and he fell in. I swear it was an accident, and I tried to save him… But it was too late. Then I panicked. I faked the suicide note on his phone. I never thought Steve would be blamed for his death—that I could've taken Jilly and Drew's father away from them with my actions. I can't bear to think I've hurt Darcy's family like this."

She took the letter with numb fingers. "Where will you go?"

"I've said enough. The storyteller in me just wants you all to have a happy-ever-after ending. As for me, I don't want to spend the rest of my life in prison. Not being able to see Darcy or my grandchildren is punishment enough. If I can, over time, over the years, I'll contact Darcy, or at least send things—money for Jilly and Drew. Please ask Steve to forgive me, too, to take good care of my girl."

"I—yes, of course I will."

"I've visited her grave many times, you know—Miranda's, your mother's. I released beautiful butterflies there. I did love her, Claire, but I've said it all now and must go. I'll call the police from the car, and they'll be here soon. Nick, too, I'm certain."

He kissed her on the cheek and ran on unsteady legs through the buffeting wind to his car. She moved out from under the shelter of the entry, clinging to a pillar, sobbing, unsure if Will was a liar and a murderer, but she believed him about being Darcy's father. How would she tell her? She was only Darcy's half sister now, but that had to be enough.

Her legs went weak, and she slid down a pillar to sit on the doorstep of Onward while the rain poured down and lightning forked to the ground nearby and thunder shook the sky.

She must be hallucinating through the rain and her tears to see a vehicle with flashing bar lights pulling in. Already? Maybe Ralston or Jedi had called for an ambulance.

No, it was a police car. It stopped so close and—yes, she must be dreaming—Ken Jensen jumped out bareheaded in this rain, and Nick... Nick right behind him.

Ken started shouting questions, but all she could do was cling to Nick.

"What was that?" Jace asked Mitch as the plane jolted. The aircraft yawed left, and Jace struggled to get it back on even keel.

"You're heading back to base through a wind and lightning storm and you ask what happened?" Mitch shot back, but his voice quavered.

Thank God, Jace thought, he could get the plane back on its radar heading toward Tampa, but it kept shuddering, listing left. And though they were flying through low clouds that were bumpy, he was certain they had actually hit something. Birds? Pelicans, maybe, brown bodies up this high, maybe trying to outrun the storm or getting sucked up into it—hit by the left engine propellers?

He held tight to his control wheel, while their little hanging mascot figure jerked wildly. He skimmed the readouts. The left engine was—was gone, dead.

He tried to restart it while Mitch opened the all-call to

the crew. Jace could imagine them back there, glad their tangling with the worst of the hurricane above the gulf was over, but tense until they landed at MacDill. But with one engine and all that distance in rocky winds, MacDill and Tampa were too damn far to make it without going down into the drink.

"Come on, baby," he muttered to the forty-nine-million-dollar plane, not to mention the valuable weather equipment and trained crew.

"It won't restart?" Mitch asked.

"Tell everybody to sit tight," Jace told him, ignoring the obvious answer. "I'm going to radio Naples Municipal because we're wobbling, and even the Fort Myers Airport with its longer runways may be too far. Besides, I'm used to the approach in Naples, and no way we'd have room to land at our little Marco spot for Fly Safe. Damn," he muttered, his voice low. "Fly Safe. Mitch, see if they can take us at Naples. Get me the radio reading for them."

As Mitch explained to the crew to strap in and sit tight, that they were going to request an emergency landing in Naples, Jace concentrated on keeping the plane from dipping the left wing or starting to circle. He had to use a huge amount of rudder to keep the aircraft flying somewhat straight. They were just a little moving blip on the radar screen in a vast ocean of black. In a brutal storm. Worse than a desert dust storm in the Middle East.

Trained to respond with cool, objective thought and action, Jace fought picturing his loved ones. Brit. Lexi. Even Claire. He had to bring this big bird in, one that must have been damaged by birds in flight.

He talked as calmly as he could to the Naples control tower. "Affirmative," he told them after they repeated his request. "Probably bird ingestion, left engine. Might not make it to Fort Myers. NOAA Hurricane WC-130 turboprop with twelve aboard. Yes, requesting emergency equipment to meet us."

"Roger that. Crosswinds a problem," the Naples controller said. "And we just heard from your NOAA headquarters that the storm will arrive here earlier than expected."

Mitch whispered to Jace, "We were right about that."

The airport controller went on. "Gusts to sixty miles per hour from southwest but swirling, but I'll bet you know that. We had a jet land that got shoved off the north/south runway before we closed."

"Roger that, but we have no choice."

"Understand. We'll talk you in. Heavy ponding on the runway surface makes for skidding, so do not overshoot your wheels down. Not certain you'll be able to see the approach and runway lights until you're very low. We will continue to give you readings."

"Affirmative. Used to fly jets in dust storms but not with twelve aboard and Cat 4 blow."

"We see you on our screen, but you're still a ways out and over water. Runway all yours."

In the sudden radio silence, Mitch said to Jace, "Hope they even have ER vehicles to send with that storm coming. Bet everybody's trying to help evacs on the ground."

Jace's hands were steady but his legs shook from handling more and more rudder.

Mitch went on. "And we thought this assignment would be a piece of cake. But if anybody can put us down all right, it's you, Jace."

"Affirmative that, my friend. *Semper Fi* and comin' in on a wing and a prayer."

CHAPTER THIRTY-THREE

"But how did you know to find me here?" Claire asked them once Nick and Ken had her in the squad car with Ken in the front seat, Nick in the back with her.

Nick said, "Will Warren phoned me to say where you were, but not why. He wouldn't say more, cut me off. And thank God I was with Ken, and we weren't far from here. We were leaving Clint Ralston's house because Jedi had called in to say Clint had been kidnapped. In the call for help, Jedi said he had a security home video but couldn't identify who took him. When we got there, Jedi was gone, but Ralston's butler told us about Onward, and we figured it was the first place Jedi would look for his boss."

"So, on the phone, Will didn't tell you what happened inside—what we found—that Clint Ralston and Jedi Brown are both injured in there?"

"No," Ken cut in. "Only that you needed help and were at this address with the big butterfly logo. Describe what you can about what I'll find inside. Go ahead. I'm turning my body cam on to go in."

"You should hire Will Warren as a detective if you catch him, but I bet you won't. He's a mastermind, but I won't tell you all the details now, so you can help the wounded, however evil they are. Will said Jedi's been shot and Ralston— I'm not sure, but Will dumped liquid nitrogen on him. He tried to hit both of them with it. Turn left down a hall to a large room. You'll be shocked to see what else is in there. Cryogenically preserved bodies in liquid nitrogen, with the intention of being revived someday. In other rooms, the missing orangetips and a dolphin Larry Ralston must have caught for his brother. But my biggest shock was that Will said he's Darcy's father. And I believe him."

Ken swore under his breath. Nick pulled her even tighter to him. Claire briefly described more of the layout inside. Ken called for two ambulances and police backup. He also radioed for officers be on alert to apprehend Will Warren if his vehicle, which he asked for a license plate number on from his controller, was spotted, though it was probably a futile request in this storm. Then, after telling Nick he should stay outside and take care of Claire, he ran alone into the building.

"Needless to say, I'm so glad you're here with Ken," she told Nick, holding tight to him. "But you should never have left the house in this dangerous weather."

"Sweetheart, you're scolding me for reckless behavior, like leaving the house in a storm? At least I was with someone on the right side of the law."

She almost laughed at that, but she was—like Darcy— too traumatized to control her emotions, and she started to cry again, shaking uncontrollably.

"Nick, I had to go with him. I had to know what happened to Darcy to help her, and I trusted him. Somehow, I knew he cared about Darcy, even for me a bit. I know now that was because he loved our mother."

"The police may not find him right away. I kind of hope they don't at all. I have to give the guy credit for all he did, each detail, even telling me on the phone that he'd left the front door of Onward open, so the police could get in. It was almost as if he knew I was with Ken, but I didn't tell him. I guess Will Warren—the ultimate enigma—wanted Ralston and Jedi to be found before Jedi bled out or Ralston managed to escape, liquid nitrogen burns or not."

"He—he didn't mention Ralston's injuries to me."

"He said he thinks Ralston is probably blind now."

Despite the storm, two big, square, red ER rescue vehicles came screaming in, and their crews rushed inside with gurneys and equipment. She and Nick had been talking about Will being Darcy's father, and how all that had come about. Nick had comforted her just as she must soon be the one to comfort Darcy—after telling her everything.

Nick said, "I wish Ken would come out to tell us that the two of them were captured and are still alive enough to be interrogated and tried in court."

"If there's a trial, I would have to testify. Nick, you won't believe the horrors of that place, bodies floating in those huge vatlike containers. If you climb a ladder, you can look in and see their faces. And that trapped dolphin that haunted Darcy is so sad. I guess I can grasp the desire to see the future, to live again, to come back from the dead, but I don't think that's for mankind to decide. Ralston tried to justify their experiments by saying their findings would help space travel, but their tactics of using animal and human guinea pigs is just plain wrong."

Sitting on Nick's lap, she held tight to him as they saw Jedi carried out on a stretcher and put in the back of one rescue squad vehicle. A police officer got in with a paramedic, and they pulled away, lights and siren on. What else had that man, Clint Ralston's guard and enforcer, done that he must pay for?

Next they watched as Ralston himself was brought out. Much of his face was bandaged. He was helped up into the back of the other ER vehicle, and an officer climbed in before it pulled away. So both men were captured now, Claire thought, just like they had captured Darcy, the dolphin, even those delicate butterflies—and those floating bodies inside, too.

Yet sitting in the gated back section of the squad car, Claire almost felt that they were prisoners, too. She knew she'd have to give extensive debriefings and, later, testify in court. From danger at least—at last—she and Darcy were free. Yet how would her half sister take the stunning news about what had happened here tonight? About Will? Darcy had already been so hurt, but she had to know and be strong enough to accept the truth. Claire had to help her mend her delicate wings, her past, herself.

"I hope Darcy's strong enough to learn about Will, to understand," she said. "And to forgive him. He protected me when Jedi showed up. If he hadn't, who knows what might have happened to me."

"I'll bet Jedi didn't know Will was the one who abducted Ralston in the video. I think Jedi just figured Onward was the place to look when his boss went missing. Jedi told Ralston's butler he didn't recognize the kidnapper from the home surveillance camera, though maybe that was just so he wouldn't be blamed if he rescued Ralston and killed Will."

"I can't wait to get home—even in this hurricane. And to get to Darcy when all this is over."

"So here you were, in the line of fire again. Ken said you continually overstep, but that's putting it mildly."

"You should talk," she said, but her voice was shaky and soft as she clung closer to him. "How many times have you put yourself in danger trying to help others through your South Shores rescue missions, starting back when we first met, before our nearly deadly time in St. Augustine?"

"Enough talk," he said, resting his chin on the top of her damp head as he pinned her to him, then tipped her face up toward his. He began to kiss her again, gently at first, then possessively, and despite all the terror and grief, it was wonderful, like riding on the wings of the wind.

They both jumped at a knock on the door of the car, and Ken got in. Before they could pepper him with questions, he said, "Another lucky detective is going to be sent to calm the masses at Germaine Arena instead of me. I'm taking you two home before this gets worse. Will Warren was seen ditching his car at a nearby gas station, which I had an officer check first. I've read Jedi Brown his rights for firing on Claire and Will, and he's heading for Naples General to have several bullets dug out along with a blood transfusion. Clint Ralston was complicit in keeping Darcy here once Jedi abducted her, so I read him his rights, too."

"But Will got away," Claire said, sliding off Nick's lap and leaning forward to hook her fingers through the lattice between the front and back seats as she spoke through it.

"The gas station cashier who saw him said he just abandoned his car and got in another one parked there and drove north. That's all—he drove north in a dark car into the darkness, so I'm not banking on him being found, at least not for a while."

"He was a kind of genius, Ken. Will arranged for me to have papers that show Darcy was abducted and brought here for testing. Jedi took her, but Ralston was all for detaining and experimenting on her. The papers are wet— where are they, Nick?"

He pulled them out of his duffel bag. "Criminal lawyers know criminal intent when they see it," he said, pushing the damp papers to Ken around the very end of the mesh screen. "But I know your police techs will be all over the files where this came from—if that place gets through this storm."

"If we all do. You know," Ken said as he put the papers in a front compartment, "as damning as his testimony would be in court, I wouldn't mind if the guy just vanished. It would be easier on your sister, too, not to mention he's been making the Collier County law enforcement guys— including me—look bad by doing a better job at turning up criminals than we have. Besides, all I have is he's a man heading north in a dark car."

"His most serious charge would probably be manslaughter," Claire said. "And faking evidence, if Will's the one who faked Larry's suicide note on his phone. But I'll bet, if you catch him, he could testify to make us all believe Larry fell in."

"And remember that old guy on the dock you two asked for directions to Captain Larry's boat?" Ken said. "He's willing to testify that a man we can now prove is Will Warren was arguing with Larry *after* Steve had a fight with

Larry and then stormed off the dock. In all this mess, I didn't have time to tell you and I didn't want to get your hopes up, but with that confession letter from Will, I'm pretty sure all charges will be dropped once we all get through this storm."

"Thank God," Claire said. "I bet Will's heading back to Japan. He made a lot of connections and money there dealing in butterfly smuggling and black market selling."

"You don't sound unhappy about that," Ken said.

"He may have killed Larry Ralston, abducted me at gunpoint, planted that smart doll in our house to spy on us, and hurt a lot of people with his actions. But he tracked down Darcy's abductors when I couldn't. Misguided as his actions were, he did it out of love. I don't want to see him charged," she added with a huge sigh.

Nick put his arm around her to draw her closer again. "That's exactly how I think of my beautiful wife. Are you sure he's Darcy's father and not yours?"

She elbowed him in the ribs. "Ken, can you get us home somehow before this hurricane hits?" she asked. "I'll answer questions when you want, but I don't know if I can even talk or walk straight right now."

"I've got one officer still inside and two more coming to guard this place along with some of the staff to tend to those bodies. As soon as I can hand the scene over to them, I'll take you both home. Waiting for more orders, always someone else's orders, and now we have to listen to the weathermen. Be back in a sec."

He got out of the car and jogged toward Onward again, but he returned quickly as promised.

"Change of plans. I've been ordered to the Naples Airport, so I've handed the scene here over to the officer in-

side. I'll take you two as far as the airport. Even though it's
closed to traffic and people," he told them as he started the
car and gunned the engine. "Maybe you can get your man
Bronco to come get you there or even Darcy's husband if
he's not going to sit this out at the hospital—and give him
the good news I predict we'll be dropping charges against
him per your future testimony."

"Yeah," Nick said, "I can have Bronco come to get us
there. Steve is going to be celebrating once all the charges
are dropped. So what's the big problem at the airport?" he
asked as Ken turned the siren and the lights on. "I heard it
was closed because of the storm."

"A NOAA hurricane hunter plane blew an engine. It's
going to try to land, but it's really dangerous in this mess,
and we'll need emergency vehicles and cops if it goes down.
Hopefully, it will even make it as far as the airport runway
because there's a big population with lots of buildings on
that approach."

Claire gasped, gripping Nick's hand so hard he winced.
Jace had to be piloting that plane. It would be terrible
enough to have to comfort Darcy, tell her who her father
really was and that he was probably gone forever.

But to have to tell Brit her new husband was gone? To
have to tell Lexi her daddy was gone after all she'd been
through?

CHAPTER THIRTY-FOUR

Claire was amazed by how fast Ken had driven them to the airport. They had explained to him that the pilot of the hurricane plane could well be her ex-husband and their friend, Jace Britten.

"Out of the frying pan and into—well, didn't mean that," Ken had said. "If I hadn't been ordered to the airport, I'd take you home."

Claire kept wiping at her tears, trying to keep her stomach cramps from making her throw up. They were both in their seat belts; Nick held her hand tight. They were safe now, but she feared for Jace, Mitch and their crew.

When would this nightmare sequence of events finally end? They had Darcy back, and Lexi had shown strength over that horrid doll, but if she lost her father...poor Brit, and Mitch was set to be married to Kris soon. Once a pilot's wife herself—this pilot—Claire knew if either he or Mitch survived but lost any of their crew, they would never forgive themselves.

As they turned onto the access road to the runways, Ken, bending close to the windshield to see through the deluge and wild wind, told them, "I'm going to pull up near the emergency vehicles in case the crew needs help exiting the plane when it lands. You two get out, go into the terminal and wait. If you can't get someone to come for you, we'll get you home ASAP."

"Understood," Nick said, and motioned for her not to say more.

Did Nick know, Claire wondered, that she would never obey that order? But then maybe he would not, either. They were going to stay back, of course, but not go inside, not as long as they could stand in this wind.

Ken jerked the car to a halt in the line of four Collier County sheriff cars and three waiting emergency vehicles. "Head inside!" he ordered, and got out. His door slammed so hard it must have been the wind.

Nick and Claire got out and staggered toward the end of the terminal, then huddled against it to escape the worst of the brutal gusts of wind and biting rain.

"I hear a plane!" she cried.

"The wind's roaring!" Nick shouted back.

They clung together. "No—listen!" she insisted. She pulled away and ran out a little ways and, shielding her eyes from the stinging raindrops, looked up.

Although Jace had the controls, both he and Mitch listened intently as the Naples Municipal Airport controller tried to talk them in. At least the flicker of flame around the dead engine had been doused by the rain. Swirling, heavy wind banged the big turboprop plane as if it were a toy. Jace's legs were shaking from trying to control the rudders.

Mitch continually scanned and read their position aloud as Jace held hard to the steering yoke. The airport controller's voice was breaking up. *Dear God*, Jace prayed, *don't let this plane break up, too, when we hit the ground, with wheels down and, hopefully, some control in this gusting wind.*

"Runway north/south at 6600 feet long," the man's voice said. "Radar readings affirmative, but hold your altitude and trajectory until you see the lights. They are all on for you. Since you know the airport, you realize the central business and hotel district is only two nautical miles before touchdown."

"Roger that. Trying to control nose lift. Wind speed on the ground?"

"Gusting between eighty and ninety, but going up steadily. Sporadic and circling, southwest feed."

"Roger that."

"Have you jettisoned fuel?"

"Most over the gulf. I know we're only getting one shot at this."

Jace could feel his heartbeat. He'd been through worse in the Middle East, he tried to tell himself, but in a jet with no crew. He felt he had so much more to live for now. A new wife, peace with the old one, though Claire would never be old to him. Always young, strong, the mother of his beloved Lexi.

Extend glide, extend glide, he told himself. Ready to raise flaps.

Mitch said, "I'm looking for the damn city lights. Hell, are we gonna be on top of the roofs before we see them?"

"Altimeter says not yet. With all their noise ordinances here, think the city council will fine us—or NOAA will fire us—for roaring in so low?"

"They'll just think it's the hurricane instead of the hurricane hunters. I'm with you, man. You can do this."

"Tell the crew to brace."

Mitch hit the all-call and said, "We'll be on the ground at Naples Airport soon. They're ready for us. Be prepared to deplane. Brace. Brace positions."

Good man, copilot and friend, Jace thought. Mitch's voice had been steady, however nervous he was, too. Training. Courage. This had to work.

"There!" Mitch cried. "Lights, blurry, but lights! Not the runway lights, but I saw them."

"Then those can't be far."

"We have you on visual descent," the calm voice came over the radio. "You are cleared for landing."

"No kidding," Mitch muttered. "They've already cleared everybody else out and shut down the place."

Jace gripped the steering yoke. All he'd ever learned flying, all he'd ever done, loved and lost, was riding with him, in his hands and on his head if he made a mistake.

The big plane yawed again. He yanked it back, tried to steady it so the left side would not hit the runway first and turn them, spin them, flip them.

Yes, he saw runway lights below, also blinking and strobes from emergency vehicles, maybe police cars along the runway. That helped, at least some.

Drift down slow, he told himself. Keep control. Feather the dead engine more to reduce drag. Cannot go around, just one try. Just one chance not to crash and burn.

One golden light, only one, was coming out of the black, shifting sky. Did they only have one headlight? Only one engine? Claire wished she didn't remember the overheard, half-knowledge of being a pilot's wife, all the worry. She prayed silently that Jace would land the plane safely, for Lexi and for Brit—for Mitch and Kris, too.

"Land safe!" she shouted as if those in the plane could hear.

Coming up behind her, Nick put his arms around her and held her tight again. Strange then, but as the big plane roared lower, tilting a bit, one wing down but still nose up, she thought about butterflies in a storm. This big plane fighting the elements, wounded, no delicate wings but so endangered.

She heard shrieking brakes, then the single engine. The plane went past them, silent now as that engine shut down. The flaps were deployed, trying to stop the huge weight and momentum. The big plane twisted, tilted, skidded sideways. Was there any runway left?

Expecting a crash or fire, she could not look. She turned and buried her face against Nick's sopping wet shoulder.

But no crash. No explosion or fire they could see as she dared to look again. They heard only the sounds of sirens.

"They're down!" Nick shouted. "It stopped rolling. No flames! Just off the end of the runway, I think, tilted, maybe turned. All the ERs are heading out there."

They held hands and ran, not onto the tarmac but just inside the fence, closer, where they could see. Amazingly, the long line of runway lights blinked, flickered, then went out before popping back on. Nick looked out to Airport Road. "Power just went out, I think, except what's on generators. We may have to hunker down here but let's make sure the passengers...our pilots...are okay."

Our pilots. Yes, they were ours, Claire thought as they held hands and tore even farther along the tall wire fence heading toward the dark plane now illumined by headlights and flashing emergency vehicles.

Even though the plane was tipped and partly off the end of the runway, the door popped open. No stairs, but a slide deployed. Close together, person after person slid down and started toward the lights pinpointing them.

In the sweep of rain, Claire could not see clearly. The pilots—if they were all right—would surely get off last, the captain last of all. She laced her hands through the wire fencing, trying to count people because she remembered Jace had said there was a crew of ten besides the two pilots.

"Ten," she told Nick, squinting through the rain. "I count ten. But with the plane slanted sideways, what if the flight deck caved in?"

But then she saw two tall forms slide down after the crew had been pulled away from the fuselage. Yes, surely Mitch, then Jace.

"Thank goodness Lexi still has her daddy!" Claire cried.

"Those men are heroes, both. You think we can take them home with us?"

"After that, probably not," Claire said, her voice still shaking. "Debriefing and I'm sure they'll stay with that valuable plane even in this mess, unless someone's really injured, and it doesn't look like it. I wish we could offer shelter to them and the entire crew, but no way. Jace and Mitch will have to wait to be reunited with their loved ones. For Jace, duty always calls."

Somehow, Ken had seen them and came striding over. She figured they were in for another dressing down for not following his orders again, but what else was new?

Ken called to them in the wind, "All in one piece, and insisting they stay near the plane. The airport's up to code, though they'll have to bunk on the floor inside. I won't even bother to mention you two ignored my orders again. The Collier County jail is up to code, too, and I ought to drop you both off there—but I give up. I just give up. Let me get you home ASAP, so I can get back here or wherever they send me next. Hell, wish they'd send *me* home."

He hurried back toward the plane in a vast darkness lit now only by the runway lights, which must be working on emergency generators. Claire and Nick were about to head for Ken's car, but she heard a voice she knew.

"Nick, I hear Jace," she cried.

She turned back, though the storm beat against them all. It didn't matter, she told herself. They had Darcy back, and somehow Claire could help her handle the shocking news about Will Warren. Kris could still marry Mitch. Jace was safe, and Claire had managed to get through a perilous night. She and Nick had come through again, and surely things must be better now, brutal storm to face or not.

Jace approached on the other side of the security fence. He put one hand through it, gripping the wires, clutching her fingers. Claire saw he had a big bump on his forehead that was turning gray or blue. He had tears in his eyes.

"Jace!" she cried. "Jace, you did it!"

With his other hand, he gripped Nick's fingers through the fencing, too. "I can't believe you two are here—and yet, I can. Tell Lexi and Brit I'll see them soon. Brit said she's going to ride out this storm with you."

"Yes," Nick said. "We'll take care of her...both of them... for you."

"Hey," Jace said, a bit of his pilot swagger and bravado back already as he loosed their hands and gave a mock salute, "this storm's nothing if you've ever had to deal with Claire. Know what I mean, Nick?"

"You don't know the half of it—why we're out in this mess tonight," Nick told him.

Tears also flooded Claire's eyes to see Jace teasing and in one piece. Yes, she knew exactly how Nick felt when she got herself into dangerous, deadly dilemmas, but he should talk. At least, thank heavens, hurricane or not, surely nothing else could go wrong now.

CHAPTER THIRTY-FIVE

They must look like drowned rats, Nick thought as Ken drove them into their driveway at about two in the morning. It had been a harrowing trip home from the airport with trees down and debris skidding across the roads as well as traffic lights out. At least the streets were greatly deserted. Headlights and the pulsating strobe bar at the top of Ken's cruiser had been the only lights in most places. Their neighborhood was a ghost town, one being battered by the elements. The houses were all dark with the electricity out here, too.

"The latest order is that not even emergency vehicles are allowed on the roads," Ken told them. "I know there was a huge traffic jam of people fleeing north earlier. I just hope everyone else is hunkered down somewhere safe. The storm is a low to mid-Cat 4. As for me, I hope I never have to rescue you two again, but let's hoist a few cold ones once we get through this. I'll bring my wife. Now get in safe and stay put. Get some sleep if you can."

When they got out, despite the rain, Ken rolled his window down and put his hand out. Holding on to Claire and the car to keep from going off his feet, Nick grabbed Ken's hand and shook it. Claire leaned in to give him an awkward half hug.

"We both owe you," she told him, raising her voice over the shriek of the wind.

He shouted back, "Never know when I might just turn to crime and need a lawyer. And that job offer always stands, Claire. Man, I can tell the barometric pressure's dropping bad because I'm having a toothache from some dental work. It's supposed to give some people a headache, too, but I already have that dealing with you two. Take care!"

He rolled up his window, and they ran to the front door, knowing the garage door probably wouldn't work. Nick fumbled to get his key in the lock in the darkness. Surely someone would be up waiting for them, Bronco at least.

Ken's headlights slashed across them as he pulled out and headed slowly away. The wind's howl had turned to a shriek. They'd been pretty sure they saw Brit's car parked down the street away from trees, so Kris must be here now, too. They'd planned to come in the morning, but this storm was worsening fast.

Before Nick could get his key in the lock, Brit pulled the door open. Shaking water off like wet dogs, they went in while she held the door for them against the force of the wind, but he had to help her close it.

"I thought I saw headlights, then peeked out," she told them. "I'd like to hug you, but I won't."

Nick saw Will's painting had been moved farther down the hall, no doubt in case the rain and wind swept in like this.

"Glad you're here," Claire said. "Yes, we won't hug you, or you might drown. Is Kris here, too?"

"Uh—yes. She's with Nita and Bronco," Brit said, wringing her hands.

Nick wondered if she could know what Jace had just gone through, what he'd done so heroically, but he guessed not. They'd have to sit her down and tell her. The storm appeared to be making her nervous. No doubt she was worried about the zoo animals as well as everyone here and fretting over Jace, who she thought was in Tampa with his plane and crew.

But maybe he wasn't going to tell her all that right now, since she looked so jumpy. He was suddenly proud of Claire again. She, too, must have realized this was not the time to tell Brit about Jace's near catastrophe. What a surprise they had for her when she calmed down.

"I'm sure you've been through a lot," Brit went on, gripping Claire by her upper arms. "But—but I guess it happens sometimes when a pregnant woman is due to deliver soon, and the barometric pressure drops. We've seen that with the big cats at the zoo."

"What?" Claire asked. "What are you talking about? Is Nita all right?"

"Okay, okay. I hope you've had your narco meds because her water broke about two hours ago, and I'm pretty sure she's gone into labor already, though I'm only familiar with pregnant felines."

Brit's voice broke. Nick could see she was shaking; Claire looked wide-eyed and speechless. How much more could she take tonight?

"Before the power went out," Brit rushed on, "they said on TV that no one is to be out on the streets, not even emergency vehicles, so we can't call an ambulance. But yes, we have an emergency right here in this house. Claire, you're the only one here who's had a baby, so please take over, and I'll help you. She says the baby's named for you, so I hope you know how to deliver little Clarita!"

Bronco was going berserk, but Claire didn't feel much better. Nita was definitely in labor. And her contractions were only ten minutes apart already. At least she said she had no desire to push yet.

Bronco kept insisting he could still drive her to the hospital. Claire finally told him no and got Nick to back her up. "What if a tree crashes down in front of your car or on your car?" she told the big, nervous guy. "And palm trees don't have a good root system. Even if your car wasn't damaged, do you want to have to deliver your baby, exposed to the elements, in the middle of a hurricane?"

He backed down a bit and quit raving after that. Claire later heard Nick speaking to him in the hall outside the guest bedroom they were using as a delivery room. "Listen to me, Bronco. The very best you can do for Nita and the baby is to keep calm, hold her hand and remain steady while Claire, Brit and Kris help her deliver this baby. Everything will be fine."

As exhausted as she was after spending some time comforting a frightened Nita, Claire washed up, ate and drank something to sustain herself and tried to bring some sanity to the birthing scene. She told Brit where to get some extra plastic pads she used for Trey's crib, and they put three of them on the double bed under Nita with an extra shower curtain under all that.

Trying to think all this through—remembering her so-different hospital deliveries of Lexi and Trey—she gathered dry towels, sanitary pads and sterilized scissors. Trey's waterproof pants and clothes would be too big for a newborn, but she gathered some anyway. She grabbed her cell phone to use the timer on it, then assigned Brit to time Nita's contractions—now about eight minutes apart. This was going fast, so fast, though she knew some women went through labor quickly. But a first birth? She prayed it wouldn't turn into an emergency C-section like she'd needed with Trey.

She helped Nita take a cool shower, sitting on a lawn chair she had Bronco bring into the bathroom from those they'd brought in from the backyard. After they got Nita back in bed, Claire finally took a quick shower herself.

She made Nita drink water and Brit sponged her off when her pains came closer together, and she continued to sweat—but weren't they all too hot between the humidity and stress and no air-conditioning? Both Kris and Brit took to fanning Nita with folded newspapers.

Claire tried not to look at the clock. She hadn't slept well since Darcy was taken or at all tonight, so she was running on fumes. Finally, she cleared the bedroom but for Brit and Kris. Claire had Kris hold the biggest and brightest of the two flashlights they had here, lifted the sheet, propped up Nita's knees on two pillows and looked at her dilation.

"What do you see?" Nita asked. "Any sign of Clarita's head yet? Years ago, I witnessed my older sister have her first son. Ah, ah—coming, another bad one!" she cried, and tugged hard at the padded ropes Kris had strung above her head from tall chairs on both sides of the bed after insisting she'd seen a prehistoric petroglyph where an ancient woman was shown delivering a baby that way.

Nita was already exhausted, but so was Claire, relying on her narcoleptic pills that were stimulants, and downing lukewarm bottled tea for the caffeine to get herself through her emotional and physical exhaustion. She fought to keep calm and keep Nita calm, so she wasn't letting Bronco back into this room until she had to.

"Tell me—tell me the truth about what is happening," Nita cried. "My body is doing its own thing! Tell me—ah!"

"You've expelled a bit of prebaby discharge, but no head yet. Yes, I'm going to tell you exactly what I think is happening so that you can help."

"I can help between the hits of pain. *Mi amiga*, what would I ever do without you? Our plans for the doctor and the hospital—aaahh! Well," she gritted out through clenched teeth, "this how my mother had me, no doctor."

Between the closer contractions and during a quick bathroom break, Claire gave a hug and more reassurance to Bronco, who was pacing up and down with Nick sitting farther down the hall on a chair he'd dragged out of their bedroom, sound asleep.

Claire peeked in for the second time at the girls. Lexi and Jilly must've been wakened by the howling wind and a fierce clap of thunder; both were in Lexi's bed. And—this touched her deeply—it appeared they had netted several butterflies to save them from the brutal winds and brought them inside. On the top of Lexi's dresser, they rested on a leafy branch in an old, empty aquarium with a screen across its top.

"Our Sleeping Beauty night-light went out!" Lexi cried, her little voice shaking.

"I'll leave you this flashlight I have. I'll put it on the dresser, see, and turn it on so it will be just like a night-light." At least they had an extra stash of flashlights in the birthing room. She decided again not to tell them what was going on across the hall unless she had to.

Looking at the girls' frightened faces, she couldn't help but recall Will's tearful expression when he had gazed at the sleeping Jilly with tears on his face. He would probably never see his beloved Darcy and her children again, but with Will, you never knew. He'd chosen to go on the run now, so did that mean he was sacrificing a life with them because he knew he could be found guilty of Larry's death and abducting Ralston—then blinding him?

Lexi said, "Mommy, that wind is screaming, but did I hear another scream? Are you okay?"

"I'm fine, sweetheart, but let me explain something to both of you."

So much for keeping these two in the dark. As Claire sat down on the edge of the bed, she saw the doll was not with them, but was on the floor, wrapped in a blanket head to foot so that even her face didn't show. That was a small victory, a first step toward getting rid of it.

"Don't either of you worry if you hear another scream. Nita is going to have her baby right here in this house during the storm. And sometimes, when a baby is born, it hurts the mother a little, but then she is so happy to have her baby, she forgets the pain."

Jilly said from the other side of the bed, her voice slow and sleepy, "I hope my mommy didn't hurt when I was born, 'cause she went through a lot when she was away last week, but she's okay now."

"She sure is going to be," Claire said, kissing Lexi's cheek, then Jilly's. "Now, listen, you two. I am going to be with Nita so I want you to stay in here even if you hear a scream or two. Both of your dads are here—and your daddy, Jace, is just fine, too, Lexi—so you please help me by keeping calm and getting more sleep. We have a strong house to withstand the storm. Lots of people are here at the house, but tomorrow, we might just have a new baby for you to see."

"Good," Lexi said, "'cause I don't want—" she lowered her voice so much that Claire could hardly hear her "—that other doll anymore. I would give it to little Clarita 'cause Nita said she's real sorry she gave it to me, but I don't want it spying on Clarita or Bronco or Nita, either. But when Heck was here earlier, I think he turned off her insides."

"Then I think she is fine right where she is, all bundled up. Now, listen to me. I love both of you and Darcy does, too. If you need someone, you call for your dads, but try to get some sleep now."

Outside their room, Claire went down the hall and, hating to do it, woke Nick. "I know you're trying to keep an eye on Bronco," she told him, "but make sure you occasionally look in on the girls and Trey, too."

"Will do, captain. Didn't mean to nod off. Claire, you okay in there? What can I do?"

"Pray and try to keep Bronco from coming in until the head at least crowns. I'll let you know. I just don't want something to go wrong with the delivery because I'm scared. But I've been scared before."

He shook himself more awake, then stood and embraced her. "Remember," he said, his lips in her hair, "she's named after you, so that baby is a fighter. I'll keep an eye on Bronco. I think he just went to get something to drink."

As she hurried back to Nita's bedside, Claire told herself that surely Jace's safe landing tonight had set the precedent. Dark storm or not, more good news had to be on the horizon.

CHAPTER THIRTY-SIX

Claire, Brit and Kris all cooed to the new baby and cried with joy and relief while they washed Clarita in the storm-tossed early morning. Bronco, big bruiser that he was, cried when Claire put the little, black-haired, brown-eyed bundle into his shaking arms. He had only been invited into the birthing room for the last few minutes of the delivery so that Nita could focus on pushing. Despite the darkness in the house and probably devastation outside, Bronco and Nita's joy brightened everything.

Even Lexi and Jilly got a peek at the new baby, and Claire noticed the next time she was in Lexi's room that not only was the doll still wrapped head to toe, but it had been shoved under Lexi's bed. So, Claire hoped, there was both light and power in a house that had neither right now.

Finally, Claire shooed the other visitors out and left the new, little family alone.

"A first baby and only about six hours of labor," Claire

told Brit. "Unbelievable. Don't know what was wrong with me to take so long with Lexi."

"She's worth it," Brit said, "and glad to hear she dumped that doll. Tough times but full steam ahead—like mother, like daughter."

Everyone sat or stood around the kitchen table while Kris wrangled removing things from the warming refrigerator. "Perfect for a new baby celebration!" she announced. "Peanut butter and jelly sandwiches, cookies and soda pop, just like we're all kids again. Or water or warmish orange juice. Nick says no adults are allowed alcoholic beverages until after lunch and then he's going to check your IDs."

How proud Claire was of these people, trying to carry on despite the dangers and dark parts of life. She and Nick were blessed to have such family and friends—and a new life in the other room she could hear crying. Maybe she should go back in and be sure Nita could nurse Clarita. No formula around here, but they would make do. Then the crying stopped, so maybe Nita or even Bronco had figured things out. She'd go knock on the door and look in later. And what tales of her delivery they would all have to share with Clarita as she grew up.

Claire thought of Will again, driving through the storm, fleeing, but worst of all, maybe never to see his daughter and grandchildren again. Yet knowing Will, he'd be back someday, delivering a package at Darcy's door, calling on the phone to tell Jilly or even Drew a tale about his adventures...

"Claire," Nick said, putting his arm around her, "you're nodding off. Let's get you to bed."

"Food first. I'm famished."

As she ate PB&J, she began to feel she was on her second—maybe third or fourth—wind after being up and through so much these last twenty-four hours. She was even mostly thinking straight, and for a narcoleptic, that was pretty good.

She had to tell Steve about Will being Darcy's father and explain all he'd done to make those who had hurt Darcy pay. Nick had only told him so far that they'd learn from Detective Jensen that the charges against him had a good chance of being completely dropped, and that Nick would look into it as soon as things returned—somewhat, at least—to normal.

When this weather stopped, they were all going to gear up to help others who did not have as strong a house. Claire nodded as everyone spoke of that. Even the new home of Bronco, Nita and Clarita would need a thorough examination, and it was possible they wouldn't have much to go home to, anyway. But they—this family and these people, including Darcy, of course—would pull together on that.

And, above all, as soon as possible, Steve had agreed that Claire should tell Darcy about Will alone, though he and the kids—Jilly, at least, since it wouldn't be possible for Drew to get back yet—would be waiting outside the room at the hospital. Depending on how Darcy took that news, she would either stay there for more counseling, or be able to go home—if she and Steve still had a home in decent shape, since their neighborhood was older.

After breakfast, Claire slept most of the morning and early afternoon. When she woke, she sat up in bed, alarmed. What was wrong? Something was very wrong!

Then she realized the wind no longer howled, and the rain no longer pounded on the roof. She took her meds

Nick must have left next to the bed and got up to look out. Windy, but not bad. Daylight, but no sun. Two palm trees had toppled over to crush their back fence, and things looked beaten down with debris strewn and snagged almost everywhere.

"Like life," she whispered. "Like my life, but I've come through, and Darcy has to come through, too."

"Wow, what a storm!" Darcy said the minute Claire joined her in her room at the hospital late that day. "I watched a lot of it out the window. I'm scared to hear what Steve finds when he checks our house. And hopefully the airport is open again in time for Drew to come home next week. The cell towers are still down, but we're going to explain everything to him in person when he gets back. I can't wait to get home with all my family there. I can't thank you enough for taking them all in during the storm!"

"Of course," Claire said. "We missed you, though."

"I hope so! Claire," she said, lowering her voice and drawing her over to the couch to sit, "I think I'm ready to leave here. To try to be normal again, even if some things I can't explain still kind of…haunt me. Dr. Spizer said you might be able to fill in some of the blanks."

"Yes, thanks to Will Warren, who did some private detective work to learn what happened to you, who took you and why."

"Will? Really? But how does he figure in?" she asked, reaching over and gripping Claire's hands so tightly that Claire almost winced.

"He figures in a lot, more than I realized. You knew he was especially fond of you…"

"True—and Jilly, too, though Drew seemed not to like him. Boys!"

"Do you remember Will from our youth, before he took off for parts unknown for a while?"

"I don't. He told me he went to Japan—research, I think—because he wanted to write about butterflies. Well, you know, that lovely book of his."

"But before he went, after Dad deserted Mother, even before that, I think, Will came to the house with books for her."

"You did tell me that, though can't say I remember. Claire, just tell me. What's all this about Will? Was he injured in the storm?"

"Okay, here's what I've learned. Our father had another woman—a common-law wife, no less—he visited on his salesman travels. But Mother, too, had an extramarital affair—with Will."

"With our mother? Meeting—in the house? But then he left? Is that when he went to Japan? Why didn't he stay and marry her? I mean, how long were they together? I'm not following you. Could that be what made her so strange—losing two men?"

"There's more. Will had things lined up to make a lot of money there, he told me, money he wanted to bring back and use to support her—and us. She said if he left, he didn't care for her, but...but he did. And he has all these years."

"Was what he did in Japan illegal? Tara told me there's a lot of smuggling and black marketing of butterflies there."

"Yes, some, I think, but that isn't the big news. There was a time when he and Mother loved each other very much. They had a love child. And that child...is you."

Darcy's hands remained in Claire's, but they went very

still. Her eyes widened, looking past Claire, who feared
what was coming next—inward retreat or an explosion.

But Darcy only heaved a huge sigh. When she blinked,
tears speckled her lashes.

"Crazy as it sounds, I feel like I knew that," she whispered, looking at Claire. "But he—he never said it. He
should have. I knew he wasn't in love with me romanti-
cally. He was so proper, yet concerned and protective—
interested in my life."

"He loved you very much—still does—and took great
care to show me the place you were kept. He wanted justice, wanted to expose those who hurt you. He loved Jilly,
too—and yes, said he noticed Drew didn't take to him and
that hurt."

"So much hurt. Mother's agoraphobia. Her reading all
those books, burying herself in them, never one word about
Dad's desertion. Not a word about Will. At first, when
we were young, of course not, but why not later? And he
should have tried to contact her, tried again those years
she was alone. But then, remember the checks she received
from a great-aunt she didn't remember every Christmas?
What if...?"

"He didn't say that, but yes. What if? He did tell me he
visited her grave more than once, even released some butterflies there. Darcy, I want us to be complete sisters for
always," she said, and started to cry herself. "So forget the
half-sister thing."

They hugged hard, held on. "Tell me all he did and every
word he said," Darcy insisted. "And tell me he's safe, that
I can see him soon."

"Let me explain from the beginning." Claire sat back,
swiping at more tears. Darcy was in for another blow, but

she was here with her and they were both going home soon. "Let me just be your sister still in every way and tell you all I know. And then, how much you tell Jilly, Drew and Steve now or someday is up to you, though Steve does already know Will is your father."

Darcy nodded. "Yes, start at the beginning. And I always knew my dear sister would be my best friend for life—forever, too."

EPILOGUE

Four months later

Because the hurricane storm surge had eroded some of the beaches, and huge dredges and barges were making noisy repairs, Kris and Mitch's wedding was held at the Naples Botanical Garden near the two-tiered waterfall.

What a lovely, relaxing sound, Claire thought as white water spilled into the small, calm lake. So much better than the shrieks of a hurricane. She and Brit, wearing peach-hued gowns and straw hats, accompanied the bride. Jace, of course, was Mitch's best man.

Kris had insisted that even the younger children come, so Nita was tending Trey and Clarita. The dig team who worked with Kris were here, along with several of the NOAA flight crew, and the manager of the Marco Island Airport where Jace and Mitch were locating their new Fly Safe flight school. The love of Heck's life, Gina, also came from Miami, and both were beaming since he had proposed and she had accepted, though that meant he'd be moving there at least until she finished med school. He'd already secured a new position with the Dade County police in their Digital Forensic Unit.

Lexi and Jilly were flower girls, beaming under their little straw hats. Claire could see Darcy and Steve from where she stood as the vows began. "Dearly beloved, we are gathered together..."

Her dearly beloved were here, family and friends, including several friends the four of them—Claire, Darcy, Brit and Kris—had made volunteering with a local hurricane disaster service group. Steve had helped Bronco put a new roof on their house, and now that it was done, Claire would be sad to see the little family moving out of the Markwood home. At least Nita would still work for them and bring Clarita with her. But their not living in the extra bedroom where Clarita was born would be another wrench for Lexi, who had announced she was too old to bother with dolls now, because Clarita was like a little doll.

Claire blinked back tears when Kris and Mitch exchanged rings, said their vows, kissed and walked up the grassy aisle together. What a rocky path she and Nick had had together, but things had ultimately worked out so well. She felt herself blush at the memory of last night in bed, for their love had grown in meaning and depth since their own shotgun wedding, and months later their reception, which had literally blown up in their faces.

No rice was to be thrown in this lovely setting amid so many stunning gardens. Some foliage had been uprooted or damaged by the storm, but trees and bushes were coming back strong. There was a butterfly house here, but they had decided against a release because that meant the butterflies had to be imprisoned first. That had made Claire happy. She'd had enough of innocent creatures being taken prisoner.

The single women gathered to catch Kris's bouquet, which she tossed over her shoulder without looking. It flew perfectly to Gina. Heck was so excited at that he hugged Nick where they stood watching. "Thanks to you and Claire getting in trouble in Cuba, boss, 'cause that led me to Gina!"

"See, Claire," Nick said, pounding the happy man on his back. "Our almost getting killed in Cuba was for a good cause!"

A lot of good had come out of their toughest times, Claire realized. Nick had even given a deposition on behalf of Lincoln Yost, who was caught up in the Ralston scandal because of his ties to the Onward projects. Hometown hero that Yost still was, he did not go to prison but did have to pay such a hefty fine that he was selling his dream home and moving into a house in Golden Gate, not far from the one Will Warren had vacated.

Clint Ralston, who had regained minimal vision, was soon to stand trial along with Jedi Brown. Of course, Nick was keeping clear of those criminal cases.

Gina ran over with the bouquet and hugged Claire as the bride and groom began to greet their guests in an impromptu reception line near the catered food table featuring a large cake.

"Mommy!" Lexi cried. "Jilly and I think this wedding is totally awesome!"

Jilly's brother, Drew, hands thrust in his pants pockets, muttered, "This isn't as cool as some birthday parties I've seen, 'specially one I went to that had paintball. But I guess there's lots of food here."

Claire thought it was a blessing Drew had not been here during his mother's disappearance, because even being told about it had made him angry. So Darcy had found herself counseling Drew while counselors—and Claire—still counseled her.

"Totally awesome?" Nick repeated what Lexi had just said when the kids ran off together again. "Why is our little girl suddenly sounding like a teenager?" He put his arm around Claire's waist to give her a little squeeze.

"Don't say that. Next you'll be signing our toddler son up for Little League or teaching him how to get clients off the hook in a court of law."

"Speaking of that, thank goodness Steve was finally cleared of any wrongdoing. And I'd bet that crazy cake over there that they'll never find Will if he doesn't want to be found."

They strolled toward the buffet table where there were chairs set up on the grass. The wedding cake was perfectly unique. Instead of the usual decorations of flowers, entwined hearts or a bride and groom, the baker had custom decorated it with a small plane on one side with *Fly Safe* written on it, and on the other side, a picture of a primitive, doll-like effigy that Kris had recently excavated from an ancient burial at the Black Bog where Claire had once worked.

"Well," Nick told her as they looked down at the design, "two unique people joining their lives."

"Like us," she said, "and look what we've made of things."

"Meaning the calm, good times, not the mess—the dangers."

"Of course, and I'm not sure what you could be referring to," she said, elbowing him gently in the ribs.

"Ah, my beloved Claire," he said with a little sigh. "We've come so far and, hopefully, have a lot farther to go."

"Dark storms or not, I predict a lot of happiness ahead. For Darcy and Steve, too."

"The two of you seem even closer than before."

"Working on it. By the way—you heard it here—I'm retiring from dangerous endeavors, just wait and see."

"Yeah, right. Heard that one before," he said, rolling his eyes.

Although Claire could hear Trey starting to cry for her across the way, and it wasn't their wedding, she stood on tiptoe in the thick grass, threw her arms around Nick and kissed him hard.

When they stepped apart, she whispered, "For better or worse, till death us do part."

Nodding with tears in his eyes, he said, "I'll take the better with none of the worse, but whatever happens, to love and cherish you, I will and I do!"

★ ★ ★ ★ ★

AUTHOR'S NOTE

I hope you have enjoyed this book. Perhaps you also read the earlier five novels in the South Shores series that lead up to the events in *Dark Storm*. But it is time for me to leave Claire and Nick Markwood and their family and friends. They have come a long way since we met them— and Claire and Nick met each other—in the first book, *Chasing Shadows*, when Claire was shot outside the Collier County Courthouse.

I will miss them as well as the Naples/South Florida setting, almost as much as I miss it in reality since, after thirty lovely years, we no longer spend our winters there. It has been fun to use settings from some of the places we visited and loved in Naples and the Caribbean for this series. In this book, for example, walking out on the rocks at Doctors Pass and the Naples Botanical Garden (www. naplesgarden.org).

I have had the idea of writing a suspense novel using the falcate orangetip butterflies as the hook since 1998, but a story never quite fit together until now. However, I thank Gary Noel Ross, butterfly consultant in Baton Rouge, Louisiana, for his research suggestions on this unique butterfly. Other research came from the lovely book *The Spirit of Butterflies: Myth, Magic and Art* by Maraleen Manos-Jones, and the *Official Guide to Butterfly World*, which we visited in Coconut Creek, Florida (www.butterflyworld.com).

I thought the falcate orangetip talent for suspended animation was amazing; later, I learned that dolphins have a variation of this gift, too. But how to blend such different animals in a story? And what to do with the intriguing subject of cryonics, the ultimate suspension of life?

I also wondered which butterflies are endangered. In my research, I learned a butterfly breed as "common" as monarchs are indeed threatened today. For example, researchers claim monarchs have decreased ninety percent over these last years, according to the Environmental Defense Fund, mostly because their milkweed habitats, necessary for their life cycle, are disappearing. Concerned citizens can visit www.edf.org/MonarchAcre to learn more about this.

Also, I find it interesting but sad that, according to an article in the *Naples Daily News* of July 26, 2018, the local butterfly population has not recovered from the battering they received during Hurricane Irma. I based Hurricane Jenny loosely on Irma, which hit Southwest Florida in August of 2017. While we owned a condo in Naples, Florida, two hurricanes visited the area, and once, we lost the roof of our lanai.

Two quick explanations of unusual things in this book—things that I hardly believed until I researched them. First of all, Lexi's "smart" doll. The info Claire discovers online is true. I was surprised to see that such a doll can be monitored via a mobile app and Wi-Fi connectivity. An attacker can send unauthorized requests and extract information through such a doll. This can lead to malicious campaigns against caregivers or the child. The doll outlawed in Germany was called My Friend Cayla.

Secondly, it is not "an old wives' tale" that the sudden drop in barometric pressure during a hurricane can cause headaches, toothaches—and yes, women who are not far from delivery can go into early labor. This most often happens to women who are at least thirty-four weeks pregnant. During Hurricane Andrew in South Florida in 1992, for example, a large number of women went into labor and flocked to hospitals, and this phenomenon has been noted elsewhere.

Thanks for support on writing this novel to my wonderful team consisting of agent Annelise Robey, editor Emily Ohanjanians, MIRA Books publicists and copy editors, to name a few. I appreciate advice from Officer Jim Parsons of the Columbus Ohio Division of Police. And to my husband, Don, for being my travel companion and proofreader.

*See you online at www.KarenHarperauthor.com
or www.facebook.com/KarenHarperAuthor*

KAREN HARPER
HOW I WRITE

How I put ideas and background research into a novel is a question I'm asked a lot. Authors write many different ways, whatever works for them. With my previous career as an English teacher and as a longtime author and rabid reader, it's something I'm always interested in.

One time I attended a signing at a bookstore by an author I really admired. But I was disappointed that he just did a reading, then autographed books, and didn't give a glimpse into how he wrote his series. I decided then that I would always try to explain to readers what method of "authoring" works for me for book-length fiction.

So, after several decades of being an author, this is basically how I write. I won't go into idea gathering, the intentional and the serendipity. Take a look at my author's note to get a glimpse of that for this novel. It all began when I stumbled on a mention of falcate orangetips.

When I'm ready with an idea for a story, I send my editor ten pages or so of the possible plot. (This is typed double-spaced, so it's about five pages long.) This is called an outline or usually a synopsis. She and I have worked together for a while, so she knows that events may change as I write, but she okays my ideas and makes early suggestions.

In the past, such feedback has been invaluable. One time an editor told me, "The sales reps just had a book that featured an actress and it bombed, so they won't want to see another one. Can you shelve this for now and do something different?" Publishing is a business as well as an art.

I do plan somewhat ahead as I write, but I do not look too far out. Some writers push quickly through the entire story, then go back to delete, add or change things. I like to have each chapter quite well-written before I go on. I see each scene and chapter as the foundational building blocks to stack the rest of the story on.

I don't print out chapters until I have read/revised them about seven times. After I have printed out part of the story, I let it sit, then go over it with a red pen—the former English teacher coming out in me again. I then make those revisions on my laptop.

Once I am all the way through the book and have it printed and corrected and input my changes, I reread the entire book online again, make final revisions and print out the final copy my husband proofreads. I then add his corrections. He knows to look for two things especially, besides typos: I am directionally challenged (even if I know one must drive north to reach a site, I might write it as south). Secondly, time spans give me trouble, so I have to watch a calendar to keep from messing up what day it is, how long Darcy had been gone, that sort of thing. Having a character pregnant for ten months in a book years ago has made me wary of dates.

Besides my and my husband's proofreading, my editor catches things and makes important suggestions. Also, a professional copy editor reads and queries any possible mistakes. It's been a long time since a "groaner" got through one of my novels after all that attention to detail. But in an early historical novel, whereas I thought I had written "along the riverbank drums rolled," what appeared was "along the riverbank drunks rolled."

The quote from another author that comes closest to an overall explanation of how I write is this one by E. L. Doctorow: "Writing a novel is like driving a car at night. You can see only as far as your headlights, but you can make the whole trip that way."

I have found that so true, discovering new plot possibilities by what already happened, finding surprises in what the characters do. A new turn and surprise in plot or my fictional people is always just around the next bend in the story.

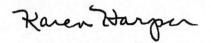